Praise for
BENTLEY LITTLE

The Summoning

"A must for those who like vampire tales with real bite. Little terrorizes us with new and nasty twists . . . the story soars—original, eerie, rough and fun."

—*Richard Laymon*

The Ignored

"What Little has created is nothing less than a nightmarishly brilliant tour de force of modern life in America."

—*Publishers Weekly* (starred review)

The Store

"Bentley Little has solidified his place at the very top of the horror genre."

—*BarnesandNoble.com*

The Mailman

"A thinking person's horror novel. *The Mailman* delivers. Very scary."

—*Los Angeles Times*

The Revelation

"Little does an electrifying job of keeping the reader in suspense."

—*West Coast Review of Books*

Books by Bentley Little

THE SUMMONING*

THE TOWN

THE REVELATION

THE HOUSE

THE STORE

THE IGNORED

DOMINION

UNIVERSITY

THE MAILMAN

*Published by Pinnacle Books

THE
SUMMONING

BENTLEY LITTLE

PINNACLE BOOKS
Kensington Publishing Corp.
http://www.pinnaclebooks.com

For my grandpa, Lloyd Little, who was there for my family through thick and thin, and who, when I needed it most, helped me out with a '74 Dodge Dart, my first reliable car.

Thanks to the regulars: Dominick Abel, Keith Neilson, Larry and Roseanne Little, Judson and Krista Little.

Thanks also to Richard Laymon, for his much-needed and much-appreciated support.

Special thanks to Wai Sau Li, for her assistance with Chinese language, customs and lore; and to the Chu family—Danny, Salina, Fanny, Henny and Susan—for giving me a glimpse into Chinese restaurant life.

Before me floats an image, man or shade,
Shade more than man, more image than a shade;
For Hades' bobbin bound in mummy-cloth
May unwind the winding path;
A mouth that has no moisture and no breath
Breathless mouths may summon;
I hail the superhuman;
I call it death-in-life and life-in-death.

    —William Butler Yeats
     "Byzantium"

Prologue

Jesus appeared to the Pastor Dan Wheeler while he slept. Tall and healthy, bathed in a shimmering glow, Jesus strode across the meadow grass and through the trees while Wheeler followed. It was day, a clear glorious day with the sun hanging warm and white in a deep blue cloudless sky. Around him, the trees and plants were green, bright green, free from dust and dirt, and the grass beneath his feet felt soft and smooth and cushiony. The fresh air was alive with the vibrant sound of birdsong.

Jesus walked around a copse of manzanita bushes, and now Wheeler knew where they were. He recognized the empty feed and grain store and the smattering of trailers which flanked Highway 370 on the north side of town.

Only . . .

Only this wasn't desert. And the trailers did not look as shabby as they usually did. Indeed, each seemed bright and shiny and new, and colorful flowers were planted in the lush ground surrounding them. The feed and grain store, while still empty, also seemed refurbished, as though waiting for someone to move in.

Moving gracefully, almost gliding, Jesus ascended the steep incline which led to the raised road and began walking down the center stripe of the highway. Wheeler followed, past the new Texaco station, past the rebuilt fence of the Williams's old horse corral, until they came to a small clearing between the empty mining administration building and the assaying office at the top of the hill.

Now Jesus stopped and turned to face him. The Savior's features were framed by beautiful hair that hung in thick curls around His shoulders, and His reddish brown beard shone in the sunlight. The expression on His face was one of infinite patience and understanding, and when He spoke His voice carried the firm yet comforting tone of Truth.

"Dan," He said, and His voice was music to Wheeler's ears, "I have chosen you for a special task."

Wheeler wanted to respond, wanted to fall to his knees and sob his grateful thanks, but he was rooted in place, transfixed by the power radiating from Christ's form.

Jesus lifted an arm, gestured toward the land around him. "This is where you will build your church."

Now Dan Wheeler found his voice. "What kind of church am I to build?"

Jesus said nothing, but the church appeared immediately in Wheeler's mind. In one epiphanous instant, he knew everything about the church to be, from its dimensions to its construction materials to the placement of items within its rooms. It was an awesome structure, overwhelming in its scope and ambition, a tremendous testament to God's living glory that rendered pale the cathedrals of old and seemed far too grandiose and spectacular to be hidden away in a town like Rio Verde.

"The Lord's greatness can be honored any place at any time," Jesus said, answering his concern before it was vocalized. "The Lord need not locate His church where people will see it; people will see it where it is located."

And Wheeler understood. The faithful, the worthy, the deserving, *they* would know where the church was built and would make the effort to visit it. Pilgrims from all over the world would flock to Rio Verde to experience the glory of Christ reflected in the magnificence of His church. The blind would be sighted by casting their dead eyes upon it, the crippled would be healed by touching its walls. Believers would be rewarded, nonbelievers would come to believe. Wrong would be righted, and the kingdom of God on earth would spread from the germ of this humble beginning.

Wheeler's eyes filled with tears, and the transcendent form of the Savior began to blur. "I . . . I love you," Wheeler stammered, falling to his knees.

Jesus smiled, a smile so radiant and beatific that it cut through the wavering wall of tears and shone full force on Wheeler's face. "I know," Jesus said.

When Wheeler awoke it was morning, and he found himself staring up at the white speckled ceiling above his bed. He lay there for a moment, thinking, then threw off the covers. He stood and walked across the cold wooden floor to the window, feeling both frightened and exhilarated. He had no doubt of the veracity of his vision, that he had seen the Lord Jesus Christ. God had spoken to him. The sincerity and fervency of his untiring efforts to spread the gospel had been noticed in Heaven, and he had been specifically chosen by Jesus to assist Him in the performance of this duty, to construct this great monument to God's glory.

Wheeler had no illusions about himself. He knew he was small time. He did not command the attention of the TV evangelists, did not have a nationwide following and probably never would. Then again, maybe God did not look favorably on the way the big-time pastors traded on the Lord's name for their own profit. Maybe He had been looking for just such a humble preacher as himself to carry out His wishes.

Wheeler was not vain enough to believe that he was the only man on earth qualified to perform in the service of the Lord, and he would not be surprised to discover that Jesus had spoken to several men of God other than himself, exhorting all of them to construct churches in different areas of the country or the world. It was unrealistic to suppose that he, Dan Wheeler, out of all of the billions of individuals on the planet, had alone been chosen to do the bidding of the Lord.

Then again . . .

He thought of Noah, thought of Moses, thought of Abraham.

Wheeler looked out the window and down the hill toward the abandoned storefront where his church had been forced to hold its first meetings. He couldn't really see the storefront, could only see a portion of its tar-papered roof between the other buildings, but he knew it was there, and its presence made him feel good. He had carved out a niche in this town with nothing going for him but his own gift of gab and an undying faith in the Lord Jesus Christ. For the past ten years he had been preaching the living gospel in Rio Verde, and despite the presence of established churches, he had found a following and formed a congregation. Donations had allowed him to eventually move out of his original storefront and purchase the old Presbyterian church when that denomination had constructed a new and bigger building on the east end of town. He had continued expanding his flock, making no concessions to modernity, refusing to follow the example of the chain churches and compromise the words of the Lord with secular notions of tolerance.

And now Jesus had rewarded him.

Wheeler turned away from the window. He knew what he had to do. The path for him had been illuminated, and he had been given detailed instructions. He would obtain a loan, sell this house, take up a collection, do everything he could and anything he had to to pay for the building of the new church. He would have meetings in the vacant lot next to the Dairy Queen, like he did in the old tent days in Phoenix.

The Lord's will would be done.

Shadows shrunk as the sun rose in the east and the desert dawn gained strength. Wheeler continued to stare out the window. The adrenaline within him was still high, but the fear and excitement he had experienced only a few moments before had metamorphosed into something like the peace he had felt when he had been with Jesus. He felt strangely calm. He would have expected to feel tense, pressured, as though the weight of the world had just been placed on his shoulders. He had met and spoken with Jesus Christ, had been instructed to build a magnificent temple of the Lord, had been asked to participate in the biggest event in the history of modern Christianity, yet he felt oddly disassociated from it all, as though he were watching it happen to someone else.

He smiled as he looked out over the shabby town. Here he was, in this small house in this nondescript desert community, and he alone knew the solution to a question that not even the world's greatest theologians could have answered. It was not an important question, not anything earth-shattering, but somehow it made him feel better than everything else he had learned during the night.

Black.

Jesus' favorite color was black.

The Lord's will would be done.

One

Sue Wing tried to be as unobtrusive as possible as she stood behind the restaurant's cash register, folding the newly printed take-out menus. Behind her, in the kitchen, she heard her parents arguing loudly in Cantonese, her mother insisting that the air conditioner be set at eighty degrees in order to save money, her father stating that he was going to leave it at seventy so their customers would be comfortable. Underneath the arguing, from farther back in the kitchen, she heard the tinkly, dissonant sounds of her grandmother's music, faint but appropriate, like a soundtrack to her parents' heated discussion.

Sue picked up another menu, matching the edges and creasing the fold. She glanced over the top of the register at the restaurant's lone customers, two yuppies who had obviously stopped in town on their way to the lake or the dude ranch. Both of them had short brownish hair, the man's a little shorter than the woman's, and both wore expensive clothes of studied casualness, fashion statements that were supposed to show that they were at once hip and weekend relaxed. The woman had pushed her lightly tinted sunglasses to the top of her head. The man's sunglasses lay on the table beside his elbow. Through the window of the restaurant, Sue could see the couple's red sports car.

She had not liked the man and woman on sight, had

not liked the condescending way in which they'd looked around the interior of the small take-out restaurant, as though they had been expecting waiters and banquet tables, had not liked the way they'd exchanged smug, derogatory glances over the contents of the menu.

She peeked at them over the top of the register. They were eating with chopsticks, and though they handled the utensils fairly well, it still seemed phony to Sue, a pretentious affectation. She had never understood what made affluent white Americans want to use chopsticks—while eating Chinese food. These people used chopsticks at no other time, did not utilize the utensils when eating American food or Mexican food or while they were cooking, but they insisted on using them when they had Chinese food. Did it make them feel more ethnic, as though they were broadening their cultural horizons? She didn't know. She *did* know that while her parents and grandmother used chopsticks exclusively, she herself used either forks or chopsticks, depending on what was on the table. Her brother John preferred forks and seldom used chopsticks at all.

The woman looked up, and Sue quickly returned her attention to the menus.

"Miss?" the woman called, raising a tan hand.

Sue stepped around the register and over to the table.

"Could we have some more soy sauce?" The woman pronounced the word "soy" in a strangely awkward glottal-stopped manner that was supposed to be authentic but resembled neither Mandarin nor Cantonese.

"Certainly," Sue said. She hurried back into the kitchen and grabbed a handful of the small foil-wrapped packets of soy sauce from the box next to the door. Her parents stopped their argument the instant she walked into the kitchen, her father moving over to the stove, her mother heading through the back door to the small room where her grandmother was chopping vegetables.

She returned to the front of the restaurant. The man and woman ignored her as she placed the packets of soy sauce next to their plates.

Moving back behind the register, she once again began folding menus. The kitchen was quiet now, the only noise her grandmother's music issuing from the cassette player. She stared down at the menus as she folded. Her parents had not resumed their argument, afraid that she would hear them. They always did this, trying to pretend in front of her and John that they always saw eye-to-eye on everything, that they were always in complete accord and never fought. Both she and her brother knew better, but they never said anything about it. Not to their parents.

Sometimes she wished that her family could hash out their problems in the open like a typical American family' instead of keeping everything so secretive all the time. It would make things a lot easier in the long run.

The yuppies departed, leaving behind an inappropriately large tip. Sue cleared the table, taking the plates back to the sink where her mother, grateful for something to do, had already started washing.

"Clean table," her father told her bluntly in English.

"I always do," she said.

She grabbed a wet cloth and wrapped it around her hand as she walked back out front. She looked up while she wiped the table, and through the front window she saw John running up the street toward the restaurant. He jumped over the small ditch next to the parking lot and ran across the dirt. He pushed open the restaurant door, causing the attached bells to tinkle, and threw his books on the table nearest the entrance before heading into the kitchen to get something to drink. "Friday," he said. "Finally."

She watched her brother without being obvious about it. He was out of breath, but he didn't appear frightened, and she relaxed a little. Last week, a couple of bullies from his junior high had threatened to beat him up, and he had run home in terror. This week, she supposed, the bullies had moved on to someone else.

He came back out a moment later, Dr Pepper in hand. "What are they fighting about this time?" he asked, nodding toward the kitchen.

Sue smiled. "You could tell?"

"Neither of them are talking."

"Air-conditioning," she said.

"Air-conditioning? Again?" John grinned and shook his head. "Let's turn it down to fifty and open all the doors so the air gets out and drive them both crazy."

"Knock it off," she said, laughing.

"It'd be fun."

She threw the washcloth at him. He caught it and tried to whip her with it, but she ran around the table.

"You can't escape me!"

They ran behind, between, and around the restaurant's four tables, chasing each other, yelling, throwing the washcloth, until their father came out of the kitchen and angrily told them to knock it off.

They stopped, and John glumly handed the washcloth to his father. "Another fun Friday evening with the Wing family," he said.

Business was slow, and instead of waiting until after the restaurant closed to eat dinner the way they usually did, they ate early. Their father brought out a platter of *chow fun* around seven o'clock and set it on the largest table, telling Sue and John, who were both reading, to get plates, chopsticks and forks. They put away their books and followed their father into the kitchen while their mother and grandmother set out bowls of rice.

The meal was pleasant, the air-conditioning argument having been resolved, and after dinner, after they had drunk the *moqua* soup, after the table had been cleared, Sue told her parents that she was going to go to the theater. There was a new Woody Allen movie playing, she explained, and this was its last day.

"Me too!" John said. "I want to go too!"

"No," Sue told him.

"Why not?" Her mother asked in Cantonese. "Why don't you want your brother to go with you?"

"Because I'm going with a friend of mine."

"Which friend?"

"Mother, I'm twenty-one, I'm old enough to go to a stupid movie without being treated like a criminal."

"A boy? Are you going to the theater with a boy?"

"No."

"Yes, you are. And you are ashamed to show him to your family, and you are sneaking around our backs."

"Fine then. I won't go."

"Go," her father said. "It's okay."

"We don't even know this boy!"

"There is no boy!" Sue told her mother, exasperated. "If I was going out on a date, I would tell you. I am not going on a date."

"Then why can't I go?" John asked.

"It's rated 'R'."

"Rated 'R'?" her mother said. "I'm not sure you should be seeing this movie."

"I've seen thousands of 'R' movies on cable. So have you. So has John."

"Then why can't I go?" John asked.

Sue threw up her hands. "Forget it!" she said in English. "God, if I knew it was going to be this complicated, I wouldn't've even brought it up!"

"You can go," her father said. "We're not that busy tonight. I don't need you here." He turned toward his wife and John. "She's old enough to do things with her friends if she wants to," he said. "And she deserves a little privacy."

She took a deep breath. "Thank you," she told her father. She glanced toward her grandmother, who smiled at her and nodded approval.

"Should I pick you up afterward?" her father asked.

Sue shook her head. "I'll walk home."

"Are you sure? That late?"

"I'll be fine."

"What time will you be back?" her mother asked.

"The movie starts at eight, gets out at nine-thirty, I'll be home by ten." She glanced at the clock on the wall. "I have to go, I'll be late." She grabbed her jacket from the chair next to the kitchen door and hurried out before her mother could think of another argument. The truth was that she was going to the movie alone, something she did far more often than she would ever admit to her parents. Usually, she went alone not because she had to, but because she liked to. This time, though, it had not been entirely voluntary. She had asked Shelly and Janine to go with her, but neither of them had wanted to see the film. She wasn't about to let the fact that no one wanted to go with her keep her from enjoying herself, however.

Her parents, she knew, especially her mother, would forbid her to leave the house if they realized that she actually liked to go to movies, go shopping and perform other supposedly social activities by herself. They would probably consider her a disgrace to the family and decide that there was something seriously wrong with her. Or something *else* wrong with her.

Although neither of her parents had ever said anything, it was clear that both of them already thought there was something amiss because she was twenty-one and not yet married. When her mother was her age, as she never tired of pointing out, she already had a two-year-old daughter. Sue never said a word, but she thought to herself that if she had gotten pregnant at nineteen, her parents would have thought her the slut of the Western world.

On this issue, her grandmother, who more often than not took her side in disputes, was in complete agreement with her parents. Her grandmother had even suggested sending her to live in San Francisco with her aunt so she could find a nice Chinese boy.

She had long since given up trying to explain that she would get married when she was ready and when she fell in love, not when tradition said it was appropriate. These days she just smiled, nodded, and waited for the discussion to end.

A car pulled up to the restaurant as she was leaving, and she moved out of its way, veering off to the right and taking the sandy path that wound through the cactus and cottonwood and acted as a shortcut through the land between the restaurant and the back of the Basha's shopping center.

The movie theater was on the far side of the grocery store, and she arrived just in time, grabbing a seat just as the lights dimmed, the curtains opened, and the first preview came on.

The movie was good, but not one of Woody's best. Not as great as Siskel and Ebert had said it was but still thoughtful and funny and well worth watching. She seemed to be in the minority in her enjoyment of the film, however. Throughout its presentation, people in the audience made loud comments which they and their friends seemed to consider amusing but which she found juvenile and obnoxious. The sparse audience laughed more at the observations of these buffoons than they did at the genuinely funny lines in the film, and it almost made her wish she'd waited to see the movie on video.

Afterward, she walked slowly across the parking lot toward the street. The lot was deserted save for a cluster of vehicles around the entrance of the theater. She stopped for a moment, looking up. The moonless sky was black, freckled with oversize stars, and the air was chill with a promise of winter. Carried faintly on the light desert breeze was the scent of a mesquite campfire.

She took a deep breath, inhaling the crisp cool air. She loved nights like these, but they always made her sad somehow. These were evenings that should be spent with others, not alone. These were nights for cuddling and comforters and hot chocolate, not nights for *moqua* and arguing parents.

Around her, couples made their way to cars and trucks, talking together in low intimate tones. They were high school students mostly, the boys younger versions of their fathers with cowboy hats, boots, and white Skoal circles outlined on the back pockets of their faded Levi's, the girls giggly emulators of their mothers' status quo subservience.

Sue shook her head, looked toward the drooping cottonwood tree at the corner of the parking lot. She was being too hard on these people, and she knew it. She was in a mean mood tonight. Jealousy, probably. Her own mother was no doubt far more subservient than these girls or even their mothers would ever be.

To her right, leaning against a red pickup, she saw a boy and girl kissing passionately, young lovers who no doubt thought their relationship would last forever. She *was* jealous. This had never been a part of her life when she'd been their age. She'd regretted it then, and she regretted it now. She thought of her senior prom, the only school dance she had ever attended. She'd gone with Clay Brown, a boy she barely knew and who barely knew her. Neither of them had been able to find dates for the prom, and they'd sort of fallen together out of necessity. After the dance, they'd tried to make out, there in the dark of the car on the dirt road next to the river. But though each of them wanted *something* to happen, nothing had. Their passion had been forced, awkward, and uncomfortable for both of them, and it was instantly clear that there were no sparks, that it was not going to work.

Embarrassed, they'd avoided each other after that. Clay had eventually moved out of town. He was probably married by now.

She watched the young lovers break their kiss and get into the pickup. They kissed again before driving off.

She continued walking, wondering whether her mother was going to be up and waiting, ready to give her the third degree when she got home.

"Hey, Sue! Wait up!"

She turned to see Shelly hurrying across the parking lot toward her. Sue stood, waiting. By the time her friend reached her, the chubby girl was panting and nearly out of breath. "I knew you'd be at the movie, so I decided to come with you, but I didn't see you in there."

"I sat in the back. I thought you didn't want to go."

"I changed my mind."

"Why? Did you get a date?"

Shelly snorted. "Very funny. Actually, I tried to catch you at the restaurant, but John said you'd already left. I thought I could find you at the theater, but by the time I got here the movie had already started, and I didn't want to walk up and down the aisles looking for you."

"Well, I didn't see you either."

"I was near the front, off to the side." She shook her head. "I almost went home. I've never gone to a movie by myself before."

Sue shrugged. "It's something you get used to." She started walking again. "So what was the emergency? Why did you have to find me?"

"I didn't. It's just that, you know, my dad didn't come home after work again, and my mom started taking it out on me, so I had to get out of there. I thought I'd go with you to the movie."

"Now you wish you'd stayed home, right?"

Shelly didn't smile. "No," she said. "It's starting to get bad. I was going to wait to leave until I could afford someplace decent, get my own trailer or something, but now I'm thinking it's better to get out no matter what. I have a half day tomorrow, and I was wondering if you wanted to come with me and see how much apartments are."

"That'll take ten minutes. What are there, those new ones over on Sagebrush, those old ones on Copperhead?"

Shelly shrugged. "I don't know. I thought we'd get a paper and look."

"Yeah, I'll go." Sue looked at her friend. "What about tonight? Are you going back? You could . . . stay over at my house."

"Yeah, right."

"You could sleep in my room."

"Sue, your parents don't like me. They wouldn't let me stay overnight."

"Yes, they would."

Shelly shook her head. "No, they wouldn't. Besides, I'm going home. My dad's probably back by now, and if they're fighting, I'll be able to slip in without being noticed."

Sue said nothing, did not look at her friend. Shelly was right. Her parents didn't like her. She had never been sure if that was because Shelly was not Chinese or because she had not made the kinds of grades in school that they considered appropriate for a friend of their daughter's. Her parents would have let Shelly stay overnight, and they would have been polite to her, but she herself would have received an extensive grilling about the details of Shelly's home life after her friend had left.

"Come on," Shelly said. "I got my car. I'll give you a ride home."

"All right."

The parking lot was empty save for Shelly's broken-down Dart and a Toyota pickup near the far side of the theater. Once again, Sue smelled mesquite, and she wondered if it was from the dude ranch or a lone camper sleeping overnight in the surrounding desert.

Shelly unlocked the passenger door of the car. Sue got in, then leaned across the seat to unlock the driver's side. She buckled her seat belt while Shelly started the car and pushed in a Clint Black tape.

Sue groaned. "Not that country crap."

Shelly grinned. "If it ain't country, it ain't music."

Sue stared out the window at the darkened buildings as the Dart sped up 370 toward Center. In the west, the silhouette of Apache Peak looked black even against the darkness of the sky. They drove in silence, listening to the music. This morning her grandmother had stated that today would not be a good day, and although Sue had dismissed the prediction at the time, she wondered now what her grandmother had meant. It was obvious that the old woman had had some sort of dream that she believed foreshadowed an important event. Had she been thinking of the crisis within Shelly's family, or had it been something else? She would have to ask.

The car pulled to a stop in front of Sue's house, and she got out, walking around to Shelly's window. "Do you want to come in for a while, just stay until things cool down?" Shelly shook her head. "It's been two hours. Either everything's okay, or the whole night's shot, and they'll be arguing until dawn." She smiled tiredly. "Or my dad hit the road and is heading down the highway singing 'By the time I Get to Phoenix.' "

"Call me tomorrow then."

"I will."

Sue stood on the cracked sidewalk and watched the taillights of her friend's car shrink in the distance, turn a corner, and disappear. She walked up the steps to the front porch. The door was opened before she had finished taking her key out of her purse. Her grandmother stood in the doorway, backlit by the light in the hall, her frizzy hair forming a dark halo around her head. The rest of the house was dark. Everyone else, including her mother, had already gone to bed.

"I'm glad you are safe," her grandmother said in Chinese. "I have been waiting. I thought something might have happened to you."

"I'm fine," Sue said, walking inside, taking off her shoes and closing the door behind her. But the troubled expression on her grandmother's face did not disappear.

"I was worried."

"About what?"

The old woman patted her shoulder. "We will talk in the morning. It is late now. I am old and need my rest. You are young and need your rest. We should both be in bed."

"Okay," Sue said. The two of them walked down the hall, stopping before the door to Sue's room. Sue yawned, then smiled. "Good night, Grandmother," she said.

Her grandmother nodded, said good night, but she looked troubled and did not smile as she continued down the hall.

Two

As always, Rich Carter awoke with the dawn.

He opened his eyes, yawned, stretched. The drapes were closed, but the bedroom was filled with hazy diffused light, a curtain-filtered distillation of the powerful Indian summer sunrise outside. Next to him, on the bed, Corrie still slept, one arm thrown over her eyes as though some part of her brain had known morning was coming and had ordered her body to preserve the illusion of darkness for as long as possible. He watched her for a moment. Asleep, she appeared almost happy, more content than she ever did when awake. The set of her mouth was softened, the lines of tension in her forehead smoothed away. She looked ten years younger, the way she had when they'd first met.

Sometimes he felt guilty for bringing her here.

Rich reached over and carefully cracked open the curtains, peeking outside. Through the chain-link fence, between the corner of the garage and the palo verde tree at the far end of the backyard, he could see the desert—the flat land, the far-off mesas, and the closer red sandstone buttes. Yellow morning sunlight threw saguaros and ocotillos into clear relief and highlighted the oversize boulders which covered the range of high hills to the north, illuminating aspects of the landscape that could only be seen at this hour on this kind of day. It was mornings like this, when the sky was clear and blue and cloudless and even the most overt intrusions of civilization seemed like only temporary incursions on a beautiful unchanging land, that he felt most acutely the rightness of his decision to return to Rio Verde.

Corrie would not agree. Which was one reason why he did not wake her up to share this moment. Corrie hated the desert. Well, maybe hate was too strong a word. But to her the beauty of the desert was not apparent, and the uniqueness of light and sky and landscape had virtually no effect on her. She had gotten used to Rio Verde, but she still required frequent weekend trips to Phoenix and drives to Flagstaff or Randall or Payson. Upon her first view of the town, he recalled, she'd instantly declared it the ugliest place she'd ever seen. Her views had modified somewhat—she now claimed to have seen several towns uglier than Rio Verde, all of them within the county—but she had never grown to love the community the way he'd hoped she would.

The way he did.

On that first trip back, he had thought the town the most welcome sight he'd ever seen. After the Valley, after Southern California, the familiar view of the ribbon of cottonwoods lining the river, the streets and structures built atop the low desert foothills fronting Sinagua Bluffs was one which filled him with comforting pleasure and a sense of contentment. He had been so happy to be back that he had rationalized Corrie's feelings, claiming that they had driven in on 370 instead of 95, coming in from the ugly east end of town, and that this had skewed her initial perceptions. But he'd known then as he knew now that she was a city girl and that life in a small town would take some getting used to.

He'd thought it would be easier than this, though.

Rich let the curtain fall. Anna was already up. He could hear the theme music for *Sesame Street* from the living room. He pushed off the blankets and got out of bed, careful not to disturb Corrie. He went to the bathroom, then pulled on a robe and walked down the short hallway to the living room. "Hey, sweetie," he said, picking up Anna from the couch and giving her a quick kiss on the forehead.

She giggled and wiped the kiss away. "Knock it off, Daddy. I have to watch my show."

He put her down.

"What's for breakfast?" she asked.

"Lizards and snakes. With bug milk."

She giggled again. "No, really."

"French toast," he said.

"Goody!" She flashed him a missing-toothed grin and sat down on the couch to watch TV.

He walked around the breakfast bar into the kitchen. If he ever did decide to leave Rio Verde, it would be because of Anna. He'd never had much sympathy for Corrie's complaints that the town was boring, since he himself was never bored, and he firmly believed that an intelligent person should be able to find something of interest no matter where he or she was located. But sometimes he worried about Anna. Rio Verde *was* a small town, and while he and Corrie tried to instill in their daughter their own intellectual values, and while cable television ensured that they were electronically connected to the cultural life of the rest of the world, he could not help feeling that she might be . . . well, missing out on something. He had complete faith in the abilities of the town's teachers—he knew many of them and liked most of those he knew— and he had no doubts about Anna's potential, but he still found himself agreeing with Corrie that their relative isolation would eventually put the girl at a disadvantage when competing with people from other parts of the country. Their isolation was geographical, not intellectual or cultural, but still the fear was there.

If anything could get him out of here, it would be Anna's welfare.

Then again, when he watched news reports of the daily murders in Los Angeles and Detroit and New York, when he read statistics about drugs and violent crime, he thought that a small town like Rio Verde might be the perfect place to raise a child, after all.

It was tough being a parent.

"Hey!" he called. "You want to crack the eggs?"

"Yeah!" Anna said, hurrying into the kitchen. Cracking eggs was one of her favorite things to do.

He held the bowl, while she used both hands to hold the egg and smash it against the rim. Half of the egg white slid down the outside of the bowl, and bits of shell accompanied that portion which made it inside, but he told her she did a great job. She grinned, then ran back into the living room to watch *Sesame Street*.

After breakfast, while Anna helped Corrie clean the dishes, Rich retired to his study. The deadline for this week's paper had come and gone, and Marge Watson had missed it again. The world would survive without this installment of *Social Scene*, which chronicled the past week's worth of Ladies' Auxiliary news, but he still had a page-two space to fill, and now he was going to have to spend half of his Saturday writing some sort of observational feature.

He turned on his PC, put in the disk for his word-processing program, and watched the screen as the computer booted up. Sometimes he wondered what the point of all this was. He knew he didn't have the resources at his disposal to put out a top quality paper, but he worked hard and did the best he could with what he had. Unfortunately, there just weren't enough permanent residents of the town to provide him with a consistent readership, and the tourists who passed through only used the paper to start their campfires. To top it off, his own contributors didn't seem to give a damn if they missed their deadlines.

It got downright depressing sometimes.

In his more romantic moments, he liked to think of himself as a tough, hard-boiled reporter, a man whose role could easily be portrayed on the screen by Bogart or Mitchum or perhaps the young Brando. But that was a fanciful daydream, one that didn't hold up even to himself. Truth be told, he was closer to a secretary than anything else. His life wouldn't be worth dramatizing on screen, not even with a soap opera star.

The phone rang, a stereo burr sounding simultaneously from the cordless next to his desk and the wall phone in the kitchen. It rang again, but he waited a moment before picking up the receiver, hoping that Corrie would answer it. She did, and, a beat later, called his name: "Rich!"

"Got it!" he called back. He picked up the phone. "Hello?"

"Rich? It's me."

"Robert?" He shifted the phone to his other ear, frowning. He could not remember the last time his brother had called this early on a Saturday. "What's up?"

"What are you doing?"

"Talking to you." He tried to keep his tone light, but he could hear the seriousness in Robert's voice.

"No, I mean this morning. Do you have any plans?"

"Not really. Why?"

Robert cleared his throat. "I want you to come out and look at something with me."

"What?"

He cleared his throat again, a nervous habit he'd had since childhood and something he did only when he was under extreme pressure. "We've found a dead body. Out by the arroyo. It's . . . Manuel Torres."

"The old guy who worked at Troy's garage?"

"Yeah. He's . . ." More throat clearing. "You gotta come out here. You gotta see this."

"Murdered?"

"You gotta see for yourself."

"All right. Let me grab my camera. I'll meet you . . . where?"

"The arroyo. But I don't know if you'll be wanting your camera. These aren't pictures that'll be suitable for the paper."

"What happened, Robert? What is it?"

"You gotta see for yourself."

There were two cars, a Jeep, and four men already at the arroyo. Steve Hinkley and Ted Thrall, two deputies, stood next to one of the vehicles, talking. Robert and Brad Woods, the county coroner, were at the edge of the over-size gully, looking down at something.

Rich pulled to the side of the dirt road and got out of the car, grabbing his camera from the passenger seat and slipping the strap over his shoulder. A cloud of red dust, kicked up by the braking tires, washed over him and continued on, carried by the warm morning breeze. He coughed and spit, wiping his eyes, then glanced over at Robert, who waved him forward.

In a normal town, a real town, he and Robert would not have been able to maintain the professional relationship they now shared. There would have been charges of conflict of interest, allegations that the police and the press were far cozier than they should have been, and he would have had to assign someone else to cover the crime beat.

But Rio Verde was not a normal town. No one here gave a damn whether or not he was the police chief's brother or the mayor's cousin or the president's transvestite son as long as their garage sale ads came out on time—a fact that played hell with his journalistic ethics but sure as shit made his personal life a whole lot easier.

He walked across the hard-packed sand, past the parked cars, to where Robert and Woods stood solemnly waiting. "Hi," he said, nodding to both.

Robert turned to the coroner. "Would you excuse us for a sec?" he asked. "I want to talk to my brother alone."

The other man nodded and began walking slowly back toward the cars. Robert looked at Rich for a moment but said nothing. His gaze was troubled.

"Is he down—?" Rich began.

Robert nodded.

Rich moved closer, standing at the top of the arroyo and looking toward the bottom. His heart began thumping in his chest. "Jesus," he breathed.

There was nothing left of Manuel Torres but a skeleton covered with skin.

He stared, unable to look away. Even from here, even from this angle, he could see the wrinkled parchment appearance of the man's face, the way his teeth, protruding between dark deflated lips, looked overlarge in his now shrunken head, the way his nose had collapsed in on itself, a crater between hard-bone cheeks. There were round black holes in the sockets where the old man's eyes had been.

Goose bumps popped up on Rich's arms. Manuel Torres was still clothed, wearing faded jeans and a greasy T-shirt, but his shoes had fallen off, his pants were partially pulled down, and the thin covering of dried crinkled skin which now outlined the infrastructure of his waist and lower legs was clearly visible.

Around the body, in an almost deliberate semicircle, were dead animals, similarly drained, similarly dried: a crow, a hawk, two jackrabbits, a roadrunner.

"What is this?" Rich asked. "How did this happen?"

Robert shook his head, looking toward the two deputies

standing by the cruiser. He had not glanced into the arroyo once, Rich noticed, not since he'd arrived. "I don't know," he said. "I don't know what's going on here. Even Brad's never heard tell of anything like this."

Rich found that he, too, was having a hard time looking back into the arroyo. He kept his eyes on his brother. "Who discovered the body?"

"I did. I saw the Jeep parked there, no one around, and I came over to check it out. I was driving the Bronco and had no radio, so when I saw Manuel down there, I hauled ass back to the station, called Brad, called you, and came back here with Ted and Steve."

"You haven't gone down there yet?"

Robert shook his head. "We have to be careful. There might be footprints. We don't want to disturb anything. We'll walk along the cliff a ways and find another way down."

Rich turned away from his brother and looked to his right, to where the arroyo curved away from town. He had not come here for a long time, but as children he and Robert and their friends had played here often, converting crevices into caves, laying boards across outcroppings of rock to make forts and hideouts. They had thought the arroyo private, had assumed that they had discovered it, and no one else knew about it. It had been their secret place, where they'd hidden from enemies and adults and imaginary antagonists.

He could not remember the last time he'd been here, but as he looked down the length of the gully it seemed different to him. It was now permanently tainted by the presence of death. Of course, he was viewing the scene with adult eyes now, seeing the dead man as an incursion of evil into what had once been a childhood paradise. As kids, he was sure that they would have had no problem adjusting to the idea of the corpse, would, in fact, have concocted some elaborate adventure story to explain its existence, a story that would have made their hideaway seem that much more forbidden and exciting.

What had they known then, though? *Nothing.* They'd been children. They would not have understood the implications of what had happened, would not have been any more frightened by this dried husk of a man and the dead animals surrounding him than they would have been by a gruesome horror story told around the campfire.

He was scared now, though. And the chill which had come upon him when he'd first looked into the arroyo had not lifted. He turned again toward his brother. "Is this a murder or is this a natural death?"

"A 'natural death'?"

"You know what I mean. Did he just die out here and get, you know, dehydrated or something?"

"I saw him working yesterday when I drove by the garage."

Rich shivered. "Then how could this have happened? How could this physically have been done?"

Robert took a deep breath. "Remember a few years back when we had those rumors of witches and satanists meeting out here? There were supposedly people in robes chanting when the moon was full?"

"But nothing ever came of it. You never found anything. Hell, you never even found anyone who'd seen the chanters. It was all friend-of-a-friend stuff."

"Yeah, but maybe this is connected. I mean, Jesus, look at him." He motioned toward the body. "This is not your average everyday murder."

"There are no 'average everyday murders.' This is the first murder you've ever handled."

"And I'm scared shitless. I admit it. I don't know who I'm supposed to inform, how I'm supposed to begin the investigation. What if I screw up? I called Brad, he's here, he'll take the body and do an autopsy. I'll tell Manuel's wife. But do I have to tell the state police? Do I have to report this to the county supervisors? What is the chain of command here? What's the procedure? Who's going to know if I'm doing a decent job of investigation or poking the pooch?"

"Call Pee Wee. He'll know what to do. He's bound to have come across something like this."

"Something like this?" Robert shook his head. "I don't think so."

"I don't mean something *exactly* like this, I mean a murder. He was chief for thirty years. I think he's handled murders before." Rich glanced again into the arroyo, his eye drawn to the shriveled bony body and its halo of empty animals. "I don't think anyone's come across something like this."

"I don't think so either." The breeze kicked up again, ruffling Robert's thinning hair. He said nothing for a moment. "What do you think happened here?" he asked finally.

Rich blinked against the warm wind, still felt cold. He cleared his throat. "I don't know," he said. "It's . . . it's not like something real. It's like something out of a damn movie, you know?"

Robert nodded. "I know." He spit, then ground the wet spot into the sand with the toe of his boot. He motioned toward the deputies and the coroner. "Come on," he said. "It's getting late. We've dicked around enough here. It's time to go down."

Rich nodded, saying nothing.

The two of them walked in silence toward the cars.

Three

Brad Woods had performed autopsies on a lot of bodies in his time. Men and women who had died of old age, children who had succumbed to illness, even victims of mining accidents and car crashes. Some had been more heartbreaking than others, some had been more gruesome than others, but all had been within the range of normalcy. None of the bodies had ever scared him.

Until now.

He stared down at the form of Manuel Torres, laid out on the table in the center of the room. Naked, the old man's body looked even more inhuman than it had when enveloped within the too-large clothes. Lying on the sand, Manuel had seemed so shriveled and shrunken that he'd resembled a predatory stick insect that had crawled into the clothing of a human being. But here, on the table, in the cold glare of the operating lights, the unbelievable distortion of the ordinary was even more frightening. Now Brad could clearly see that the insectile limbs of the body were severely attenuated human arms and legs, that the sunken body cavity and strangely shriveled genitals were the products of acute emaciation, that the fright-mask face was the result of dehydration without decay.

He reached out and poked a tentative finger into the body's stomach region. He could feel the dryness even through the gloves, and in the silence of the room, against only the low hum of the lights, the skin made a sound like that of a newspaper being crumpled.

He pulled back, nervous despite himself. The old man's bones were broken in several spots, his rib cage crushed, and in these places the skin had cracked open. None of the dermal layers had retained enough moisture to maintain flexibility. No blood had escaped from any of the openings.

What could have drained the body of all fluids so completely?

And in a single night. According to Chief Carter, Troy had said that Manuel worked until five o'clock yesterday evening.

In the arroyo, Brad had given the body a cursory examination, visually inspecting the corpse for obvious signs of violence. That had been difficult enough. Surrounded by other people, by the police and the press, he had still not wanted to handle the body, still had to force himself to touch the old man. But now, here, alone, he was finding it almost impossible to begin his work.

Brad felt goose bumps on his arms and on the back of his neck. The bodies of the animals were in bags at the back of the room, and those he would examine later with Ed Durham, the vet.

But Manuel Torres was his and his alone.

He turned on the tape recorder, picked up the scalpel, took a deep breath, then turned off the tape recorder, put down the scalpel, and took a drink of water from the squeeze bottle on the tray next to him. He didn't want to do this autopsy. That's what it came down to. He'd been procrastinating for over a quarter of an hour, laying out instruments, testing his tape recorder, performing the ordinary prep duties that should have taken no more than five minutes. He wished he had an assistant or a coworker to help him. He wished he'd called Kim, his secretary, and told her to come in, although there was nothing she could do to help with the procedure.

He wished there was someone in the building besides himself.

He glanced around the room. Though it was empty and well lit, though there were no shadows, there was something about the room that put him on edge, that made him feel more than a little uneasy. He had never been one of those people who were afraid of death, or who considered a lifeless body something sacred to be left reverentially alone. To him, dignity and dissection were not mutually exclusive. The idea of cutting open a dead person had never bothered him, which was why he had not had any problem deciding upon his chosen profession. To him, a corpse had always been the shed husk of an individual, what was left after the soul had departed. A body had value only in its ability to shed knowledge upon death. Its sole function was to impart medical or criminal information to those qualified to look for it.

But Manuel Torres's body did not seem to him like a shed husk. Despite the fact that it was physically the most husklike corpse he had ever come across, it did not feel to him like an abandoned vessel, and he could not help thinking that the soul of Manuel Torres, whatever that spark might be that made a person a person, was still alive in this dried form and had not been able or allowed to escape.

It was a silly thought but one he could not shake. And it was why he could not seem to bring himself to cut into the body, why he kept postponing that first incision. It felt too much like murder. Each time he picked up the scalpel and looked at the body, preplanning the cuts and crosscuts he would make to open up the chest and abdominal cavities, he saw in his mind a scenario in which Manuel suddenly sat up and started screaming, howls of agony escaping from between those flattened lips as shriveled disintegrating organs fell out through the flaps of dried skin.

Brad's gaze darted quickly toward the old man's left foot. Had he seen a toe wiggle? He stared at the foot for a moment, but the pinkish toes remained stubbornly unmoving against the background of the silver steel table.

What frightened him the most was the fact that he kept expecting the body to move.

It was stupid, and he knew it was stupid. The reaction of a child who'd been watching too many fright flicks. But the feeling would not go away. He had opened up a hundred bodies in this room. Two hundred maybe. He'd worked mornings and nights, weekdays and weekends, but he had never experienced anything like this.

What the hell was the matter with him?

He told himself to maintain his professionalism, to simply go by the book and, step by step, objectively perform each of the simple medical procedures required for a legal autopsy. Again he turned on the tape recorder, again he picked up the scalpel. He breathed deeply, through his nose, in a conscious effort to calm himself. He looked again at Manuel Torres. He could see bone beneath the wrinkled translucent parchment skin, the white bone of skull and skeleton, and that was something he knew, that was something he could handle. There was no monster here, only a dead man. A body built around a structure of bone. The condition of the corpse might be unusual, but its composition was not.

It was time for him to put aside his foolishness and get to work.

This time, he used the scalpel to make an incision in the chest, and his chill abated, superstitious dread replaced by the familiar and welcome feeling of dispassionate competence.

He described each procedure as it was performed, documenting the entire process on tape. The body was indeed dehydrated, and to an unbelievable degree, but this fact did not now seem as horrifying as it had only a few moments ago. He was again the coroner, doing his job, recording his findings, and while afterward he might again be affected by emotions, he was now on autopilot, observing and chronicling the facts as he encountered them.

He turned the body over to examine its lateral and posterior segments. He adjusted the corpse, then blinked, staring down at Manuel Torres's neck. There was an open gash directly below the base of the head, a large missing chunk of flesh.

How could he have missed such an obvious wound in his preliminary examination?

He shook his head, embarrassed by his oversight, and described the wound in detail, carefully measuring its width and length. There was a dried residue around the opening, a crusty pinkish substance that he carefully excised and placed on a slide, setting it aside for later examination.

He already knew the makeup of the substance. He had seen the combination before, on the lips of people who had had seizures, dried on tongues that had been bitten.

Blood and saliva.

He frowned. The combination might not be that unique, but a wound on the back of the neck was a very unusual place to find saliva in a concentration so large. Very unusual.

He looked more carefully at the wound. The skin around it was so dry that no specific finding could be verified as completely accurate, but he thought he could see the imprint of teeth on the epidermis.

Human teeth.

His own mouth felt suddenly dry.

Blood and saliva.

The chill was back, the fear, and he quickened his pace,

40   *Bentley Little*

cutting more quickly, talking faster, hastening the procedure. He knew it was important that he discover the true
cause of Manuel Torres's death, but right now he just
wanted to get this damn thing over with.

And he wanted to make sure he was out of the building
before nightfall.

Four

The buildings surrounding the church were run down almost to the point of condemnation. Entire painting histories were revealed in chipped layers on the peeling stucco walls of the tiny houses. The hard dirt ground was littered with the sparkling shards of broken bottles. In the building next door, a sagging wooden structure with wire mesh over the windows and a faded sign above the door identifying it as the "South Phoenix Social Club," several black men wearing white T-shirts and gang colors stood in the doorway unmoving.

Pastor Wheeler did not notice the neighborhood or its inhabitants. His attention was concentrated solely on the church in front of him, which was remarkably well preserved for its age and for this part of town. It wasn't the most beautiful church he'd ever seen—with its flat roof, squat structure, and lack of stained glass, it looked more like a government office than a house of worship—but it could easily be moved, and its design could readily accommodate additions. The church was currently owned by the First Southern Baptists, but the land was owned by a developer out of Seattle, and the developer wanted to raze the whole block and put up an apartment complex. Despite all the pleas, prayers, and petitions, the developer had given the Baptists only two months to find a new home for the church. An impossible task.

Although many South Phoenix residents were Baptist,

very few of them could afford to donate the kind of money required to save the building, and the pastor of the church had approached the Arizona Church Construction Council with the offer to give the building away to any congregation able to afford moving costs. The pastor had reached an agreement with the Methodists, who were going to allow him to give his sermons in their chapel on Sunday afternoons, after their services were over, but he still wanted his old church to be saved. And Pastor Wheeler was here to save it.

Praise the Lord.

Wheeler had received a call yesterday from the chairman of the ACCC, who'd told him about the church. He had filed a request for assistance from the council over a year ago, before he had independently worked out his deal with the Rio Verde Presbyterians, and he'd heard nothing from them until now. He'd assumed that the council had rejected his proposal and forgotten about him.

It was the hand of God, Wheeler realized. The Lord was working to ensure that His house of worship would be completed on time and in the manner He desired. God *wanted* him to have this building.

And the church was perfect. Certainly it was ugly, but its nondescript flatness would complement the small town homeyness of his Rio Verde chapel, and the two of them together would blend into the background and form the foundation of the new house of the Lord that Jesus had told him to build.

He looked at Paul Davis, the restoration coordinator for the ACCC who had accompanied him to the site. "It's perfect," he said. "We want it."

"Don't you even want to look inside?" Davis asked.

Wheeler smiled. "No."

"Suit yourself. I've already been in, to examine the structure, and I don't think the moving itself will pose much of a problem. This thing was built in the fifties, and it was done sectionally. We'll take it apart the same way and transport it in two segments on flatbeds. The only possible setback will be your lack of a foundation at the Rio Verde site. This here's resting on a flat reinforced concrete base, and you really should have something similar ready for it, as well as plumbing hookups in the proper locations."

Wheeler continued to smile. "We will arrange the building to our satisfaction once it's in place. We'll take care of everything. All you have to do is move it."

Davis nodded, though he looked more than a little uncomfortable. "If you don't mind me askin', what are you going to do with two churches out there? Your congregation can't be very big in a town that small."

"I mind you asking," Wheeler said. He turned away from Davis, and now he glanced around at the neighborhood surrounding the church. He saw about him graffiti, garbage, and other familiar, unmistakable signs of a slum. He knew this place. He had begun his evangelical career in a neighborhood not unlike this, in the poor part of Dallas, although there the ethnic makeup had been heavily Hispanic rather than black.

Not that it made any difference. They were all trash in the eyes of the Lord.

He had come to Dallas at the tender age of twenty-two, unschooled, untried, and inexperienced, and he had learned by doing, preaching at first from the bus stop bench of a street corner, then from a portable podium of his own making. He had attracted attention as an object of curiosity, had become an object, of ridicule, and had graduated to an object of interest. People began to listen to what he had to say, and he preached to them, converting many to the teachings of the Lord, though, truth be told, he had never liked any of his followers. He had often wondered why. It was not a question that had kept him up nights—he knew his purpose was to educate, not befriend—yet he wondered why he took no joy in the conversion of these heathens. Why did he not enjoy bringing a new soul into the fold? He truly did not care one way or the other, did not care if these people believed or disbelieved, although he would never show that in public. Indeed, he became quite adept at hiding his true emotions while in the pulpit, at masking his disgust for these dirty, ignorant savages.

He prayed on it, and he came to realize that these people were merely practice subjects, that the Lord had provided him with warm bodies so that he might hone his skills and develop his talents before moving on to the *truly* worthy.

Most of his current flock were worthy. Oh, there were a few who would not be joining the rest of them in the kingdom of heaven. Taz Penneman, for all of his do-gooding, was an unrepentant heathen. And he didn't like Mary Gale, who always looked lustily at him with her harlot's eyes. She'd burn in hell. Marge Howe—

"What you looking at, motherfucker?"

Wheeler blinked, focused. A large overweight black man was staring belligerently at him from the doorway of the adjacent house, a small wooden structure painted shocking pink. He had not been aware that he'd been looking at the man, and he glanced quickly away.

"Motherfucker!" the man yelled.

Wheeler smiled, said nothing. This entire section of the city would be destroyed when the Lord Jesus Christ established His kingdom on earth. It would be leveled and weeded, then seeded with goodness and populated by the righteous, people who understood the ways of the Lord and had a healthy fear of God.

That was the root of the problem, he knew. Not enough people had been instilled with the fear of God. Even many so-called Christians these days seemed to see God as some sort of benevolent hippie, kindly smiling down on all of their humanistic endeavors. Those men and women had strayed far from the scriptures, had let their conceptions of the Lord be influenced by the ungodly secular interpretations of mealymouthed liberal atheists, yet they still dared to say they believed. They'd forgotten that the Lord was a great and terrible God capable of exacting a steep toll for transgressions. They'd been raised to think like Catholics, to believe that the Lord forgave all, that they could steal, murder, whore, and blaspheme, then apologize and all would be forgotten.

He had been raised differently.

He was glad of it now, though he had not been at the time. He had been swayed as a youth by false companions and had wanted to share their simple easy rationalizations, had wanted to believe that he could confess his sins to the Lord and be forgiven, or that the Lord was not concerned with the petty misdeeds of youth at all. But his father had set him straight, and had lectured him and beaten into him the fear of God. His father had understood that the Lord would accept no losers, no sinners, no transgressors, that He had provided His son to the world as an example, to show that it was possible to live on earth as a perfect, unblemished human being, and the old man had made sure that Wheeler understood that as well.

Even if that meant using The Scourge.

His father had also made sure that Wheeler knew, from the beginning, the truth about his mother. So while he had never known his mother, he had always known of her. He had known exactly what she was. His father had told him. Many times his father had told him.

His mother was a harlot, a strumpet, a brazen wanton woman. A whore.

One of the wicked.

She'd always been that way, his father had explained—

even when he'd first met her—but he'd foolishly thought he would be able to convert her, to make her change. He'd been seduced by her striking beauty, her soft voice, her even temperament and easy ways. It had been the sole mistake of an otherwise exemplary life, and it may very well have cost him entrance to Heaven. But if it was the last thing he did, he was going to make sure that his son did not follow in his footsteps.

Wheeler had grown up knowing that his mother was damned to hell. Then again, most women were going to hell. His father made him realize that. Most women were wicked. All they wanted was sex. All they wanted was to feed that unquenchable fire between their legs. Like animals, they were, slaves to the lusts of their bodies.

Wheeler had not seen a photograph of his mother until after his father's death, and when he finally did see what she looked like, he was surprised to discover that she did not resemble the evil temptress he had imagined at all. He'd always thought she would look like a vamp, one of those pouty, slutty women who hung around outside the bars on Seventh Street, a painted lady with enormous breasts and tight dresses that outlined the curves of her slatternly body. But instead, she looked like a mousy librarian, a plain, average, slightly underweight woman of approximately middle age.

He'd burned the photograph after he'd looked at it, throwing it into the fireplace along with a rubber-banded stack of old letters he'd found in his father's dresser.

You could never tell. That was one thing his father had taught him. You could never tell what lay beneath appearances, what hid behind people's outer masks, what they were really like inside. That was something only God could see.

But Wheeler had found out later that he *could* tell, that he could somehow see behind the mask and into a person's soul, that he could see through the facade to the truth beneath. It was a gift God had given him, a reward for his achievement in spreading the word of the Lord.

And now Jesus had seen fit to visit him personally.

There was a new day coming.

Wheeler looked again at the church, then at Davis next to him. The restoration coordinator was one of those false Christians, all piety and obsequiousness on the outside, all bleeding heart humanist on the inside. Wheeler smiled to himself, felt warmed. The man would soon find out on which side his bread was buttered.

Davis finished making calculations in a small handheld notebook and looked up. "The earliest we can have it moved is next Friday," he said.

Wheeler nodded. "That will be fine," he said, smiling. He continued to nod. "Next Friday will be fine."

Five

The restaurant was closed on Monday. Even workaholics like her parents needed a day of rest, a day to themselves, and since they couldn't very well take off on Saturday or Sunday—the two busiest days of the week—they closed the restaurant on Monday, taking their weekend a day late and a day short.

This was the day Sue allowed herself to sleep in.

She lay in bed now, curled on her side, staring at the bottom right corner of the framed Sargent print on the wall. John was already up, getting ready for school. She could hear him brushing his teeth in the bathroom. Farther off, in the kitchen, she heard the rattling of pots and the rhythmic staccato sound of her mother's attempts to sing along with a commercial on the radio.

Usually, she liked to stay in bed for a while after she awoke, enjoying that peaceful transition between sleep and wakefulness, her mind thinking clearly and without distraction while her body still enjoyed the comforts of slumber. But today she felt restless, constitutionally unable to remain inert beneath the covers. She sat up and stretched.

Sue glanced around her room, at the Impressionist prints on the walls, at the carved antique dresser, at the small nightstand covered with lace. More than anything else, her room symbolized the difference between herself and the rest of her family. She had decorated the room according to her own independently acquired aesthetic standards, with ideas obtained from books, taste molded by movies. The rest of the house was filled with gaudy throw rugs and pillows, fake jade carvings and tacky Buddha figurines, the cheap bastardizations of Chinese culture sold in curio shops and originally meant for American tourists but embraced wholeheartedly by her parents.

Her room was different.

If there was anything to reincarnation, she thought, she'd been a Victorian Englishwoman in a previous life.

Getting out of bed, she walked across the room to her closet. She did not know what she was going to do today. It seemed to her that she had had something planned—at least it felt that way—but she could not for the life of her remember what it was.

She took her robe from its hook inside the closet door and put it on. Her parents usually used this day to shop for supplies, to work around the house. Sue read, watched TV, or did her own shopping, although she invariably felt guilty that she was not doing something more productive. In the two years she'd been out of school, she had still not adjusted to the fact that her free time was truly free, that there was no homework hanging over her head, no assignments or projects due. She kept wanting to work on something, and she'd considered trying to write, trying to paint, trying to do something creative, but instead she'd let herself become lazy, doing nothing with her days except hanging out.

Was this what life was like for most people? Drifting, merely existing? It all seemed so pointless and purposeless. She'd worked so hard to do well in school, to learn, to get good grades, and where had it gotten her?

In Cantonese, her mother yelled for John to come to breakfast.

Sue, too, headed down the hall toward the kitchen, bumping into her brother along the way.

"Watch it, retard," he said, bumping her with his hip in return.

"Die," she told him.

They walked into the dining room. Three bowls were already set on the table. Her mother, who had obviously assumed that Sue would sleep in today, was surprised to see her but hurriedly returned to the kitchen and brought out another bowl.

"What about Grandmother?" Sue asked in Cantonese. "Isn't she eating?"

"She is not feeling well," her mother said as she placed the bowl on the table. She did not elaborate but returned immediately to the kitchen. That worried Sue. Usually, if her grandmother was ill, her mother would describe in detail the precise nature of her malady, whether it be *toh se* or *tao tung*. Her mother's silence made Sue feel uneasy, and she could not help thinking of what her grandmother had muttered last night before settling painfully into bed.

Wai.

Badness.

She had not been sure at the time whether her grandmother meant sickness or evil, and she had not asked. She had not wanted to know. But she had a suspicion that her grandmother was not referring to physical illness. For the past few days, ever since the mechanic had been found in the arroyo, her grandmother had seemed worried and preoccupied, had spent more time than usual in her room, and when she'd spoken to the family at all, her conversation had been peppered with thinly veiled hints of signs and omens. While Sue often scoffed at the superstitiousness of the old woman, she was also more than a little afraid of what her grandmother called *Di Lo Ling Gum*, the sixth sense. She had never been able to satisfactorily explain to herself how her grandmother was able to tell when it was going to rain when even the weathermen did not know, or how she could predict with amazing accuracy the deaths of relatives who lived far away. She liked even less her grandmother's references to spirits and *tse mor,* demons.

She remained standing as John sat down. Her father was already sitting at the head of the table, but he had not yet spoken, and neither she nor John dared address him. He was not a morning person, and though he always awoke early, he seldom spoke before breakfast and never before his first cup of tea. He preferred to sit in undisturbed silence and listen to the news on the radio or, on Thursday, read the newspaper.

Looking at him now, at the way he stared crossly at nothing, she wondered if he even spoke to her mother before breakfast, or if the two of them simply woke up when the alarm went off, got out of bed silently, and got dressed without speaking.

It was a depressing thought, and she pushed it out of her mind.

John began drumming on the table with his spoon and fork as he waited for breakfast, pounding out the rhythm to some rock or rap song running through his mind. Sue walked into the kitchen to see if her mother needed help with the food. Her mother was just finishing scooping fried rice from the wok onto a plate, and she told Sue to get the teapot from the stove. Sue picked up the teapot, her mother picked up the plate, and the two of them walked into the dining room.

John looked up as they entered. He frowned when his mother put the plate on the table. He put down his fork and spoon. "How come we never have breakfast food for breakfast?" he asked in English.

His father glared at him. "Eat!"

"I want pancakes or something. I don't want rice. We have rice every day. I'm sick of it."

"John . . . ," Sue warned.

But the argument had already started, her mother joining her father in lecturing John on nutrition, telling him that he was ungrateful and disrespectful. The argument was bilingual, her parents speaking in Cantonese, her brother speaking in English in order to annoy his parents.

"When I'm eighteen," John said finally, "I'm getting an earring."

"You are not. Be quiet and eat your food."

John lapsed into silence, slumping down in his seat.

Sue said nothing but scooped some fried rice onto her plate. She worried about her brother. Right now he was still young, and he still showed his parents some respect, but he was much more Americanized than even she was and much more than her parents understood. Her parents were going to have a very tough time with him in the next few years. He was going to want to do the same things his friends did, and he was going to chafe and fight against the restrictions her parents would place on him. That's what concerned her. John was easily swayed, too concerned with fitting in, too worried about what his peers thought of him. She, too, had been torn between the two cultures, not feeling fully a part of either, but she had had enough self-confidence that she had done what she thought was right and had never succumbed to peer pressure. John was different.

"That's it," he muttered under his breath. "When I'm eighteen, I'm hitting the road."

Neither of her parents heard his remark, and Sue just let it lie. She didn't want to inflame the situation even further.

John finished eating quickly and, without waiting to be excused, pushed his chair away from the table. "I gotta catch the bus," he said. He ran down the hall to his bedroom to get his books, and a moment later yelled, "Bye!"

The door slammed behind him.

"Tieu pei," her father said, more to himself than anyone else.

Her mother finished eating, and she took her own and John's bowl to the kitchen. A few seconds later, the phone rang, and Sue heard her mother answer it. " 'Lo?" There was a short moment of silence. "Sue?"

"Coming!" She pushed back her chair and hurried into the kitchen, taking the receiver from her mother. "Yes?"

"Sue, it's me."

"Janine?"

"Yeah. My car died again this morning, and I have to be at work in five minutes." Her friend's words were rushed, her voice on the edge of panic. "I called Shelly, but her mom says she's not home. Do you think you could get your dad's car and pick me up?"

"Sure. I'll be there in a few minutes. Where are you? Home?"

"Yeah."

"Okay, I'll be right over."

She asked her parents if she could borrow the car to take Janine to work. Her father said okay, but her mother said no, they had shopping to do. She explained that she'd be back in ten minutes, two hours before the grocery store even opened.

"The keys are on the dresser," her father said.

Before her mother could disagree, Sue hurried into her bedroom, put on a pair of jeans and a T-shirt, grabbed the keys from her parents' room, and hurried out to the garage.

Janine worked at The Rocking D, a dude ranch situated at the foot of Poundcake Hill that catered to young rich couples from the Valley and out of state who liked to pretend for a week or a weekend that they were living in the Old West.

The Old West with swimming pools and cable TV.

The ranch was Rio Verde's sole claim to fame. A four-star resort, it had been built in the 1950s by a hotel mogul from back East who had been suckered into buying investment land in Rio Verde sight unseen. Determined to turn a lemon into lemonade, the mogul had built the Rocking D and had then proceeded to place advertisements for his "guest ranch" in such unconventional places as *National Geographic* and *Modern Equestrian* magazines. His strategy had worked, and while Rio Verde had been too far from civilization to ever make it a resort mecca, the Rocking D did generate a consistent profit. Ads for the ranch still appeared periodically on TBS and other cable stations, although, like the rest of the town, the ranch had lately fallen on hard times and had seen much of its business defect to Scottsdale and Laughlin.

Janine was waiting in front of her house in her cowgirl uniform, nervously banging her purse against her thigh, when Sue pulled up. She had the passenger door opened and was inside almost before Sue had stopped the car. "Let's go."

"What's the hurry? We'll make it."

"Yeah, but I have to be there on time. I was already late once last week, and let's just say my supervisor is not exactly my best friend."

Sue turned around at the end of the cul-de-sac and headed back toward the highway. They passed a corner where three raggedy-looking elementary schoolchildren waited for the bus.

"Did you get that schedule for Pueblo College?" Sue asked.

Janine shrugged. "I think so."

"I'm thinking of taking a few classes this semester. Classes start next week."

"You're driving all the way to Globe—?"

"Of course not. They have extension classes at the high school here on weeknights. Didn't you read the schedule?"

Janine shook her head. "No. But it doesn't matter. I wouldn't go back to school anyway. I'm over, done, and through with that crap. I promised myself on the day I graduated that I would never set foot in another classroom again."

Sue smiled but said nothing. Her friend's attitude was not entirely foreign to her—it was an attitude shared by most of her ex-classmates—but she still thought it terribly shortsighted. Credits from the extension courses were accepted at Arizona State University, Northern Arizona University, and most of the community colleges throughout the state. There weren't many classes being offered right now, but there would be, and she knew that she could earn nearly enough credits to get an AA degree without leaving Rio Verde.

Of course, she had always planned on going to college. Her parents had wanted her to go to college too, but there simply hadn't been enough money. She'd received two partial scholarships based on her academic achievement and SAT scores, one from ASU and one from Pitzer College in California, but the key word had been "partial." Each of the scholarships would have paid for half of her tuition, but she would have had to come up with the other half herself, as well as money for books, food, lodging, and transportation. On the advice of her high school counselor, she had applied for a student loan, but for the past few years both the state and federal governments had been cutting back on the number of loans made available, and her application was rejected. When she'd called the Financial Aid Office at ASU to ask why, she was told that her parents had too much equity. They owned both their house and their restaurant, and although her family barely managed to eke out a living each month, on paper they had assets in excess of $100,000—which made her ineligible for financial aid.

She had been doing everything she could over the past

two years to save money for college: living at home, working full time, allowing herself only an occasional movie for entertainment. But while she still wanted to go to college to learn, her parents' priorities had shifted a bit. They now thought of college as a place where she could look for a good husband.

Janine looked at her. "Night classes, though . . ." Her voice trailed off.

"I don't want to think about it," Sue said quickly.

Janine shivered. "They said his body was totally drained of blood. Like a vampire got him or something."

"That's a cheerful thought first thing in the morning."

"Well, you brought it up."

"No, I didn't. You did. I just said I might take some classes."

"Well, that's why I have to get there on time. I don't want to get transferred to the night shift. I may have to do some brown-nosing for a while, but I don't want to work all alone at that counter in the middle of the night. Not with some loony running around."

Sue turned off Highway 370 onto Rocking D Road, glancing at the dashboard clock. Janine might be a minute or so late, but that was all. "Do you need a ride home this afternoon?" she asked her friend.

Janine shook her head. "I'll catch a ride with somebody."

"You sure?"

"Yeah. Thanks for the lift, though. You saved me."

Sue pulled to a stop in the parking lot in front of the ranch house that served as a lobby. She looked from the western-style buildings to the fake boulders surrounding the two sculpted swimming pools. It always amazed her that people from other cities were willing to pay exorbitant amounts of money to spend a few nights here in Rio Verde.

She would pay money *not* to spend a few nights in Rio Verde.

"What are you doing Friday?" Janine said as she got out of the car.

"No plans yet. Why?"

"Let's do something then. Catch a movie, maybe."

"Sounds good," Sue said. "Give me a call."

"Okay. Later."

Sue watched her friend walk up the porch steps of the ranch house, then turned around, put the car into gear, and headed toward home.

Six

There was plenty of used underwear at the Goodwill, and Sophocles Johnson bought it all.

Ordinarily, they sorted the clothes by color here, putting blues with blues, whites with whites, browns with browns. But the underwear they lumped all together, regardless of the color or style, and he gathered up the rows of hangers from the rack without bothering to check the undergarments. Many of the panties and girdles were probably soiled and worn through, most of the men's briefs were probably stained, but he didn't care. He piled them high on his arms, made his way down the aisle past an overweight woman who smelled of yesterday's sweat, and dumped the underwear on the taped cracked glass of the checkout counter. The old woman working at the cash register eyed him strangely, seemed even to be a little frightened of him, but he refused to give her any reassurance or any hint as to why he wanted the underclothes, and he stood silently, watching the numbers ring up on the electronic cash register.

"Nineteen-fifty," the woman said.

He paid the money, watched mutely as the clerk placed the undergarments in an oversize plastic bag, then carried his purchase out the door and to his car. Grinning, feeling proud of himself, he drove through town and back to the bank. He was late—the lunch hour had officially ended twenty minutes ago—but it didn't matter. That was one

of the perks of presidency. He got to make rules and
didn't necessarily have to follow them.

Sophocles parked at the side of the bank, near the instant teller machine, and took the bag from the passenger
seat. The top of the bag had opened during the ride, and
he could smell the undergarments inside, the fragrance
at once acrid and somehow comforting. He got out of the
car, slammed shut the door, and flung the bag over his
shoulder, giggling because the act made him feel so damn
much like Santa Claus.

And he was going to be like Santa, in a way. At least to
his underlings.

No, his subjects.

If he was the president, they were his subjects.

He walked through the front door of the bank and
across the lobby, the bag still slung over his shoulder.
He nodded to Susan Richman, the customer service officer, and said hello to Tammette Walker, the teller on
duty. He was still grinning, unable to keep from smiling.
He felt so damn good, so proud of himself, so excited,
so happy. It was hard to keep his plan a secret, hard
not to blurt it out to everyone in the entire building,
but he managed to restrain himself, and made it to his
office without spilling either the beans or the bag. He
closed and locked the door behind him. Pressing the
intercom button on his phone, he told Marge Norson,
his secretary, to hold all calls and fend off all comers,
he was not to be disturbed.

He breathed deeply. *This* was a project. It would take
him several days, maybe the entire week, but he would
see it through, he would get it done.

He dumped the contents of the bag on the floor of his
office, took the sewing kit from the bottom right drawer
of his desk, and got right to work.

* * *

He sewed the underwear together himself, making uniforms for the tellers and the loan arranger and everyone else who worked at the bank. He neither washed the underwear nor dyed it a different color, but sewed the material together as it was, rayon to cotton to silk. While he called the clothes he made "uniforms," they were, in reality, nothing of the sort. If there were similarities between any two garments, it was strictly coincidental. He sewed without any plan or pattern but according to the dictates of the underclothes he found. The results, he had to admit, were spectacular. Before this, he had never picked up a needle or thread in his life, and he found himself imagining what he could have accomplished had he received formal training and guidance.

He placed the completed uniforms on hangers, which he hooked over the nails he'd pounded into the wall behind his desk. Bob Mackie could not have done any better. The uniforms were marvels of style over substance, each retaining the essence of the bras, briefs, or panties from which it was designed, yet somehow transcending its humble origins to become a unique and stylish customized bank outfit.

Sophocles had no idea whether or not the uniforms he was creating corresponded to the body sizes of his employees, but he didn't care. That did not matter. The workers could adjust their sizes to fit the clothes—gain or lose weight as necessary, wear platform shoes or flat sandals—and if they were not able or willing to do so, then new workers would be found.

Anything was possible. Anything could happen.

Anything.

He had learned that the other night. When he had been out in the desert with his telescope, waiting for the meteor shower.

When he had seen Jesus.

When he had seen Jesus kissing Manuel Torres.

He looked up from the uniform he was working on, feeling suddenly uneasy. An uncomfortable sensation came over him, and he had the feeling that he had forgotten something or had done something wrong. He frowned, trying to think, to remember. Then he saw his handiwork hanging from the hangers on the wall, and he relaxed as, once again, all seemed right with the world.

It was dark outside, and the clock above the desk said it was ten-thirty, but he was not yet tired. He grabbed a pair of skivvies from the pile. He could continue sewing for hours. He could work through midnight with no problem. Maybe until dawn.

He grinned. With any luck, he would be finished with the uniforms by Friday.

Seven

The door to the town council chambers was open when he walked by, and Robert stopped for a second to peek inside. The room was dark, save for the line of dim ceiling lights above the council members' seats, and the gallery was shadowed, the aisles next to the walls bathed in gloom. There was something creepy about the partial illumination of those empty chairs behind the raised circular desk, and he felt the hair on the back of his neck prickle. He hurried on, not looking back. He had passed by the council chambers a hundred times before on evenings such as this and had never thought anything of it, but tonight was different. Tonight everything seemed creepy.

Part of it was that damned autopsy report. That thing had been haunting him now for two days, ever since he'd first received it. Woods had declared the official cause of death to be, in layman's terms, exsanguination—loss of blood—but the circumstances surrounding that blood loss were truly frightening. For it was not only blood that had been removed from Manuel Torres's corpse, it was water, spinal fluid, saliva, semen, bile—every liquid that the human body produced or retained. And all of these fluids had been sucked out through a single hole bitten into the mechanic's neck.

Vampire.

That was the word they had tiptoed around, had been

afraid to say. It was ludicrous, of course, but it was also scary as hell. He had quizzed the coroner on the findings, asking if it would be physically possible for a deranged individual to suck out all of those fluids by placing his or her mouth on the wound. He knew from seeing Manuel's shriveled body that such an idea was absurd, but Woods had replied seriously that, yes, it would be possible with the aid of a pump strong enough to collapse interorgan membrane walls but not so strong as to significantly damage the organs themselves—although the coroner had to admit that he had never heard of the existence of such a device, and he didn't know how such a device could do exactly the same thing to the infinitely more fragile body structures of the animals found next to the corpse.

The truth was, neither of them had any idea how it had happened. The only theory that offered any explanation was vampirism.

But there were no such things as vampires.

Robert felt cold, though the night was not particularly chilly. The short peach-fuzz hairs on the back of his neck prickled. He was glad that Ted was on duty tonight. He would not have wanted to be alone in the police office right now.

Pussy, he told himself.

He shook his head, smiling wryly as he pushed open the glass door. *Robert Carter: Pussy Sheriff.* Might be a good title for his autobiography.

He walked inside, nodding at Ted, who was sitting behind the front counter. "How's it going tonight?"

"It's not."

"Good."

Ted stood, stretched, held his back. "Mary Beth Vigil called again, though. She says Mike's still missing."

Robert frowned. "What'd you tell her?"

"I told her she had to wait twenty-four hours to file a

missing persons report. She said it's been twelve hours already."

"Shit."

Mary Beth had phoned earlier in the afternoon to tell them that her father had not returned from a rig run to Casa Grande. He'd called her from the Casa Grande Dairy Queen before heading back to Rio Verde and had told her that he'd be home in two hours, but when three and a half hours had passed and he still hadn't arrived, Mary Beth had called them. They'd contacted the Department of Public Safety to see if there'd been any accidents on the highway, but none had been reported, and they'd assumed that Mike had stopped off at a truck stop for a piece of pie, or maybe just stopped off for a piece. He had been known to frequent Nicole's and was not above picking up hitchhikers in his more desperate moments.

Now Robert was not so sure. It wasn't like Mike to disappear for this long without letting anyone know where he was, particularly once he'd called and specifically said he was coming home.

"Did you call DPS again?" he asked Ted.

The deputy nodded. "No accidents, no stalls. Their helicopter flew the route an hour or so before sundown."

Robert felt the chill return. It was probably unrelated— he hoped to Christ it was unrelated—but he could not help thinking that whoever had killed Manuel Torres was still at large.

He imagined Mike lying at the bottom of the arroyo, his body shriveled and shrunken and dry.

The worry must have shown on his face, because Ted looked at him sympathetically. "You seem pretty worn out."

"Yeah," he admitted.

"Go home then. Get some rest."

He shook his head. "We have to come up with some leads on this murder."

"Tonight? There's nothing we can do tonight. Go home."

Robert ran a hand through his hair. He looked at the deputy, felt the sting of tiredness, and was forced to rub his eyes. "You're right," he said. He reached over the counter and picked up a rubber-banded stack of forms. "I'll take the answering machine off so I can hear the phone. If DPS calls or anything else comes up, give me a ring."

"Will do."

It was late, and the streets were empty as Robert drove home. He passed Rich's house and was going to give his usual shave-and-a-haircut honk as he drove by, but he saw that all of the lights were off and figured his brother and the family were already asleep. He turned onto Sagebrush, feeling slightly lonely. The moon was out, reflected in the front windows of all the homes on the right side of the street, and its dim bluish glow made the street look vacant and abandoned, like part of a ghost town.

The road curved at the foot of the hill, winding out toward the desert. The houses here were farther apart, with stretches of sand in between. In his parents' time, this had really been the boonies, and the school bus had had to make a special trip out this way just to pick up him and Rich. More homes had been built since then, but this was still the least populated section of Rio Verde, and cactus here still far outnumbered people. Most of the time he liked it this way—it meant he could crank up his stereo to maximum volume without disturbing his neighbors; it meant he could target practice in the desert behind his house without fear of hitting anything but rocks—but sometimes he felt isolated from the rest of the town, from the rest of the world, and at those times he wished that, instead of buying Rich out, he had sold the old homestead and both of them had moved closer to town.

He swung the car next to his mailbox, rolled down the

window, and checked to see if he'd gotten any mail. Pulling out three bills, he tossed them on the passenger seat next to him, then drove over the old boards that covered the culvert, and pulled to a stop on the dirt driveway in front of the toolshed.

As always, the house was empty, the living room dark and silent as he walked through the door. He had been alone longer than he'd been married, but somehow he'd gotten used to certain aspects of married life and had never been able to wean himself of them.

One was coming home to a warm lighted house.

He threw his keys on the coffee table and turned on the lights in the living room, dining room, and kitchen. The house seemed quieter than usual, and he walked over to the TV and turned it on, grateful for some noise. On HBO, a police detective was inviting a pretty young woman back to his apartment.

He went into the kitchen, got a beer out of the refrigerator, and stood in the doorway for a moment, watching the television. He could not remember the last time he'd invited a woman over. There had been a few after Julie, one-night sluts he'd corralled in the roper bars, but those he'd brought home more for spite than pleasure, as ammunition to use as return fire in case he and Julie ever got back together again.

They never had gotten back together, though, had never even *seen* each other after that last court appearance, and he had gradually stopped bagging the bimbos, realizing that there was no point to it.

The frightening thing was that he did not really miss them. Sex had just sort of drifted out of his life, and he had not even cared. He could not even remember the last time he'd beat off.

He sat down on the couch, feeling depressed.

Sometimes he wondered if he wasn't just wasting his life in Rio Verde. He had never lived anywhere else, had never even been out of Arizona for more than a few days at a time, and he wondered what it would be like to move to a different state. Rich often told him he was lucky not to have made the mistakes he himself had made in moving away, but Robert wondered. Rich was different, always had been. Rich could be happy in prison if he had enough books to read. He, on the other hand, lived in the real world more than in his mind, and he needed physical, material things to make him happy.

Periodically, he toyed with the idea of running away: packing a suitcase and taking off, not telling anyone, not looking back. It was a nice dream, but that's all it was. The idea was romantic enough to appeal to him, but he was practical enough to know that it could never be anything more than a fantasy. He had responsibilities here. He wasn't some nobody who would not be missed. He was the damn police chief.

And there was a murderer at large.

A vampire.

He finished off the beer and dropped the can into the wastebasket. He remembered that he'd told Ted he would turn off the answering machine. Reaching over the arm of the couch, he switched the phone over to manual. He put his feet up on the coffee table and tried to watch TV for a few minutes, but he felt restless, fidgety, and he kept flipping the channels, unable to concentrate on anything.

Finally he stood up and walked outside.

The night was warm, the slight chill that had infiltrated the past few evenings gone. He stood at the edge of the porch, leaning on the railing, and looked up at the stars. Venus was visible, and the Big Dipper, and the belt of Orion, but the light of the moon had forced many of the minor stars to fade into blackness. His eyes moved from the sky to the ground. To the north, he saw an army of multiarmed saguaro silhouetted in front of the faint glow of town lights. He shifted his weight, and a porch board

creaked, scaring the cicadas into silence. From the area
out toward Apache Peak came the faint howl of a far-off
coyote, a lonely eerie sound that, even after a lifetime of
desert living, he still associated with horror movies.

Vampires.

The chill returned, and as he glanced around, he realized that because of the lay of the land, he could not even
see the lights of his neighbors' houses from the porch.
The coyote howled again, its cry low but clear even above
the buzzing of the restarted cicadas.

Shivering, Robert walked back inside the house, locking
the door behind him.

Eight

Corrie dropped Anna off at preschool, then stopped by the video store to return the tapes they'd rented over the weekend. She was supposed to have dropped the tapes off yesterday, but she hadn't felt like doing it, and they'd sat in the backseat of the car until now. She'd been low and kind of melancholy for the past few days, and, truth be told, hadn't felt like doing much of anything. Usually, when she felt down, she was able to cheer herself up by reading or exercising or playing with Anna, but lately her mood seemed to remain constant no matter what she did, and she could not figure out why. She'd thought originally that it might be PMS, but she'd checked her calendar and that was still a week and a half away.

It was Rich, she decided. It was their relationship. They were drifting apart.

Or rather, she was drifting.

Rich was staying exactly where he'd always been, anchored securely in place.

The problem was that she did not seem to be drifting *toward* anything. She had toyed with the idea of going back to school to get her Master's. She had even halfheartedly considered having an affair. But nothing sounded good, nothing seemed right. Rich, of course, was oblivious to it all. He was as happy as ever, puttering around with his little paper, writing feature stories on ranchers who were making methane gas from steer manure and little old ladies who had once dated the cousins of B-movie actors. She didn't know if he actually thought his job was important, but she knew that he was content with it. He had no desire to do anything more ambitious, no desire to be anything more than the unread chronicler of these unlived small-town lives. And there was nowhere he would rather be than Rio Verde.

She wanted more. She'd known that from the beginning, from the first time he'd brought her back to this town to meet his brother. She'd tried to make a go of it for Rich's sake. She could see how much this meant to him, she knew how much he'd hated California, and she'd wanted him to be happy. But, damn it, *she* deserved to be happy too, and perhaps it was time for him to do a little sacrificing for her.

And for Anna.

She was not sure what she wanted for their daughter. She wasn't sure Rich was either. She could see his point about the crime and the drugs and the gangs in the cities, but she knew that he could see her point about the intellectual disadvantages of small-town life as well.

She sighed. Great parents they were turning out to be.

The bottom line was that she was not happy. It was time for a change. Even if she didn't know what that change was. Something in her life had to be altered. She was feeling stifled, smothered, though by what she didn't know. She did know that if something was not modified soon, she was liable to crack under the pressure.

It had occurred to her more than once recently that she should try to find another job, get away from Rich and the paper and do something separate, on her own. She had not mentioned this to Rich, but the more she thought about it, the more reasonable it seemed to her. A new job might not solve all of her problems, but it might be a step in the right direction.

She stopped at the crosswalk by the post office, waiting

for an old cowboy to cross the road, and looked past the end of the street to the flat desert beyond. To the right, she could see into the unfenced backyards of houses on the next street over: colored shirts and ragged white underwear hanging on crooked clotheslines, rusted cars and parts of cars sinking into sandy lots, discarded bikes and Big Wheels strewn carelessly about depressingly undergrown lawns.

God, this was an ugly town.

An ugly dying town. Despite the influx of Phoenicians on summer weekends, despite the presence of the Rocking D, Rio Verde was slowly but surely turning ghost. It had never been a thriving business community or cultural showplace, but with the closing of the mine in the late eighties and the loss of jobs, what little economic stability the town possessed had been decimated. Rio Verde could not survive on tourism alone, particularly not the kind of weekend recreational tourism attracted to this area of the state, and gradually businesses had started to bite the dust as people began to look elsewhere for work. In the past year alone, three stores had closed, and there were now six empty buildings in the two-mile stretch that constituted the downtown business district.

The old cowboy reached the curb, and Corrie applied pressure to the gas, moving forward. She turned left at the next corner, onto Center, and slowed down in front of the cafe, pulling into the parking lot of the newspaper office.

She was conscious of another feeling beneath the vague discontent and dissatisfaction. *Dread.* A murky, intuitive premonition that disaster was on its way. Her mind skittered over the emotion, preferring not to dwell on it. The feeling was strange and darkly alien, having nothing to do with Rich or herself or their relationship but with something bigger, something on the order of an earthquake or a war, and though it scared her to even consider the source of such a strong but undefined impression, she could not help but wonder if this feeling of dread was somehow contributing to her own personal sense of un-ease.

She turned off the ignition and grabbed her purse from the seat next to her, getting out of the car, locking it, and walking around the side of the building to the front entrance. She nodded to the receptionist as she entered. "How are you today, Carole?"

The older woman smiled. "It's still too early to tell. Ask me again after lunch."

"Ah, one of those days." Corrie smiled at the receptionist and walked around the modular office divider that separated Carole's desk from the newsroom. Rich, as usual, was on the phone, scribbling furiously on a scratch pad he had somehow managed to find amidst the mountain of paper before him, and he waved good morning to her as she dropped her purse on the desk against the opposite wall. Ordinarily, she would have sat down and sorted through her mail to see if there were any items of local interest that she could put in one of the columns she edited, but today she simply leaned against the desk and waited for Rich to get off the phone.

She found herself looking around the newsroom, at the pasteup tables at the far end, at the printer, waxer, and dryer, and she realized for the first time how truly sick she was of this place. She stared at the wall decorations— one Pena print, an aerial photograph of the town, and two framed issues of the paper that had won minor awards in the Arizona Press Association's annual newspaper competition—and wondered why she had never put her own stamp on this room, why she had never attempted to decorate even her own desk area.

Perhaps because she had never considered it hers.

There was a crackle of static from the police scanner on the shelf above Rich's desk, and he automatically reached up to increase the volume as he continued speaking on the phone. The police dispatcher recited a list of garbled numbers, then fell silent. Rich once again turned down the volume.

A moment later he hung up the phone, and she walked over to his desk. "We need to talk," she said, sitting down in the chair opposite him.

He frowned. "What's wrong?"

She looked at him, sighed, and shook her head. "Rich," she said, "I want to get a job."

"What do you mean? You have a job."

"No, a real job. One where I get paid. I'm tired of having to scrimp and save for every little thing. I'm tired of only eating food that we can get on double coupons."

"But I need someone to help me paste up and type out the columns. If you get another job, I'll just have to find someone else to take your place, and that'll cost us even more."

"No, it won't. I'll get a full-time job, you hire a part-time person. You only need someone one or two days a week. Besides, you'll be teaching. That'll bring in some extra cash."

"But what about Anna?"

"She gets off school at noon. You can pick her up and let her hang around the paper with you. Or we'll see. It depends on my hours."

He shook his head. "Well, what kind of job are you thinking of getting? The economy in Rio Verde is not exactly booming. You think there's actually an opening in this town for a woman who got her degree in Liberal Studies?"

She met his gaze. "That's not the point."

"Then what is the point?"

"I want another job. Away from you. Away from the paper."

"Why?"

"Because if I don't," she said, "I'll go crazy."

They stared at each other across the desk. Rich broke the stalemate first, shrugging, picking up his pen. "Fine." His voice was resigned, his attitude dismissive, and though he sounded as though he was too weary to continue arguing with her, she knew from experience that this meant he was going to emotionally cut himself off from the rest of the family for the next week or so, speaking only when spoken to, spending most of his time alone in the den, hiding. Pouting.

Right now, that suited her fine.

She stood. Part of her wanted to make an effort to explain things more clearly to him, to try to make him understand what she was going through, even though she didn't really understand herself, but another part just wanted to take the path of least resistance and that was the part that won out. "I guess I'd better start looking then."

"Let me know if you find anything."

She nodded. "I will. And I'll pick up Anna after school." She walked over to her desk and picked up her purse. She was about to walk out and throw a short "goodbye" over her shoulder, but something made her stop. She tried to smile at him. "We'll talk about this later, okay?"

Rich was already writing on his scratch pad and did not even look up. "Fine. Whatever you say."

She stood there, waiting for something more, but it was obvious that nothing was forthcoming, and she started walking.

"Good luck!" Carole called out to her as she walked out the door.

Nine

"Wait a sec. He just walked in." Steve put his hand over the mouthpiece of the phone as Robert stepped into the office. "Chief? I've got a woman here who thinks she might've seen the guy who killed Torres."

"Who is it?"

"Someone I don't know. She said her name's Donna Sandoval."

Robert's eyebrows raised in surprise. "I know Donna," he said. He walked around the side of the counter and took the phone from the deputy. He'd been half-expecting a crank: a panicked old lady who'd seen an unfamiliar man on her street, one of the small handful of do-gooding loonies who claimed to know the perpetrator of every crime. He had not expected to hear from someone like Donna Sandoval, who worked at First Interstate and was, as far as he knew, intelligent, trustworthy, reliable, and utterly devoid of imagination.

A perfect witness.

Maybe he would get some breaks here after all.

"Hello?" he said into the receiver.

"Chief Carter? This is Donna Sandoval. I . . . I heard what happened to Mr. Torres, and I think I might've seen the man who killed him."

"On the level?"

"I saw a man walking with Mr. Torres that night, just before he was supposed to've been killed."

Robert's pulse began racing. He pressed a button on the phone and another button on the connected tape recorder. "I'm going to record this conversation, Donna. If it's okay with you, I'll take this as your statement, have it transcribed, and you can come down to the station and sign it at your convenience. Would that be acceptable?"

"Sure. Whatever."

"All right. Please state your name and address, then tell me exactly what you saw."

"My name's Donna Sandoval. I live at 55 Gila Lane." She cleared her, throat. "On last Friday evening, around six o'clock, I was driving down Copperhead Road toward home. I'd stopped by the store to buy some groceries after work. The street was empty, but I saw two men walking along the side, away from Troy's Garage. When I got closer, I saw that it was Mr. Torres and another man. Mr. Torres . . . I don't know if I should say this, I don't want to impose my own feelings on what I saw—"

"Tell me everything. We'll sort out later what's important and what's not."

"Mr. Torres seemed nervous. At least to me. That's why I remembered seeing him. He was . . . sort of moving slowly and looking over his shoulder, like he didn't want to be walking with the other man, like he was looking for a way out of it."

"What did the other man look like? Did you get a good look at him?"

"Yes." She paused. "He was about six feet tall, about 250 pounds, and he was limping. He had a big thick mustache, a walrus mustache, and he was completely bald. He was wearing jeans and no shirt, just a Levi vest."

They were both silent. Robert was aware of the fact that the tape recorder was running, but did not know what to say. He stared down at the top of the desk as the hope he'd held dissipated and disappeared. Donna had just described Caldwell Burke, the man accused and convicted of molesting her daughter Charlotte in 1979.

There was only one problem.

Burke had died five years ago in a knife fight in the state prison in Florence.

"Donna," Robert said quietly. "You know who you just described."

She was silent for a moment. "Yes," she said.

"Burke's dead."

"I know that. I'm just telling you what I saw. I'm not saying it was Burke. I'm just describing the man I saw with Mr. Torres."

"How dark was it? Maybe you didn't see—"

"They were under the streetlight next to the garage. I had my glasses on. I could see perfectly."

There was something in Donna's tone of voice, a believability in her matter-of-fact declaration that caused a subtle chill to caress the back of his neck, an echo of his feelings from last night. He glanced down at Steve, who was looking at him expectantly, trying to follow the conversation from this side. "Did you see where the two of them went?"

"No. They were walking west, away from the garage, then I drove past them and turned off onto Gila to go home. When I heard what had happened, I thought I'd better call you and tell you what I saw, in case it might help."

"Were they walking toward a car or a truck, or did you see any unfamiliar vehicles parked near the garage?"

"That's all I saw. I've been wracking my brain all morning trying to remember something else, but that's all I could come up with."

"Did you see anyone else on the street or in the general area who also might have seen something?"

"Like I said, the street was empty." She paused, and when she spoke again her voice was quieter. "That really is what the man looked like. That's why I remember it so clearly."

"What was Mr. Torres wearing?"

"He had on jeans and a dirty T-shirt."

The chill was resurrected. That was exactly what he had been wearing when they'd found the body.

Robert glanced again at Steve, who raised his eyebrows hopefully. He wanted to follow up with more questions, to go over every point of Donna's story in detail, but he sensed from her voice that such an attempt would not be successful right now. He would cruise by later, maybe this afternoon, maybe tomorrow morning, and talk to her in person. "I think we have enough for now, Donna, but I may need to ask a few additional questions later. Would it be more convenient for you if I contacted you at home or at the bank?"

"Either one is fine."

"Thank you for calling, then. I'll have this transcribed into a statement. I may add whatever additional information you can give me later, and then I'll need you to come in and give us your John Hancock, okay?"

"Sure."

He hung up a moment later and walked across the office to his own desk.

"Anything there?" asked Steve.

"Hard to tell."

"Is she reliable?"

"Donna Sandoval doesn't have an imaginative bone in her body." He sighed. "I believe she saw someone, but I don't believe she saw who she thinks she saw."

"What's that supposed to mean?"

"Do you remember Caldwell Burke?"

Steve shook his head.

"Biggest crime we've had since I've been on the force. He was a child molester, and he was sent to Florence in seventy-nine for molesting Donna's daughter."

"That's who she saw with Torres?"

"That's who she described. But Burke was cut and killed five years ago in a yard fight."

"So you think she saw some guy with Torres, didn't get a look at him, and put the molester's face on him?"

Robert shrugged. "Could be. I don't know." He glanced out the window. There were a few thin white wisps of cloud near the hills on the horizon, but other than that the sky was a deep dark unbroken blue. It was going to be a hot one.

"So what's the plan?"

He thought for a moment. This morning he wanted to go over Troy's Garage once more, and then the length of street between the garage and the arroyo, see if he could find anything they'd passed by on first inspection. He would send Steve, and maybe Ted, to help out the DPS with the search for Mike Vigil. This afternoon, he planned to lead a full and complete search of the arroyo, from beginning to end. They'd examined the area immediately adjoining the segment in which they'd found the body, but little else, and he had a hunch they might've missed something. "Call Jud and Ben," he said. "I need every man out here. I want a full force today."

"But it's their day off."

"They'll get comp time." He looked at Steve. "You don't think a murder and a missing person's enough of a reason to adjust the regular work schedule?"

"I didn't say that."

"I hope not. Or I was going to suggest you give up police work and try your hand at shoe sales."

Steve grinned sheepishly.

"We're going to make a thorough search of the garage, the arroyo, and the area between the two. I want you and Ted to assist the state in looking for Vigil."

"What do we do? Just call them up and tell them we're coming over?"

"Basically."

"I don't—"

"I'll call Finn in Casa Grande and tell him to expect you two around noon."

"Thanks."

"Just don't let those guys push you around. Vigil's *our* missing person. They're working for us here."

"Gotcha."

The phone rang again, and Steve answered it. Robert listened to his deputy's side of the conversation and felt the chill return. He thought of Woods's report.

Exsanguination.

Steve hung up. "Man wouldn't give his name, but he says he knows who the vampire is."

"The vampire," Robert repeated.

Steve nodded slowly. "This is getting pretty weird," he said.

"Yeah." Robert put his feet up on the desk and once again looked out the window. "It is."

The temperature in the afternoon was even more unbearable than Robert had expected. He stood in the shade of the west wall of the arroyo and chugged the last half of his canned Coke. When was this damn Indian summer going to end?

He watched the two closest men walk slowly across the arroyo floor. There was no way that the shifting, loosely packed sand could have held a footprint, but he'd hoped to find something: a thread caught on a jojoba branch, a strand of hair pulled out in a struggle, hell, even a discarded gum wrapper.

But vampires don't chew gum.

Damn it, he had to start taking this seriously.

They'd found nothing new at the garage, and the detritus along the side of the road had been impossible to differentiate. He'd called off that search early in order to concentrate efforts down here. He had a gut feeling that they might find some sort of clue in the arroyo. The deliberate placement of the dead animals about Torres's head suggested to him that the mechanic had not been killed and then his body dumped, that most of the action had instead taken place down here, away from any possible witness's line of vision.

"Chief!"

He looked up to see Stu Thiebert hurrying around the curve of the arroyo, his feet pumping furiously in the shifting sand, his body moving forward at an incongruously slow pace, looking almost like a cartoon figure.

"We found something!"

Robert stepped away from the wall, placing his Coke can on the sand where he could retrieve it on his way out, and headed toward Stu, motioning for Jud to follow. His own feet moved slowly through the sand, but he hardly seemed to notice. "What is it?" he called.

"Mice! Dead desert mice! They're about a hundred yards down!"

Robert stopped walking, frowned. "Mice?"

"They look like they've been drained! You gotta come and see it!"

Robert felt his stomach clench up. He suddenly wished he'd brought Rich along. He followed Stu around the corner, Jud hurrying close behind. Ahead, he could see the other three men in a huddle next to the arroyo's eroded east wall.

"Here!"

Robert, Stu, and Jud reached the spot almost at the same time.

"Ben found them." Stu pointed toward a crack in the arroyo wall. "In there."

Robert's gaze followed his deputy's pointing finger. On the floor of the upward sloping fissure, reaching all the way to the surface, were twenty or thirty desert mice. They had indeed been drained of blood and fluids. Their bodies looked like deflated sacs of fur, their heads like hairy eyeless skulls.

Surrounding the top half of each mouse was a semicircle of shriveled, dried black beetles.

"Mother of shit," Jud breathed. The other men were silent. He looked at Robert. "What do you think this means?"

The knot in his stomach tightened. "I don't know," Robert said. "But go up and get the camera. And radio for Woods. I want him to see this."

He stared for a moment at the dead mice and their halos of beetles, then turned away.

Ten

After shutting off the lights, closing the blinds, and locking up the office, Rich walked around to the rear of the building, sorting through his overstuffed ring for the keys to the pickup. The sun had almost set, was little more than an orange half circle on the flat border of the cloudless western horizon, and the ground, the cactus, the buildings, and the mesas behind were all bathed in a muted amber glow that lent the town a fake, cinematic quality.

He stood next to the pickup, fingers on the door handle, watching the sun's slow descent, knowing that if he stood here long enough he would see the sky directly above shift from white across the red spectrum to purple. This was his favorite time of day, this hour of dusk between daylight and dark. He breathed deeply.

God, he loved this land.

Especially the horizon. He loved the horizon. Standing here in his parking lot, he could see the curve of the earth, a gentle rounding of the corners between north and west and south that somehow dwarfed the entire landscape. There were desert mountain ranges in the distance, and isolated mesas, but they were like bumps on a log, noticeable but not large enough to affect the totality. What he liked most was the open space. There was room to breathe here, the vistas were spectacular, the air was clear, and the sky covered three-fourths of the world.

That was one thing he'd noticed when they'd lived for that first year with Corrie's parents in California: The sky had seemed so small. It had been white there instead of blue and was revealed only in small segments between buildings and houses and trees. Even in the flatter areas of Los Angeles, the sky had still seemed low, claustrophobically close, not wide and expansive as it was in Arizona. He had never said so to Corrie, but it was that smallness of space, that feeling that he didn't have enough room to stretch even in the open air, which as much as anything had made him want to return to Rio Verde. It was a stupid reason for returning, he supposed, an immature attachment to the emotions of place. But strange as it might sound when articulated, it felt right, and he had never regretted coming back.

He opened the pickup door and slid onto the seat. He'd wanted to call Robert this afternoon, but things had been so busy with Corrie gone that he just hadn't had the time. Something had been nagging him. He should talk to his brother and find out what was going on with the investigation, but he'd rationalized his inertia by telling himself that if anything important happened, Robert would call. Besides, the scanner had been silent the entire time he'd been in the office.

He would phone Robert when he got home.

Rich looked at the clock on the dashboard as he turned the key in the ignition and the truck roared to mufflerless life. Six-forty. His new class started at seven. That gave him only twenty minutes to grab some chow and dig through the pile of papers on the seat next to him for the lesson plan he'd roughed out last weekend.

Buford's Burgers was on the way, and while it wasn't a drive-thru, it was the closest thing to it. He could sort through his papers in the pickup while he waited for his order.

He threw the truck into reverse, pulled out of the parking lot, then jammed it into gear and took off down Center, slowing only for a moment at the corner, then speeding down 370 toward Buford's.

He passed the small brick American Legion hall and saw that both the U.S. and Arizona flags were at half-mast, their colors altered and darkened by the setting sun and the growing twilight.

The obit for Manuel Torres he'd written this afternoon had been pitifully inadequate. He had spoken to Troy and Manuel's other coworkers at the garage, but they had not been very articulate in their expression of grief. Manuel's widow had not wanted to talk to him at all, and he had respected that, leaving her alone. He'd done the best he could under the circumstances, but he had not really known the man himself, and that distance, combined with the bizarre circumstances of his death, had cast an almost tabloid air of sensationalism over everything he'd tried to write.

Maybe he would go over the obit tomorrow, try it one more time before putting it permanently to bed.

He found himself thinking about the autopsy report and what Robert had told him. It had not been a surprise, really. But somehow the written confirmation—typed, dated, and signed in triplicate on official county forms— gave it an air of authenticity and turned what had been merely a suspicion into frightening fact. He'd been right when he'd told his brother that it was like being in a horror movie.

The coroner, he knew, had pressured Mrs. Torres into having the body cremated, and although, as a devout Catholic, she had wanted to see her husband decently buried, she had reluctantly agreed to the cremation, electing to bury the ashes afterward in a traditional cemetery plot instead of having them interred. This capitulation of faith worried Rich because he knew the impetus behind it. He had heard all day the whispers, the thinly veiled references. He knew the word in everyone's mind.

Vampire.

It was a belief that such a creature really could exist which had led Woods to suggest cremation and Mrs. Torres to agree to this otherwise unsatisfactory burial alternative.

Cremation was insurance that Manuel Torres would not rise from the dead.

Rich wanted to be angry at this superstitious regression on the part of what would seem to be rational people, but he too had seen the body, he too had seen the halo of animals, and he could not drum up as much anger as he would have liked. The shriveled and empty form of the old man had frightened him far more than he would have thought possible.

He was equally frightened at the prospect of mass hysteria and paranoid panic. Deep down, he did not believe in vampires. Not really. Something strange had happened to Manuel Torres, but he had no doubt that once the murderer was found, a rational explanation for the death would be forthcoming.

He drove into the dirt parking lot of Buford's, pulling next to a dusty Jeep with a round NRA sticker on the corroded back bumper. He turned off the ignition and got out. Reading the lighted menu, he realized that he was hungrier than usual. Tonight he wanted more than just his usual hamburger and medium Coke.

Stress always made him hungry.

It was Corrie's fault as well. She could have waited until things calmed down a little before bailing out on him. He told himself not to be so harsh on her, not to be so unsympathetic; he was her husband, not just her editor; he should be able to understand her side. But, as she never tired of pointing out, that was one of his chronic problems: He was too selfish and insensitive to sympathize with her feelings.

But, damn it, she should've given him warning.

She'd already found a job. That surprised him. She'd been lucky enough to be in the right place at the right time, and she was now the secretary for the Church of the Holy Trinity. That was okay, he supposed, but the fact that she was going to be working for Pastor Wheeler bothered him a little. He did not know the pastor, had had no real contact with the man aside from a few short phone conversations regarding events for the "Church Notes" column of the paper, but he'd always had the impression that Wheeler was something of a sleaze and a charlatan, a man who aspired to and was perfectly suited for televangelism. He didn't like Wheeler, and he didn't like his wife working for Wheeler, but at this point it was probably wiser for him to say nothing about it.

He was not sure if he could bring himself to be supportive, though.

Buford himself, a blond crew cut ex-Marine gone only slightly to seed, stepped up to the window. "Whatcha want today?"

"I'll take a double cheeseburger, large fries, and an extra-large, super-thick chocolate shake."

Buford grinned. "Bad day, huh?"

"And it's not over yet."

"That'll be four forty-five."

Rich broke out his wallet and handed him a five-dollar bill.

Buford gave him back two quarters and a nickel. "So, do you think there really is a vampire?"

"What?" Rich stared at him.

Buford shrugged. "Rumors."

"There're no such things as vampires."

"Well, even if there are, I've got enough garlic in here to hold them at bay until dawn." Buford laughed.

Rich forced himself to smile. "Look, I have a few things to do, so when my food's ready, give me a holler. I'll be in the truck."

"Will do."

Rich walked slowly back to the pickup. Even Buford was talking about vampires.

He would call Robert tonight when he got home.

The two of them had a lot to discuss.

Eleven

Sue stood next to the gym, looking down the hallway. It felt strange being back here again. She had not returned to the high school since graduation, and although it had only been two years and she had not, to her knowledge, grown, everything seemed smaller: doors, drinking fountains, lockers. It was like visiting a school built for munchkins.

It also seemed somewhat threatening, and that was not something she would have thought possible. For her, school had always been a refuge, a haven where even the uncivilized were forced to behave in a civilized manner. The microsociety created by teachers, administrators, and the other adults in authority had created for her a very pleasant environment, a sharp contrast to the rougher and more chaotic world outside the school boundaries.

But everything had changed. That familiar society had shut off for the night and left in its wake this scaled-down and darkly alien travesty of her old stomping grounds. She glanced to her right at the door to the girl's restroom and was thrown off by its surprisingly diminutive stature. It was probably just her imagination, but, like everything else, the doors in the buildings looked as though they had shrunk and been reduced to dimensions more appropriate to a junior high school.

She stared straight ahead. The hallways had not shrunk, however. They seemed to have grown much longer.

And darker.

She shivered, turning around, and looked back toward the parking lot, but hers was still the only car in sight. Once again, she faced the hallway. It looked like a tunnel or a cave, the staggered shadows forming stalactites, stalagmites, and outcroppings of stone. The shadows overlapped, created shapes where there weren't shapes, darkened areas that were already dark. There were lights on, but they were few and far between, and Sue wondered if perhaps she'd misread the class schedule and come on the wrong day. The only illumination seemed to come from downward trained vandal lights on the corners of each building and from single bulbs housed in protective mesh which hung down from the ceilings of the hallway at long intervals. The lights near the lockers were off, and the windows in all of the classrooms were black.

She peered down at the schedule in her hand, trying to read in the gloom. No, today was the fourth. The class was supposed to start today.

So why was the school so empty? Why was no one else here?

And why was she afraid to walk down the hall?

Silence.

That was the primary reason she kept standing here. The silence. Not a sound disrupted the complete quietude of this place, not a voice or footstep disturbed the perfect noiselessness. It was like being in a vacuum, or a tomb. Even outside sounds from the other parts of town did not appear able to penetrate the invisible sonic barrier which seemed to surround the school.

This was stupid. She was just being dumb. The reason everything was dark and silent was because night classes were all held on the other side of the school. Out of habit, she'd parked in the student lot on the south side of campus. She should've parked in the faculty lot on the north side. All she had to do was walk down the hallway, past the lockers, and through senior corner to get where she was supposed to be.

But she didn't want to walk down the hallway.

She peered into the dimness. Was it her imagination, or were the hall's irregularly spaced lights less bright than they had been just a moment before? And had the shadows shifted? She cleared her throat, and the noise was like a gunshot in the stillness. Why couldn't she hear any noise from the other side of campus?

Then something moved at the far end of the hallway.

Her heart lurched in her chest. A black amorphous shape had passed through a patch of dull light, moving from one shadow to another. She thought she could still see it, darker than its surroundings—jet against charcoal—but the specifics of its form were so vague that she could not be sure.

Sue took a deep breath. She was not afraid of the dark, had never been plagued by that traditional childhood fear. But she could not shake the feeling that someone—*something*—was waiting for her at the far end of the hall.

She had an impression of size. And tremendous age.

It was the vast age that frightened her the most.

Her mouth was dry, her hands shaking. She turned around and hurried back out to the parking lot, to the car. She fumbled with her keys, trying to open the door, certain that if she turned around she would see, coming up behind her, that ancient black shape, large and getting larger.

She found the right key and unlocked the door, banging her knee on the metal as she pulled it open. She scrambled into the car as quickly as she could, locking the door before daring to look where she'd been.

There was nothing there. The parking lot was empty.

Still hyperconsciously aware of the fact that she was alone out here, that if something happened there would be no one to hear her scream, she slipped the key into the ignition, started the engine, and peeled out. She did not know why she'd been so stupid, why she hadn't realized immediately that the parking lot was empty because night classes were held on the other side of the school. She'd told Janine and promised her parents that she would be careful, and instead she'd behaved like a complete idiot.

She thought of Manuel Torres, tried to imagine what a man would look like who'd been totally drained of blood.

She drove down the small dirt road around the school to the faculty lot. Here there were lights, and other vehicles, and small groups of people walking toward their classrooms. She pulled into a parking space next to a Dodge van. The terror and the panic subsided somewhat. A moment before she'd been half ready to run screaming through a group of strangers, warning that the monsters were coming. But now, though the fear was still strong within her, though when she looked toward the darkened southern half of the school she could still see in her mind that black and shifting shape, the idea that some sort of . . . monster lay crouched and waiting within the confines of the campus seemed absurd and melodramatic, the product of an overactive imagination.

Still, she could not shake the feeling that she had been in very real danger.

Maybe she would tell her teacher that she'd seen someone suspicious lurking in the hallways and let him find someone to check it out.

She walked toward the office, following two old women armed with paintbrushes and sketch pads who were obviously here to attend an art class. Outside the office, they parted ways, the two women heading toward the multipurpose rooms to the left, Sue going toward the right.

She found room 211, her old sophomore English classroom, easily enough and entered. Again, everything seemed smaller than she remembered: the desks, the blackboards, the room itself. So far, she was the only student here. The teacher, a clean-shaven man in his early to midthirties who looked vaguely familiar, stood next to the front blackboard at the head of the rows of empty desks and smiled at her. Both of them glanced up at the wall clock at the same time.

"Five minutes to go," the teacher said. "I don't think we're going to have a very big class."

Sue smiled politely back at him and sat down at a desk in the middle of the room.

He looked down at the roll sheet in his hand. "You're Susan Wing?"

"Yes." She nodded. "Sue."

"Well, you're the only one who's actually signed up for the course. I did have two other people on the list, but they both cancelled. I was hoping I'd get some walk-in registrants, but I don't think so." He gave her a wry grin. "Journalism's not the hot draw it was after Watergate."

"What if no one else shows up?" she asked.

"Then the class is cancelled. We need at least six people to keep a class open." He looked again at the clock. Three minutes to seven. "By the way, my name's Rich Carter. I'm the editor of the *Rio Verde Gazette*. You can call me Rich."

Sighing, Sue looked down at her desktop. "I really wanted to take this class."

"I really wanted to teach this class. I need the extra money."

"I need the credits. I'm trying to get some of my general ed done at Pueblo before I transfer to ASU, but not that many applicable courses are offered."

Rich walked down the middle aisle, stuck his head out the door, looked both ways. He glanced back up at the clock. "Seven. I don't think anyone else is coming."

Sue stood.

"Have you ever taken a journalism class before? Were you on the school newspaper or anything?"

Sue shook her head.

"Well, did you sign up strictly for the GE credits, or are you really interested in journalism?"

"Both."

"The reason I'm asking is because I can give you some real hands-on journalism experience. We'd be able to kill two birds with one stone. I just lost one of my reporters, and I need a replacement. You'll get to do a little typesetting, a little pasteup, a little of everything, learn all aspects of the newspaper biz. It'll be part time, of course, but I'll pay you. By the hour or by the column inch, whichever is more."

"Will I still get credit for the class?"

He laughed. "Sure. I'll talk to the dean. We'll call it 'Independent Study' or something."

"Thank you."

"If it's not too presumptuous, may I ask why you're not going to one of the Valley community colleges for your general ed? It seems kind of backward to just wait around until Pueblo offers transferable courses. You might have to wait for years."

Sue reddened. "I have no choice. We can't afford anything else."

Rich nodded. "I hear you." He looked at her. "Don't you work at that Chinese restaurant?"

"My family owns it," she admitted.

"I thought so." He pulled a piece of paper from the pad beneath his roll sheet and wrote something down. "Here," he said, handing her the paper. "This is the number of the paper. Give me a call tomorrow morning around ten or so, and we'll set something up."

"Okay."

"I'll talk to you tomorrow, then."

Sue started toward the door, saw the night outside,

black in contrast to the light of the classroom. She turned back toward Rich. "Are you leaving now too?"

He shook his head. "I'm required to stay here until twenty after, just in case someone else shows up."

"Well, I'll see you later, then." She swallowed, her heart pounding, and forced her feet to carry her through the door.

Outside, it wasn't that bad. Other classrooms were lit, and there were plenty of late students and teachers walking around. She hazarded a glance toward the darkened other half of the school, and goose bumps popped up on her arms. It seemed stupid now to tell anyone what she'd seen, or to even hint that she'd seen anything, but the fear was still there.

She ran through the lighted parking lot to the station wagon.

She did not relax until the school was receding in her rearview mirror.

Twelve

Pastor Wheeler was awake the second time Jesus appeared.

He was locking the door of the vestibule for the evening when he sensed a subtle change in the quality of the air. It seemed suddenly easier to breathe, and his head felt light, open, as though all oppressiveness and negativity had been lifted from his mind, and the full potential of his thoughts was suddenly allowed to flower freely and unrestrained within his brain.

He turned around but saw nothing there, only the empty pews in their parallel rows, the last of the afternoon sun glowing in weak rainbows around the edges of the stained glass windows.

He turned around again—

And there was Jesus.

The Savior was standing in front of the altar in all of His glory, gazing up at the cross that hung above the pulpit, the cross that the pastor had found rotting in the desert near Goldfield and had refinished himself. Wheeler held his breath, not daring to move. He gazed, transfixed, at the back of Jesus' head, at His long, gorgeous reddish brown hair. Pride was a sin, Wheeler knew, but he felt proud nevertheless, knowing that the Savior would be pleased with his efforts. The cross had been constructed from discarded railroad ties, and the wood had been weatherworn and faded nearly white when he'd found it outside the ghost town, the whorled grain dried and raised by exposure into ridges. He had dragged the cross over his shoulder, as Jesus had, only through the desert to his car instead of through the streets to Golgotha. Days and nights he'd spent sanding the cross, finishing it, coating it with the finest oils, and when it was finished, he'd known that it was something special. He'd known that it was good.

He had been preaching in Phoenix at that time, had moved twice since, but the cross had remained a constant in his life and had always accompanied him.

Now Jesus turned to him, smiling, and Wheeler felt an ecstatic pride swell within his breast. "You have created a thing of beauty," Christ said. His voice filled the air of the silent church like music, caressing the empty space between the beams in the peaked roof, falling gracefully down to spread lightly through the lower half of the chapel. "Men will volunteer to be crucified on your cross. Women will plead to be allowed to be nailed on such wood."

"Yes," Wheeler whispered. He stood unmoving as the warmth of rapture flooded through him. The feeling in real life was much stronger than it had been in his vision and much more immediate, a physical sense of extraordinary well-being that spread throughout his body, manifesting itself in his head, in his heart, his fingers and toes. It was a feeling like no other, and he knew with utter certainty that it was not something that could be duplicated by drugs or sex or any human-generated states of euphoria. It could only be found in the presence of the Lord.

"You have heeded my words," Jesus said. "But there is still much that needs to be done."

There was something both great and terrible in the countenance of Christ as He spoke, and though it was sublimated and subdued, translated for his benefit into

human terms, Wheeler could, sense the awesome power
of God in the arrangement of those familiar features. As
before, there were questions he wanted to ask, things he
wanted to know. But also as before, the impulse was
quashed, and he was intimidated into silence by the Savior's presence.

Jesus nodded His understanding. "All of your questions
will be answered," He said.

Tears of gratitude filled the pastor's eyes. "Thank you."

Jesus smiled again, and His smile brightened the interior of the darkening church with the light of goodness.
He gestured with one graceful hand toward the world outside the stained glass windows. "This town is home to sin.
It is filled with evildoers. It must be cleansed before it can
become host to the house of the Lord. It must be cleansed
with the blood of the guilty."

Information flooded into Wheeler's brain, the totality
of the concepts that Jesus only touched upon with His
words, each course of action instantly magnified and clarified. Wheeler saw tortured faces, scarred and scored and
bleeding, contributing to the greater glory of God with
the pure and exquisite beauty of their deaths. He saw
gracefully severed heads and arms, artfully eviscerated torsos, streams of corrupted blood flowing into a river of
forgiveness that led straight to Jesus Christ. He saw slaughtered sinners, immolations, decapitations, and crucifixions. He saw the virtuous rejoicing at the passing of the
wicked, wielding weapons of pain in the war of the righteous, the pure and the chaste granting welcome release
to the tortured souls given them by the Almighty.

Wheeler found himself buoyed by the images, suddenly
filled with strength, but still it took all of his courage to
raise his head and address Jesus directly. "I bought some
things for the church," he said. His voice was little more
than a cracked whisper. He turned and fumblingly opened

the door to the storeroom behind him to display what he had purchased in Phoenix.

The fetters. The rope. The bear trap. The knives.

Jesus smiled, and the radiant glow which always seemed to surround Him grew brighter. Wheeler sensed in the Savior a hunger, a craving, an almost tangible desire. Christ's gaze took in the assembled instruments of bondage and pain, and He looked upon Wheeler with approval, eyes shining. "You have done well, my son."

Again, the minster was filled with an almost unbearable sense of pride. His actions had pleased the Lord!

"You have forty days," Jesus said. "Forty days to complete your task."

Wheeler nodded dumbly. Forty was the Lord's favorite number. When he destroyed the earth the first time, wiping the slate clean of wickedness and iniquity with the flood, it had rained for forty days and forty nights. When Christ went alone into the wilderness, he went for forty days and forty nights.

Now Jesus was giving him forty days and forty nights to complete His church.

Woe to him if he failed.

Jesus turned away and, for a brief second, Wheeler thought that the Savior looked like his father. He saw the familiar heavy lantern jaw, the thin delicate nose. A wave of cold washed over him and he shivered, unnerved by the resemblance. Then his attention was distracted by a black shadow that interrupted the rainbow glow, flitting past the series of stained glass windows.

When he looked back, Jesus was gone. There was only a soft vague luminescence in the air where He had been.

Wheeler's eyes were filled with tears, his heart with joy, and he knelt down to kiss the floor where Jesus had stood before closing the door to the storeroom and locking inside the blessed instruments with which the Lord's will would be done.

* * *

The shell of the Baptist church arrived early Friday morning in twin flatbeds, a third truck with an attached crane carrying the interior fixtures and other nonstructural items in its half van. There were three volunteers from the ACCC in addition to the truck drivers, and Wheeler had engaged two workers from Worthy Construction for the day. Four other men from the parish had volunteered their own time to help reassemble the church.

Wheeler stood next to the crane operator, a burly dark-tanned man wearing a CAT hat, as the flatbeds were maneuvered into position on the vacant lot next to the existing church. The crane operator frowned as he watched the proceedings. He turned to the pastor. "Where're we going to put the structure?"

Wheeler pointed to the empty section of property on the north side of the existing church. Ten parish members had spent the better part of the week clearing and leveling the ground. "Right there."

"You got no foundation. You got no hookups."

"We're going to put it there."

The crane operator looked around, then turned suspiciously back toward Wheeler. "You got any permits? Building permits? Structural permits? Electrical permits?"

"We're going to put it there." Wheeler smiled calmly at the man.

"You can't do this. You have to go through the proper channels. You have to follow the proper procedures. I'm going to talk to Davis. The council can't deliver a church to a location without any permits."

"Talk to Davis," Wheeler said. The permits were all in order, he had obtained them from the county several days ago and had already shown them to the coordinator, but he was not about to tell that to this ignorantly officious nonentity. He watched the crane operator stride across the dirt toward the trucks, then looked slowly around in satisfaction. He saw the town as it had appeared in his vision, the hard desert ground covered with soft grass and beautiful flowers, the dusty, run-down buildings restored better than new with gleaming fresh paint and clean, shining windows. At the center of this new town, at the center of the new world, he saw the Church of the Living Christ, a glorious monument to the greatness of God.

He smiled benignly at the group of onlookers who had gathered in the street to see what all the fuss was about. They would soon be dead, he knew, consigned to the pit of hell by the wrath of the Almighty. No more would they dog his heels with their petty annoyances, intruding into his life with the mundane strictures of their secular world. They would be dealt with by the hand of God. He saw in his mind Lang Crosby flayed alive, his eyes white and bulging bug-like in his bloody red-muscled face. He saw Jane Page with a ragged hole ripped between her legs where the source of her sin originated.

He breathed deeply, feeling good. This was going to be a special day.

A very special day.

Even with the help of the ACCC workers, the church volunteers, and the men from Worthy Construction, it took all morning and most of the afternoon to attach the two sectional halves of the building and get the shell settled in place. There were a few minor mishaps—a window broke when the crane dropped the first section too jarringly on the ground, and a small portion of the lower east wall was accidentally damaged when a corner of the flatbed bumped against it—but for the most part things went very smoothly, and by nightfall the reconstructed church, on the outside at least, looked almost the same as it had when he'd viewed it back in Phoenix.

It was after dark before Pastor Wheeler finally told everyone to call it quits. The bulk of the fixtures still remained in the third truck, but the two flatbeds were empty. The first phase of the work would be completed tomorrow.

The ACCC workers were put up in the homes of willing parishioners for the night, and Wheeler saw them to their hosts' houses, giving each his hearty thanks. Afterward, he returned to the church. He picked up his plastic iced tea cup from the hood of one of the trucks and walked into the empty husk of the new addition. The wooden floor had been placed directly atop the dirt, and while he had been lectured on the disadvantages of such a move by all of the construction workers and ACCC men, it looked good. In the next few weeks, they would tear out a portion of one wall and connect it to the existing church. In his mind, he saw the completed project, the finished Church of the Living Christ, a house of worship so large and unique that it would appear on the desert horizon taller than Apache Peak, more substantial than the surrounding bluffs, acting as a beacon to the multitudes who would come to praise God.

He felt a tingle of excited anticipation course through his body. On Sunday he was going to tell his flock that the Lord Jesus Christ had returned. He was going to tell them what he had seen, what he had been told. He did not know how they would take the good news, but that only contributed to his excitement.

This would separate the wheat from the chaff in his congregation. This would determine the future of his flock.

He took a sip of his iced tea and grimaced as something grainy and foul-tasting rode the wave of liquid over his tongue and down his throat. He pulled off the plastic lid and held the cup toward the refracted light that streamed through the door and windows. On the single floating slice of brown lemon were dozens of small furiously crawling flies, each about the size of a pinhead. More small specks floated in the dark tea between the ice cubes. Some sort of fruit fly, he assumed. He was about to walk outside and toss the contents of the cup on the ground when he realized that, like everything else, this too was part of God's plan.

If Jesus hadn't wanted him to drink the flies, he wouldn't have allowed them into his tea.

Wheeler thought for a moment, then gave a short prayer of thanks, replaced the lid, put the straw to his lips, and drank.

Thirteen

The last hour at the restaurant had been slow, so they'd eaten pork fried rice and an order of chicken *chow fun* that had been phoned in but not picked up, and had cleaned up early. Sue and John wiped the tables and swept the floor in the dining area, while their mother and grandmother washed dishes. Their father took care of the woks and the cooking area. They left on time for once, and it was only a few minutes after nine when they pulled into their driveway.

Although it was dark out, Chris Chapman and Rod Malvern were standing on the strip of brown grass that separated their properties, talking, and Sue waved at them as she got out of the car. They waved back and returned immediately to their conversation. Neither of them acknowledged her parents at all. She shut the car door and followed her father and mother around the willow tree, up the short walk to the house. Such behavior was something she'd gotten used to over the years, and though she supposed she should be angry about it, she really didn't care. She accepted the situation as part of The Way Things Were.

The Way Things Were.

She told herself that The Way Things Were were that customers did not become overly friendly or overly familiar with shopkeepers, restaurant owners, or other individuals with whom they did business, that there was a wall automatically erected during the establishment of such a business relationship that discouraged more intimate contact. But she knew that wasn't really the case. Mike Fazio, who owned Mike's Pizza Place in the Basha's shopping center, seemed to be good friends with many of his customers. Hank and Tara Farrel, who operated the video store, often socialized with their patrons.

It was because her family was Chinese.

She didn't like thinking about that. It made her uncomfortable, and she couldn't help feeling that she was being overly sensitive. On TV, when she saw Asian groups protesting showings of Charlie Chan movies or cartoons with Oriental stereotypes, she always felt uneasy, wanting to agree with the protestors—knowing she should agree with them—but not being able to fully take their side. She had a hard time convincing herself that, in this day and age, race made any difference at all in the way people were viewed or in how others behaved toward them. After all, the sports heroes of some of the biggest rednecks in town were black football and basketball players. Their kids spent their music money on the tapes of black pop stars. Was it reasonable for her to think that her family was treated differently merely because they were Chinese?

Yes.

Because, after all these years, her family still did not fit in, were still treated more like outsiders than members of the community. Even the nicest customers, those who joked and laughed with her, who were friendly and respectful toward her parents, seemed awkward and standoffish outside the confines of the restaurant. They would nod, sometimes smile, at the most say a quick "hi," but the relaxed informality of their behavior as customers disappeared when the roles of waitress and patron were no longer in effect. Her family was not shunned, not even actively disliked, it was just that they were treated . . . differently.

And it was because they were Chinese.

Sue had never had a problem with prejudice. She'd always had a group of close friends, had never been treated unfairly, had never been discriminated against, had always been accepted by her peers and by the kids she'd grown up with. Her parents, though, had no friends in town, had always been socially ostracized. More than the skin color, more than the Oriental eyes, more than any aspect of physical appearance, it was the language that seemed to separate them from everyone else. Their accents and broken English served to emphasize that they were from another country, an alien culture. And when they spoke Cantonese, it actually seemed to offend people.

But that was The Way Things Were.

The night was warm, without a breeze, and the moonless sky was dark, the stars like tiny prisms against their black backdrop. Sue glanced up as she followed her parents into the house. She noticed that the constellations had changed position since the last time she'd looked, shifting closer to their winter locales, and it made her realize how quickly time was speeding by. Summer had just ended, and soon it would be Christmas. Then summer again. Then Christmas. Years were now moving by in the time it had once taken seasons to pass.

Inside the doorway, her father took off his shoes and carried the leftover food from the restaurant into the kitchen. John, without pausing, walked into the living room, turned on the television, and immediately draped himself over the couch. Her mother and grandmother took off their own shoes and followed her father into the kitchen.

Sue stood for a moment in the entryway as she slipped off her sandals, staring at a pink-flowered fan hanging on the walls She was not sure whether she should go to her bedroom or help her parents and grandmother in the kitchen. Instinct told her to go to her room. Something was not right tonight. She'd felt weird all evening, spooked—though not quite as badly as she had been the other night at the school—and she wanted to go to bed and forget about it.

Wai.

Badness.

She heard her grandmother speaking quietly to her parents in the kitchen. All evening her grandmother had been uncharacteristically silent, not even listening to her tapes as she chopped vegetables in the rear of the restaurant. Several times, upon turning around, Sue had caught the old woman staring at her strangely, and she'd seen her grandmother bestow equally cryptic looks upon her brother. Her parents, too, had noticed the change in her grandmother's mood—she could tell by the way that they were polite to each other instead of bickering—but neither of them had said a word about it, and they'd continued about their business as usual.

She looked toward the kitchen, then decided against going there or to her bedroom, opting instead for the coward's way out. She walked over to where John lay sprawled on the couch, his head leaning against one armrest, his feet pressing against the other. "Move over," she said. "Let me sit down."

"Mo cho," he told her.

"Shut up yourself."

"Hit the road. You're blocking my view."

"Fine then." She sat down on top of his legs.

"Hey!" he yelled, trying to wiggle out from under her. "Knock it off!"

"Tieu pay."

"You're too fat. It hurts!"

"Then move your feet so I can sit down."

"Get up so I can move my legs."

She stood, and he gave her a quick kick in the buttocks before rolling off the couch and out of her way. He looked back over his shoulder to make sure she wasn't going to retaliate, then spread out on the floor in front of the television. He wrinkled his nose. "I can't sit next to you. You reek."

"You're the one who smells," she said. "Take a bath."

"Susan."

Sue turned her head at the sound of her grandmother's voice. The old woman was standing in the doorway, framed by the light from the kitchen, her frazzled white hair forming a fuzzy penumbra around the silhouetted shape of her face. For a brief second, she looked to Sue like a witch, and an instinctive shiver passed down Sue's spine as the image imprinted itself on her brain. Then her grandmother walked all the way into the room and once again she looked like herself.

Sue forced herself to smile. "What is it, Grandmother?" she asked in Cantonese.

"Will you come with me to my room? I have something I want to give you."

"Yes." She was puzzled, but it would not be polite to question her grandmother, so she got up from the couch and followed the old woman down the hall. Behind her, John immediately jumped up from the floor to retake his seat.

Her grandmother's room smelled, as always, of must and medicine and herbs, the odors of old age. On the small teak nightstand next to her bed were two bottles of ginseng, the source of the room's dominant scent. One of the bottles, the smaller of the two, was filled with dried chopped slivers of the root. In the other, a full root floated in clear liquid, looking like a little man trapped inside the glass with its branching offshoots at arm level and its downward growing rootlet legs.

Sue had always liked going into her grandmother's room. Slightly warmer than the rest of the house, it seemed to her exotic, like a little piece of China transplanted here to Arizona, in stark contrast to the Americanized Chinese decor of her parents. She liked the dark three-paneled screen that separated the sleeping area from the sitting area, the huge hand-painted vase in the corner, the ornately carved furniture. Tonight, though, that exotic, mysterious quality seemed a trifle disquieting, the dark room a little too dark.

Wincing as if in pain, her grandmother sat down awkwardly on the edge of the bed. Her shoulders slumped as the bed settled beneath her weight, and for the first time she looked old to Sue. Really old. The deeply etched lines surrounding her mouth and eyes, which had remained unchanged for as long as Sue could remember and had always seemed a permanent part of her face, had altered, shifted course, moving downward into her chin, upward into her cheeks and forehead, and were now intersected by newer spiderweb wrinkles that gave her skin an almost mummified look.

Sue looked away, not wanting to see her grandmother in this light, and instead concentrated her attention on the old photographs from Hong Kong that were aligned on the dresser between newer photographs of herself and John. There was a picture of her grandmother and her mother standing in front of a junk in Hong Kong harbor, a picture of her grandfather holding up a live chicken purchased from one of the vendors on the street, a picture of her grandmother and two friends clowning in front of the black steam engine of a train. Hundreds of times over the years, on boring nights, on rainy days, her grandmother had told her the stories behind each of those photos, promising that one day the two of them would visit Hong Kong together, but Sue realized now that the two of them would not be taking any such trips. The thought depressed her, filling her with a bleak hopelessness and making her feel sadder and more empty than she'd ever felt in her life. She wished that she'd gone to her bedroom as soon as they'd come home and pretended to be asleep when her grandmother came looking for her.

"Susan."

She looked back toward the bed.

"I want you to have this." Her grandmother withdrew a necklace from the top drawer of her nightstand. She held it forth with two slightly trembling hands. In the still-open drawer were wads of tissue and small empty bottles of old medicine.

The necklace, with its thin gold chain and small white jade pendant, looked vaguely familiar, and Sue turned it over gingerly in her hands as she took it. She examined the jade. "Is it real?"

Her grandmother nodded. "It is from the K'un Lun Mountains in Khotan. It was given to me as a wedding present." Sue recognized the necklace now, from the pictures. "I wore it as long as your grandfather was alive, but when he died, I took it off. I was planning to save it, to give it to you as a wedding present, but I have decided to give it to you today."

Sue tried to hand the necklace back. "I'll get married eventually. Give it to me then."

"No." Her grandmother held up her hands in refusal. "I want you to have it now."

Sue looked more carefully at the object in her hand. The jade was white, milky, of the rarest variety. In the shape of a circle, it contained two carved figures, the dragon and the phoenix, joined together, symbolizing the male and female joined together in marriage. "I can't accept this," she said.

"You must. I will not take it back."

"I'm not getting married yet."

"I may not be alive when you are married."

Sue stared at her grandmother, realization slowly dawning on her. She felt an unpleasant churning in her stomach. "You're not going to die, are you? You're not giving away all of your stuff because you're—"

Her grandmother smiled. "I'm not dying."

"Then why are you—"

"But I will die one day. I may even die soon."

"Grandmother . . ."

The old woman sighed. "I am giving you this necklace for protection. I know you do not hold the same beliefs I do, but I beg you to do me this one small favor. Wear the necklace. It will protect you against evil. You may not understand now, you may think I am being foolish, but I think one day you will understand and you will be grateful."

Evil.

Sue looked at the necklace in a new light. Her eyes saw not the beauty of the intertwined figures but the teeth of the dragon, the claws of the phoenix. Instead of making her feel safe and secure, instead of reassuring her the way it was supposed to, the necklace caused the hair on the back of her neck to prickle, sent a shiver of coldness through her. She might not hold the same beliefs as her grandmother, but she was not the skeptic she aspired to be, and the idea of wearing something that was supposed to have supernatural powers frightened her. She thought of the strange shadow in the dark hallway of the high school.

Evil.

"Did you put a . . . spell on this?"

Her grandmother laughed, a tinkling, musical sound. Her eyes were laughing too, and for the first time since entering the room, Sue relaxed a little. Maybe she was overreacting.

"I know no spells. I am not a witch." Her grandmother grinned. "Do you think I am?"

"No," Sue admitted, embarrassed.

"The necklace will protect you because it is jade. Not

because of any spell that has been put on it or because it has been treated with herbs or because the carving has symbolic meaning. Anything made from jade will protect you."

"Oh."

"I am giving you this necklace because I was going to give it to you anyway. I have simply decided to give it to you early." Her smile faded. "But I don't want you to mention this to John or your parents. This is between you and me. Do you understand?"

Sue nodded.

"Good. And you will wear the necklace?"

"Yes."

"All the time?"

"Even when I'm asleep or taking a shower?"

"All the time."

"For the rest of my life?"

"Until it is safe to take it off."

Sue looked at her grandmother, saw again how old she looked, saw the thinness of her hair, the boniness of her frame. "Yes, Grandmother," she said.

"Good." The old woman smiled. "You are my favorite granddaughter."

Sue smiled. "I'm your only granddaughter."

"Even if you weren't, you would be my favorite." She rubbed her eyes and yawned, realistically, but with more dramatic flair than usual. "It's getting late now. Go to bed. I will see you tomorrow. We will talk more about this later."

Sue understood that she was being dismissed, and she gave her grandmother a quick hug, noticing as she did so that the old woman was wearing a jade bracelet around her skinny wrinkled wrist. "Thank you," she said, holding forth the necklace. "I will treasure this always." She said good night and left the bedroom, filled with conflicting feelings, not sure if she was scared or sad, relieved or worried. She was definitely tired, and she wanted to go to bed, but instead she returned to the living room, where John was on the floor again, her parents on the couch.

She stood silently in the doorway, watching, until she found what she was looking for.

John, wearing a white jade ring on the middle finger of his left hand.

Her parents, wearing matching white jade necklaces.

Fourteen

Two pairs of footsteps on the hardwood floor of the hallway. Heavy and light.

Rich set his fingers on the keyboard of the PC and stared intently at the green words on the top half of the screen, as though he'd been doing so all along. He felt Corrie's presence behind him even before seeing the blur of white movement in the glare of the VDT, even before her shadow fell across his papers. He typed a sentence that he had no intention of using but that would seem legitimate if read over his shoulder.

Corrie stood, silent, waiting, trying to force him to be the first to speak, but it was Anna as usual who unwittingly broke the stalemate. "We're going to church, Daddy." Her small soft hand grabbed his neck. She kissed his unshaven cheek, giggled at the roughness.

"That's good."

"Are you coming with us?" Corrie asked.

He turned toward her, shook his head, motioned toward the PC. "I have to finish this article. If I don't get it done today, there's going to be a big hole on the front page."

She looked at him blankly, saying nothing. He was embarrassed by the obviousness of his excuse and wanted to look away, but he forced himself to meet her gaze. They'd been playing this game for a long time. When they'd first gotten married, he'd told her that he wasn't a churchgoer, but she'd said that if he really loved her he'd go with her. She said that sometimes she did things she didn't want to do because he wanted to do them, and that he should do the same for her. So he'd gone. Then Anna had come along, and they'd both agreed that it would be good for the child to go to church. But gradually, over the years, he'd begun worming out of his Sunday morning duties, pleading work, fatigue, sickness. He'd started going every other week, but when the pattern had become too obvious he'd varied it, attending two weeks and missing the next, attending one week and missing the next two.

These days, he hardly ever went to church at all.

It had nothing to do with religion, really. It was church itself. He just couldn't help feeling that he was wasting his Sunday mornings by going to services. Sunday mornings were for eating waffles and lying around, reading the *Republic* and listening to music. Not sermons.

Not the Pastor Dan Wheeler.

That was a big part of his refusal this morning. Now that she was Wheeler's secretary, Corrie felt obligated to attend his services. It was not an obligation he shared. The Methodist church had been bad enough, but testicle hooks could not drag him to one of Wheeler's sermons. He could think of nothing worse than spending his only real day off sitting on an uncomfortable bench with a bunch of self-righteous strangers listening to a hellfire-and-brimstoner tell him that he was damned for eternity.

He would rather stay home and work.

"Come with us, Daddy," Anna pleaded. "You haven't gone to church with us for a long time."

"That's okay. He has more important things to do." Corrie took Anna's hand to lead her from the room.

He did not dignify that dig with a response, but smiled and blew Anna a kiss. "Don't worry, sweetie. I'll be here when you get back. And if I finish my article in time, we'll go out for ice cream."

"Yeah! Ice cream!"

Corrie glared at him. "Come on," she said. "We'll be late."

He watched the two of them walk out of the room, Anna bouncing and happy, Corrie determinedly flat-footed and grim. What the hell was wrong with him? He knew Corrie hated it when he wasted money taking Anna out for ice cream. Why had he so purposefully and deliberately baited her? He sighed, staring blankly at the screen. He wasn't sure. They'd had a fight last night, a fairly big one, but when they'd awakened this morning the wounds seemed to have healed. They'd kissed, almost made love, probably would have had Anna not been awake already. But something had gone wrong during breakfast, something had changed, shifted, something he could not quite put his finger on. He had sunk deeper into the words of the *Republic*'s sports section, Corrie had prepared the food in silence, and the two of them had spoken only to Anna, who had continued to chatter away, blissfully unaware of the change in atmosphere.

The front door slammed shut. He saw twin movements of white, big and little, on the porch.

Corrie did look good in her Sunday dress, he had to admit. He felt a twinge of regret that he had not told her so. In the old days, if he'd thought what he was thinking now, he would have acted on it, running outside, dragging her back into the house, throwing her over the back of the couch, flipping up her dress, pulling down her panties, and taking her from behind.

And she would have let him.

But now . . .

Now things were different.

He watched through the window as Corrie led Anna across the driveway to her car.

Her car.

When had it become *her* car? And *his* truck? When had

they started assigning individual ownership rights to their joint property? Or had they always done so? He couldn't remember.

He watched his wife and daughter get in the car, close their doors, buckle up, and drive away. Anna waved at him as they left. Corrie did not even look in his direction.

He hadn't really lied to Corrie. He did have a lot of work to do. She knew that. He had to coordinate her columns as well as do his usual work. And there'd been a lot of news the past few weeks. He wished she would be a little more sympathetic.

The girl from his journalism class was supposed to come in tomorrow, and that would definitely help out the production side of the paper—she seemed bright, and he had no doubt that she would quickly pick up the technical aspects of typesetting and pasteup—but he did not yet know if she could write. When she'd called on Friday, he'd asked her to bring in a writing sample, and she'd said she would try to dig something up, but it sounded to him as though whatever writing experience she'd had had been in high school.

Rich picked up his notepad from the top of the desk and glanced at the notes he'd jotted down. The top story was going to be Mike Vigil. The truck driver was still missing, although his rig had been found on the highway some forty miles out of Casa Grande. Rich just needed to call the DPS for a current status report, and then tap Robert for a few local police quotes.

Robert, he knew, was pissed at him. Although his brother had never before attempted to interfere with the content of the paper, he hadn't wanted Rich to run the story on the dead mice and had actually asked him to pull it. Rich had almost caved in on this one. With all of the vampire talk, he, too, was afraid of starting a panic, and he could definitely see the issue from his brother's point of view. But he hadn't bought the argument that the story would jeopardize the investigation into Manuel Torres's death, and he'd finally decided that it was interesting and offbeat enough to be newsworthy. He'd compromised, placing the article on the second page and treating it as a feature, but Robert still hadn't liked it.

Hell, Rich thought, it *was* a good story. He stood by his decision to run it. If the paper subscribed to one of the wire services, it probably would've been picked up by now. Besides, despite what Robert had predicted, there'd been no panic—although the tourist value of the arroyo had gone up considerably since publication of the article. For the past two days, small groups of people, mostly teenagers, had made pilgrimages to the site and had been combing the surrounding area trying to find their own mysteriously murdered animals.

Rich hadn't spoken to his brother since the paper had come out, had thought it best to wait and let Robert call him first. Now he wondered if he should call Robert at home for a quote, or call him later in the day at the station. He wondered if his brother would give him a quote at all.

He put down the notepad and picked up his empty coffee cup, heading into the kitchen for a refill. The front of the house still smelled of breakfast: syrup and peanut butter, buttermilk waffles and jam. Corrie had washed, dried, and put away the dishes, but the waffle iron sat cooling on the counter, drying drips of batter decorating its lower half.

He put the waffle iron in the cupboard beneath the sink and poured himself the last cup of coffee. The house was quiet, the only sounds his own, and for a second he wished he'd accompanied Corrie and Anna to church. Then he reminded himself that he would have had to listen to Wheeler rant for an hour and was instantly reassured that he'd made the right decision.

He walked into the living room, turned on the stereo,

put an old Jethro Tull album on the turntable, and went into the bedroom to call Robert.

The church was filled, the street outside lined with cars and trucks, the pews inside nearly all taken. Corrie stood in the entrance, holding tightly to Anna's hand, looking for a place to sit. She was surprised by the size of the congregation. She had not realized that the Church of the Holy Trinity was so popular. She'd come here today because she worked for the church and thought it part of her responsibilities to attend Sunday services. In the back of her mind, she'd also half-thought that she would be doing Pastor Wheeler a favor. He seemed so . . . awkward with people, so standoffish, that she found it hard to believe that he had much of a following. It was a shock to discover that there were more people at this single early service than there had been at all the combined services at the Methodist church.

No wonder Wheeler wanted to expand the building.

She thought of her old church, of Pastor Franklin giving his benign sermon in his benign way to a half-empty chapel, and she immediately felt guilty. Maybe she should explain to Pastor Franklin why she was now attending the Church of the Holy Trinity. She did not know the pastor well, had never spoken to him on a one-to-one basis except at the obligatory palm-pressing at the end of each service, but he'd always seemed to her to be a kind, gentle, and rather fragile old man, and she felt the need to let him know that she was now attending another church, not because of anything he had done or because of any lack in his sermons but because she had gotten a job as Pastor Wheeler's secretary.

Maybe she should attend services at both churches.

She felt Anna tugging at her sleeve, and she looked down.

120 *Bentley Little*

"There's a seat, Mommy. See? Next to that fat woman?"
"Shhh," she admonished her daughter.

There was indeed a section of empty pew near an over-weight elderly woman in a loud floral print dress, and Corrie led Anna down the carpeted aisle. She felt very conspicuous as the two of them walked through the center of the church, almost like an intruder, though she knew that the church was open to everyone. She did not know why she hadn't insisted that Rich come with them. If he had time to take Anna out for ice cream later this afternoon, he had time to go to church now. But that was just like him. He didn't stop to think that this was her first day at a new church and that she might like some moral support, a hand to hold as she entered this building filled with strangers.

She knew that, though. She knew what he was like. And, after all these years, she should have known that if she wanted him to do something, she had to come right out and say it. He never figured it out on his own. He never would.

That was the main problem with their marriage. Mis-communication. A stubborn unwillingness on both their parts to adapt to each other's ways of doing things.

She could have and should have come right out and asked him to go with her and told him why. She could have brought it up yesterday or last night. He would have come. But some vain, quixotic, and hopelessly idealistic part of her had made her hold out, to see if *this* time he would volunteer on his own. And another part of her had relished the thought of taking him to task for not doing what she wanted him to do, even though she knew ahead of time that he wouldn't do it.

God, why was everything so complicated?

She sat down next to Anna. There was no hymnal in the rack on the back of the pew in front of them, no book at all, only xeroxed sheets of paper stapled together. She glanced at the people sitting about her. She recognized a few faces, people she'd seen and did not know, but there was not a single friend or acquaintance in the congregation.

Anna tugged at her sleeve again. "Look at the cross," she whispered, pointing.

Corrie looked. She'd been in the church every day since being hired, but she'd spent her time in the office and had not really taken the opportunity to examine its interior before. Now her gaze strayed to the huge wooden cross displayed on the wall above the pulpit. Far from being merely an ornamental symbol, a sculptural representation of the Crucifixion, the huge wooden cross looked as though it could be instantly pressed into service. It was nearly twice the size of a man and, though resting on the floor, reached almost to the ceiling. She shivered. There was something about the cross that didn't seem right, something in the proportion of its sections or the luster of its wood that made her uncomfortable.

She turned her attention away from the cross, to the stained glass windows, finding solace in the familiar normalcy of their colored designs.

"Mommy," Anna whispered, "I think it's starting."

"Yes," Corrie said.

The congregation grew hushed, murmurs fading into whispers, then trailing off into silence as Pastor Wheeler entered through the vestibule. Corrie was unfamiliar with the specific rituals of this denomination, but she'd been to enough Sunday services in enough churches that she knew what to do and when to do it. She and Anna stood with everyone else for the invocation, bowed their heads to pray, stood politely when it was time to sing.

Then Wheeler began his sermon.

He stood at the pulpit, Bible in hand, and scanned the faces of his congregation. His eyes passed over Corrie, and he smiled at her. There were a few muffled coughs, the rustling sound of people shifting in their seats.

"I have seen Jesus Christ," he said, and his voice was low and filled with both awe and pride. "He has spoken to me."

Pastor Wheeler paused for a moment to let the import of his words sink in and then began recounting the text of his conversations with Christ. He told of his dream and of the meeting in the church.

Corrie watched the preacher as he spoke, and she was afraid. She wanted to leave, wanted to run, but was too scared to do so. There was no doubt in her mind that Wheeler had seen Jesus—the proof was in his face, in his voice, in the aura of rapture which now enveloped him— but the news did not fill her with joy the way it should have. As she looked between the heads of the people, over the backs of the pews, at the preacher's eyes, she was filled with fear and a deep, intense feeling of dread.

What was wrong with her? She had always considered herself a good person and a moderately good Christian. As a child, she had accepted Jesus into her life and had done her best since then to obey His teachings. Her feelings for Christ had always been uniformly positive and unambiguous.

So why was she afraid?

"He has a plan," the preacher continued. He was smiling now, getting into his rhythm. "Jesus has a plan. He is going to establish the Kingdom of Heaven on earth, and He has chosen our humble town and our humble church as the seed from which this greatness will grow. We have been selected to be the first citizens of the Kingdom of God, and, as foretold by the prophets, Jesus will bring light and right to this troubled chaotic world and the fallen will be fodder for the cannons of Christ . . ."

Corrie felt Anna grab her hand and squeeze. "Mommy, I'm scared."

Corrie was scared too, but she gave her daughter a reassuring smile. "There's nothing to be afraid of," she
whispered.

"I want to go home."

"Shhh." She put an arm around Anna's shoulder and
again focused her attention on the pastor. Around her,
she could hear the crying and whining of other frightened
children, the reassuring whispers of their parents. The
fear in the church was almost palpable, though she was
not quite sure why the pastor's words should produce such
a response.

The sermon continued, a hypnotic intermingling of the
pastor's conversations with Jesus, prophecy from the Bible,
and personal interpretation of both. Wheeler described
in detail his plans for the Church of the Living Christ,
and he urged everyone to assist in raising funds and volunteering time to help complete this project, this project
that would forever change the course of human destiny.

Wheeler was a stirring speaker. She had to admit that.
The fear in the air shifted, changed, metamorphosed into
anticipation and excitement as he spoke. Like the other
people surrounding her, the men now chanting "Praise
God!" the women now yelling "Hallelujah!" Corrie found
herself caught up in the emotion of the moment, moved
and inspired, despite her fear, by the power of the pastor's
words.

Only . . .

Only in the back of her mind, she wondered why Pastor
Wheeler needed to resort to mundane pleas for money
and volunteer workers if Jesus had really asked him to
build this church. Did Jesus, who could cure the sick and
resurrect the dead, really have to rely on simplistic evangelical techniques to ensure that His will be done?

The Pastor Dan Wheeler's gaze again fell upon her and
Corrie shivered, feeling guilty for even considering such

blasphemy. Who was she to question the ways of the Almighty?

She spent the rest of the sermon concentrating on the back of the pew in front of her, trying not to listen to the preacher's words.

After the service, she and Anna walked quickly out to the car. Anna, usually animated and excessively talkative following the forced silence of church, was quiet and subdued, and the two of them walked without speaking. The other members of the congregation were quiet, too, and she heard very little conversation from the other families heading out to their vehicles.

Corrie strode toward the Nissan. She was walking normally, holding Anna's hand, a bland, placid expression on her face, but she felt anything but normal inside. She was frightened, deeply and truly frightened, and she felt like a character in a movie she'd once seen who'd known that the end of the world was imminent but had not been able to share the information with any of the blithely happy people around her.

Only why should the Second Coming make her feel this way?

The Second Coming.

She wanted to share this burden with Rich, to tell him what was happening, and have him reassure her that everything was going to be all right. But she knew that Rich would not believe that Jesus was coming. He would put it down to religious fervor, would think that Wheeler was either lying or had had some sort of fanatic's delusion. She'd probably think that herself if she did not know Wheeler and had not heard for herself the way he'd spoken to his congregation, but there was no way to fake the certainty of that otherworldly elation, that sense of jubilant intimidation that he had so clearly possessed.

And had possessed all week, now that she thought of it.

They reached the car, and Corrie fished her keys out of her purse, opening Anna's door.

"Did Jesus really talk to the pastor?" Anna asked.

No, He didn't, she wanted to say, but she found she could not lie to her daughter.

Why would she want to lie?

"Yes, He did," she said. She walked around to the driver's side of the car. Anna crawled over the seat and unlocked her door.

"Is Jesus scary?" Anna asked.

"Stop asking so many questions."

Anna folded her arms stubbornly over her chest. "Fine. I'll ask Daddy, then."

Corrie sighed. "No, Jesus is not scary. Jesus is nice. Jesus loves you."

" 'Like the song?"

"Yes." Corrie started the car.

"You don't want me to ask Daddy, do you?"

"No. I don't think we should tell Daddy. He has a lot of things to think about right now and . . . I just don't want you to say anything to him about what the pastor told us. I'll tell Daddy when it's time, okay?"

"What if he asks me?"

"He won't ask you."

"You want me to lie to Daddy?"

"No, I don't want you to lie," she said, exasperated. "Anna, just button up your seat belt."

"Jesus is scary, isn't He?"

They pulled away from the curb.

"Mommy?"

"I don't know," Corrie admitted. "Maybe He is."

Fifteen

The phone woke Robert in the middle of a dream.

He'd been the only living creature left on earth, and he'd been wandering through an endless desert, stepping over the dead dry bodies of men and women, children and pets, keeping his eyes focused on the flat horizon far in front of him because he knew that if he looked down he would see thousands of empty eye sockets focused on his face.

The ringing of the phone saved him, drawing him out of that hellish world, and he picked up the receiver on the first pause, instantly alert. His eyes found the glowing numerals of the clock in the darkness, registered the time. Ten-forty. He'd only been asleep for twenty minutes? "Carter," he said.

"Chief?" It was Stu.

"Yeah. What is it?"

"There's been some vandalism over at the cemetery."

"For Christ's sake, you woke me up for that?"

"I—"

"You don't have to call me every time some drunk teenager knocks over a tombstone—"

"Graves have been dug up."

Robert sat up, kicking off the covers. "Graves? Plural?"

"A lot of them."

"I'll meet you there in five." Robert hung up, put on his pants, slipped into the still-buttoned shirt he'd taken off by pulling over his head, and ran a quick hand through his hair. He pulled on his boots, grabbed his keys and wallet from the dresser, and hurried outside, strapping on his holster.

The night blackness of the desert was obscured in his rearview mirror by the cloud of red taillight-tinted dust kicked up by his tires as he peeled out.

Stu's cruiser was already at the cemetery, parked directly in front of the wrought-iron gate, and Robert knew from radioing the station that Ted was with him. The red-and-blues were off, but the twin white spotlights on either side of the patrol car were trained on the graveyard and illuminated everything that faced the entrance, creating an eerie illusion of flatness. In the high-powered halogen beams, the cemetery looked like a painting or a stage set, an exaggeration of reality, all shadows and highlights—though that sharpness of contrast made it virtually impossible to distinguish the extent of the damage through the dusty windshield of the car.

Robert pulled next to Stu's vehicle, opened his door, and stepped out.

"My God," he breathed.

All of the graves had been dug up and desecrated. Not a single plot remained undisturbed. Behind the bars of the fence, the formerly flat and well-maintained lawn was now a jumbled series of irregular holes and hills of dirt. Many of the headstones had been smashed or knocked over, and scattered randomly about were opened coffins and pieces of coffin, bones and decayed body parts lying atop wood, half-buried in dirt, thrown onto stone. One skeletal hand and connecting radius hung from the low branches of the cemetery's lone palo verde tree, looking fake in the sterile light of the halogens.

Robert turned on the twin beams of his own spotlights, adjusting them so they shone on an area to the left of that already lit. There was no movement within the cemetery, no sign of Stu or Ted, and he looked around, spotting the silhouettes of the two policemen in the lighted doorway of the caretaker's house across the street. Turning his back on the cemetery, he walked over to the house, gravel crunching loudly beneath the heels of his boots. Behind Stu and Ted, he could see Lee Hillman, the caretaker, just inside the house. The old man looked worried, and he shifted nervously from one foot to another, his hands traveling unthinkingly up and down the inner molding of the doorsill.

Robert strode up the cement walk. Like a lot of single old men, Hillman insisted on wearing the hip clothes of the last fashion cycle, which somehow made him look more pathetic and out of it than if he had simply worn the fashions of his own era. Robert had always felt a little sorry for the caretaker, who had never seemed to him to be a particularly happy or well-adjusted man, and he felt even sorrier for him now.

"Gentlemen," Robert said, nodding his greeting as he stepped onto the porch.

"I don't know how it could've happened!" Hillman said. "I swear to God!" His voice was higher than usual, his words spoken too rapidly, and Robert realized that he was not only worried but badly frightened.

"What happened?"

Stu closed the notebook in which he'd been writing. "He says he locked the gate at nine, the way he always does, and everything was fine. He called out and shone his flashlight around, to make sure no one was still inside the cemetery, then he came back home. He took a shower and, when he went to close his drapes, noticed that the cemetery gates were open. He got dressed, walked across the street to investigate, saw that the graves had been dug up and called the station."

"That was exactly how it happened!"

"Within an hour? All of those graves were dug up within a single hour?"

"I swear to God, everything was normal when I closed up at nine."

"Let's go out and take a look," Robert said.

Stu nodded. "We were just waiting for you."

"Do you need me to come?" Hillman asked. "Couldn't I just stay here—"

"We'd like you to come with us, Mr. Hillman."

The old man nodded, not daring to argue, and closed the screen door. The four men trekked across the street, Robert in the lead. "Does the cemetery have any lights? We'll radio for some portable high-intensities, but until then I don't want to wear down our batteries."

"We have floodlights, but they're not very strong. Not as strong as yours."

"Turn them on anyway. We'll use one car at a time." He nodded toward Stu. "Turn your beams off."

Robert and Ted stood at the gates of the cemetery as Stu ran over to the cruiser and Hillman knelt next to a black box on the ground. From this angle, the tall saguaros behind and to either side of the graveyard looked like alien sentries standing stiffly at attention.

The halogens suddenly snapped off, leaving Robert's now off-center beams the only illumination. The powerful white spots shone strongly on the left portion of the cemetery, making the larger right part of the graveyard seem even darker. There were shadows within shadows, oddly formed sections of blackness amidst the rubble and debris. A moment later, the cemetery floodlights came on. They were indeed as poor as Hillman had indicated, mounted on the fence at regular intervals and weakly shining on small segments of ground with a faded yellowish glow.

Robert walked slowly through the wrought-iron gates into the cemetery. *All of this in an hour?* It was unbelievable, but he had no doubt that Hillman had been speaking the truth. Whatever else he might be, the caretaker was not a liar.

That's what was so frightening.

Robert looked carefully around, stunned by the thoroughness of the desecration. Between the time Hillman had closed the gates and called the station, nearly a hundred gravesites had been torn apart, their contents unearthed and discarded. The partial skeleton of what appeared to be a small child lay atop the dirt mound in front of him. The not-quite-decomposed body of an old man lay folded over itself to his side.

He continued forward, skirting the holes, rounding the mounds, Ted and Stu following. Stu had brought a flashlight from the car, and he shone it randomly about. The most horrifying thing was that Robert recognized several of the corpses. Lying atop an irregular pile of chunked dirt he saw Connor Pittman, the contours of his young face still visible even after the years of degeneration, the patchy filaments of his hair a parody of his once long blond locks. When the boy had died of a freak heart attack on the school track, Robert had come with the ambulance and helped load the body onto the stretcher. Connor had seemed dead to him then, his body nothing more than a discarded vessel from which the soul had fled. But looking at him now, seeing echoes of the teenager he had been in the staring fright mask of a face, Robert was struck by what little change death had really wrought. He found himself thinking morbidly that perhaps there was no such thing as a soul, no mystical invisible essence of being that left the body at the instant of death. Perhaps whatever it was that made a living thing alive died when the body died and simply lay used and spent within the decomposing form of its biological host.

His gaze moved on, and he saw Putter Phillips and Lavinia Bullfinch and Terry Feenan. The most jarring sight

to him was Sally Hicks. Or rather, her head. Sally had died
of a heart attack a few years back, and her family had
insisted on an open casket funeral. He'd hated to admit
it, but she'd looked nearly as good in death as she had
in life. Now her head, rolled onto its side, sat alone near
the base of a century plant, skin peeling off in patchy
flakes, black lips curled over her once beautiful mouth in
a permanent gap-toothed sneer.

There were low, scuttling sounds in the darkness, but
whether they were caused by lizards and beetles or by the
slight breeze that blew from the north, Robert didn't
know. He did know that the breeze was not strong enough
to dispel the odor of death, decay, and mortuary chemicals that hung thickly over the cemetery. He, Stu, and Ted
all had their hands over their noses, but the stench had
so heavily permeated the, air that they could taste it. Stu,
to his left, spit continuously. Ted closed his eyes, trying
bravely not to let the smell affect him, but was soon gagging. A moment later he bent over and threw up loudly
next to a spiny cholla.

Robert felt like retching himself, but he willed himself
not to. He turned around, looking for Hillman, and saw
the caretaker standing just inside the gate, next to one of
the lights. He was about to walk back toward the old man,
when he looked down at the broken red-finished wood of
a smashed coffin and the realization suddenly hit him: *all
of the graves had been dug up.*

All of them.

His head jerked instantly to the left, his eyes easily picking out the familiar spot, even with the altered topogra-
phy. There, in the far corner, next to two smashed caskets,
a broken skeleton had been tossed over a thin, partially
clothed wraith.

Dad and Mom.

He took a step toward that section of the cemetery,
then stopped. Fingers still pinching shut his nostrils, he

took a deep breath, tasting death. He did not want to get any closer. He did not want to see. Already the familiar, healthy figures of his parents, so lovingly preserved in his memory, were being superseded in his mind by the two callously mistreated corpses in the dark corner of the desecrated graveyard.

He stood there trembling. The sanctity of his parents' memory, the dignity of their deaths, the privacy of his own feelings had been violated, and the fear he had felt was replaced by anger and outrage.

Whoever had done this was going to pay.

He knew he should call Rich, let him know what had happened. But he didn't want to call his brother. He wanted to protect him from this, to spare him, although he knew that was impossible.

He closed his eyes. When they were little, he ten and Rich five, he'd found the dead body of their cocker spaniel Roger in the ditch in front of their house one morning. Roger had obviously been hit by a car and had dragged himself out of the road and into the ditch, where he'd died during the night. The dog's black and white fur was matted with drying blood, blood so red that it looked like catsup, and there was a wet streak of smeared dirt on the road where the dog had pulled himself forward.

The loss of Roger had hit him hard, and he'd wanted to run back inside and tell Mom and Dad and have them somehow make everything okay, but he'd known that, this time, everything would not be okay, *could* not be okay, and he'd sat down on the edge of the ditch and cried, for Roger, for himself, for his parents, and, mostly, for Rich, who'd loved the dog more than anything else in the world.

He had buried the dog himself, not telling his parents, not telling Rich, preferring to let them think that Roger had simply run away. He'd placed branches and dead leaves over the dog's twisted lifeless form in the ditch that morning and had returned at night alone, picking up the hard bony body, the gluey blood sticking to his hands, and carrying the dog out to a spot in the surrounding desert near a particularly large saguaro where he'd already dug a hole.

He had never told anyone the truth, and forever afterward Rich and his parents had believed that Roger had run away and had not come back because he had found another friendly family to live with. They had never given up the hope of getting Roger back, had always thought they would run into him someday in town or hear his bark from someone else's backyard, for years had even made weekly pilgrimages to the small corral behind the vet's that passed for a pound in Rio Verde, but of course they had never found the dog. He had successfully spared them the horrible truth of Roger's death.

But he could not spare Rich this.

Robert opened his eyes, glanced back toward his men. Ted, especially, looked stricken, and Robert remembered that the young patrolman had lost his own mother a few years back.

She was doubtlessly one of the disinterred corpses now littering the landscape.

"Ted?" he asked. "You want to take a breather?"

The patrolman shook his head. "I'm fine." He ran a hind through his short brown hair. "Who you figure'd do something like this?"

"I don't know," Robert admitted.

Stu looked toward them, the flashlight pointing down at his feet. "Where do we start? I mean, do we dust the tombstones for fingerprints?"

"We look for tire tracks in the road. We take soil samples. Footprints should be our best bet. Whoever did this had to walk out of here. He had to step on this dirt somewhere."

"Unless he flew." Stu's voice was quiet.

"Knock that crap off." Robert looked from Stu to Ted.

Both were pale, frightened. They were just kids, he realized. Hell, out of all his men, only he and Ben had any life experience to speak of. The rest of them were just . . . babes in the woods.

He was just being overprotective. Equally young cops in inner cities dealt with worse things than this all the time. But he didn't know those young cops in inner cities. To him, they were faceless men in blue uniforms, like the police on TV crime shows, somehow better trained, more mature, and more competent than his own men. He *did* know Stu and Ted. They were good men, good cops—good small-town cops—but they had never had to face something like this.

On the other, hand, neither had he.

"What are we going to do about the bodies?" Hillman asked from behind him.

Robert turned to face the caretaker. He felt tired all of a sudden and realized that it must be getting close to midnight. "After we're through with our investigation, we'll hire some men to redig the graves and return the bodies to their proper plots."

"How'll we tell who's who?"

"We'll have family members come out and identify the . . . remains. If that doesn't work, and if we can't tell by the placement, we'll have to go by dental records." He nodded toward the corner. "My parents are over there."

No one spoke.

Robert bent down to examine the body closest to him, an ancient skeleton wearing the rotted remnants of a dress. He found himself focusing his attention on the exposed left femur. The bone had been snapped in half. Frowning, he motioned Hillman over. "Is this usual? Do bones usually break like this?"

The caretaker dropped to his knees and squinted at the skeleton's leg. "I can't really say. My job is just to take care of the cemetery grounds. I don't know nothing about the bodies."

"Maybe it broke that way when she fell out," Ted offered.

Robert shook his head. "I don't think so. Look at how the body's positioned. It's been taken out of its coffin and deliberately placed here. That leg hasn't even been bent. How could the bone have broken?"

Stu climbed a small dirt mound nearby. "Come here," he said.

They followed him. His flashlight shone on the femur of another skeleton. This one, too, had been broken. "Looks like we have a pattern here." His flashlight beam moved on to another corpse lying next to an open new coffin on the other side of the mound.

Hillman gasped. "Jesus."

Robert moved quickly forward, sliding down the pile of dirt, the others following. The body at his feet, though fully clothed and obviously interred only recently, had been shriveled and shrunk and bore an uncanny and uncomfortable resemblance to Manuel Torres's exsanguinated corpse. The same wrinkled parchment skin clung moisturelessly to the skull, the same deflated lips surrounded the overly toothy mouth. It was Caleb Peterson, Robert realized. He'd forgotten that old Caleb had been buried last week. He'd read about it in the paper, but he hadn't known the miner that well and hadn't gone to the funeral.

Only Caleb looked as though he'd died decades—not days—ago.

Robert put forth a tentative finger. The skin he touched was dry and brittle.

The vampire had smelled fresh meat.

He pushed the thought from his mind. "Ted," he said. "Get on the radio to the station. I want Jud out here with a camera. Get Woods here too. I want a medical opinion on this."

"Yes, sir."

"And see if we can use Globe's K-9."

"You're not going to want to hear this," Stu said quietly. "But I think it was a vampire."

Hillman nodded fearfully. "I think so too."

"Don't be stupid."

"Stupid? This whole place was uprooted. In an hour. Mr. Peterson's body has been sucked dry—"

"The vampire got a mouthful of embalming fluid then."

"Those bones were broken open because he was looking for the marrow."

Robert kept his face as impassive as possible. "We're here for ten minutes, we haven't even started our investigation, and already you're jumping to conclusions. Idiotic conclusions, I might add."

"You don't think all this is weird? Mr. Torres—"

"Yes, it's weird. But we don't know what's doing this, and until we do know, I want you to keep your mouth shut. There are going to be enough rumors as it is. I don't want any of them to originate with the police department. You got that? If you have theories, you keep them to yourself."

"Are you going to tell your brother?"

Robert glared at him. "Yes, I am. I think he has a right to know since his parents are lying over there with their graves dug up."

Stu looked down at the ground. "Sorry. I just meant that, since he's on the paper and all—"

"I know exactly what you meant. Now if you don't think you can handle this investigation without blaming everything on monsters, I'll get Steve out here and assign you to the desk."

"I can handle it."

"I hope so." Robert looked at the young officer, then sighed. "While we're waiting, why don't you take Mr. Hillman's statement."

"Why? Am I a suspect? I swear to God, I didn't do it—"

"You're not a suspect. But you're the closest thing we have to a witness. We just have to record what you saw and when you saw it."

He blinked. "Oh. Okay."

Robert stood alone next to Caleb's dehydrated body and empty coffin as Stu and the old man headed back through the cemetery toward the caretaker's house.

Looking for bone marrow.

The idea made sense.

Shivering, he looked again at the tight, grinning face of the corpse. There was the sound, far off, of a coyote howling. A clichéd noise at a clichéd time, but it did its work, and the peach fuzz on the back of his neck bristled, turning into goose bumps on his arms.

Turning to face the bright beams of the car, he followed the others out of the cemetery.

It was time to call Rich.

Sixteen

Sue stood for a moment in the middle of Center Street, looking at the front of the newspaper office. Stenciled white lettering in a rainbow curve on the window read: RIO VERDE GAZETTE. Beneath that, the chipped and faded ghosts of previous letters could be seen on the dusty glass. A lone pickup was parked next to the door.

She had passed by the newspaper office plenty of times but had never really noticed it before. It was located in one of the nearly identical sandstone brick buildings that made up most of the town's business district, lost amidst the proliferation of lawyers' offices, insurance offices, real-estate offices, and title companies. Across the street was a small house that had been turned into a beauty salon, and next to that a metal quonset hut that was home to the American Legion Thrift Store.

She walked slowly across the asphalt, wondering if Mr. Carter—Rich—was watching her through the window. She felt exposed and a little embarrassed, and she wished she'd had her father drop her off farther away. Her palms were sweaty, and she wiped them on her jeans. Jeans? She glanced down at her pants. She should have worn something dressier the first day. A skirt. A nice blouse. Earrings. Jewelry.

At least she'd thought to put on makeup.

The door to the office opened, and Rich walked across

the hard dirt parking lot toward her. He *had* been watching. "Hello," he said. "I'm glad you're here."

"Hi." Sue nodded at him. He looked tired, she thought. The other night, at the school, he'd seemed vigorously healthy, but now there were dark circles around his red-rimmed eyes, and his face seemed thinner, though she knew that he could not have lost weight since Thursday. His clothes were wrinkled enough to have been slept in.

He must have caught her looking at him and correctly interpreted the expression on her face, because he gave her a wan grin. "Forgive my appearance. I'm not usually this seedy, but I've been up most of the night. The graves at the cemetery were all dug up, and I had to cover the story. I was at the cemetery until one, and then I went back home to write the article." He cleared his throat, and his smile faded. "Also, two of the graves were my parents'."

"I'm sorry." Sue looked away, not knowing what to say. She focused her gaze on an oversize beetle scuttling across the dirt. "You know, if this is inconvenient, I could come back another time—"

"Inconvenient? You're a lifesaver. I need someone right now."

Sue licked her lips. "I'm not sure how much help I'll be."

"Don't worry about it. I'll teach you what you need to know. Right now, I'll take you on a tour of the facilities." He opened the door and stepped aside to let her in.

Inside, the newspaper office seemed bigger than it looked from the street. Next to the window was a low naugahyde couch and a wire rack filled with copies of last week's edition. Across from the couch, a kindly looking old lady sat behind an overlarge desk sorting through what looked like bills or invoices. There was a modular room divider in back of the woman's chair, and a cat calendar and various photos of cats clipped from magazines were tacked to the fabric wall. Over the top of the divider, she could see into the room beyond.

"This," Rich said, gesturing elaborately toward the old lady, "is Carole Taylor. My right arm. She mans—or womans, or persons—the front desk, answers all phone calls, deals with all walk-ins, is in charge of circulation and billing, and does many other things too numerous for me to mention and too complicated for me to understand."

Carole giggled. "Knock it off, Rich." She smiled at Sue. "How are you, dear?"

"Fine."

"Rich never has been able to do a proper introduction. You're Susan Wing?"

"Yes. Sue."

"Well, I'm glad that you're here. We're both glad that you're here."

Sue immediately liked the woman. She had a soft, almost musical, voice and a natural air of friendliness. She looked the way Sue had always imagined Santa's wife would look: white hair in a bun, plump happy face, small wire-rimmed spectacles.

Rich walked behind the desk and put an arm around Carole's shoulder. "If you have any questions about anything and I'm not here, ask Carole. Come to think of it, even if I *am* here, ask Carole."

The old woman giggled again.

The editor walked around the side of the room divider, motioning for Sue to follow. "Enter the newsroom."

The "newsroom" was not as glamorous as she'd thought it would be. In fact, it seemed depressingly mundane, even slightly run down, looking more like the tired office of a failing realtor than the bustling information vortex she'd seen in cinematic newsrooms. Four parallel rectangles of fluorescent light were inset into the stucco ceiling. One of the bulbs in the middle rectangle had burned out, and while there was no lessening of illumination, the darkened light bar added to the office's overall air of shabbiness. She followed Rich across the faded gray carpet. There were only three desks and one table, all piled high with mail and typing paper. A third table lay overturned against the wall to the left, a clamp on one of its upward-pointing legs. Adjacent to the largest desk was a small stand on top of which was situated a computer terminal.

Two open black doorways disrupted the otherwise perfect white of the back brick wall.

"It's not much, but it's home."

Sue nodded, saying nothing.

"You were expecting 'Lou Grant'?"

She reddened. "No, it's not that—"

"Of course not. Look, I know this place doesn't look great. But you'll get used to it. It's like a cheap car. It'll get you where you want to go."

Sue gave him a halfhearted smile.

"Over here is my desk." He walked over to the large desk with the adjacent computer. "Over there"—he pointed toward the desk with the least amount of clutter—"is where you'll be working. The other desk is Jim Fredricks's."

"How many people work here?"

"You're looking at 'em. This is strictly a two-man operation—or a two-man-one-woman operation, now that you're here. Jim works part time and covers sports. Four or five people contribute weekly columns, and, of course, we print letters, but all of the news stories, features, and editorials are written by me."

"Why did the other person quit, the person before me?"

"My wife? She got a job at the Church of . . . at Pastor Wheeler's church."

"Oh."

"Do you know Pastor Wheeler?"

She shook her head.

"I don't either. Anyway, this is it. This is the *Gazette*. A few years ago, we did have another reporter, a kid about your age from the U of A. Tad Pullen. I don't know if you remember reading his byline. It was just about breaking us to keep him on. As I'm sure you've noticed, there's very little real news in Rio Verde. There's also very little real advertising. The *Gazette* is not a big money-making operation. Tad eventually found a job up in Flagstaff."

Sue nodded.

A kid about her age.

Other people her age had already graduated from college, were already starting careers, and here she was, still living at home, still clearing tables, taking night courses that didn't have enough people to keep them open. The optimistic enthusiasm she'd felt when she'd awakened this morning had entirely dissipated.

Rich put his hand on top of the computer. "We have only the one VDT, so if you're going to be writing articles for us, this is where the deed will be done. Of course, you can write your original out in long-hand or on a typewriter at home, whatever makes you feel comfortable, but you'll eventually have to retype it on the VDT because this is where we put your story on disk. We'll then take the disk over to the Compugraphic, which prints out a camera-ready copy." He nodded toward one of the open doors in the back wall. "Come on, I'll show you."

They walked across the worn carpet to the doorway. Rich went in first, flipped on a light. "Pasteup."

Sue glanced around. The entire left side of the room was taken up by two upward slanting tables with tops of cloudy glass. Against the facing wall was a huge blue machine on top of which was situated a strange black object that resembled an overlarge film canister.

"The Compugraphic," Rich said, following her gaze.

He walked over, flipped up a corner panel of the machine, and placed the black canister in the niche. He shut the panel. "Your disk will go here," he said, pointing toward a narrow horizontal slot next to a series of square green and red buttons. "We flip the switch, there are some noises and gyrations, and, *voila*, exposed paper rolls into that black doohickey I just put inside there. We take that to the darkroom, put it in another machine, and camera-ready copy comes out." He moved beside a flat table to the left of the Compugraphic, touching a low silver object that looked like a rolling pin welded to a paper cutter. "We wax the copy here, and paste it up on the light tables. Once the entire newspaper is pasted up, it goes to the printer.

"Any questions?"

Sue shook her head.

"Don't worry. You won't be tested on this. I just wanted to acquaint you with the place. You'll have plenty of opportunity to learn how everything works later."

Rich led the way out of the room, shutting off the lights behind them. He peered into the next doorway over. "Darkroom," he said. "Not much to see there." He reached in, closed the door. "And that's it. That's the tour." The two of them walked back to Rich's desk. He seated himself behind the desk, motioned for her to take the metal folding chair opposite. "Now the question is, do you still want to go through with this, or do you want to quit?"

"Drop the class? Never."

"Good." He picked up a round piece of flat white plastic, spun the smaller concentric circle attached to it, reading the numbers on the edge of the circle. "Do you know how to work a pica wheel?"

She shook her head.

"Do you know what a pica wheel is?"

"No."

"Do you know what a pica is?"

"No. I thought this was going to be a beginning class."

"It was, it was. But the lesson plans have changed. Which is probably to your advantage. You're going to get a crash course covering beginning, intermediate, and advanced journalism. Only instead of learning the subject the way the book says you're supposed to, you'll be picking up things as needed. Your academic journalism may suffer, but you'll learn what it takes to put out a real newspaper. When you do get into a regular class, you'll be way ahead of everyone else. By the way, did you bring that writing sample I asked for?"

"I couldn't find anything," she admitted. "But I did write a short story about my parents' restaurant."

"Short story?" He frowned.

"Nonfiction."

"Then it's an *article*, not a short story. First lesson: terminology."

"Should I write that down? Should I be taking notes?"

"Not unless you want to."

"So what is this exactly? A job or a class?"

"Both."

Sue sighed. "I told my parents it's a class. They think there's a field trip today to the newspaper. I didn't tell them that's what was happening, but I sort of let them think it. I should've corrected them, but . . ." She shook her head. "My father will be cool, as long as it doesn't affect my work at the restaurant, but I'm not sure what my mother's going to say."

Rich smiled sympathetically. "Do you want me to talk to your parents?"

"No," she said quickly. "I'll do it. But I do need to know what my hours are and all that sort of thing."

"The hours are flexible. You come in when you can, work when you want to. I'll give you assignments and deadlines, and as long as you meet those deadlines, no problem."

"How is the grading going to work? Are there still going to be tests?"

"Every Thursday. The newspaper's going to be your test. And don't worry about grades. This is strictly pass/fail."

"Do you have an assignment for me yet?"

He grinned. "Glad you asked. You get to go through all that mail on your desk over there, separate the press releases from the ads, then pick out one with a local angle and rewrite it as a feature. That was the first assignment I was given when I was an intern."

"Did it teach you anything?"

"Not really. But that mail does need to be sorted, and it'll give you something to do while I go over your article."

"I guess you want the article, then."

"It would help."

She reached into her purse, pulling out several folded pages paper clipped together and handing them to him. "Here."

He scanned the top page, then looked up at her. "I'm impressed. You've got the right format and everything."

She smiled self-consciously. "It's amazing what you can learn on a trip to the library."

He smiled back, but above his mouth his eyes were troubled. Now that she looked, she saw that the easy good humor that had been so natural to Rich the other evening seemed forced today. She suddenly remembered what had happened, where he'd been all night. She glanced away from the editor, unable to meet his gaze. She tried to imagine how she would feel if her parents' graves had been dug up, but she didn't even want to think about her parents dying and immediately pushed the thought from her mind. "I'll, uh, start looking through that mail," she said.

"Okay. I'll go over your article."

Sue went to the other desk, her desk, sat down, and began opening envelopes. Before she was even a fourth of the way through the pile, Rich was calling her back. She walked over, and he handed her the pages. She sat down in the folding chair, feeling as though she'd been kicked in the stomach. She'd spent the better part of yesterday working on the story, revising and rewriting it until she felt it was as good as she could make it, but obviously it hadn't been good enough. The top page alone was covered with red pencil—squiggles and circles and unfamiliar marks.

"Not bad," Rich said. "I'm impressed."

She looked up to see if he was being facetious, but his smile was gentle and understanding and not at all sarcastic. She felt confused and flustered. "Not bad? Then what's all . . . this?"

"Copyediting symbols. Some are corrections, but most are just symbols that tell the typesetter what to do. You'll be doing your own typesetting here, but I thought it was important for you to learn the symbols anyway. Typesetters don't go by the appearance of the manuscript, they go by what you tell them, so you should learn how to prepare your copy. The story itself, though, is pretty good. You're not a bad writer."

"Really?"

"You're not a journalistic writer yet. This reads more like a report for an English class than a news article, but I think you'll be able to make the transition without too much trouble."

He spent the next half hour explaining to her the basics of copyediting, telling her what the symbols on her paper meant and when and how they were used. He then gave her a short assignment: copyedit one of the press releases she'd come across in the mail.

He opened the middle drawer of his desk, then the

drawers on the side, searching for something. "I was going to get you a pen, but I don't seem to have any extras here. Why don't you ask Carole to get you some."

Sue had almost forgotten that the secretary was out front. She walked around the room divider and saw the plump woman gathering a handful of multicolored pens and pencils from the bottom right drawer of her desk.

"He's always losing pens," Carole confided. "I just gave him a box last week. I swear I don't know where they all go." She handed Sue the pens she'd taken from the drawer. "Here you go, dear. This should tide you over for a while."

Sue smiled at her. "Thanks."

"You're more than welcome."

She returned to the newsroom and went directly to her desk. She found a suitable press release in the pile—an article from the Forest Service about an infestation of ips beetles in the northern part of the state—and began dutifully transcribing the symbols from her own paper to the release.

"I have a deadline to meet," Rich told her. "So I'll be working on my own article. If you need any help, give me a holler."

Sue nodded.

The two of them worked in silence. Sue kept glancing over at the editor. She couldn't help thinking that she should initiate a conversation, but she had no idea what to say. She wondered if he felt as strange and awkward as she did and hazarded another glance in his direction. He appeared to be busily working on his story, apparently unconcerned with the silence.

He glanced up, caught her looking at him, and smiled. "How would you like to do 'Roving Reporter'?" he asked.

"Me?"

"I'm busy, I'm tired, and I'm not sure I'll be able to get to it this week. If I don't put it in, though, I'll be getting calls from everyone and his brother. The people in this town don't like their regular features to be missing."

"What do I do?"

"You know how to work a camera?"

"A little."

"Either you do or you don't. We have a Canon AE-1."

"I don't," she admitted.

"No problem. I'll show you how." He opened his bottom desk drawer and pulled out the camera by its strap. "I should warn you, though, that 'Roving Reporter' is not as easy as it looks. People think we just stake out a spot, ask the question, take a few photos, and that's it. But you're going to find that there are a lot of people in this town who don't want their opinions published or who are afraid to express their opinions even on innocuous subjects. And there are even more who don't want their picture taken. I remember standing in front of the bank for two hours one day looking for five people to tell me whether they prefer ice cream or frozen yogurt. Not a controversial subject, but I stood there for half the afternoon trying to find someone to respond. Everyone likes to read the 'Roving Reporter,' but no one wants to meet him. Or her . . ."

Sue smiled. "Adversity and I are no strangers."

Rich chuckled. "We'll make a reporter of you yet."

Since she didn't have a car, Sue was forced to stake out a location within walking distance. She considered the post office, but Rich told her he'd been there two weeks ago and didn't want to repeat this soon. He suggested the Shell station, but she said she didn't feel comfortable hanging out there. They finally decided on Mike's Meats, the butcher shop.

Sue first walked inside and told Mike Grayson, the

owner, what she was planning to do and asked his permission to stand on his front walk. He said he didn't care, and she went back outside and waited.

And waited.

An old man ignored her completely, not responding to her request or even looking at her. Two women agreed to answer the question but refused to allow their pictures to be taken. A cocky-looking teenager laughed at her.

It was going to be a long morning.

By the time she returned to the newspaper, it was after one. Carole's seat was empty—the secretary was obviously on her lunch break—and Rich was at his desk, eating an apple. Sue sat down in the folding chair and placed the camera on top of his desk. She wiped the sweat from her forehead. "You're right. No one wanted to talk to me."

"What'd I tell you? How many responses did you get?"

"Four."

"How many people did you ask?"

"Twenty."

Rich smiled. "Were the responses good?"

She shrugged. "I guess."

"Anybody give you advice, tell you what you should be asking instead?"

"Three people told me I should be asking about vampires."

Rich's smile faded. "Vampires?"

She nodded.

"They were joking, weren't they?"

"I don't think so."

He frowned. "What did you tell them?"

"Nothing. I smiled, nodded, told them thank you, then went on to the next person."

Rich stared silently at the camera, making no move to pick it up.

Sue cleared her throat. "Maybe we should ask about vampires. It seems to be on a lot of people's minds. I think—" She broke off in midsentence, suddenly remembering the events of the night before. She mentally kicked herself, looking quickly away.

"We may," the editor said quietly. "We may have to."

"Hey, Daddy!"

Sue turned her head at the sound of the voice. A young girl with long blond hair came speeding out of the door to the pasteup room.

"Oh," the girl said, stopping short.

Rich stood. "Sue, this is my daughter Anna. She's going to be visiting us for a few hours in the afternoons. Anna, this is Sue Wing. She's going to be working here."

"I know you!" Anna said, coming closer. "You work at the restaurant!"

"I recognize you too," Sue said. She turned toward Rich. "I know who your wife is. She's a regular customer."

"Yeah. We like your food."

"How come I've never seen you in there?"

"I've been in, a couple of times. You probably just didn't notice."

"Or I was in the back."

"I like the fortune cookies!" Anna announced. Sue laughed. "Me, too. You want me to bring you some tomorrow?"

"Yeah!" Anna grinned at her father.

"You've got yourself a friend," Rich said. He sat down again. "Now there are two of us who're glad you're here."

"Three," Sue said, smiling.

Seventeen

The FBI agent and the representative from the state police left at the same time. Robert saw them to the door of his office, shook hands with both men, and gave them a smile and a hearty "thank you."

The second the door closed, he stuck out his middle finger, thrusting it upward in the air for emphasis.

Assholes.

He had never before had to deal with state or federal law enforcement authorities, and he hoped to Christ he never had to deal with them again. He walked across the room and watched through the slats of the miniblinds as the two men got into their respective cars. A chain of command had been established, and for that he was thankful. The buck no longer stopped with him. He was now merely a link in the chain, and if he couldn't handle the situation, he could pass that buck on up to the state police and the FBI.

But he regretted giving up his autonomy. Last week he'd been confused, not knowing what he should do or how he should do it, but a week of responsibility had given him a taste for serious decision making, and now he felt resentful toward the big boys for trying to horn in on his territory.

Especially since they were such complete and total assholes.

The state policeman had said almost nothing during

the meeting, had simply requested duplicates of everything asked for by the FBI agent. It was the FBI agent who
had done most of the talking, who had laid out the recent
events in Rio Verde in such a patronizingly arch manner
that the emerging picture, though factually correct and
chronologically accurate, made Robert and his department look like Joe Doofus and his Goober Patrol.

God, he hated the smug attitude of that business-suited
geek.

To make matters worse, Robert had snuffled and
sneezed his way through most of the meeting. The handkerchief on his desk was soaked. Fall was always the worst
time of year for his allergies, and, unfortunately, they'd
picked today to start the season. He would've taken a pill
had he known, but in that instance the cure was almost
worse than the disease. Even the mildest over-the-counter
allergy medicine knocked him out. If he had taken a pill,
he probably would have dozed off halfway through the
FBI agent's diatribe.

Not that that would have been a bad thing. He and the
agent, Greg Rossiter, had experienced an immediate an-
tipathy toward one another. That was strange. Ordinarily,
he was a fairly easygoing guy and got along with practically
everyone. But something about Rossiter had instantly
rubbed him the wrong way. He'd known from the moment he'd laid eyes on that blond brush-cut Nazi's head
that he wouldn't like the man. And his response to Joe
Cash, the state policeman, had not been much different.

Both men had seemed to take a perverse pleasure in
making him feel as inept and incompetent as possible.
After allowing him to describe the coroner's findings on
the death of Manuel Torres and relate his own firsthand
knowledge of the cemetery, Rossiter had said only, "Rio
Verde only has ten thousand people. Anything new or different would be noticed immediately by you or your men,
wouldn't it?"

The implied criticism in that condescending query had made Robert bristle, but he'd forced himself not to become defensive, had made sure his voice remained professionally impersonal. "Not necessarily. Our town may be small compared to Phoenix, but we still don't know everyone in it. And we're not in the habit of keeping tabs on people when they haven't done anything wrong."

"But they've done something wrong now, haven't they?"

"Who?" Robert had tried to keep his voice even. "We're a couple hours' drive from Florence, Globe, Miami, Superior. We're four hours from Phoenix. Five from Payson and Randall. Seven from Flagstaff and Sedona. Who's to say someone's not cruising into town, doing his business, and leaving? We get a lot of tourists passing through here on their way to Roosevelt Lake. It seems more than likely to me that this is being done by someone who does not live in Rio Verde."

"Really?" The agent had looked at him with a bored expression. "I think it highly unlikely that any criminal or psychopath would specifically make a series of runs all the way out here merely to perform activities he could do in his own hometown."

He'd sneezed and said nothing more.

The thing that had galled him the most was the importance both men seemed to place on anything that happened in Rio Verde, their almost nonchalant attitude toward the horrors that had occurred here. A man had been murdered. A man with friends, a family. The bodies of hundreds of the town's departed loved ones had been disinterred, their resting places desecrated. Wild animals had been killed. But none of this seemed to make any sort of impression on either Rossiter or Cash. It was almost as though they considered events in Rio Verde too trivial to be taken seriously, the province of children rather than adults, hardly worth bothering with.

He half considered calling up both men's superiors and leveling a charge of racism against them, claiming that they were dragging their feet because Manuel Torres was Hispanic. *That* would get a response.

Only he wasn't sure he wanted any deeper involvement from those people. The FBI had installed a fax machine in his office, a direct line to the federal building in Phoenix so he could send copies of all reports and paperwork.

That was enough meddling in his business, as far as he was concerned.

He would keep them informed of his progress, let them know when something was discovered, but that was it.

The intercom beeped, and Robert moved away from the window and back to his desk. He held down the white "Talk" button, leaning into the receiver. "What is it?"

Steve's voice came through clear and strong. "We have a slight, uh, situation. I think you'd better come out here."

"Be there in a sec." Robert let go of the button, wiped his nose with the wet handkerchief, and collected the forms and pamphlets the FBI agent had left him, carrying them out to the front office.

In the waiting area, six or seven people were clustered on the other side of the counter near the front door. They were standing close together, obviously upset. At the receptionist's desk, LeeAnne was trying to look busy, shuffling through recently typed papers, not looking up. Robert scanned the group of people and noticed that they were all from the Central Arizona Bank.

Almost as one, the faces turned toward him. Robert dropped the handful of pamphlets on Steve's desk and bent down. "What is this?" he asked quietly.

Steve shook his head, grinning. "I'll let them tell you."

"Mr. Johnson wants us to wear underwear!" Tammette Walker said.

"Uniforms!" Maxine Gilbert added.

Robert straightened up and stared at them uncomprehendingly.

"He wants us to wear uniforms made out of underwear!"

"He's gone crazy! There must be a law against—"

Robert held up his hands for silence. "Whoa, whoa, whoa! Hold on now, just hold your horses. One person at a time." He nodded toward Maxine. "Maxie? Why don't you try telling me what this is all about?"

The elderly teller pursed her lips and nervously clicked the clasp on her handbag open and shut. "Mr. Johnson has not been himself lately, not for the past week or so. Usually, he's very involved in the operation of the bank, but for the past several days we haven't seen him at all. He just stays cooped up in his office. This morning, though, when we arrived, he was there waiting for us, and he had his . . . uniforms on display."

"It was disgusting!" Tammette said.

Robert held up his hands. "Let Maxie finish. Please." He nodded at Maxine. "Go on."

"They were—" She shook her head, as though unable to come up with an adequate description. "They're made out of underwear. He sewed panties and bras and boxer shorts all together, into pants and shirts—well, they're not really pants and shirts, but they sort of have sleeves and legs and necklines—and he calls them uniforms. He said that all bank employees now have to wear one of his uniforms. He said if we don't wear them, we'll be fired."

"I think they're made from used underwear," Mort Emerson added, grimacing. "They have stains on them."

Robert cleared his throat. "I don't quite understand what you want me to do about this."

"Pee Wee would know what to do," Stephanie Bishop said through pinched lips.

"I'm not Pee Wee."

"We want you to arrest him!" Tammette said. "It's not

legal to force us to wear uniforms made out of underwear."

"I don't think an actual crime has been committed here. I'll go over and talk to Mr. Johnson if you want, but I can't arrest him. My suggestion would be to call the head office and talk to the bank president, tell him your problem—"

"There is no head office," Mort said. "Sophocles Johnson is the president."

"Well, if worst comes to worst, if Mr. Johnson really does fire you, you may have to take him to court—"

"We need our jobs," Tammette said. "And what do you mean court? Isn't there a law against forcing your employees to wear uniforms made out of underwear?"

"Used underwear?" Art added.

Robert sighed. "I'll talk to Mr. Johnson. I'll try to get this cleared up. If I can't, I'll call the Better Business Bureau and the state wage and hour commission. I'll get this thing sorted out, okay?"

"He's crazy," Maxine said. "He won't talk to you."

"It sounds as though he's a little whacked out," Robert admitted, "but I'll see what I can do. Right now, why don't all of you leave your numbers with LeeAnne over there at the front desk. I'll give you a call this afternoon."

Maxine clicked and unclicked her purse clasp. "What about the bank? It's going to stay closed?"

"I can't afford to lose a day of work," Janice Lake said.

"I'll do what I can," Robert told them. "I'm going to go call Mr. Johnson right now. Just leave your numbers with LeeAnne." He turned away, forcing the receptionist to deal with the bank employees. He looked over at Steve, who was still grinning, rolled his eyes, and walked back down the hall to his office.

The first thing he saw when he strode through the door was the fax machine on his side table.

This was turning out to be a hell of a day.

Eighteen

Before he retired and moved back to Arizona six years ago, Bill Covey had been an architect. Senior Architectural Supervisor at Sippl, Doyle and Dane in Irvine, California, to be exact. He never had any illusions about himself, and he would have been the first to admit that his architectural efforts had been less than inspired. Many of the small stores and restaurants that he had designed in the fifties and sixties had, in fact, been bulldozed over and replaced with splashier, more eye-catching structures in the wave of redevelopment which swept over Southern California in the seventies and eighties. The condominium plans he had laid out before retiring, his last project for the firm, were probably the best work he had ever done, yet even they were hardly original.

Now, however, he was inspired.

Covey, pumped up with caffeine from the massive amounts of coffee he'd been gulping all evening, raced through one sketch after another, not bothering to do cleanup work, not bothering to smooth out the rough edges or draw to scale. He was creating here, setting down ideas for the Church of the Living Christ, the future physical home of the Son of God on earth, and he could not be bothered with petty technical details. He could fix the small stuff later, right now he was on a roll, and he had to try to record these ideas as they came to him, before they were lost.

He had never been a churchgoing man, had always thought of belief in a higher power as a crutch used by people who couldn't manage their own lives, but something had made him start attending Pastor Wheeler's church a few weeks ago, and he was prepared now to admit that it was the hand of the Lord guiding him. When he'd heard the pastor describe his plan to build the ultimate house of worship right here in Rio Verde, Covey had known that the reason he had been put on this earth was to design Christ's church.

He'd talked with the pastor after the sermon, prepared to beg for the assignment if need be, but he hadn't had to say much at all. It was almost as though the pastor had been expecting him to approach and volunteer his services.

They'd met once since then, a single quick informal conversation. They had not talked specifics, but the two of them had understood each other. He knew what the pastor wanted without being told, and when he'd explained a few of his ideas, Wheeler too had realized how closely aligned were their goals.

He'd been drawing ever since, putting onto paper every thought that occurred to him, designing doorways and naves, chapels and chambers, altars and pews.

Living quarters for Jesus Christ.

All of which could be constructed within forty days.

He wondered what Jesus was going to do when He established His kingdom on earth. Was He going to abolish war and hunger? Was he going to make the world a paradise? Was He going to reunite families with their dear departed loved ones? Covey put down his drafting pen.

Was He going to resurrect Judith?

No, he thought. Jesus wouldn't do that to him. Not when he was designing His church.

Would He?

Just to be on the safe side, maybe he would try to talk

to Jesus when all this was over. Maybe he could ask for a favor. Maybe he could get Jesus to make sure that Judith burned in hell for eternity.

Covey had not yet seen the Savior, but he already knew that Jesus was nothing like he had imagined. He had bought the Hollywood conception of Christ, had always seen Him as kind and loving, tolerant and forgiving. But he knew now that Jesus was judgmental and unforgiving, that He was ruthless in His dispensation of power, and although this was not what Covey had expected, it seemed right to him. This was the way it was supposed to be.

Which was why he knew Jesus would understand about Judith.

Covey finished the last of his cold coffee and looked over what he'd drawn. It was a sacrificial altar, a carved and decorated block of stone not unlike those he'd seen in Bible movies, where offerings could be made to Jesus.

Jesus liked sacrifices.

Covey rubbed his tired eyes, looked at the clock, and decided to call it quits for the night. Next to the clock, on top of the television set, was the pickle jar in which he planned to keep his lizards. He'd caught the first one this morning in the backyard. It, and another he had caught at noon, were now caged in the jar. He would offer these, and the others he intended to catch, to Jesus as a sacrifice. Maybe, if he had time, he would even capture some bigger animal.

Maybe that would ensure that Judith would be taken care of.

Covey stood up, turned off his desk light and, feeling exhausted but happy, he headed toward his bedroom.

Nineteen

Ginni saw the green sign before she could read the words on it, and she prayed that the number of miles to Rio Verde would be under twenty.

No such luck.

She sped by the sign and swore softly to herself as she saw that the town was still fifty miles away. She'd promised her sister that she'd be there before noon, and now it looked as though she wouldn't be there until after three.

She put her hand in the ice chest next to her, feeling around, but her fingers encountered only cold water and half-melted ice cubes. She'd finished the last of the Diet Cokes some miles back, and she was thirsty again. The small Hyundai had no air-conditioning, and even with the windows down the desert heat was stifling, the wind which blew against her face warm and hellish.

She also had to go to the bathroom, and she wasn't sure she would be able to wait until she reached the next gas station, the pressure on her bladder was becoming too insistent to ignore. She glanced outside the window at the barren landscape and didn't even see any bushes she could squat behind if worse came to worst. There were only tumbleweeds, cactus, and thin leafless trees. She pressed down on the gas pedal, edging the car up another five miles an hour.

Mary Beth, she knew, was going to be frantic that she was late. Ever since their father had disappeared, her sister had, understandably, been a bundle of nerves—tense, jumpy, always on edge. Although she had not let Mary Beth know it, Ginni too was worried sick. She had not been surprised when their father disappeared for a few days—it was not as though he hadn't done it before—but when a week had passed, and he hadn't contacted anybody in the family at all, she'd become worried. Now she was convinced that her sister was right, that something *had* happened to him.

Ahead, on the right, she saw a blue sign, and though it was still too far away for her to make out the words, Ginni knew from experience that the sign announced a rest area coming up. She sighed with relief.

A few miles later, she saw a trio of picnic tables covered by cheap metal awnings and, between them, a low brick building. A bathroom! She pulled into the rest area and parked next to the only other car there, a red Fiat. Its occupants, a young man wearing a white tennis outfit and his blond girlfriend, were eating at one of the picnic tables.

Ginni fairly ran through the doorway marked WOMEN. The smell hit her the instant she stepped inside, but she didn't care. She saw, in the second before she sat down, that the metal toilet did not have a chemical disposal system but was positioned directly over an open septic tank. Then there was relief, and she closed her eyes gratefully.

She heard a loud sickening plop from the tank below.

She jumped up, stared into the open hole. It was dark down there, and she could only make out a vague dark lake of human waste. She thought she saw something white swimming through the sludge.

Then her father popped up from the sewage, grinned at her, and resumed swimming in the filth.

The Fiat people had been just pulling onto the highway when she ran screaming out of the bathroom. She'd run instinctively after them, but before she had even reached the parking area they were gone.

Now she sat on top of one of the picnic tables, staring at the bathroom. The small tan building looked threatening to her now. Standing alone in the middle of the desert, the only sign of human encroachment in the flat empty wilderness, the structure seemed out of place, wrong. Ginni took a deep breath. She knew she was just being paranoid. Her perceptions had been altered by what she'd seen in the cavernous hole beneath the toilet.

She shivered. Had she really seen what she'd thought she'd seen? It was so off-the-wall crazy that it did not seem even remotely credible. If she'd heard about it from someone else or had read of such an occurrence, she would have dismissed it as ludicrous. Even now, her rational mind was telling her that she'd imagined it, her worry and concern having overshadowed her reason. Could her father really be living in a septic tank under a woman's bathroom in the middle of the desert?

No.

But she'd seen him swimming through the shit.

He'd grinned at her.

She knew she should get out of here, tell Mary Beth, tell the police, but despite what she'd seen, despite the fear within her, she was still not certain that her father was really down there. How could he be? No human being could live in such an environment. And it didn't make any sense. Why would he disappear from home to live under a toilet?

Ginni pushed herself off the plastic tabletop, pulling her shorts out of the crack of her buttocks. She started walking slowly down the winding cement walkway. She had to make sure. She had to see.

The inside of the bathroom was dark, the only light coming from the diffused rays of the sun through a battered translucent skylight and the open door. Her heart pounding crazily, Ginni approached the toilet. The smell was as bad as before, maybe worse, and she almost gagged.

She forced herself to look into the open septic tank. "Dad?" she called hesitantly. The lake of filth remained undisturbed. She cleared her throat. "Dad?"

Her father's head broke through the surface of the effluence, white and grinning.

Ginni backed up, her heart feeling as though it would burst through the walls of her chest. She realized she was screaming, and she forced herself to stop. Gathering her courage, she approached the toilet again, looked down into the opening.

Her father stared up at her, waste dripping down his exposed forehead, brownish liquid running out of his grinning mouth. "Don't come back!" he hissed. His voice was cracked and wheezy.

Ginni looked around wildly. What should she do? Should she—

A middle-aged woman wearing a fashionable blue business suit stepped into the bathroom. She stared at Ginni, standing over the toilet, looking down, and cleared her throat. "Excuse me," she said awkwardly. "I need to use the facilities."

Ginni whirled on her. "You can't! My father's down there!"

The woman backed up, a look of startled incomprehension on her face. She exited quickly, and Ginni looked back down. There was only darkness, only brown.

"Bitch!" her father's voice hissed from somewhere in the septic tank.

Frightened as much by the hatred in that voice as by the circumstances in which they were spoken, she moved hesitantly away from the opening.

An excrement-encrusted hand shot upward from the seat of the toilet.

Ginni made it back to the car and barely managed to lock the doors before fainting.

The hours after she came to were a blur. She remembered being revived by a uniformed police officer—someone had apparently seen her lying slumped over the wheel, unconscious, and had called the police. She remembered telling and retelling her story. She remembered the influx of policemen and sewage workers and, later, the television cameras.

She remembered nothing of the capture, but she remembered Mary Beth. Mary Beth hugging her and holding her, crying with her, talking for her to the police. Mary Beth taking care of the details and formalities.

And she'd always thought *she* was the strong one.

Ginni stared through the bars as her father paced restlessly back and forth across the cement floor of his cell. She was alone back here except for a uniformed guard. Mary Beth was in the front office, talking to the police chief.

Her father's eyes were bright, alert, and filled with a demented sort of excitement. She could feel the kinetic energy radiating from him. He stopped pacing, turned to look at her, then rushed the bars, hitting them with his head and grinning. "Bitch!" he screamed.

"Settle down in there," the guard ordered.

Tears welled in Ginni's eyes—tears of pity for what he had become, tears of loss for what he had once been. The man before her still had her father's form and face, but the words, the movements, the expressions were those of a different person entirely, an alien. A tear escaped, rolling down her right cheek, and she wiped it away with a finger. "Why . . . ?" She swallowed hard, trying to keep her voice steady. "Why did you do this?"

His grin became wider. "I'm a shit. I've always been a

shit." He shoved his head in the toilet, swishing it around. Ginni turned away. She closed her eyes, saw in her mind her father's hand emerging from the septic tank.

She left the detention area crying, escorted by the guard.

Robert stared hard at the fax machine, still not sure if he should immediately inform the feds about Vigil or if he should wait. They probably knew already, probably had people whose job it was to monitor radio and television newscasts for crime reports, but no one from either the FBI or the state police had yet contacted him. He was tempted to hold off for a few days, wait to fax them the information, but no, he couldn't do that. He thought of Mary Beth's face when she'd seen her father in the cell: a bleak barren landscape.

She deserved the best men and resources that could be mustered.

Rich walked in, and Robert nodded tiredly at him, moving back behind his desk and sitting down. "How's the news biz?"

"Pretty good. How's law enforcement?"

"Takes it up the ass."

"Different strokes for different folks."

The two of them were silent for a moment. Robert leaned back in his swivel chair, which creaked with an exaggerated opening-door-in-a-haunted-house sound.

"You oughta get that thing oiled."

"Yeah."

Rich walked over to the fax machine. "I wish I could afford to get myself one of these things."

"It's the FBI's. If it was up to me, it wouldn't be here."

"Have they been able to find anything out?"

Robert shook his head. "Who knows? If they did, I'd probably be the last person they'd tell. I'm sure they're

running everything through their computers and what-
not, doing whatever it is they do."

Rich leaned against the windowsill, faced his brother.
"So what *is* happening?"

"If I knew, I'd tell you."

"The cemetery made it into the *Republic* the other day.
Did you see that?"

"I've been too busy to read the newspaper lately. I haven't even gotten to your article yet."

Rich grinned. "You don't have to read it. It was brilliant."

"They think they're going to be able to rebury all of
the bodies based on the plot map. Nothing was moved
too far."

"Thank God."

Robert cleared his throat. "Did you ever go out there
to see—?"

"I didn't look."

Robert focused his attention on a topographical map
of the county that hung on the left wall, not wanting to
see his brother's face. "I didn't either. But now I think
maybe I should've. It just doesn't seem right to me that . . .
I wasn't there. That neither of us were there."

"Mom would've understood."

"Dad wouldn't've."

There was a knock on the door frame. "Am I interrupt-
ing anything?" Brad Woods stood in the entryway, holding
by his side a manila folder stuffed with papers.

Robert shook his head. "Come on in."

Woods walked across the worn carpet and dropped the
folder on top of Robert's desk. "Here're copies of my
reports. I already sent copies to the county. I ended up
examining eight of the bodies in detail, the ones that appeared to have been specifically, for lack of a better word,
operated upon. You were right. The marrow had been
removed from several of the corpses, although most of

that marrow was already dried. But I could find no evidence of any surgical procedures, no telling marks upon bone or flesh, no trace of chemical substances that shouldn't be there, no method, no indication even whether this was done by a human or an animal."

Robert sighed, picked up the folder, glanced halfheartedly at the top page and dropped the packet down on his desktop once again.

Woods took a cigarette from his shirt pocket and examined it. "What have you found out? Do you have any idea who could have done this or why?"

"No. I was hoping you'd help me out with that."

Woods stopped examining the cigarette and placed it, unlit, in his mouth. He looked from Robert to Rich and began pacing. "What if we really do have a vampire on our hands?"

Rich snorted. "Come on, now. Not you too."

"No. Hear me out. I've been doing a little research on exsanguination techniques, and the way Torres's body and the bodies of those animals were drained was . . . Let's just say it was highly irregular. It also shouldn't have been able to work as it did."

"Brad—"

"I know this is crazy. I understand how you feel. But, medically, this stuff does not happen. And I'll be honest with you. Examining those corpses from the cemetery gave me the creeps. The technical aspects and examination results are in those reports, but what's not in those reports is the weirdness. It just spooked me to work on them. I kept wondering why anyone would suck the dry bone marrow from a corpse."

Robert stood. "Maybe it's a cult. Who the hell knows?"

"Exactly. Who the hell knows? All I'm saying is that right now we need to keep an open mind about this." Woods took the still-unlit cigarette from his mouth and replaced it in his shirt pocket as he stopped pacing. "What about Vigil? What did County Psych say?"

"The guy's in there right now. I'm just waiting for him to report back."

"Who is it?"

"Jacobson."

Woods nodded. "He's good. A little flaky, but good. The county doesn't usually get shrinks of that caliber." He moved next to Rich, turned toward Robert. "Can I wait around here until the results come in?"

"Sure. Why not?"

"What about me?" Rich asked. "Is this going to be on or off the record?"

"Your call. I'm not going to tell you what to do."

"That's a first."

Robert picked up a paper clip, threw it at him.

Ten minutes later, the three of them met Dr. Jacobson in the conference room. The psychiatrist, an unusually tall, bald man with earrings in both ears, did not even wait until they were seated. "Are you familiar with the Medusa Syndrome?"

Robert and Rich looked dumbly at each other. Woods shook his head, since the question was clearly directed to him. "Can't say that I am."

"It is exceedingly rare. It refers to a trauma-induced personality change, or, more specifically, aberrant behavior produced by exposure to a traumatic incident. What differentiates the Medusa Syndrome from other trauma-induced personality disorders is the fact that it is not merely triggered by a single incident but is actually caused by that one-time exposure, the shock is so great that the individual is not able to cope with what he or she has seen, and the defenses of the ego break down completely. The person experiences what might be referred to as a personality restructuring. I've never before come across it myself, but I can tell you this: I've never even read of anything this severe. Mr. Vigil's name is going to live in textbooks for years to come. If he survives, if he didn't catch some fatal disease down there, we're going to have ourselves quite a study."

Robert cleared his throat. "Excuse me for asking, but how can you be sure? Maybe Mike—Mr. Vigil—has been crazy all along. Maybe he just snapped."

"I'm not a hundred percent positive. I only met the man today and only examined him for a few hours. But the signs are there. To be honest, we may not be absolutely certain of the diagnosis for some time to come. But I'll tell you this: There's a high probability that Mr. Vigil is suffering from the Medusa Syndrome." Jacobson ran his index finger over his top teeth. "You know, I was at the conference where the syndrome was named. I wanted to call it the 'Tommy Syndrome,' after The Who's rock opera because Tommy becomes deaf, dumb, and blind after witnessing the murder of his mother's lover by his father. But the other psychiatrists were all quite a bit older and were not even familiar with The Who. I doubt if most of them knew who The Beatles were. Besides, they had to get in the obligatory Greek reference. Psychiatrists love classical references—"

"What about Mr. Vigil?" Robert prodded.

"Well, it's clear that this individual has been severely traumatized. To the point of precipitating radical behavioral changes. From the brief conversation I had with his daughters, and from my own discussion with him and observation of his behavior, it appears quite likely that he saw or experienced something that so shocked or frightened him that his psychological defenses were shattered. He retreated into the person you discovered in the septic tank."

Woods looked at Robert, then at the psychiatrist. He cleared his throat. "What if a person saw a vampire? Do you think that would produce the sort of shock necessary to cause this change?"

Jacobson frowned. "A vampire? What do you mean?"

"A monster," Rich said. "A guy with a black cape and fangs who sucks blood."

"This is not a joking matter," the psychiatrist said, standing. "I don't have time to play games with you. I was called in here and asked to look at this man, and I've given you my opinion. My recommendation will be for him to remain at the hospital in Florence for further examination."

Robert stared at Woods and found himself hoping that the coroner would pursue this line of reasoning, would say, "We're not joking," would press the psychiatrist on the vampire issue, but Woods remained silent, eyes downcast. Robert glanced at his brother, who looked away.

Jacobson began gathering his papers.

"What sort of thing could frighten a man this badly?" Robert asked. "I know Mike—knew Mike—and he is not an easily frightened man."

Jacobson looked up, shook his head, his left hand toying with one of his earrings. "I don't know," he said. He thought for a moment, and a slow smile spread across his face. "But we'll find out. And when we do . . . that's going to be interesting. Very interesting."

Twenty

"Susan."

The words were a whisper, spoken with a Cantonese accent. *Soo-sun.*

"Susan."

She opened one eye, peered into the darkness. There was an unfamiliar weight on the end of her bed, an indentation that affected a gravitational pull on her feet. Outside there was wind, a sibilant dust storm that played around with the defenses of the house but was not strong enough to attack. The pillow next to her face smelled faintly of breath.

Stretching up and out of the fetal position in which she slept, Sue saw her grandmother sitting on the edge of the bed, a small hunched shape in the too large darkness. She rubbed her eyes. "What is it?" she asked tiredly in English, then, correcting herself, in Cantonese.

Her grandmother was silent for a moment, the only noise in the room her labored breathing, which blended perfectly with the sandstorm outside. Sue felt a dry cold hand touch her cheek, trace her chin. "I dreamt again of the *cup hu girngsi.*"

Sue said nothing.

"I have dreamed for five nights of the *cup hu girngsi.*" *Cup Hu Girngsi.*

Sue knew the sounds, knew the words they formed, but she had never before heard them spoken together, and their combination sent an icy shiver of fear down her spine.

Cup hu girngsi.

Corpse-who-drinks-blood.

She looked carefully at her grandmother's face, searching for a sign that the old woman was joking. But her grandmother's gaze remained unwavering, her expression deadly serious, and Sue knew from the fact that her grandmother was here, in her bedroom, at this time of night, that this was no joke. She reached up, instinctively touched the jade around her neck.

"Yes," her grandmother said, nodding.

Sue felt cold, and she wrapped the sheet more tightly around her body. She wanted to be able to laugh off what her grandmother was trying to tell her, wanted to be able to fall back asleep and forget that this conversation had ever taken place, but sleepiness had left her completely. She found herself thinking of Manuel Torres, of Rich's parents and the others in the cemetery.

Of what she had felt at the school that night.

Her grandmother suddenly leaned forward, eyes wide. "You have sensed it too!"

Sue shook her head. "No."

"You have. You cannot hide it from me." Her grandmother was whispering, and her voice was nearly indistinguishable from the wild wind outside "You know of the *cup hu girngsi.*"

"I have never heard that name before."

"It is called something else in America."

"Vampire," Sue said.

"Vampire. Yes." Nodding. "But we know it as the *cup hu girngsi.* I have dreamed of it now for five nights, and it is here. You have sensed it too."

"I have not sensed anything."

"You have."

"I cannot 'sense' things."

"Yes, you can. You have *Di Lo Ling Gum.*"

"I do not!"

"Your mother does not. Your father does not. John does not. You do."She reached for Sue's hand, tightly clutching the sheet, and squeezed it. "Do not be afraid."

"I am not afraid, because there is no *cup hu girngsi.*"

"There is. I have seen it." Her grandmother was silent for a moment. The wind outside seemed to grow louder and sounded almost liquid. When she spoke again, Sue had to lean forward to listen. "I was eight years old when the *cup hu girngsi* came. We lived in Cuangxun, a small village in Hunan. I was young, and it was a long, long time ago, but I remember it all. I can still see the houses on the hill in the early morning mist, standing like silent sentries in the fog.

"I can still hear the screams of Wai Fan echoing through the valley."

She stared in Sue's direction but past her, not at her. "We were awakened by the echoes of those screams. I was frightened and confused, and I ran into my parents' room. Father and Mother knew immediately what had happened. They knew it was the *cup hu girngsi.* That frightened me even more, the very words terrified me. I had never seen my parents scared—I had never seen them not be in complete control—and the haunted looks on their faces made me more afraid than anything I had ever seen. I realized, that whatever was happening, they could not protect me from it. They were yelling but not arguing, and that was scary also.

"They did not want to bring me with them, but they were more afraid to leave me alone, so Mother grabbed my hand, and we ran down the path, through the cold mist to the house of Wai Fan. The air felt different to me as we ran, not the way it usually did, and I could smell something strong that I did not like. We were running south, away from the open end of the valley, but it felt as though we were running north, and I knew that something had happened to my sense of direction.

"When we reached the house there was already a crowd, and Mother left me outside with Father and the other men and children, and went inside with the women. I was too afraid to talk or ask any questions—all of the children were—but I understood from what the fathers said and the few words I could hear from inside that all three sons of Wai Fan had been killed by the *cup hu girngsi*.

"We stood, waiting. The air became even colder, the bad smell stronger, and then we saw it, floating down the path in front of the house in the mist: the *cup hu girngsi*. Father whispered and said it was Chun Li Yeung, who had died the year before, and someone else whispered that it was Ling Chek Yee, but I saw something that no one else saw, and I did not say anything because the figure I saw floating through the mist was not the corpse of anyone we knew. It was not a corpse at all. It was not human. It had never been human. It was a different creature entirely, older than any human corpse could have been. A monster. It looked at me and saw me, and it knew that I saw it for what it was. And then it disappeared into the mist and was gone."

"What did it look like?" Sue asked.

"You do not want to know."

"Yes, I do."

"No, you do not." Her grandmother was silent for a moment, staring not into space but into time. Sue said nothing, waited for her grandmother to continue.

Finally the old woman did, and her voice was sadder, softer. "I knew after that that I was different from everyone else, that I had *Di Lo Ling Gum*. The knowledge comforted me, but it also frightened me. I talked about it to my father and mother, to the wise men of the village, hoping that someone could teach me, train me, tell me what to do, but there was no one in Cuangxun who understood.

"I had thought, I had hoped, that the *cup hu girngsi* would go away after that, after killing the sons of Wai Fan, but it did not. It remained in the hills, feeding off the *hong mau*, growing stronger. In the day, the men went looking for it, hunting it. In the night, we all stayed locked in our houses. A baby was taken from one of the young women in the village. One of the hunters did not return. The land itself began to die. The trees dried up, and the bamboo, and the rice in the fields. There were no more animals to be found. One old man, Tai Po, wanted to offer a sacrifice to the *cup hu girngsi*, believing that would appease it. He suggested that we offer a virgin to the monster, but I knew this would not work, and I said so, and because of my power they believed me.

"In the end, we decided to leave. Father thought that it would be better to begin a new life in Canton than remain in Cuangxun or anywhere in Hunan. Several families left at once, ours and six others. I do not know what happened to those who remained behind.

"We survived. In Canton, I found a teacher. I learned the ways of spirits and *tse mor.* I learned how to protect against the *cup hu girngsi*, but I never again saw one."

The wind outside had stopped, and the house seemed suddenly quiet, too quiet. "There are such monsters, Susan. There always have been. There always will be."

Sue shifted uncomfortably against the backboard. She did not know what to say. She did not exactly believe in vampires, but her grandmother's story had frightened her, and she could not say that she entirely disbelieved it.

Her grandmother patted her hand. "We will speak more of this later, when you are not so tired. We know what is out there, and it is our responsibility to make sure that it is stopped." She stood and moved away from the bed, walking into the darkness.

It is our responsibility to must make sure that it is stopped.
What did that mean? Sue wanted to ask, but her grandmother was already out of the room and closing the door,
and she knew that she would have to wait until morning
for an answer to that question.

She listened to her grandmother return to her own
bedroom. She remained sitting, no longer tired. She
heard her parents talking in their room down the hall,
their voices little more than low, muffled mumbles. Had
they been talking before? She'd thought they'd been
asleep. She held her breath, trying not to make any noise,
but though she strained to hear what they were discussing,
she could make out nothing.

She sat in the darkness, still clutching the edge of her
sheet, staring out toward the curtained window, feeling
cold. She was not sure whether or not she believed her
grandmother, but she had to admit that ever since she'd
gone to the school that night she'd felt something in the
air, an indefinable sense of wrongness, the impression that
everything was not as it should be.

Maybe her grandmother was right. Maybe she did have
a touch of *Di Lo Ling Gum.* She lay down again, her head
sinking into the fluffy pillow. She thought back, trying to
recall if she'd picked up on any supernatural vibes at any
time in her life, but could not.

She fell asleep soon after, and she dreamed of a rotted
corpse, blood dripping from its grinning lips, floating
through fog in a Chinese mountain village, searching for
her, calling her name.

The next day, at the restaurant, Sue tried to stay as far
away from her grandmother as possible, making an extra
effort not to be alone with the old woman. She felt bad
about it, ashamed, but in the clear light of day the talk
of *Di Lo Ling Gum* and the *cup hu girngsi* seemed down-

right silly. She felt embarrassed for her grandmother and found herself wondering, guiltily, if perhaps the old woman's mind was slipping.

By lunchtime, the kitchen was almost unbearably hot and humid. The ventilation system was on, but her father was cooking on four woks at once, as well as deep-frying two orders of shrimp, and the air, recycled or not, was sweltering.

Sue took the plastic bowl of chopped onions from the back counter and handed it to her father.

"More chicken," he said in English.

She hurried across the palleted floor and opened the oversize freezer, taking out the bag filled with sliced breasts that he had prepared that morning. She passed by John, who leaned against the counter and stared up at the TV. "Why don't you help out?" she asked.

He grinned at her, raised his eyebrows.

"Father!"

"John, help your sister!"

"Why do I always have to do all the work? It's not fair. She gets to spend all day at that dumb newspaper, and I have to stay here and do everything."

"You do nothing around here," Sue said. "I could have five other jobs and still help out more than you do."

"Stop arguing," their father said in Cantonese. "Susan, you help me. John, you help your mother out front."

"God!"

"John!"

"Have fun," Sue said in English.

"Susan!"

John stormed out of the kitchen, and Sue turned back toward her father. He was scowling at her, but she could tell from his eyes that it was an act, and as he flipped the shrimp onto two plates, he was smiling.

John returned a few moments later, polite, humbled,

and obsequious. He lightly tapped her shoulder. "Sue, greatest sister ever to walk the face of the earth—"

She smiled. "What do you want?"

"Trade with me. Let me work in the kitchen. There's a guy from my science class out front, and I don't want him to see me."

"Why?"

"Because."

"Because why?"

"Mother's trying to talk to his parents."

The past came rushing back in a wave of emotional recognition, and Sue nodded, understanding what her brother meant without him having to spell it out. She too had been embarrassed by her mother, by her father, by everything her parents did or said, a magnification of the mortification all teenagers felt in regard to their parents' behavior. She had spent most of her grammar school years trying to deny any association with her family.

She recalled even being embarrassed by their yard, wondering why her father had chosen to draw attention to himself by imposing his own artificial conception of nature on the desert instead of adapting to the local terrain like everyone else. All of the other houses on their street had had sand or gravel with rearrangements of existing vegetation: cactus, sagebrush, succulents. Her father had planted a yard—grass, flowers, and two ludicrous willow trees which flanked the sides of the driveway.

Even now, she still wasn't quite sure how she felt about her family. For years she had not wanted to be seen in public with her parents, avoiding shopping trips, dreading open houses and back-to-school nights. She'd seen the smirks on the faces of her classmates, heard the snickers, when her mother had come to pick her up from school and called out to her in Cantonese. For a whole year, third grade, the year that the schoolyard rhyme "Chinese . . . Japanese . . . Dirty knees . . . Look at these!" had made the rounds, and Cal Notting had teased her unmercifully by pulling taut the corners of his eyes and sticking out his front teeth in imitation of a stereotypical "Chinaman," she'd prayed each night before going to bed that her parents would wake up in the morning and speak perfect English. She had never been to church in her life and did not really understand the concept of God, but she'd heard enough about praying from her friends and from television to have gotten a general idea of what she was supposed to do. So she'd folded her hands, closed her eyes, started off with "Dear God," followed that with her wish list, and signed off with "Amen." It hadn't worked, though, and she'd given up the prayers when she'd graduated to fourth grade.

That embarrassment had ended somewhere along the line, but those years had taken their toll.

John was still stuck at that hypersensitive stage, and she was a little worried about him. By the time she was his age, she had already started growing out of it and coming to terms with her family and her background.

She wondered if that was something John would ever be able to reconcile within himself.

It was hell living in two cultures.

"Okay," she said. "I'll trade."

"If mother says anything, tell her it was your idea."

She was about to argue with him, then changed her mind. "All right," she agreed. She caught her father's eye, and he gave her an approving nod.

He understood.

Her mother wouldn't understand, and Sue was glad that she had not been in the kitchen with them. It would only have resulted in an argument.

Her parents were so dissimilar in so many ways that Sue often wondered whether their marriage had been arranged—although she'd never been brave enough to ask. She realized as she picked up a completed order from the low shelf next to her father that she did not really know how her parents met. All she knew was that they had been living in Hong Kong and had married there. That was it. Her friends all seemed to know the intimate details of their parents' courtships and were able to recite specifics the way they would the plot of a movie. She and John knew no such stories of their parents' past.

Her mother came in through the door to the dining room. "Hurry up, John. Customers are waiting."

"That's okay, John," Sue said. "I'll get it."

He looked at her gratefully as she handed her mother the plates and followed her out to the front.

"You owe me," Sue said over her shoulder as she walked into the dining room.

John nodded. "Deal."

Twenty-one

Corrie watched through the window as Pastor Wheeler got into his car, backed up, and pulled onto the street. She put down the pen she'd been writing with and flexed her fingers. Being a church secretary was different than she'd envisioned. She'd thought it would be a leisurely, slow-paced job: writing Thank-you notes to little old ladies, scheduling appointments with parishioners, calling people during the holidays and asking them to donate food for the poor. But she seemed to spend most of her time filling out permit applications, making out invoices, and filing requisition forms.

Not that she minded.

Just as the subdued pastel light of the church office in which she worked stood in sharp contrast to the harsh fluorescents of the paper office, the simple unstructured demands of her new position were a welcome change from the rigid deadlines of the *Gazette*. She might have a lot of work to do right now, but the labor was not mentally taxing, and she felt as though she finally had time to think, to sort things through in her mind.

She had also grown to like Pastor Wheeler, although she knew that the mere thought of that drove Rich crazy The pastor could be a little aloof, a little preoccupied, but he was a good man, with good ideas, and he really was dedicated to serving God.

I have seen Jesus Christ.

She pushed the thought from her mind and looked down at the paper on which she'd been writing. There was going to be a big church fund-raiser a few weeks from now, a picnic, and it was her responsibility to make sure that the event was publicized in the *Gazette*. Rich would cynically suggest that that was the reason she'd been hired, her close ties to the paper and the publicity which that relationship could provide. But he knew as well as she did that, in Rio Verde, anyone who wanted publicity got it. There simply wasn't enough real news to take up the slack.

At least not until recently.

She added a line to the description of the fund-raiser she'd been preparing, and glanced up at the clock on the bookshelf. Three-thirty. Out of the corner of her eye, she saw the darkened doorway that led down the hall to the chapel, and she quickly focused her attention back on her paper.

She didn't like being left alone in the church. It was a strange thing to admit, but it was true. She felt comfortable and at ease when the pastor was around, but as soon as he left, the whole tenor of the place seemed to change. Noises that had been unobtrusive became disconcertingly loud. The hallway and chapel seemed darker, the locked doors to the vestibule and storage room appeared to be hiding something. Her office remained unchanged, but the atmosphere in the rest of the church altered palpably, and the empty hulk of that new addition seemed downright threatening.

He has spoken to me.

Corrie reached over and turned on the desk radio, found the faint rhythmic static of a powerful Top Forty station out of Phoenix. She shifted her chair so that in her peripheral vision she saw the window facing the street rather than the doorway opening onto the hall.

She focused her attention once again on her work and began writing.

The spider was still there when she got home.

Corrie stared at the hairy black body in the upper right corner of the living room as she took off her shoes. She knew Rich had seen the spider that morning, and she'd watched him studiously avoid that entire section of the room as he prepared for work. She had purposely not touched the spider, had waited for him to take care of the creature, though she'd known that he wouldn't kill it. Sure enough, he'd left it there for her to deal with.

A grown man afraid of a bug.

She heard Rich talking to Anna in the kitchen, and she felt suddenly annoyed with him. Why did she always have to be the one to take responsibility in this relationship? Whether it was their finances, their domestic arrangements, or even a simple spider, she always had to make the decisions, she always had to take action. Anything outside of the precious newspaper automatically became her responsibility.

If he worked as hard on their marriage as he did on that damn paper, they might be able to have a fairly decent relationship.

She heard Anna laugh, heard Rich say something to her. His voice was light, happy, relaxed. As always, he was acting as though nothing was wrong. That annoyed her too. It was fine to behave that way around your daughter; children needed their parents to be strong. But it was quite another thing to put on that same happy face in front of your wife.

Part of her felt guilty for resenting his behavior. It wasn't up to her to tell him how to deal with his feelings, how to cope with his grief. But then again, maybe it was. She'd been sympathetic with him. She'd been there for him. She knew how he must feel having the graves of his parents desecrated—she knew how *she'd* feel if her parents died and their bodies were dug up—but he had not shared his feelings with her, had not opened up to her the way she'd expected.

The way he should have.

The way, at one time, he *would* have.

That angered her.

What made her even angrier was that she knew he wasn't even discussing it with Robert. She knew that the two of them, when together, would tiptoe around the subject, talk about it like reporter and cop, not talk about it like brothers, not talk about the way they felt inside.

What the hell was wrong with that family?

She picked up one of her shoes and, standing on her tiptoes, smacked it against the spider. The black body fell down onto the carpet, where she hit it again, pressing the heel down as hard as she could to make sure it was dead.

Anna heard the sound, came running out from the kitchen. "Mommy!"

Rich looked at her over their daughter's head. "What was that you just killed? A spider?"

Corrie picked up Anna, gave her a kiss on the forehead, then looked flatly at Rich. "Yes," she said. "It was."

At the church, the days passed quickly, much more quickly than they had at the paper. The work was by no means challenging, but she felt less stifled than she had working with Rich all day, and some of the edge seemed to wear off of her dissatisfaction. She still wanted to get out of this town and move back to civilization, to raise Anna in a more culturally enlightened environment, but some of the urgency had gone out of her need. She was more laid back now, more willing to take things easier, to wait a little.

Perhaps it was the influence of Jesus.

She preferred not to think about that, tried desperately hard to keep it at the back of her consciousness. If she allowed herself to even consider the idea that Jesus had returned to earth, had come here to Rio Verde, she would become so frightened that she would not be able to function. She knew that Anna was still worried, still scared— she'd had nightmares every night this week—and she wished she could do more to set her daughter's mind at rest. To set her own mind at rest as well. In truth, she was not sure what to think. She and Pastor Wheeler discussed only the practical matters of the parish, the day-to-day operation of the church. She knew from Wheeler's bearing and attitude, from the assumptions underlying his statements, that he truly believed he had seen Jesus Christ. But her own certainty had waned with the week, the almost palpable belief that had been imparted to her and the rest of the crowd by the pastor's sermon now seeming more and more like the by-product of a good speech.

But if she didn't believe, why was she dreading this Sunday's services?

Why couldn't she reassure Anna that there was nothing to be afraid of?

And why was she keeping it all from Rich?

She had the feeling that if she could just talk to Rich, if she could just tell him what was going on, if she could just share her confusion with him, everything would be okay. Wasn't that what marriage was about? Sharing and support?

She pushed such thoughts away. The bottom line was that, despite the fear, she enjoyed working here, and she felt better now than she had in a long time. The words that came immediately to mind were "tranquil" and "at peace."

Church words.

He is going to establish the kingdom of heaven on earth.

"Jesus loves you," the Pastor Mr. Wheeler said.

Corrie looked up. The pastor was smiling at her. There was something a little off about that smile, a hint of fanaticism in its too wide parameters, and it would have frightened her had he not spoken, had he not said those words, had he not addressed the doubts inside her head.

But he *had* spoken, he *had* said those words, *he had addressed her doubts*. And his voice was comforting, soothing, making her feel warm, wanted, and content.

The Pastor Dan Wheeler had truly been blessed by God.

Wheeler stood and walked out from behind his desk, holding in his hand the pristine white Bible from which he drew his sermon topics. "Glen Lyons did not show up last night," he said. "He was supposed to take over the night shift from Gary Watson and construct that installation in the walkway to the addition. I am very disappointed in Glen. Very disappointed. Would you call him and tell him that? Would you call him and tell him that the next time he volunteers his time and reneges on his promise, I will personally rip his balls out by the roots and feed them to Jesus?"

The pastor was still smiling. Somewhere in the back of her mind, a warning buzzer sounded, telling her that these words were not normal, not right. But her perceptions seemed to have been encased in Lucite, and that warning was just a dull hum somewhere far in the background.

Corrie nodded. "I'll tell him."

Behind the preacher, on the wall, she could see a calendar for the year. Small black X's filled the squares for the months of January through September. October 31, the date of the Second Coming, was circled in red.

The rest of the year had been whited out.

Corrie found Glen's number in the church directory, picked up her phone, and dialed while the pastor watched. She realized that there was less than a month left until the Second Coming.

That suddenly seemed very important to her.

Very important.

Glen, obviously hungover, answered the phone after six rings. She told him in a cold voice that the next time he volunteered his time and did not show, causing construction of the church to fall behind schedule, Pastor Wheeler would rip his balls out by the roots and feed them to Jesus.

She liked saying that word: "balls."

And she found that she liked hearing the terror in Glen's voice as he desperately and pathetically tried to apologize.

She hung up on him in the middle of his apology, and looked up at the pastor. He grinned at her. "Very good," he said. "Very good."

Her doubts seemed to have disappeared, and in their place she felt only a quietly unobtrusive bliss. She was smiling to herself as she returned her attention to the invoices on her desk.

Twenty-two

He saw it again. *The Face in the Sand.*

Cutler closed his eyes and gripped the sides of the sink for support. Outside the restroom of the Shell station he heard the blowing wind, a whooshing noise that would have sounded like water were it not for the tiny granules of sand that scraped against the metal door and the small dirty window above the wastebasket. From inside the gas station itself, muffled by the wall, he heard the dinging of the bell as a late-night customer ran over the cable and pulled up to the pumps.

Cutler opened his eyes, looked again at the mirror. Over his shoulder, he could still see the reflection of The Face, peering in at him through the window.

He looked down into the sink, concentrating on a rust stain connected to the drain directly below the faucet. *The Face in the Sand.* The malevolence of its gaze and the unnaturalness of its composition had been burned permanently into his brain, and after all these years had lost none of its terrifying power. Seeing it again, Cutler felt like a small frightened child, and he was dimly aware that he had wet his pants.

The whooshing sound seemed to grow louder.

It was The Face in the Sand that had kept him from setting out and searching for the Lost Dutchman when he was eighteen. Along with Hobie Beecham and Phil Emmons, he'd been planning to take a year off after high school and before college, to search for the fabled gold mine. Having grown up in east Mesa, practically under the shadow of the Superstition Mountains, the three of them had spent most of their grammar school years obsessed with the Lost Dutchman, dreaming of becoming rough, tough, rich, and famous prospectors. For six months in fifth grade, after they'd pooled their allowance money one week and purchased a weathered "Genuine Lost Dutchman Treasure Map" from the tourist trap on Main Street, they'd thought the mine was theirs. The obsession had cooled somewhat by high school, but they were still seriously planning to spend a year prospecting in the Superstitions beginning the summer after graduation. They didn't really expect to find the mine, but they *were* expecting to party, live off the land, and generally enjoy their last gasp of freedom before becoming responsible adults.

Then he'd seen The Face in the Sand.

Cutler had never told his two friends what he'd seen, knowing they would think him pussy—or worse. Instead, he'd given them a transparently false story about growing up and putting away childish things, a story neither of them bought. Both Hobie and Phil had tried desperately, together and separately, to change his mind, playing on his sympathy, on his memory, on his loyalty, but he'd refused to budge. They'd ended up fighting with him, then fighting with each other, and the whole idea had died an ignominious death. He hadn't seen either of them after that, was not even sure if they'd kept in touch with each other. At the end of the summer, carrying only the stuffed backpack that he'd planned to bring with him into the Superstitions, he'd hit the road to Denver, where there was supposed to be an airplane mechanic's school. He had some half-baked idea of becoming a jet mechanic, but he'd lasted there about nine months before moving on to Colorado Springs, where he lasted about nine

months before moving on to Albuquerque, where he
lasted about nine months before moving on . . .

And always The Face had haunted him.

He'd seen The Face in the flat desert outside Apache
Junction. It had been a hot Saturday afternoon, and he'd
been walking alone, down one of the old Indian trails that
wound through private property and reservation land to
the base of the Superstitions. The sky had been spectacu-
larly, unnaturally blue, so blue that he had specifically noticed it, though that was not something that often
captured his attention. He'd felt slightly dizzy, and he'd
stopped to rest on a low mound of sand, taking off his
T-shirt and using it to wipe the sweat from his face, knowing from touch that his nose and forehead were already
burned. He'd glanced down at his feet.

And he'd seen The Face.

Twice the size of a normal human face, it had looked
like a sculpture protruding from the ground. The chin
and cheeks, eyes and mouth, nose and forehead had all
been formed from sand and had a strange, grainily
smooth texture. For a brief second he'd wondered why
he hadn't seen it before and what its creators had used
to hold the sand together. Then he'd seen that the face
was moving, muscles outlined in ridges beneath the
cheeks stretching taut, lips spreading out into a silent
scream, eyes rolling wildly.

He'd jumped up, nearly tripping over his feet in his attempt to scramble away from the mound. Even as he moved
frantically back, he kept his gaze on the face in the sand.
Or The Face in the Sand, as it had immediately become.
He would have screamed, wanted to scream, but was afraid
of what The Face would do in reaction. The sweat pouring
down his face was cold, and his heart was pumping crazily.
It was not merely the fact that sand was sentient that scared
him so; it was the structure of The Face itself, the contours
of its form. There was something about the cruel shape of

the mouth, the way the eyes were positioned above the nose that seemed wrong, unnatural. *Evil.* The effect was all the more terrifying because of the monochromatic nature of the sand. The eyes that were glaring at him, the mouth that was grimacing at him, everything was the same light tan-white color, and the imposition of a three-dimensional form on a two-dimensional substance was monstrous.

Above the beating of his heart and the pounding of blood in his temples, he'd thought he heard a noise, a hiss issuing from those shifting sand lips. He held his breath, tried to hear the sound above the panicked rasp of his own breathing.

The words were faint, but audible: "I will find you."

The eyes had met his, locked, and though he'd tried to look away, he couldn't. The Face had strained, grown, pushed outward, as though trying to break free of the confines of the earth, then had sunk back into ordinary sand. There'd been a brief moment of respite, a few confusing seconds in which he'd put it all down to heat prostration and an overactive imagination. Then The Face had reformed in the sand at his feet, thrusting upward from the ground. A small cactus was sucked into the opening mouth. The horrible eyes had glared at him, then the mouth had grinned and whispered his name.

"Cutler."

Again: "Cutler."

And: "I will find you."

He'd run then, back down the trail on which he'd come, knowing that at any moment The Face in the Sand might reappear, might pop up before him, might whisper his name.

Might do something worse.

He had not known why The Face had promised to follow him, but it was instantly clear that he had to get away from the desert, away from Arizona, away from the sand. Whatever it was, whatever its purpose or motives, it would not be able to find him if he stayed in forests or cities, if he got away from the stuff of its substance.

He'd done a good job of keeping away from the desert before coming to Rio Verde to work at the Rocking D. But somehow, he had never traveled far. He had never gone to the East Coast or the South or the Pacific Northwest or another country. He'd always stayed in the Southwest, near Arizona.

And now he'd returned.

Why hadn't he stayed away forever?

Again he closed his eyes, willing The Face to go away, praying to God, promising He or She or It that he would be good, that he would never so much as swear if he could just get out of this restroom with his sanity and his life.

It was late and the gas station would be closing soon. Surely the attendant would come back here to see what had happened to him, to inform him that they were getting ready to close.

But the Face in the Sand might get the attendant.

But then the police would come.

But what if the police couldn't stop The Face? What if nothing could stop it? What if it would not give up until it had him, no matter how many others it had to kill first?

"Cutler."

The voice was rough and whispered, barely audible above the grainy liquid sound of the wind.

He wanted to scream but could not. He opened his eyes, and in the mirror his mouth was open, although no sound was coming out. Over his shoulder, outside the small window, was The Face. The features changed, the wall of sand on the other side of the dirty glass shifting, rippling, now grimacing, now smiling, now screaming, the movement not smooth and fluid but still and jerky.

Hadn't it been more fluid before?

"I found you."

He plugged his ears, trying to keep out the voice, trying

not to hear it, but though the sound of the wind was shut out, the voice echoed in his head. There were only the two phrases, repeated—"Cutler" and "I found you"—but for some reason that frightened him more than if a coherent series of threats had been leveled at him.

The glass in the window shattered, flying inward, and, reacting instinctively, Cutler hit the floor, curling instantly into a position under the sink that was half fetal, half duck-and-cover. Now he was screaming: short, high, feminine bursts.

He stopped screaming when the first grains of sand tickled the back of his neck.

There hadn't been a single car on the highway for the past fifteen minutes, and Buford wanted to close up early. He had never closed the stand before ten o'clock in the nine years it had been operating, and he didn't want to start now, but something was wrong here. He could feel it; he could sense it. He glanced over at the clock, but he could see the order window in his peripheral vision, and he looked immediately away. Licking his lips, he started singing. Military songs. *"I'll pick the lock with my enormous cock, said Barnacle Bill the Sailor."* His voice sounded strange in the silence, and he stopped almost immediately. He reached over, flipped on the radio, turned the knob, but there was only static.

Something was definitely wrong. He didn't like the color of the sky or the sound of the breeze or the fact that his was the only business open this late in this part of town.

He scraped the grill with his spatula, concentrating all of his attention on the square of dark metal and the brown hardened grease, trying not to think of that blackness beyond the order window. There were goose bumps on his arms, and he had to admit that he was spooked. Hell, a few moments ago, he'd nearly jumped out of his shoes when the phone rang. It had only been Jacy, and for the few moments they talked he'd felt fine, but the second he hung up the receiver the chill had returned.

He'd thought he'd seen movement outside the window, but when he'd looked more closely there'd been nothing there.

He'd avoided looking out the window since then.

He'd pretended to himself that he hadn't heard the noises.

He finished scraping the grill and used the spatula to pick up the congealed grease and drop it in the empty coffee can on the floor. He had never before been this scared. Not in 'Nam, not nowhere.

But there was nothing to be frightened of, nothing out there.

Buford reached for his cup on the edge of the grill, picked it up and drank the dregs. He should close up, let Taco Bell or Dairy Queen get the extra business. How much could he make between now and ten anyway? If he was lucky, a couple of kids would stop by for Cokes and fries after the movie got out, but that was the most he could hope for. And considering the fact that the theater was showing a "serious" film this week, not an action flick or a comedy, and that this was a weeknight, not a weekend, the chance that any kids would come by at all was damn near zip. He could close up now and not notice the difference.

But he didn't want to close up, and he was forced to admit to himself that he was afraid to leave. His truck was parked in the rear, facing the desert, and the outside bulb in the back had burnt out some time ago.

The stand was surrounded by darkness.

He could call Jacy, invent some excuse, tell her to come over and meet him here. But she'd probably taken her bath and was in bed already. Besides, he wasn't such a pussy that he had to have his wife save him from the boo-geyman, was he?

Was he?

He found himself thinking of Manuel Torres and all those animals lying in the arroyo with the blood sucked out of them. The arroyo stretched only a few dozen yards behind the stand. He knew that a posse had searched the area thoroughly, but he also knew that nothing had been found. He imagined the arroyo at night, a huge black gash across the desert, its floor invisible in the gloom. In his mind, he saw the top of the arroyo, saw white fingers reaching upward from the blackness, grabbing the dirt edge of the cliff, saw the vampire pulling itself upward.

Vampire. Jesus Christ, he was turning into a little old lady. What the hell was wrong with him? He should just knock this shit off, close up, and get his ass home to bed.

But as he stood next to the grill, he heard rustling in the sagebrush outside, the light whisk sound of moving gravel, and he concentrated once again on the square of the grill, afraid to look up, not knowing when he would build up enough courage to leave the stand and go home.

Twenty-three

After dinner, Rich helped Anna with her spelling flash cards. Her class was studying "at" words this week—cat, hat, fat, and bat—and she could recognize them all except "bat," which for some reason she missed each and every time. She kept confusing it with "fat." He tried to explain the difference between the two, and she could get it correct if he repeated the flash cards in identical order, but the minute he shuffled the cards, she would miss it again.

They quit studying after fifteen minutes, when he sensed that Anna was getting restless, her attention starting to wander, and he told her she could watch TV until bedtime. The two of them sat next to each other on the couch. A few moments later, Corrie came into the room. Rich had thought she was in the kitchen doing something, but she came in from the hallway.

She walked in front of the television. "Here," she said. "I want this in the paper." She tossed two paper clipped pages on the coffee table.

He picked up the pages, glanced at the top one, shook his head. "Can't do it."

"What?"

"Joking," he said, raising his hands in apologetic self-defense. "I'm just joking." He read through the copy. "A fund-raising picnic for Wheeler's church? We don't have to go to this, do we?"

"I'm going. Anna's going." She looked at him coolly. "I would appreciate it if you would accompany us."

He dropped the papers on the table. "I suppose."

"It's for a good cause."

"Yeah," he said. "Right. Could you move over a little? You're blocking the screen."

Corrie's mouth hardened into a straight line. "Anna," she said, "I think it's time for you to go to bed."

"But the show's not over yet!"

"Anna . . ."

Rich patted her leg. "Listen to your mother," he said. She hesitated.

"Anna . . . ," Corrie repeated.

"I want a story."

"A story? I thought you said you were too old for me to read you stories."

"I'm not too old anymore."

Rich looked at Anna, but she wouldn't meet his eyes. He glanced over at Corrie, who was frowning. "Are you afraid to go to sleep by yourself? Is that it? Have you been having bad dreams? We could leave your light on for you."

She shook her head emphatically. Too emphatically. "I'm not 'fraid."

"It's all right, honey," Corrie said softly. "We're here to protect you."

"I'm not 'fraid!" Anna pulled away from her father, jumped off the couch, and stalked out of the room.

Rich and Corrie looked at each other. The anger, the unborn argument that had been building between them had dissipated, and all they saw in each other's faces was concern for their daughter.

He stood. "I'll find out what it is."

"No, I will," Corrie said.

He followed her down the hall. "We both will."

Twenty-four

Arn Hewett stared into the muzzle of the cocked pistol for what seemed like hours before finally turning it away from his face. He slowly uncocked the gun and placed it on the table in front of him. His hands were wet with sweat, and perspiration streamed down his forehead, stinging his eyes, dripping onto his nose.

He really *had* been planning to kill himself, to blow his brains out, but at the last minute something had held him back; the feeling—no, the *knowledge*—that his life would be better sacrificed some other way.

Donna was going to the police. He had no doubt about that. She'd packed all of her clothes and personal belongings and had taken Dawn with her, and the two of them were probably in the police station right now, spilling their guts, trying to make him look like some sort of sick pervert.

Or were they?

If Donna had planned to press charges, the cops would have come to him by now, would have shown up at the store or, at the very least, would have been waiting for him when he arrived home. Besides, why would Donna pack all of her clothes if she was just going to turn him in? There would be no reason for her and Dawn to move out or find someplace else to stay if he were in jail.

Maybe they weren't going to the police. Maybe they were just running away.

Head pounding, he stood up and walked from the kitchen, through the living room, to Dawn's bedroom. Leaning against the door frame, unwilling to disturb the sanctity of her sanctuary even though she was gone, he took visual inventory of her room. She'd taken her clothes and her books. She'd taken her stuffed Winnie-the-Pooh. She'd taken her high school photos, the ones she'd taped to the edges of her dresser mirror, as well as her old transistor radio. She'd left her Walkman. And her unicorn picture. And her camera.

Everything he'd bought her.

He felt a twinge of unreasonable hurt, a flash of pain in a vacuum of emptiness, but he was glad of the hurt. It meant that he still loved her.

He stared at the reflection of himself in the newly revealed mirror. He blamed Donna. He would bet a dollar to a donut that it was Donna who'd made her leave all those things behind. The bitch was jealous; that's all it was. She wasn't concerned about her daughter. She didn't give a rat's ass in hell about Dawn's welfare or happiness. She just wanted to get back at him. She was hurt and she wanted to hurt back.

It was her own fault. She should've known what to expect. She should've seen it coming. He liked them young. Always had. She knew that. She'd been sixteen when he'd married her; he'd been twenty-six. She'd known that it was her youth that had been one of the chief attractions for him, and she should have known that when she crossed that line into middle age, he would be forced to look elsewhere for his pleasure.

Only he hadn't meant for it to be their daughter.

He stared at Dawn's bed, remembered all of the good times they'd had there.

It had started innocently enough: he'd seen Dawn masturbating.

It had been a Friday night. He'd gotten out of bed after

the ten o'clock news to go to the bathroom, and as he walked by his daughter's room, he saw movement through the crack of the open door. He had not looked closely, but that one quick glimpse had been enough. He'd seen Dawn's hand, massaging between her legs, backlit by the small wall night light.

He had not been able to get that image out of his mind—his daughter rubbing herself—and he began to notice, at breakfast and at dinner, that she was growing up, starting to fill out. That she was becoming a very attractive young woman. He began thinking about her when he was taking off his clothes, when he was taking a shower, when he was with Donna.

One day he came home from work at lunch to find a note from Donna waiting for him, explaining that she'd gone to the store with a friend. He'd started to make himself a peanut butter and jelly sandwich when he noticed a rolled up pair of Dawn's white cotton panties on the tile floor next to the washing machine. Putting down the butter knife, he'd walked over to the washing machine and bent to pick up the panties. He stood slowly. They were small, delicate, and they felt soft and sensuous to his touch. He unrolled them, and pressed the thin material to his lips before guiltily dropping them into the washer.

He began coming home at lunch more often after that, secretly hoping that lightning would strike twice, but not daring to admit such a desire even to himself. He ate his lunches at the counter, staring toward the washing machine. His hope soon graduated into an obsession, and after two weeks he gave up all pretext of innocence, contriving as often as he could to get Donna out of the house before quickly sifting through the hamper for Dawn's panties. They hadn't had much of a smell at first, only cloth, but he'd soon begun to discern through the material the faint fishy scent of female arousal.

He hadn't intended to have sex with her, and probably

would not have done so had she not caught him. He probably would have continued playing with her panties, fantasizing about her when he was with Donna, masturbating. Perhaps he would have eventually found a girl who looked like her.

But she'd come home one day at lunch, and he'd been sniffing the crotch of her underwear, inhaling the delicious perfume of her panties as she'd walked through the door into his bedroom. Dawn hadn't said anything, hadn't done anything, had simply stood there, staring. He'd slowly lowered his hands, feeling the guilty red heat of embarrassment flush across his face. He'd wanted to say something, wanted to apologize, but he hadn't been able to speak.

She'd backed up, started to move away, but he found his voice and said in his stern Father tone, "Dawn! Stop right there!" She'd stopped, turned ashamedly around to face him, and then he had rushed forward, taken her in his arms and held her, hugged her, pressed against her, kissing her full warm lips. He knew that she could feel his hardness against her and that made him even harder. He slid his hand under her shirt, feeling the tiny nipples of her firm young breasts. She was whimpering, crying, her eyes closed, but she was not fighting back, and he knew that she wanted it, and he pushed her to the floor, slid her shorts down and felt the rough hair of her vagina beneath his fingers.

He'd taken her there, on the carpet next to the bed.

She'd stiffened at one point, and he knew that she'd come.

He'd wanted to roar in triumph; he'd wanted to cry in shame. He'd wanted to hug her with gratitude; he'd wanted to beat her in disgust.

They'd done it regularly after that, at least twice a week for the past year. He had not told Donna; of course, but he had not forbid Dawn to tell her mother, and he'd assumed that she'd known.

More than once, he'd even considered a threesome.

But Donna had *not* known, until yesterday. Despite the extra attention he'd shown Dawn, the extra things he'd bought her, the obviously unpaternal kisses he'd bested upon her, the stupid bitch still hadn't figured it out. If she hadn't been snooping where she wasn't supposed to, sneaking through Dawn's diary, she probably never would have found out.

But that was all water under the bridge now, and after reading Donna's letter, he'd known that his time was up.

That's when he'd taken out his gun. There was no way in hell that he was going to go to prison. Especially not as a short eyes.

He'd rather just end it before it got that far.

But a bullet in the brain was not for him. He walked back into the kitchen, looked down at the gun lying seductively on top of the table. No, he was not to die this way. He was supposed to die, his time had truly come, but the manner and method of his death was not to be so meaningless, so trivial. He knew that. He knew it not as a conscious thought but instinctively, deep inside, the way he knew that tonight the sun would set and tomorrow it would rise. He closed his eyes, feeling a sudden pressure on his brain, fearing a headache. But no headache came. Instead, he had the impulse to go outside and walk into the desert in back of the house.

He frowned, wondering if his mind was going. His eyes focused again on the gun, and he found himself thinking that there was no reason to kill himself at all. He was safe; Donna had obviously not gone to the police—

The pressure kicked in again. He shut his eyes so tightly that tears came, and in a clear instant he understood that it was his time to die.

He walked out of the kitchen, through the back door,

through the yard, past the rusted barbecue, and crawled through the hole in the chain-link fence. He stood up on the other side of the barrier, not bothering to dust the sand and burrs from his clothes, and began walking across the open desert, heading in the general direction of Apache Peak. Behind him, the sun was setting, and the ground was bathed in an orangish red glow, the saguaros and ocotillos black shapes against the color.

Death.

He stopped walking. The pressure in his mind strengthened, but he pushed back against it. He knew he should continue moving forward, keep walking, but he sensed that Death was near, and he was now scared. Death, he suddenly realized, was not merely the absence of life but the presence of . . . something else. It was not a natural cessation of mind and body functions but an actual, physical entity. He turned his head, looking toward the darkened north, his terror growing. It was coming, moving across the desert toward him. He couldn't see it, but he could feel it, a blackness on the horizon, and as it drew closer he knew that it was very big. And unbelievably ancient.

The pressure in his mind no longer seemed to have any hold over him, and he suddenly gathered his wits, turned, and ran. He ran not toward home, not toward shelter, but away from the onrushing . . . thing, away from Death, scrambling madly through the sand in an effort to escape its coming. What the hell had possessed him to come out here in the first place? Temporary insanity? What had compelled him to—

He slid, fell, tumbling arms over head over legs down the soft sand to the bottom of the arroyo, still looking behind him. His shin hit a rock, the side of his face a bush, and he landed hard on the arroyo floor, hearing and feeling the bones in his right arm crack beneath him. He was stunned for a moment, but then he remembered what was after him, and he stumbled to his feet. He looked upward, wondering if he should chance a climb up the cliff or run through the gulch.

There was a noise from around the curve behind him. A whooshing hiss. It was a sound not unlike water, and for a brief second he thought a flash flood was sweeping through the arroyo, though there'd been no rain. He started to stagger away from the sound, then a blanket of peace settled over his mind, and he felt no worry. He stopped, turned around, and began walking toward the noise, growing more docile, more tranquil with each step he took.

He did not even cry out as he rounded the curve and saw the face of Death.

Twenty-five

Sue awoke feeling tired, her mind a conflicting jumble of images from several disparate dreams. There was something about a hole in the earthen floor of a building, a hole that led into a tunnel. There was a man nailed to a willow tree, screaming. There was a river of blood that ran uphill.

She sat up in bed, fluffing the pillow behind her and using it to brace her back against the headboard. She'd gotten to sleep late last night. Janine had come over after work to talk and had stayed until nearly midnight, ignoring the not-so-subtle hints of Sue's parents, who tried to kick her out at eight, nine, and ten before finally giving up and going to bed.

John had already gone to school by the time Sue walked out into the living room, but her grandmother was still in bed. She found herself wondering, not for the first time, if maybe her grandmother was ill, if she was dying.

She forced herself to think of something else.

After breakfast, she accompanied her parents to the market.

There was only one other car in the parking lot this morning, an old green Torino, and her father pulled next to it, parking so close that she and her mother could not open their doors all the way and had a difficult time getting out of the car. She maneuvered her way between the two vehicles and walked up the curb to the store sidewalk.

Her father grabbed a shopping cart, and she held open the door to the market as her parents went inside.

She noticed the difference immediately.

The market had changed.

She had always enjoyed coming here; had always found the atmosphere to be pleasant and friendly; had always liked Mr. and Mrs. Grimes, the owners of the store. But today something was wrong. The atmosphere was different, the air filled with an unfocused hostility that she sensed the second she walked through the door. She felt unpleasantly uncomfortable, and she desperately wanted to walk back outside into the cool fresh air.

She watched her parents walk down the first aisle toward the produce section at the far end. They obviously felt nothing out of the ordinary, sensed nothing wrong, but her muscles grew tense as she watched them, her uneasiness and anxiety increasing. She noticed for the first time that Mr. and Mrs. Grimes were nowhere in sight. Ordinarily, the checkout stand was never left unattended.

There were a series of burnt-out lights above the meat counter that cast an entire section of the market into semidarkness. Her parents walked into the shadow.

"Hey there!"

She jumped at the sound of Mr. Grimes's voice and turned quickly around to see him standing directly behind her, smiling. There was nothing false about his smile, nothing sinister, but the fact that he had been able to sneak up on her like that, without her being able to hear him, scared her.

"How are you and your folks today?"

"Fine," Sue said, forcing herself to smile at him.

The negativity in the air had not diminished, the atmosphere within the market remained unchanged, but she *knew* that the impressions she was receiving had nothing to do with a *cup hu girngsi* or *tse mor*, were entirely unrelated to the supernatural.

Di Lo Ling Gum?

She suddenly wished her grandmother were here.

Her parents had turned the corner, and Sue moved across the front of the store to the next aisle, looking toward the far end. They were not there, and she continued on to the next row.

Mrs. Grimes rushed toward her from between the stacks of canned foods.

Sue stepped back, feeling as though she'd been physically pushed. This was where the hostility was coming from, the source of the negativity within the market. She could feel it rolling off the woman in nearly palpable waves.

Mrs. Grimes moved past her, frowning, saying nothing.

Sue walked quickly down the vacated aisle and found her parents in the produce section, stocking up on cabbage for the restaurant. Her mother looked up at her, annoyed. "Why are you just standing around? Help us. Get a gallon of milk."

Her mother had a list for the house, her father for the restaurant, and they walked through the market, picking up everything they needed for both before heading back to the checkout stand. Again, the register was unattended, Mr. and Mrs. Grimes nowhere to be seen.

Her father began taking items from the cart and placing them on the unmoving black rubber conveyor belt. "Wait," her mother said. "We forgot to get cereal for John."

"Cereal?" her father said.

"He doesn't want rice every day."

"You're going to spoil that boy," he said, but he followed her back down the first aisle to the breakfast foods.

Mr. and Mrs. Grimes emerged from the shadowed meat department, both of them moving behind the register. "All ready to go?" Mr. Grimes asked.

"Almost," Sue said. "My parents are just getting some cereal."

Mrs. Grimes cleared her throat loudly, melodramatically, and nudged her husband. Mr. Grimes looked embarrassed and pushed her arm down, but he faced Sue. He smiled, tried to make his voice casual. "How come your mom and dad're always talkin' Chinese?" he asked.

She blinked. "Because they're Chinese."

"But they're in America now."

Her cheeks were hot, and she could feel herself becoming defensive. "What does that mean? They're in America so they should be speaking American? What is American? What language is native to this country? Navajo? Hopi?"

He laughed. "You got me there." He looked at his wife and rubbed his chin. She could hear the rough skin of his fingers scraping against the stubble. "No, I just mean that, well, since they're in an English-speaking country they probably oughta be speaking English."

"They do," Sue said, her face growing warmer. "When they need to. But Cantonese is their native language, and when they have personal conversations it's easier for them to speak Cantonese." She shifted her weight uncomfortably. "It's like if you and your wife moved to China. You'd speak Chinese when you had to, to get along in society, but when you were home alone you'd speak English. It's your native language, it's easier for you. There'd be no reason for you to speak Chinese in private, would there?" She motioned toward her parents. "Same thing."

He nodded thoughtfully, still rubbing his chin. "I see your point."

Next to him, his wife leaned forward, thin lips pursed. "Well, I'll be honest with you. I don't like it. I mean, your parents are good folks and all, don't get me wrong. But sometimes . . . well, sometimes I can't tell what they're talking about when they talk like that. I can't help thinking that they're talking about me."

"Right now," Sue said drily, "they're talking about corn flakes."

Mrs. Grimes frowned. "You know what I mean. I have nothing against your parents, but what if there were some of them who weren't so nice, who weren't such good people?"

"Some of who?"

She colored. "You know, foreign . . . people from other countries. I mean, how would we know what they were talking about?"

Mr. Grimes turned toward his wife. "I think her point, Edna, is that some conversations are private. Some things you don't need to know about."

Her parents returned with a box of Rice Krispies, and both Mr. and Mrs. Grimes smiled pleasantly at them, she totaling the purchases on the register, he bagging the groceries. "Come again," Mrs. Grimes said as they left.

Sue had often wondered what it was that had prompted her parents to settle in Rio Verde. After moving to the United States from Hong Kong, they had lived for a few years in Chinatown in New York—where she was born—before heading west when she was two. But what had made them decide on Arizona? And why had they decided to live in this town instead of Phoenix or Tucson or Flagstaff or Prescott?

She had never come out and asked her parents why they were here. Partly because she did not want to admit to them that she was not completely happy here, and partly because she suspected that her father had been suckered into buying land in Rio Verde.

But as they walked out to the car, as the oppressiveness that had hung over her since she'd stepped into the market lifted, she found herself wondering if there were other reasons they had come here. Had it been *laht sic*, fate? Or had her grandmother's *Di Lo Ling Gum* steered them here?

She pushed these ideas out of her mind.

Her father unlocked her mother's door, then popped open the back of the station wagon, and he and Sue loaded the groceries. Her father closed the hatch, then went around to the driver's door. "We'll stop by the restaurant first," he said.

"I need to go to the newspaper office," Sue told him.

"All right."

"Actually, I think I'd rather walk. I can use the exercise. And you won't have to go out of your way."

"Are you ashamed of us?" her mother said from inside the car.

"No."

"Then why won't you come with us?"

Sue sighed. "Fine." She opened the back door of the station wagon.

"If you want to walk, walk," her father said. "It is not a problem."

"I don't want to cause an argument."

"Go," he told her.

She smiled at him. "Thank you."

Sue moved out of the way, and as the station wagon backed up, she expected to hear the sound of her parents arguing, but even her mother must not have considered this a big deal since both parents waved and smiled through the windows as the car pulled out of the parking lot.

Sue looked around. She was standing alone now by the green Torino, facing the smoked glass of the market door, and she turned away and hurried across the cracked and broken asphalt of the parking lot, wanting to get as far away from there as possible.

She began walking toward the newspaper office, but instead of heading down the highway, she found herself turning onto Jefferson, then onto Copperhead. She did not know why she was going this way—it was longer and slower and led through the crummier part of town—but her feet were leading and her head was following, her directions running on instinct.

She turned left onto Arrow.

And there was the black church.

She stopped. There was something about the way the buildings fit together that she didn't like, that set her on edge. It was nothing specific, nothing she could put a finger on, more of a general feeling—a sense that the architectural aesthetics of the union were wrong.

Although it was daytime, the street was deserted. A scrap of paper blew across the asphalt, drifting from the construction site to the empty feed and grain store, making everything seem like part of a ghost town.

Ghost.

That was it exactly. There was an air of unreality about this street, the sense here of something supernatural.

She wanted to go back the way she had come, but a fog seemed to have settled over her brain, and her feet took her forward instead, toward the church. There was the sound of pounding, hammering, sawing, the noises of construction unnaturally loud on the otherwise silent street. Sue looked up, saw men at the top of the church roof, on a makeshift scaffold at its side. The men looked gaunt and haggard and far too white for laborers used to toiling in the sun. Two of them had taken off their shirts, despite the cold, and across the broad back of one she could see red welts that looked as though they were made by lashes from a whip.

She forced herself to walk faster.

On the steps of the church she saw Pastor Wheeler. He stared at her as she hurried by, and she shivered, chilled. There was something predatory in the pastor's gaze, something that didn't sit well with her, and she quickened her pace. Although she did not really know Wheeler, she knew she didn't like him. The few times she'd met him, he'd seemed sneaky and somehow sleazy, like a car salesman or a child molester, and that impression only intensified now.

"Miss?" the pastor said.

Sue didn't want to stop, wanted to run, wanted to pretend as though she hadn't heard the call, but she turned. "Yes?"

A slow grin spread over the pastor's face. "Chink," he said softly. "Fucking chink."

She backed up a step, swallowing.

Wheeler's grin grew wider. "Fucking slant-eyed heathen slut. Why are you walking by my church?"

She shook her head. "I—"

He walked down the steps toward her. "I'll teach you a lesson, you cock-teasing bitch."

She ran. The slight numbness that had seemed to come over her when she'd stepped onto the street lifted, and she was free to act, free to move. She ran like hell.

She heard the pastor behind her. She did not know if he was following, but he was definitely shouting at her, though the sound of her breathing mercifully muffled his cries into an indistinguishable drone.

She turned left at the corner, and though her legs and lungs were hurting and it was getting hard to breathe, she did not stop or slow down, and she continued running until she reached the highway.

Twenty-six

Rich didn't want to go to the picnic, but Corrie had to attend, and he and Anna had been formally invited. It *was* a legitimate news event, he reasoned, and he would have been obligated to go and take a few photos for the paper anyway. Rather than argue with Corrie, he agreed to make it a family outing.

They argued anyway, on the way over. They were driving toward the park, he and Corrie traveling in silence, Anna in the backseat singing to herself, when Corrie said, out of the blue, "People here say 'man-aise.'"

He glanced at her, puzzled. "What?"

"They say 'man-aise.' Either they have reading problems or speech problems. It's 'may-o-naise,' not 'man-aise.' How do you get 'man' out of 'mayo'? Tell me that. Is this the kind of thing that you want your daughter to grow up emulating?"

"What are you talking about?"

"I'm talking about our daughter's future."

"What does colloquial speech have to do with Anna?"

"Everything. Children are products not just of genetics but of their environment. I think she's growing up in the wrong environment."

"I bet Pastor Wheeler says 'man-aise' too."

She stared at him, face muscles tightening. "What's that supposed to mean?"

He shook his head. "Nothing."

"No one's forcing you to go to this picnic, you know. If you don't want to spend time with your wife and daughter . . ."

"Jesus. Just shut up for a while."

Corrie did not respond. Anna's singing had stopped, and the silence in the car seemed unbearable. Rich reached over and pushed a cassette into the tape player. Allman Brothers. Corrie hated the Allman Brothers, but she didn't say anything, simply sat staring straight out the windshield, arms folded over her breasts.

They drove to the picnic without speaking.

The park was crowded, much more crowded than he would have expected, and he had a difficult time finding a parking place. He finally found a spot a block away on the opposite side of the street, and they walked back. Lines had already formed in front of the barbecue grills, and there were people everywhere. Wheeler's church was not one of the major denominations and Rich would not have expected this many people to show up for a fundraiser, but then again not everyone here was from Wheeler's congregation. Most of them were probably people who had read about the picnic in the paper and had come out of curiosity, or because nothing else was happening in town this weekend.

Still, the turnout was impressive.

The picnic did seem to be well planned and put together, he had to admit that. A large banner proclaiming this the "First Annual Rio Verde Picnic and Church Social" was strung between the park's two dusty oaks, and all of the benches and picnic tables were festooned with yellow crepe paper. There were booths and cordoned-off areas for organized games, and plenty of name-tagged church members were on hand to direct newcomers to the appropriate section of the park. The air smelled of burning charcoal, beer, relish, insect repellent, and suntan lotion. Rich glanced up again at the banner. He was a little leery of the fact that this was being called *Rio Verde's* church social rather than the Church of the Holy Trinity social, but the banner's grammatical error and its implications didn't seem to be troubling anyone else, so he let it ride.

Taking Anna's hand, Corrie started off across the dried grass toward the barbecues, without giving him so much as a backward glance. He considered remaining where he was, or even going back to the car—just to give Corrie a little scare—but he didn't want to drag Anna into this, so he followed his wife and daughter through the crowd.

The day was hot. There was very little shade in the park, and what shade there was had been usurped by church families who'd staked out the benches underneath the occasional trees. He glanced around as the three of them headed toward the food, smiling, nodding, waving, saying a few quick "hi"s, but though he saw several acquaintances, he saw no friends. Most of the people here were strangers to him.

Ahead, behind the middle barbecue, in a white apron and comical chef's hat, spatula in hand, stood Pastor Wheeler. The preacher was grinning hugely, joking with the men and women who waited in line, paper plates in hand, but there was something about his manner, about the way he talked to the people in front of the barbecue that seemed forced, false, and slightly patronizing. It was unnerving to see such unapologetic glad-handing, and Rich felt even more ill at ease when Wheeler noticed Corrie and turned some of that guile on her.

He did not follow Corrie and Anna around the barbecue but remained where he was. Anna, he noticed, seemed wary of the pastor. She didn't blanch or pull back when he smiled and patted her head, but she wasn't as friendly or forthcoming as she usually was, and he could tell from her posture that she was afraid of the man.

Apparently, she had inherited his own good sense and instinctive ability to judge character.

The strange thing was that Corrie, too, seemed somewhat frightened. Her beaming smile and friendly tone of voice betrayed no such reservations, but her body language told another story. She stood stiffly, awkwardly; even her usually expansive hand gestures appeared reserved.

Rich watched Wheeler for a few moments, making no effort to move any closer. The pastor was of medium height and medium build, but carried himself as though he were something more, something special. There was about him an indefinable air of sleaziness and opportunism common to all salesmen. Rich watched him clap hands on backs, overreact to jokes. Try as he might, Rich failed to understand how people could find such a man charismatic.

And how people could believe that such a man knew The Truth was totally beyond his comprehension.

Rich caught Corrie's eye, motioned to her that he was going to look around, but she simply looked away. She'd seen him, he knew, though she wouldn't acknowledge it. He started off through the crowd toward the booths at the edge of the playground. He wondered if he should have brought his notebook, but then decided that any factual material about the picnic he might need he could get from Corrie. He'd go back to the car a little later, get out his camera, and take a few crowd shots. Maybe a small kid eating a big slice of watermelon. Or a dog playing Frisbee. Something cute and heartwarming.

To the side of the first booth—a ringtoss game—was a table covered with red crepe paper. From the front edge of the table hung a sign on which was printed a single word, "Raffle," and a price, "$5." He walked around the line of people in front of the table to where the ticket sellers sat and looked down at one of the raffle tickets.

As a fund-raiser, the church was raffling off a car donated by Whit Stasson's Chevrolet.

A car?

Sure enough, a new white Blazer was positioned in the street behind the table, half hidden from this angle by the ringtoss booth.

Rich frowned. Churchgoer or not, a car was one hell of a donation for a person to make, particularly in this town where raffles were usually for video rental coupons or, at best, toaster ovens. One hell of a donation. Whit had cut back on his advertising in the paper earlier this year, and Rich knew firsthand that the dealership was not doing all that well.

How could Whit afford to do this? And why *would* he even if he could? Whit was no Holy Roller.

What was the money going to be used for? Rich found himself wondering. Judging on past actions, Wheeler was not going to donate it to the poor or use it to help needy families.

The woman seated behind the table looked up at him, smiling a Stepford smile. "Would you like to buy a chance to win a new Blazer? It's only five dollars."

Rich shook his head, moved away from the table. "Not today."

The afternoon dragged on. He and Corrie and Anna ate together, standing with the crowd watching the relay races, then played a few of the games. He wandered around taking a roll of photos, letting Anna carry the camera case. Several men on the fringes of the festivities grew progressively drunker, progressively louder, as the hours passed, and members of Wheeler's congregation kept sneaking furtive glances at the pastor to see what his reaction would be. But there was no reaction, no sermonizing, no lecturing. Although Wheeler's eyes seemed to grow blank when he looked over at the drunks, he remained cheerfully tolerant of their excesses, choosing to put up with them rather than make them an example. Rich found himself thinking that, in con artist terms, it was easier to take a drunk mark than a sober one.

That's what Wheeler reminded him of. A con artist.

"What's the money being raised for?" Rich asked Corrie as they walked back to the car. Behind them, the announcement of the raffle winner was about to take place.

"The church just purchased more construction materials from the Valley," she said. "Pastor Wheeler is in a hurry to build the Church of the Living Christ."

Great, Rich thought, another monument to a shyster preacher's vanity. What was next? A prayer tower? A broadcasting tower? A TV show? But he said nothing.

The three of them walked back to the car in silence.

Twenty-seven

The Branding Iron, Rio Verde's only real bar, was the last building on the desolate east end of town, a low nondescript structure on the highway to Casa Grande that was separated from the Shell station—the end of the town proper—by a good half-mile of empty desert. The building was brick, with a small lone window next to the perpetually open front door through which shone the neon lights of red and blue beer signs. There were hitching posts around two sides of the building, and on summer weekends, for two days straight, an army of motorcycles remained parked in front of the posts, chrome shining in the desert sun, gleaming under the desert moon.

Tonight there were no hogs in front of the bar, only a few broken-down pickups. And Brad Woods's Buick.

Robert pulled next to the coroner's car and got out, yawning. He was tired. He'd spent most of the morning on the phone and most of the afternoon on his feet, and he'd been planning to go home and go to bed when Woods called and asked to meet him at the Branding Iron. He would've begged off, but the coroner had sounded half-crocked, and the fact that he refused to discuss what was bothering him over the phone alerted Robert's police sense.

He didn't want to meet Woods, but he had to.

Robert walked around to the front of the bar and through the door into the darkness. He heard the coroner's voice before his eyes had completely adjusted, and he made his way toward the far corner, feeling his way around the tables.

There were three empty glasses in front of Woods and a half-full glass in his hand. He did not look up as Robert approached but moved over on the vinyl seat, patting the bench. "Pull up, have a sit down."

"Knock off the B-movie crap." Robert swiveled the end of the table so he could fit in and slid into the seat. "What's all this about?"

"Vampires."

"Shit."

"I'm serious."

"About vampires?"

"You know me, Robert. I'm not a superstitious man. But I'm also not a stupid man. I'm open-minded enough that I'll discard theories if they don't work, or adjust my worldview if evidence shows that I've been wrong." He swallowed a healthy amount of his drink. "And I have been wrong."

"Come on, you're drunk."

"I am drunk, but I'm not thinking this because I've had too much to drink. I've had too much to drink because I've been thinking this. There are vampires, my friend. And we've got one here. Or more than one. Who knows?" He finished his glass, called for another.

Robert felt cold, but he kept his voice even, rational. "What brought this on?"

"I've been thinking on it for a while. Since Manuel's autopsy. I'm sure you know I was the one to suggest he be cremated. And I'm sure you know why."

Robert said nothing, suddenly wishing he'd ordered a drink as well.

"I got a call from Ed Durham this afternoon. Ed, you know, autopsied the animals. He didn't seem to be as spooked by them as I was by Manuel, maybe because they were animals, not people, but he sounded weird and plenty scared when he called today. He told me to come over right away, he had a big problem. I knew something was up, so I hurried over there as quickly as I could.

"When I walked into the animal hospital, the place was silent. Silent. You know what that place's like. Usually it's so noisy that you can't even hear yourself think: meowing, barking, braying, what have you. But there was nothing this time, and I'm telling you it gave me the creeps. Ed came out, and he looked like a damn ghost. He didn't say anything, just held open the door into the back, and I followed him.

"The animals were dead, all dead. Drained. Just like the ones from the arroyo. I could see them lying in their cages, the dogs and the cats and the hamsters and the rabbits, and outside, through the window, in the dirt, the horses. I've never seen anything like it. For a second, I thought maybe it was some sort of unknown virus. I thought maybe some government biological agent had been accidentally released into the wind and doused us, and that I hadn't detected it in Manuel's autopsy because I hadn't known what it was. But I looked into the cage next to me, a tabby cat who'd been shaved around the neck for surgery, and I saw the wounds, and I knew it was a vampire. I *knew* it. I kept wondering if the vampire had opened each and every cage, had grabbed the animal inside, bit into it, replaced it, and locked the cage.

"Ed asked me how he would tell people that their pets had died. He asked me about his insurance. He was worried about all this small stuff, and I told him he had something bigger to worry about, and he became silent. I think he knew it all along but didn't want to admit it."

"Great," Robert muttered.

The bartender arrived with Woods's drink, and Robert ordered a Scotch. Double.

"What I want to know is what are we going to do about

this? We know what's going on here, and we can't just walk around with ocular rectalitis—"

"Is that what you think we're doing?"

"Don't get your damn feathers all ruffled. I know you're trying to find the murderer—the vampire, let's be honest about it—but I'm talking about offensive, not defensive measures. We should be practicing some preventative medicine."

The bartender returned with Robert's drink. He paid the man and downed it. "You really think there's a vampire here?"

"Don't you?"

Robert shook his head. "I don't know."

"But you admit it's a possibility?"

He nodded. "Yeah."

"We need to start planning." He grinned. "Remember *Jaws*? If I've learned anything from movies, it's that people in power should not stonewall the public if they have facts in their possession."

"Facts?"

"We have to come up with some sort of civil defense plan. Publicity should be no problem. We have your brother—"

"We can't panic people."

Woods finished his drink. "You think there is a vampire, don't you?"

Robert took a deep breath. "Maybe."

Woods looked at him, nodded.

They both ordered another drink.

Robert drove himself home. It was stupid and irresponsible, having had several drinks, but he was the police chief, and there was hardly anyone on the road at this time of night.

Robert staggered into the house and immediately

locked the door behind him. He turned on the lights in the living room, then the kitchen, the dining room, the den, the bedroom, the bathrooms. Just in case.

The house was empty.

He took a piss, walked over to the sink, splashed some cold water on his face, and felt a little better.

Walking into the bedroom, he stood just inside the door for a moment and scanned the videotape titles in the bookcase. A lot of them were movies he'd seen once and didn't care to see again. When he'd first gotten his VCR, in the throes of what for a few years had been a full-fledged mania, he'd taped anything and everything, consumed with an absurd desire to own all that he watched. The history of his videotape obsession sat spread out in chronological order on his shelves.

Now, reading those titles, he was reminded of Julie.

He moved slowly through the room and lay down on the bed, not bothering to take off his clothes or even kick off his shoes. He rolled on his side and stared at the unfinished oak dresser and the pink flowered print in the frame on the wall above it. He realized that he had never bothered to redecorate after Julie left. The furnishings and decorations had all been chosen by her, were all to her taste. For years he had unthinkingly continued to clean and straighten and live among the abandoned belongings of his ex-wife. This was *her* world, not his. It was funny how he'd never noticed that before. Well, it wasn't actually funny. It was sad, really. He was like one of those pathetic old guys who kept their wives' memories alive by holding on to clothes and perfume and personal items after they had died.

Was that what he was trying to do? Hold on to Julie's memory?

He didn't think so, but he found himself thinking of her now, wondering where she was, what she was doing, who she was with.

He closed his eyes, tried to will himself to think of something else, couldn't. He slowed his breathing, tried to fall asleep, couldn't.

He opened his eyes, stared into space. He thought of getting out of his clothes, taking a shower or a hot bath, but he did not move, did not do anything. He simply lay there.

It was well after midnight before he finally dozed off.

Twenty-eight

In the dream he was a little boy, and he was sitting in a bathtub in the middle of a church. His father was standing before him, the Bible in one hand, a switch in the other. The man was lecturing him, but he could not understand the words; they all ran together in a loud, blurred, dictatorial drone. Behind his father, on the altar of the church, his mother was doing a striptease. Her face was calm and bland and plain, the face he'd seen in her photo, but her gyrating body was slick and supple and fantastically well endowed. Her top was already off, her large firm breasts bouncing, and only a thin line of cloth covered her dark pubic area. He tried not to look at his mother, tried to concentrate fully on his father, to focus his attention on his father's lips in order to match the movements with the sounds and decipher what was being said, but he kept sneaking peeks at his mother on the altar, and his father's droning never resolved itself into coherent words.

Pastor Wheeler awoke with an erection.

The throbbing between his legs was painful, demanding, but he ignored it. Slowly, calmly, he pushed the sheet off his body, got out of bed, and walked into the kitchen. In the refrigerator, next to the milk, was the pitcher of ice water he kept for just such occurrences. He carried the pitcher to the bathroom and set it atop the closed lid of the toilet as he took off his pajamas. He climbed into the bathtub, grabbed the pitcher, and poured the ice water slowly over his already fading erection, gratified to see his organ shrivel beneath the stream of cold liquid.

He stepped out of the tub, patted dry his pubic area with a towel, and once again put on his pajamas.

It was still dark outside, and Wheeler walked into his study, glancing at the liquid quartz numbers on his desk clock.

Three-thirty.

The time when Joseph of Arimathea laid Christ's body to rest in the tomb.

He had awakened at three for the past five nights, and though he had not seen Jesus, he knew from the significance of the time that the Savior was speaking to him.

He assumed that Christ was happy with the way things were progressing. If He had been displeased, He would have confronted Wheeler with his inadequacy and failure. But things were progressing as planned.

Wheeler stared down at his desk, at the plans spread out there. The first addition was not yet completed, but the materials had arrived yesterday for the third section of the new church, and he saw no reason for the work to be done in stages, no reason why one phase of the church's construction had to wait for a completion of the old. Jesus needed the entire complex completed before October 31, the date of His rebirth, and heads were going to roll if it was not done to His satisfaction. So Wheeler now had the skilled laborers working on the frame of the new room while the unskilled workers, within the congregation painted the original building black.

The Church of the Living Christ was going to be the finest structure ever built. The most perfect building on the face of the earth.

Wheeler looked up from the plans, and his eyes passed over the world atlas above the desk. The thought occurred to him that his makeshift conglomeration of two rather

ordinary churches and additions could not hope to match
the majesty and power of the cathedrals of Europe or even
such heathen structures as the Taj Mahal, that perhaps
he would not be able to pay God the respect He deserved,
but Wheeler quickly pushed that thought from his mind.
He was thinking in Old World terms. It was a New World
now.

There would never be anything like the Church of the
Living Christ.

Wheeler sat down at his desk and picked up his white-
bound copy of the Bible, turning to his favorite book,
Isaiah. He read the entire book, from the first verse to
the last, backtracking several times to reread his favorite
passage: *"Through the wrath of the LORD of hosts the land is
burned, and the people are like fuel for the fire; no man spares
his brother. They snatch on the right, but are still hungry, and
they devour on the left, but are not satisfied; each devours his
neighbor's flesh."*

Smiling to himself, Wheeler closed the Bible and placed
it on top of the church plans, feeling restful and con-
tented. He stood, stretched. He had to go to the bathroom, and he walked back across the hall. He pulled up
the toilet seat, slipped his penis through the pajama flap,
and urinated.

A stream of red flowed out of his body into the toilet.

Wheeler stared down at the swirling red water. He was
surprised, a little shocked, but not scared. The blood in
his urine would have panicked him a month ago, would
have made him go immediately to a doctor to find out
what was wrong.

But he knew now that Jesus was showing him His gratitude for all he had done.

And the blood of Jesus cleanses us from all sin.

Wheeler finished, flushed the toilet, and returned to
his bedroom.

There was a lot of talk of blood in the Bible. He had

noticed that recently while preparing his sermons, although it was not something that had jumped out at him before. Blood was important to God in the Old Testament, important to Jesus in the New Testament. What was it that Jesus had said at the Last Supper? "Drink of it, all of you; for this is my blood."

Jesus liked to drink blood.

Soon, when he was worthy enough, when the Church of the Living Christ was completed, Jesus would ask Wheeler to dine with Him, and they would feast on the blood of the sinners. The blood would be purified within their bodies, the bad made good.

He would have to get used to the blood first, however. He did not want to embarrass himself before the Lord Jesus Christ.

Maybe he would try some blood. Start off with something small. A bug maybe. Then work his way up to a rat. A cat. A dog.

Wheeler smiled to himself. He would make Jesus proud of him.

He closed his eyes and fell asleep instantly.

Twenty-nine

They awoke before Anna for once, and Rich placed a tentative hand between Corrie's legs, testing the waters. His fingers pressed against wiry pubic hair and soft flesh, and then Corrie's muscles tightened, her legs closed, and she firmly pushed his hand away. He lay there for a moment, silent, unsure of whether to press on or give up. It had been weeks since they'd last had sex, and it depressed him to realize that he could not even remember the exact day.

How had they let their love life deteriorate to this point?

He turned toward her, spoke softly. "Anna's not up yet, you know."

She gave him a disgusted look, then rolled over to face the other direction. "I'm still tired. I need more sleep."

He sighed, got out of bed to make breakfast.

The day was long. In the morning Rich hacked out two columns, typeset a want ad, and went over Sue's story, making only minimal changes to her lead, surprised and pleased by the relatively high quality of her writing. Jim Fredricks came by and dropped off a roll of film and three sports articles, staying for only a few minutes to shoot the breeze. Corrie brought Anna by after lunch, saying hello to Carole and not bothering to come into the back to see him, and for most of the afternoon Anna sat in the front, next to the secretary, reading a book, while he ran out what he had and began pasting up the pages.

After work, Rich took Anna to Mike's for pizza. To her it was a special treat, and he was glad she felt that way, but they were going out tonight more out of necessity than desire. Just before five, Corrie had called from the church and, for the third day in a row, said she would not be home for dinner. The mere thought of having to eat another one of his own meals made him feel like gagging, so he'd asked Anna if she would like to go out for pizza, and of course she'd said yes.

She stood now with a group of her school friends, watching a thin, dirty, tough-looking boy kill row after row of aliens on a video game. Rich sat on a hard bench at the table by the front window, fiddling with a glass shaker of Parmesan cheese, glancing idly around. He had not realized that the pizza parlor would be so crowded on a weeknight, or that so many parents let their children out unattended. Fully half of the kids clustered around the video game were on their own recognizance, with no parent or older sibling in sight.

His gaze shifted from the video game crowd to the parking lot outside the window. Before leaving the office, he had called Robert and asked him to meet them here, but his brother hadn't been sure he would be able to make it. So far there'd been no sign of Robert's car.

Rich stared blankly out at the vehicles in the parking lot, wondering why Corrie was having to spend so much overtime at the church. Surely Wheeler couldn't have that much work piled up—at least not work that required immediate attention. So why did Corrie feel compelled to stay late instead of finishing things up the next day?

The thought briefly crossed his mind that she was having an affair, but he dismissed that ludicrous idea immediately. He'd been watching too many movies.

Besides, Corrie seemed to find the idea of any sex at all these days fairly repulsive.

He found himself listening to the talk of the people around him, tuning in one discussion, then another, his ears conversation hopping. Reporter's instinct. At the table behind him, an old man he couldn't see and hadn't noticed upon arriving was talking about his heart problems: ". . . I woke up naked as a jaybird with a tube shoved up my nose. There was a doctor there, and I asked him what was happening, but he just told me to take a deep breath, and then I was out again. I woke up and I had a big ol' scar down the side of my leg, and my chest hurt like a son of a bitch . . ."

A cowboy-hatted man at the table to the left of him, wearing a turquoise bob tie, was talking about a dog race in Phoenix: ". . . He said he got the skinny on one of them fixed races an' said he'd cut me in on it. I shoulda known right there that he was a crooked . . ."

A braless woman wearing a black tank top, standing with her equally braless friend at the counter: "Rob said he's going to make some stakes and crosses . . ."

Stakes and crosses.

He tried to zero in on that conversation, but the women moved away from the cash register toward the fountain. He thought of following them, trying to eavesdrop, but just then Robert walked through the door, looking around the crowded restaurant, and Rich waved his brother over.

Robert sat down. "Where's Anna?"

Rich nodded his head toward the video game.

"Oh." He picked up Anna's water glass.

"That's her glass."

"I'll get her another one. I'm dying of thirst." He downed the water in a single swallow, leaving only the ice cubes. "God, that tastes good. The drinking fountain crapped out on us this morning at the station, and we've been having to make do all day. I'm telling you, you don't realize how much you rely on something like that until it dies. Especially in this weather."

"When do you think this heat wave's going to end?"

"Who the hell knows?"

Rich took a sip of his own water. "So what's happening?"

Robert chuckled. "You know, I'm never sure if you're asking that as a brother or a reporter."

Rich smiled. "Both."

"You heard about the animal hospital, didn't you?"

"That's my front page story."

"Well, that's not the half of it. Norbit over at the Shell station said it looked like a sandstorm hit his bathroom last week. Said the floor, the sink, everything was covered with a foot-high layer of sand. He thinks teenagers are responsible, only he claims that it happened while he was working, and he didn't see or hear anything. He came bitching to me about it this morning, asking me what I'm going to do about it. He waits a week to tell me, cleans it up before letting me look at it, doesn't even take any pictures, and expects me to tell him the culprits are about to be caught? I straightened him out, let me tell you. You know Arn Hewett?"

Rich shook his head.

"Works over at Basha's? Liquor department?"

"Tall guy? Balding?"

"Yeah. That's him. Anyway, he's gone. The whole family's up and disappeared. I don't know if they just pulled up stakes and left, or if something happened to them. I got a call from Bailey, his boss, who said he'd already called neighbors and Hewett's sister, but no one knows anything. I ran a check on Hewett, and he's done some time, but it was years ago and for small stuff. I cabled the sister and told her she could file a missing person's, but she sounded real squirrely, so I don't know what the hell she plans to do." He shook his head. "There's a lot of weird shit going down, a lot of weird shit, and I don't like it."

"Whatever happened with Sophocles Johnson?"

Robert looked into his glass, shook the ice cubes.

"Did he ever let you talk to him?"

"Yeah, I talked to him. He's crazy as a damn bedbug. He put on a normal act with me, told me that he knew he had some problems to work out and was seeking help, but I could tell it was a load of horse pucky."

"Sounds like you have your hands full these days."

"That's why I came over here tonight. I need a break."

"What about the FBI? Aren't they supposed to be giving you help?"

Robert snorted. "Rossiter has the attention span of a fucking gnat. He and his boys came in here all hot to trot, acting real official, threw their weight around, told me they were going to put their resources behind this, and I haven't heard word one from them since." He popped an ice cube in his mouth. "Not that I'm complaining. The FBI and the state police investigating crimes in Rio Verde is kind of like the old bull in the china shop routine. I don't think they understand the place or the people well enough to tread as carefully as they need to in order to find this . . . whatever it is."

"Well, isn't that your job? To acquaint them with the town, act as their liaison?"

"Whose side are you on?"

"No one's side. This just seems a little out of your league. I mean, murders and grave robbings are not—"

"No graves were robbed, and for your information this is not out of my league. I'm not the rube you seem to think I am."

"I didn't say that, and I don't think it. Don't get all worked up over nothing. Jesus."

"Well . . ."

"I just thought that the FBI probably had the resources to deal with all of this."

"Yeah, but it's too close to tabloid territory. I don't think they want that sort of publicity. Not in these budget crisis times. They'd rather have us solve it and not have to explain why they were spending time and resources looking for a . . . vampire."

"Aha. It's finally said. The 'V' word."

Robert didn't reply.

"That's what a lot of people are talking about, you know."

Robert looked at his brother, thought for a moment, then shrugged. "Maybe it is a vampire."

"Knock off the crap."

"Maybe it's crap, and maybe it isn't. We both know that the supernatural exists—"

Rich shook his head. "Wait a minute here. How did the conversation get around to this?"

"It's true."

"Why?"

"You know."

"Because we thought we saw a ghost in grade school?"

"Because of The Laughing Man."

Rich was silent.

"There are things we don't understand."

"Bullshit."

"All I'm saying is I'm keeping my eyes open."

"Weren't you going to get Anna another glass of water?"

Robert sighed. "I didn't come here to fight."

"Me either."

"Fine. Let's drop it." He glanced toward the register. "Did you already order?"

Rich nodded. "A small cheese pizza for Anna. A large pepperoni for us."

"How long 'til it's done?"

"Five minutes or so."

Robert tore a strip from his napkin, rolled it into a ball on the tabletop. "Donna Sandoval said she saw Caldwell Burke with Manuel Torres before he was killed."

"I thought we were going to drop it?"

"Fine."

They sat for a moment in silence, Rich looking down at the table, tracing water rings with his finger, Robert chewing on his ice.

Robert glanced out the window, then back at his brother. "So Wheeler's claiming he saw Jesus, huh?"

Rich looked up sharply. "What?"

"You didn't hear? I thought Corrie was working for him."

"She is. But she never said anything about that."

"Apparently he's telling his flock that Jesus spoke to him in a dream, and then in person, and told him to rebuild his church—"

"Where did you hear this?"

"One of my men goes to his church."

Rich glanced toward Anna, who was watching another girl work the joystick of the video game. "How come Corrie didn't say anything about this?"

"She probably knew you'd react this way."

"Well, how would you react?"

"The same." Robert tore another strip from his napkin. "I thought maybe you hadn't heard. That's why I told you." He sighed. "I don't like Wheeler. If I thought he was just an opportunist, I'd hate him and be disgusted by him, but I think he's a true believer, and that scares me. He probably really does think he's seen Jesus. We have enough problems around here right now without someone like that working people into a witch-hunting frenzy."

"Is that what he's doing?"

"It's only a matter of time. Murder victims drained of blood? Grave desecration? You think he's not going to bring God and Satan into this? My job's hard enough without having to deal with that shit."

Rich took a deep breath. "The thing that concerns me is that she takes Anna with her to his church."

"Corrie? That doesn't sound like her."

"She's been behaving differently lately."

Robert looked over at Anna. "I'd put my foot down on that if I were you."

"Anna?"

"I wouldn't want her hearing that stuff."

"She's not going to that church anymore." Rich stared at his daughter. "But what exactly is Wheeler telling people? That Jesus told him to remodel his church and that's it? Or that this is supposed to be the Second Coming?"

"I could find out."

"That's okay. I'll look into it. I'll talk to Corrie."

"What about Anna? What are you going to say to her?"

"I don't know."

The waitress arrived with the pizzas and plates. Robert went to the fountain to get drinks, and Rich walked over to the video game to get Anna. He tried to pretend like nothing was wrong, but he watched her carefully as they ate, listened to her, and worried.

By the time they arrived home, Corrie was back. She was angry, sitting in the living room with the TV off and only the table lamp on, but she did a good job of hiding her anger as she took Anna to bed, helped her daughter change into her PJs, and tucked her in.

Her demeanor changed completely when she returned to the living room. "Where the hell were you?"

"You know where we were. I left a message on the machine, and I heard Anna tell you just a minute ago."

"Why did you go out for pizza when we had plenty of food in the refrigerator? It's a school night."

"I didn't feel like cooking. Now the question is, why weren't you here?"

"I told you. I had to work late."

"Yeah, I guess the Second Coming does involve a lot of preparations."

She'd been moving toward him, but she stopped, the words she'd been about to speak dying in her throat.

"Yes, I know about it." He stood, approached her. "You thought I wouldn't find out?"

"I didn't think you needed to know."

"Oh. Your boss is telling everyone that Jesus has been resurrected and has dropped by Rio Verde for a visit, and I didn't need to know?"

"I knew how you'd react."

"Really? And how's that?"

"The way you're acting right now."

"You don't think I might be a little concerned because you're working for a man who claims he's engineering the Second Coming? You don't think I might be worried because you're taking our daughter to church and exposing her to this?"

"Did Anna tell you?"

"Why? Did you tell her not to? Did you bribe her?" He glared at Corrie. "Or did you threaten her?"

She stared at him, then pushed past him and stormed out of the living room into the kitchen. He followed her, watched her take a can of Diet Dr Pepper out of the refrigerator and slam the door. She whirled on him. Her eyes were red and wide, her mouth a small thin trembling line. "How dare you say something like that!"

He held up his hands. "Okay. I'm sorry. I was angry—"

Corrie glared at him. "When I went for that mammogram two years ago, I had to drive myself!"

He frowned. "What does that have to do with anything?"

"It has to do with our relationship and the way you treat me!"

"What?"

"I didn't tell you about Jesus because I knew you wouldn't understand. You never understand anything."

"How can you say that? You know I—"

"Yeah, like the mammogram?"

"I don't know why we're even arguing about this. You know I offered to drive you—"

"Offered, not insisted."

"The paper was coming out the next day. You told me to finish it up, you'd go to the doctor by yourself, you'd be fine."

"I didn't think you'd actually listen to me! I expected you to argue, to insist that you drive me. I wanted some support. But you were only too happy to worm out of your responsibility and hide at the paper and leave me to face it all alone. I thought I had cancer! I thought I was going to die, and you weren't even there!"

Rich said nothing.

"Sometimes what people say they want you to do and what they really want you to do are two different things. Sometimes you have to *feel* what's happening and not just listen to the words. Sometimes you have to dig beneath the surface to find the meaning. You've never understood that. I keep waiting for you to take the initiative, to understand how I feel without me having to spell everything out for you, but you never do." She slammed the Dr Pepper can down on the counter. "That's why I didn't tell you about Jesus!"

She shoved him against the door frame and strode through the living room into the hall. He heard the door to their bedroom slam shut.

He stared after her, unmoving. He felt cold and empty inside. It was obvious to him that she bought Wheeler's story, that she really believed Jesus had talked to the preacher, but he wondered how that was possible. Corrie was neither stupid nor gullible; she had always been more of a leader than a follower, and she was not easily persuaded by smooth talkers. She was religious, but her faith had always been based on the Bible, not the words and interpretations of others.

Until now.

Was he partially responsible for pushing her into this religious zealousness, into Wheeler's church? The thought disturbed him. He didn't want to think about it, but he could not push it from his mind and could not discount its possibility. The things she'd said hit close to the bone, and the anger he'd felt at her had fled, leaving him feeling curiously drained.

He hoped Anna hadn't heard their argument.

But he knew that she had.

Walking slowly, feeling tired, he moved through the living room and into the hallway, where he opened the linen closet. He took out a pillow and two sheets and walked back into the living room to make up the couch for his bed.

Thirty

Cheri Stevens.

Aaron looked over at his date, the perfect smooth-skinned features of her beautiful face lit in soft focus by the bluish moon and the green dashboard lights, and realized that this was at once his biggest triumph and his biggest mistake.

He looked in the rearview mirror, tried to see his own face, but from this angle could only make out the huge slab that was his nose and the dark spot in the center of his nose that was a pimple.

What had ever made him think that Cheri Stevens would go out with him?

She *had* gone out with him, though.

That was the weird part.

He had admired Cheri from afar for years. Since seventh grade, to be exact, when he'd first started to notice girls. She'd been in his beginning band class, had played the clarinet, and even then had had that sophisticated sort of sexiness that, until that point, Aaron and his friends had seen only in girls on the screen. He'd watched her become a Song-And-Yell girl, a cheerleader, and then head cheerleader. She was smart, too, in the high achievement classes, and it was in those classes, which they shared together, that he got an opportunity to view her close up. Of course she had not noticed him at all. From the beginning, her interest had been in older boys, ninth graders, and her appeal soon spread beyond that. As an eighth grader, she'd gone out with a senior in high school. The captain of the basketball team, no less.

Aaron still could not believe that she had agreed to go out with him. She'd gone through a lot of guys over the years, from jocks to cool kids, all of them studs, and he had only asked her out because she was between boyfriends, and he had been dared to do so. Phil Harte, the friend who had dared him, who had promised to fork over fifty bucks if he asked her out and she said yes, had tried to convince him that most beautiful girls spent their Friday nights alone because guys were too intimidated by them to ask them out. Aaron knew that was not the case with Cheri—he'd heard the bragging of jocks in the locker room who *had* gone out with her—but he'd gathered up his courage anyway, licked his lips and ignored his pounding heart, and asked if she'd like to go to a movie with him.

She'd turned those eyes on him, that smile, and said yes.

Now they'd gone to the movie, and the time had come to decide what to do next. He was beginning to think he'd made a big mistake. Of course, the evening had been great so far. His friends, sitting together in a group in the movie theater, dateless, had seen him with Cheri, hand in hand, arms around each other. And a lot of people he didn't like, boys and girls, had seen them together as well.

But now the movie was over, the crowds were gone, and they were alone, cruising. He found himself wondering if he wasn't being set up, if Cheri was only going out with him in order to humiliate him, perhaps as part of a dare by her own friends. He'd seen it before, in movies. Beautiful girl goes out with nerdy guy, gets him in a compromising position, takes pictures or videotape, friends jump out laughing. An extended practical joke. April Fool's in October.

Was that what was going to happen here?

He didn't know, but somehow he didn't think so. He was scared, nervous, but he had to admit that the relationship between them had seemed pretty natural so far. She hadn't treated him like God's gift to girls (the way she would if she was planning to set him up), and she hadn't acted like he was a charity case either. The two of them might be social unequals, but mentally they were fairly compatible, and they had found plenty to talk about, the long and awkward silences he'd feared and dreaded never materializing.

He turned to her now, tried to make his voice casual. "So what do you want to do now? The night's still young. We don't have to go home yet. We could grab a bite to eat or—"

"The river," she said. "Let's go to the river."

The river? This was better than he had hoped for in even his most wildly optimistic moments. He studied her face out of the corner of his eye. Was this for real?

It looked like it was.

"Okay," he said.

He turned around in the Radio Shack parking lot and headed back through town, passing the theater, passing her street, passing the turnoff to his house. In a few minutes the lights of Rio Verde were behind them, only darkened trailers and occasional run-down houses discernible in the darkness along the highway. Just before the bridge, he turned onto the dirt road that led to the river. The car bumped over ruts and potholes, the road sloping sharply down to the water. There were other cars and pickups parked here, between the trees and bushes, the orange glow of cigarettes visible through some of their windows, and Aaron continued on until he found a secluded spot far past the last parked car.

He shut off the car engine, the radio and air-conditioning dying at the same time, and suddenly there was silence. He could hear his own breathing in the closed car. And hers. He rolled down his window, smelled the skunkweed, heard the water, the cicadas.

He was not sure what to say, what to do, so he looked over at Cheri. She was leaning her head back, her eyes closed, breathing deeply. "I love the water," she said.

He tried to talk, couldn't, cleared his throat. "Me, too."

She opened her eyes. "Let's go skinny-dipping."

He blinked, thinking that she was joking, quickly realizing that she was not. Panicked, he tried to think of an excuse, a way to get out of it, but he had never been good at thinking on his feet, and he could only stammer, "I, uh, don't think we should."

"Why not?" she said teasingly. "Embarrassed?"

Yes, he thought, but only smiled wanly.

She opened the car door, got out. "Come on. It'll be fun." She began making her way through the brush and down the low bank to the water.

He got out of the car and followed her. He started down the slope, and his shoes slipped on the dirt. He grabbed a branch to keep from falling, and lowered himself to the shore.

Cheri was standing in front of the river, facing him, smiling, her features soft and clear in the moonlight. "Let's do it."

This is where they come out laughing, he thought. I take off my pants, and the football team rushes out and grabs them, and I have to go home in my underwear.

But no one emerged from the bushes as Cheri pulled the T-shirt over her head, and he could hear only his own breathing and the rush of the water as she reached around to unfasten her bra.

"Are you sure—?" he began.

"Come on. It'll be fun. Don't worry."

Her bra was off now, joining her T-shirt on the sand, and her breasts were perfect: large enough that they made her look like a woman but small enough that they did not droop even a centimeter once freed from the confines of the bra.

He forced himself to look away. "Did you ever wonder why they named this town Rio Verde? Rio Verde means 'Green River' in Spanish. It makes it sound like it's in the middle of some lush valley, but it's just an old desert town with this pathetic little river running by it. And the river water's brown, not green." He was babbling and he knew it, but he couldn't stop himself. "Maybe it's like Greenland, you know? They named Greenland 'Greenland' to attract people, even though it's really not green at all."

Cheri unzipped her pants, pulled them down. He looked back at her. Her panties were white and lacy. Through the transparent material he could see the thick triangular darkness of her pubic hair.

She grinned at him. "Your turn, bud. Drop 'em."

She's done this before, he thought. With Matt and Mike and Steve. Guys with *bodies*. How can I hope to compare?

But he was already taking off his shoes, his socks.

He began unbuttoning his shirt. What if she laughed? What if she told all her friends that he wasn't . . . big enough?

She put a tentative toe in the water, shivered. "Cold!"

"Maybe we should skip it."

"Never." Laughing, she leaped into the water.

He quickly took off his pants and jumped in after her before she could see him. The water was indeed cold, unexpectedly so, and his penis shrunk instantly. He quickly reached between his legs and pulled on it, trying to make it grow, trying to make it big enough not to embarrass him, but his body wouldn't cooperate, and his organ remained soft and small. The river was shallow at this point, enough for them to stand, but they remained floating, and Cheri swam over to him. Her wet hair looked muddy in the moonlight, but he thought that she was the most beautiful thing he'd ever seen.

Her breasts brushed against his arm, soft and giving, and she put a hand around his neck and gave him a short kiss on the mouth before laughing and swimming away. His penis sprang instantly to life, his erection strong even in the cold water, and he paddled after her, feeling happier, more alive than he could remember having ever felt before. He no longer worried about her past, was no longer concerned about being compared to other guys she'd known. Tonight she was here, with him. And she was happy.

He swam across the river toward her, chasing her, and she squealed and pushed off from the opposite bank, heading upriver, away from him. He sped after her, paddling furiously, and caught her near an overhanging cottonwood, grabbing her right foot. She laughed, tried to twist away, and he saw the white smooth skin of her buttocks. He held onto her foot, and she stopped trying to escape, righting herself. She stood, he stood, and they kissed, his tongue slipping easily and effortlessly into her mouth, tasting warm mint and fresh breath.

They drew apart as quickly as they had come together, both breathing heavily. He had felt her breasts against him again. He wondered if she had felt his erection. He hoped she had.

She looked away from him, looked up, and Aaron looked up as well. Above them, the cottonwood branches were moving, whipping to the left as if propelled by an unusually strong wind.

But there was no wind.

The temperature changed, instantly dropping a good ten degrees. Goose bumps popped up en masse on Cheri's bare shoulders, and she shivered, hugging herself for warmth. Should he be hugging her? Should he be keeping her warm? He didn't know, and he didn't have time to make a decision one way or the other because she suddenly looked behind him, past him, and yelped in surprise.

Her eyes widened in horror. "Daddy!"

Her father!

Oh, God. How was he going to explain this? His penis shriveled to nothing, and he turned around, looking toward the opposite bank. But it was not her father. He could not tell who the figure was—it was too dark to see much of anything—but he knew that it was not her father.

Because it was not human.

The form, big and black and shadowy, slid smoothly down the dirt and into the water.

In the second before it entered the river, he saw lips and teeth and wavy wattley arms.

He and Cheri both began paddling simultaneously and desperately toward the opposite shore, toward their clothes and car and safety.

"It's not what you think, Daddy!" she was screaming, but she did not slow down in her effort to escape, did not make an effort to confront the creature.

Oh, God, Aaron thought. What if that thing really was her dad? What if she was some sort of half-human creature, and now her father had caught her with a real human being and was going to punish her?

And him.

Cold slime slid against the bottom of his feet, pressed against his lower leg. In the dark water his fingers touched flesh the consistency of Jell-O. He stopped swimming, stopped paddling, stood. He saw humps of jet break the water, saw a black tentacled hand reach out and grab Cheri by the shoulder.

"No!" she screamed. "Daddy!"

There was a syncopated crack, then a squishy sound, as of wet pages being torn from a waterlogged book. Cheri thrashed wildly in the water, going down, another dark deformed hand grabbing her blond head. She was jerking crazily, hands, head, and feet flailing in furious counter-rhythms, as though the parts of her body were all controlled by different and competing brains. Desperate screams came in staccato bursts between splashes, and Aaron remained rooted in place, unable to move, unable to scream, hoping that one of the other parked couples could hear them, hoping that he was dreaming and this wasn't really taking place.

He smelled gas and excrement, and then he noticed that the thrashing had stopped, the screams had been silenced. Cheri and the creature were gone.

Then the hideous black shape emerged from the river, drawing to its full height, making a strange whistling, sucking sound that was quiet but could somehow be heard over the rush of the water. A dark, irregular object bobbed in front of the creature, floating down the river toward him, and Aaron saw immediately that it was Cheri—only her breasts were gone, her arms had shriveled, and as she floated past him he noticed with horror that she had the wrinkled crone face of an old woman.

The creature splashed through the water toward him.

He couldn't breathe, couldn't think, couldn't move. He tried to run, tried to swim, but his muscles wouldn't obey his brain, and he remained frozen in place as the creature advanced, whistling, hissing, splashing. Water flew into his face, and then a Jell-O hand wrapped around his shoulder and pulled him into the water toward a mouth that had far, far too many teeth.

"We used to swim here, too. Remember that?" Rich looked over at his brother, who nodded thoughtfully.

Rich watched the water flowing past his feet, swirling around the exposed cottonwood roots at the edge of the bank. "So what do you think happened?"

"You really want to know?"

Rich didn't answer.

"I think it's time we admit it. We've got ourselves a vampire here."

"Come on," Rich said, but his voice had no heart in it.

"Look, Rich, I'm a cop. I deal in facts. I don't spend my time trying to jigsaw the facts so they jibe with my view of things. I don't give a shit about preserving the integrity of my philosophy. The fact is, we have two more bodies drained of blood. That's pretty convincing evidence in my book."

"Don't give me that 'I'm a cop. I deal in facts' crap. Who do you think you are, Joe Friday?"

"Fine. Have it your way." Robert walked away from his brother, toward the two sheet-covered bodies on the bank. Beneath the thin cloth, the angular outlines of the forms looked like skeletons.

Woods, standing on the other side of the bodies, looked over at the police chief. "You're right," he said. "We do have a vampire here."

"You through with the on-site?"

The coroner nodded.

"Take 'em away."

"You find anything?" Woods asked. "Tracks?"

"Not yet."

"There must've been other kids parked out here. Maybe you should ask them if they saw anything."

"You do your job, okay? Don't tell me how to do mine."

"Sorry." Woods was silent for a moment. Looking down at the ground, he cleared his throat. "Let me talk to the families. It's their choice, of course, but I think the bodies should be cremated."

Robert started to say something, then thought the better of it and nodded.

"Thanks." Woods nodded to Ted, pointed toward the bodies. "Help me load these in the wagon."

Robert turned away, stared at the water. He found himself thinking not of the murders, but of the river. At one time, it was supposed to have become part of the Central Arizona Project, and for years there'd been talk of damming it up somewhere down the line, but the job had always proved too cost prohibitive. Their river simply didn't have the volume of the Salt or the Verde, and it did not flow through an area that would make its water easily accessible to Phoenix. Miles of concrete aqueducts would have to be built to connect the river to the rest of the Project, and in these tight fiscal times such funds were not available. Hollis and his partners in the Rocking D had been grateful for that. The river, along with Rio Verde's close proximity to Roosevelt Lake, were big selling points for the dude ranch. And big moneymakers for the town. Rio Verde survived the winter from money earned during the summer season.

Robert wondered how tourists would feel if they found out that a vampire was prowling the river.

Rich stepped up behind him. "Do their parents know?"

"They're on their way over."

"Who had to tell them?"

"Who do you think?" Robert looked up. There was the sound of tires skidding on dirt, car doors slamming. "They're here."

Rich glanced toward the police vehicles parked in the clear area behind them, saw a van next to that, a frantically running man and woman hurrying away from the van toward them. A station wagon pulled in seconds behind the van.

He turned away, looked back toward the water as Robert walked over to talk to the dead teenagers' parents.

* * *

Rossiter was already waiting for Robert at the station when he arrived two hours later.

Robert got out of the cruiser, adjusted his belt. The FBI agent was standing in front of a white unmarked government car next to two other equally obvious plainclothes agents. All three were blond, had matching haircuts and government issue sunglasses, and it was only a slight differentiation in the shade of their dark suits that enabled him to tell them apart.

The state police officer stood by himself, next to his brown, not-so-new car, pretending to look through a notebook.

Robert walked directly up to Rossiter. He was hot, sweaty, and tired, there were mud stains on his pants and sweat stains on his shirt, but he didn't give a damn. "So are you actually going to try to help me, or are you just going to hang around and get in my way?"

"You need more help than I can provide." The agent's voice was flat, but there was an undercurrent of resentment in it. Robert got the impression that Rossiter was angry at him for not yet solving the case. He was angry at himself for the same reason, but he was even angrier at this suited asshole who was supposed to be providing him with help and support but instead was giving him only pressure.

Rossiter took off his sunglasses, coolly put them into his jacket pocket. "I'm afraid we're going to be taking over this investigation from here on."

"What the hell do you think you're—"

"You will still be involved and participating in a hands-on basis, but the investigation will now be coordinated through our office. It's out of your jurisdiction. Because of the very specific and idiosyncratic nature of these crimes, and the fact that a large number of victims are involved, this has been classified by the Bureau as the work of a probable serial killer and has been given a number two priority level. Our territorial rights have been established with the consent of the state police." He nodded toward Cash, still standing next to his car. The officer nodded back.

"What the state police say doesn't mean shit around here." Rossiter sighed condescendingly. "Mr. Carter, you know how the hierarchy works—"

"No, I don't."

"Despite what you seem to think, you are not the head honcho here. You are answerable to the mayor and the town council. If I have to, I'll go through them. I'll bring court orders and federal injunctions, and I'll have you out of office so fast it'll make your head spin. The Bureau does not deal lightly with intransigent law enforcement officers." He withdrew a folded sheet of paper from the inner pocket of his jacket. "I have here a list of things that I need you to provide. Documentation related to the case. We are both working toward the same end, and I think it would benefit us both if you would cooperate."

Robert stared at the agent, hating the bastard even more than he had before, but realizing Rossiter had all the cards, and Robert could play only if the agent deigned to deal him a hand.

Robert reached out, took the sheet of paper.

"I'll need everything by noon tomorrow. If there's anything that you forget or can't find, you can fax it to me." Rossiter motioned to the other agents. "Let's look at the scene."

Thirty-one

Rich shifted uncomfortably in his seat. He tried to tell himself that it was merely a leftover reaction from his own high school days, a residual fear of the principal's office that he had never quite outgrown, but he knew that was not the case.

It was something else.

He stared across the desk at Principal Poole. The older man was appropriately subdued, the expression on his face suitably mournful, but there was nothing subdued or mournful about his eyes or body language. Rich had talked to a lot of people over the years, and he had developed a sort of sixth sense about these things. He could tell when people were holding back or were outright lying by observing the way they sat, the way they moved, the way the other elements of their faces responded to the words coming from their lips.

And he knew that Principal Poole was not saddened at all by the deaths of the two teenagers.

"It's tragic," the principal said, shaking his head sympathetically. "It is always tragic when life is taken from people so young."

Rich dutifully wrote down the quote.

"Both Aaron and Cheri were model students, were irreplaceable members of our student body family, and they will be greatly missed. Mr. Cheever, our yearbook adviser, has informed me that the new yearbook will be dedicated to these two fine students."

Rich closed his notebook. Ordinarily, he would have stuck around longer, asked a few more questions, just in case he needed to fill some extra space on the front page, but right now he just wanted to get out of this office. The principal was making him very uneasy. The air in here felt stifling, and the way the older man kept staring at him, studying him, set his teeth on edge.

He stood, smiled professionally. "Thank you, Mr. Poole. I think I have enough here. If I have any follow-up questions, I'll give you a call."

The principal smiled. "You do that." He stood, extending his hand. Rich shook it. He started toward the door, had almost reached it, when the principal cleared his throat. "Mr. Carter?"

Rich turned.

"Can I tell you something? Off the record?"

"Sure."

"Aaron and Cheri? They deserved what they got."

Rich stared at the principal. There was no dichotomy now between the eyes and the expression on the rest of the face, between the words and the body language. Everything was in sync. Rich felt the hairs bristle on the back of his neck.

"They were engaging in premarital sex, and they were punished for their sin."

Rich put his pen in his pocket. He tried to keep his voice light. "I don't think they were killed because of a skinny-dipping session at the river and a little backseat boogie."

"The Lord does not look upon moral transgressions so lightly."

Rich smiled thinly. "I'd have to say we disagree on that subject, Mr. Poole. But again, thank you for your time." He turned to go.

"Your wife would not be so quick to dismiss this warning."

"My wife?" Again, he faced the principal.

"Your wife is a devoted servant of the Lord Jesus Christ. I have seen her at church—"

"Don't talk to me about my own wife."

"She is preparing herself for the Second Coming. You should prepare yourself too."

Rich walked out of the office without saying good-bye. He did not stop to look back until he was safely beyond the administration building. Outside, Rich realized that he had been holding his breath, and he exhaled. Through the partially darkened window of the principal's office, he saw two figures watching him: the principal and his secretary.

What the hell was going on here?

He walked out to his pickup, got in, and took off. He did not look back.

Thirty-two

Sue stared out the window of the cafe, seeing not the highway and desert outside but the reflection of her face and the faces of her friends, transparent ghosts against the solid blackness of night.

Shelly, Janine, and Roxanne were talking—about music, about guys—but Sue wasn't really paying attention. She was thinking of what her grandmother had said, about the deaths, about the *cup hu girngsi*. It was ludicrous to think that a vampire was stalking the town, and she should have been able to laugh it off, but the disbelief wasn't there.

She thought of Aaron and Cheri, of the photos Rich had taken of their bodies.

Somewhere outside, in the darkness, something was stirring. A monster. A *cup hu girngsi*. It was crazy, but it was true. She knew it. She could feel it. Her grandmother was right; she *had* sensed the creature before, at the school that night, and though she'd wanted to deny its existence, she could not. She did not know if the creature was prowling through the town, slinking through the shadows in search of victims, or lying in wait out in the desert, but she knew that it was somewhere in the night, somewhere close. And tonight or tomorrow or the next night it would strike again.

She shivered and looked away from the window, picking

up a French fry from the plate in front of her and dipping
it into the smeared puddle of ketchup.

Shelly was complaining about her mother again, hint-
ing broadly that she needed a roommate if she was going
to be able to afford her own apartment.

Sue looked around the cafe. They had spent many a
weekend evening like this, hanging out, ordering soft
drinks and fries, commenting cattily on the groups of guys
and girls at the other tables, friends and enemies alike.
But she noticed for the first time that, except for one
elderly couple and families in booths, the cafe was empty.
That was strange. The cafe was never empty on Friday
night.

There was a lull in the conversation, and Shelly silently
ate a soggy French fry while the others sipped their drinks.
The silence lengthened, dragged. Sue glanced over at Janine, who gave her a halfhearted smile. She'd noticed too.
There never used to be any dead time when they got together; the conversation never used to flag. Either they
were drifting apart, the common interests they'd once
shared disappearing as they grew older, or they knew each
other so well that there was nothing left to say.

Whatever the case, Sue thought, it was depressing; and
she found herself looking at her friends in a new light,
wondering whether she would be friends with any of them
if she met them now for the first time.

It was Janine who broke the silence. "What's at the theater this weekend?"

Roxanne shrugged. "Some cop movie."

Sue forced herself to smile. "That's why God invented
video."

"Yeah," Shelly said, "only you always want to see those
boring obscure movies no one's ever heard of."

"Like what?"

"*A Room With a View?*"

"That's not obscure. And it's certainly not boring."

"Not to you maybe."

Roxanne laughed. "But you liked the naked guys, didn't you?"

Shelly shook her head. "Two seconds can't save a whole movie."

"You're hopeless," Sue said.

The conversation was back on track, the awkwardness gone, and as the talk shifted to upcoming movies, Sue knew that she would still be friends with these three if she met them now. Sitting here, she felt as close to them as she ever had. She looked from Janine to Shelly to Roxanne. Part of her wanted to tell them about what her grandmother had said, about the *cup hu girngsi,* but she was acutely aware of how ridiculous it would sound. A week ago, if one of them had suddenly told her that a vampire was killing people in town, she wouldn't have taken it seriously either.

But the temptation was strong.

Maybe she could talk to them one-on-one.

Make sure that it is stopped.

Her brain suddenly felt heavy, slowed with the weight of responsibility as she recalled her grandmother's words. Her grandmother was right. If she knew what was happening, it was her moral duty to tell everyone she could, to let them know so that they could protect themselves against it. But how could she make anyone believe her? People were already talking about vampires—the subject was not that far from people's minds—but what could she say that would convince them that it was true?

And what did she know about protection against a *cup hu girngsi?*

She absently fingered the jade around her neck. She would have to talk to her grandmother, get some more information.

"I don't like any of them," Roxanne was saying. She turned to Sue. "What about you?"

"Huh?" Sue blinked, caught off guard.

"Horror movies. Do you like horror movies?"

Sue slowly shook her head. "No," she said. "I don't."

"See?" Roxanne grinned triumphantly. "Sue doesn't like them either."

Roxanne and Shelly had already left in Shelly's Dart, and Sue walked with Janine across the parking lot to her car. There was the hint of a chill in the air, a promise that the unnaturally warm weather would soon shift back to its normal patterns. It was not that late and across the street, at the theater, the early evening show was just getting out while the line for the second show was beginning to form at the side of the building. Even amidst all this, activity, Sue felt nervous. Her attention was concentrated on the pools of shadow next to each car, the darkened area next to the dumpster at the side of the cafe, the alley next to the movie theater.

The places a monster could hide.

She wanted to tell herself that she was being stupid. But she didn't think she was.

They reached the Honda. Janine opened her purse, withdrew her keys. She looked up at Sue but did not quite meet her eyes. "Can I ask you a question? A personal question?"

"Of course. You don't even have to ask."

"Have you . . . have you ever done it?"

"Done what?"

"You know, had sex?"

Sue's face felt hot, flushed. "Not . . . exactly. Not all the way. Why?"

"I'm pregnant," Janine said.

Sue stared at her in shock. "Really?"

Janine nodded.

"Who is it?"

"No one you know."

"God." Sue leaned against the Honda's hatchback. "This is serious stuff."

"I didn't want to say anything in front of Shelly or Roxanne because . . . well, you know Shelly. She'd give me a twenty-minute lecture. And Roxanne . . . It'd be all over town in an hour."

"Have you told your parents?"

Janine shook her head.

"Are you going to?"

"I don't know."

"Are you"—Sue's voice was too high, and she coughed—"going to keep it?"

Janine shrugged, and the gesture suddenly seemed so adult. "I don't know."

"How did it happen?"

Jane smiled wryly. "I know your family doesn't like to talk about sex, but I thought you'd learned about the birds and bees by now . . ."

"You know what I mean."

She sighed. "He was staying at the ranch, and he thought I was staying there too, and . . . I didn't bother to straighten him out."

"God, this sounds like a TV show."

Janine smiled. "Yeah, *The Flintstones*. The one where Fred and Barney first meet Wilma and Betty at that hotel where they're working?"

"So what happened?"

"I was off work, in my street clothes, and I was standing by the bar. He was waiting to get in, and we sort of struck up a conversation. I ended up having dinner with him. He'd come to the ranch with two friends, but they were on the overnight Cowboy Campout. He hadn't wanted to go, so he'd stayed behind, you know, to swim and hang around. After dinner, he asked if he could walk me back to my room. By that time, I didn't want to admit that I worked there, so I said no. He asked if I wanted to come up to his room."

"And you said yes."

"Yes."

"How could you?" Sue shook her head. "What if he had AIDS? You knew nothing about this guy."

Janine smiled. "I knew he was cute."

"I'm serious."

"It's been a long time, you know? I mean, I broke up with Jim almost two years ago, and there hasn't been anyone else who's even interested. That's the problem with this damn town. When you're born here, you know everyone in it. I mean, do you think you're actually going to find someone here?"

"No."

"Me either. And this guy . . . I don't know. I liked him; he liked me. We just sort of hit it off."

"What are you going to do now?"

"I have no idea."

Sue stared up at the sky, at the wash of stars against the moonless backdrop of night. She felt strange, adrift, disassociated from the events around her. The world she had lived in, the world she had known, had changed, moved from clearly defined black-and-white into a shifting realm of shadows. Janine was pregnant by a stranger. Yet she was not a slut or a whore, merely a frightened friend who was being unjustly punished for an understandable transgression. The supernatural, which had been merely the fictional basis for books and movies, a conceit of popular entertainment, had suddenly moved from the periphery of make-believe to the arena of reality.

Reminded again of the *cup hu girngsi,* she looked behind her, through the back window into the car. The Honda's seats were hulking black shapes in the enclosed darkness of the interior. The area in front of the vehicle was completely obscured by the night's gloom.

"Let's drive around for a while," she said.

"And talk?"

Sue nodded. "There's a lot to talk about."

"I wish there weren't." Janine moved around to the driver's side, opened her door, and got in. She unlocked the passenger door for Sue.

Maybe I'll tell her about the cup hu girngsi, Sue thought as she buckled her seat belt. But then she looked at the hopelessness on her friend's face and decided that this was not the time.

Janine started the car, backed out of the parking lot.

"Are you sure you're pregnant?" Sue asked.

"Positive. I took an EPT."

"Those things aren't supposed to be that reliable."

"I'm a month late."

"Oh." Sue didn't know what to say to that.

They headed down the highway.

It was after midnight when Sue finally arrived home. Janine dropped her off in front of the house and waited until she had reached the porch before taking off. Nothing had been decided, no resolutions had been made, but Sue knew that her friend felt better for having talked it all out.

Everyone was asleep, and the house was silent as she let herself in. She had hoped that her grandmother would be awake, but there was no sound coming from her room, and no light shone from beneath the door. In her mind, Sue saw her grandmother lying in bed, arms folded across her chest, bone white and drained of blood, her face that of an ancient mummy. She was tempted to knock on the door just to reassure herself that the old woman was still alive, but she knew that it would probably wake her parents as well, and she continued down the hall to her own room.

She locked her door, checked her window to see if it was closed, and felt the half-circle lock on top of the sill to make sure it was fastened before taking off her clothes, putting on her nightgown, and crawling into bed.

Thirty-three

Janine wheeled the towel cart down to the laundry. The laundry room door was open, and the visibly escaping steam humidified the hallway outside. She quickly pushed the cart through the doorway to Ramon and backed away before she started to sweat and her makeup began to run. She was scheduled to work the desk this afternoon, and she couldn't very well take care of guests looking like the Bride of Frankenstein.

She waved to Ramon and Jose, then ducked out of the building and walked outside, around the boulder-enclosed pool, to the vending machines. She popped two quarters and a dime into the coin slot, pushed the button for Diet Coke, gave the machine a quick kick, and her can tumbled down into the cradle. She popped the tab and took a long drink.

She turned around, watched the two couples at the pool for a moment. The two guys and one of the women were swimming, but the other woman, obviously pregnant, was lying on one of the chaise lounges in a maternity one-piece, casually reading a magazine.

One of the men said something, the pregnant woman turned, looked at Janine, and their eyes met. Janine glanced away and started walking toward the main building, moving behind the boulders so she couldn't be seen.

She walked slowly, sipping her drink, trying to finish it before she got to the lobby steps. She was still not sure how she was going to explain her pregnancy to her mom. She was not even sure how her mom would react. Her parents had gotten married when they were both seniors in high school, because they'd had to, because her mom had been pregnant with her. It was amazing to Janine how much her parents seemed to have forgotten from their younger days, how rigid and moralistic and unyielding they'd become in their attitudes toward her.

Janine felt bad about what she'd told Sue. She'd given her friend an overly romantic impression of what had occurred, and she knew she shouldn't have. But she simply had not been able to bring herself to tell the truth because the truth was so sleazy and sordid and cheap. The truth was that she'd been filling in for Patty Pullen, cleaning one of the rooms, and Cutler, the new handyman, had seen the open door, walked in, and come on to her.

They'd done it there on the unmade bed.

She had not been sure then or afterward why she had done such a thing, why she had gone along with his crude suggestion. She wasn't a slut, at least she didn't think of herself as one, but she couldn't deny the fact that she'd agreed, with very little prompting, to have sex with a guy she barely knew, didn't really like, and whose first name she didn't even know.

And now he seemed to have disappeared.

She'd fucked up royally this time.

There'd been close calls in the past. The time after the Winter Formal in high school when she'd gotten drunk and nearly rolled her mom's car, making up an elaborate excuse about a crazy hit-and-run driver who'd forced her off the road. The time one of her mom's friends had seen her topless in the backseat of Bill Halley's Buick, and she'd had to go to the woman's house and actually burst into tears to get her to promise that she wouldn't tell her mom. But there'd been nothing like this. Those were minor inconveniences. This was a major problem.

This could affect the rest of her life.

She looked down at her abdomen, which, thankfully, was still not showing. She was leaning toward getting an abortion, she thought it was probably the quickest and cleanest way out of this mess, but the idea frightened her, and she had no idea how to go about it.

She needed to talk to her mom.

Janine finished her Diet Coke, wiped her wet hands on her jeans, and straightened her cowgirl vest before walking inside.

Sally Mae was working the front desk, and the older woman greeted her with a relieved smile when Janine walked through the door. "I was afraid you weren't going to show up."

Janine frowned. "I'm not late."

Sally Mae laughed. "No, I didn't mean that. It's just that I have a big date tonight, and I had this horrible feeling that something was going to happen to ruin it for me. Let's face it, dear, my luck with men hasn't been all good."

Janine smiled. "Go on. Get out of here."

"My shift isn't quite—"

"I'll cover for you."

"You're a good girl."

"That's debatable," Janine said. She glanced down at today's event schedule, posted on the counter. "So where did you meet this guy? Not here?"

"Oh, no. We met at church." Sally Mae lowered her voice. "He's one of the men who volunteered to work on the church for the Second Coming."

Janine's smile froze on her face. She stared at the older woman, not sure how to respond. "Oh," she said non-committally.

"He's going to introduce me to Jesus."

Goose bumps arose on Janine's arms. "Well, you'd better get going," she said. "I can handle things here."

Sally Mae put an arm around her shoulders and gave her a quick squeeze. "Thanks. I owe you."

Janine stood behind the counter, unmoving, and watched as the other woman grabbed her purse and, waving, walked out the door.

She looked down at her stomach and, for the thousandth time that day, placed her palm on it.

Thirty-four

It was a somber rather than festive Columbus Day. A three-day weekend for many people in the state, Columbus was the only holiday between Labor Day and Thanksgiving, and a lot of local businesses counted on the extra influx of tourists to get them through the season. But though the tourists were here today, the businesses weren't. An inordinate number of stores were closed, and there was a general feeling of confused disorder along both the Highway 370 and Highway 95 shopping districts.

There were also a hell of a lot of crosses propped up in the closed storefront windows, and the funny thing was that Robert was not sure if the crosses were being displayed to ward off vampires or as a show of faith in Jesus Christ. People were not about to tell him which one it was, either. The sheriff had never been the most popular man in town—generally speaking, when he came in contact with people it was because they had done something wrong—but he was usually treated with respect. Not these days, though.

Things had changed.

He stood next to his cruiser in the Basha's parking lot, looking out over the forked intersection of 370 and 95. The afternoon was hot, and the highways were crowded, the gas stations and the parking lot of the Circle K filled with campers and motorcycles, boat and jet ski trailers. People from the Valley. Weekend warriors. Most of them were probably going up to Roosevelt, but some, he knew, would be off-roading. A few might even decide to stay in the area and spend the day at the river.

With a sinking feeling, he tried to imagine what would happen if a man or woman or, worse yet, a child from Mesa or Tempe or Phoenix, was found lying in the brush, drained of blood.

Robert stared at the mini–traffic jam on Highway 370 immediately in front of the shopping center. He felt as though things were out of control, and he was at the whim of events he could not influence. There was no way in hell that his men could keep tabs on everyone. They could only hope that there were no attacks. No deaths.

He'd ordered all policemen on duty today, Saturday, and Sunday to eschew the usual ticketing of minor violations and concentrate instead on preventative law enforcement: making sure that high-risk areas of the town and surrounding desert were adequately patrolled, keeping track of anyone or anything suspicious. Rossiter had told him that attempting to keep tabs on recreationers was a fool's errand, but despite what the FBI agent said, Robert felt obligated to try. This was *his* town, goddamnit, and he couldn't be expected to stand around and wait for someone else to get killed without trying to do something.

Earlier in the week, he'd told his men to cooperate with the feds, but his manner must have spoken louder than his words because that cooperation had been grudging at best. He was sure that someone, somewhere down the line, was going to piss and moan about his attitude, and as he stared at a line of brake lights and listened to the sound of angry car horns, he wondered if there would be repercussions. His job certainly wasn't in danger—the town's police force and the FBI ran on different tracks in regard to personnel matters—but he had no doubt that Rossiter, could drown him in a shit storm of bureaucracy.

Hell, maybe he would be better off if his job was taken

away. It would force him to get out of this town and do something with his life.

Robert waved to Mona Payne, who passed by on her three-wheeled bike. Once again, he thought of the rumor a few years back that satanists had been meeting by the river. He'd heard the story from Garden Teague, not the world's most reliable source, and he'd put the old man's account of robed figures, bonfires, and ritualistic chanting down to the DTs. If Garden had seen anything, he reasoned, it had been some high school football players trying to score with their dates around a campfire, and it was only his inebriated mind that had cast it in such a sinister light.

Now he was not so sure.

He knew that the rumors had never entirely gone away, and that people other than Garden Teague believed them. On slow nights, he and Frank Teller had made occasional trips out to the river, just to check out the situation. They'd never found anything, had never even come across the smoldering remains of a campfire, but he found himself wondering now if perhaps Garden had really seen something. Maybe there were a group of satanists in Rio Verde who were into human sacrifice and blood drinking. It was certainly more plausible than the idea that a vampire was running around loose.

Vampire?

Or vampires?

Robert ran a hand through his thinning hair, took another look at the traffic, then got into his cruiser, started the engine, and waited for a break between vehicles to speed across the highway. He cut through the dirt alley on the side of the Dairy Queen and turned right on Copperhead, pulling into the parking lot of the public library.

As usual, the place was empty. Mrs. Church, the librarian and the only other person in the building, was sitting behind the front desk reading a Sue Grafton novel. The only noise was the faint sound of an air conditioner.

People in Rio Verde didn't read much, Robert knew. They weren't illiterate, Mrs. Church had told him once, they were postliterate. They knew *how* to read—but books simply were not part of their lives. Robert wasn't sure he agreed with her, but the fact remained that aside from a core group of senior citizens, the only people who consistently used the library were students with report deadlines.

It had been a while since he'd been in here himself, but when he opened the door and stepped inside, it was like stepping into a familiar home—his grandparents' perhaps—so strong were the emotional echoes and sense of belonging. As always, the comforting odor of books was mixed with that faint lemony scent of furniture polish he'd never encountered anywhere else. On the walls were posters for the library's summer reading program, the Reading Olympics. The same posters had been used for the past thirty years. He remembered winning a bronze medal in the summer before sixth grade for his vacation reading efforts. Rich had won a gold medal.

"It's been a while, Robert Carter."

He looked up at Mrs. Church, who had put down her novel and was smiling at him. He nodded sheepishly, feeling like a ten-year-old in the presence of the old librarian.

"You haven't been in here in quite some time."

"I've been buying my books," he said to defend himself.

She laughed, and her laugh wasn't intimidating at all. "I wasn't criticizing you, Robert. I know you and your brother both read."

He stepped across the shiny waxed floor to the front desk, boots echoing on the tile.

The librarian stood. "You want some books on vampires, don't you?"

That was one thing he'd never gotten used to: Mrs. Church's ability to know, before you asked, why you'd come in here and what you wanted. As children, he and Rich had speculated on that subject. Rich's theory had always been that their mother called ahead and told the librarian what books the two of them were interested in that week. But, Robert had argued, why would their mother go to such lengths? It made no sense. He'd thought it was some form of ESP.

"Yes," he said. "Vampires."

"It's a popular subject this week. I'm not sure we have any books left. Why don't you check that middle aisle in back of the card catalogue. Top shelf, right side. We have our nonfiction volumes there. I assume you're looking for nonfiction?"

"Yes."

"Check there."

In all of his visits to the library over the years, Robert could not remember ever having used the card catalogue. Each time he had wanted a book on a particular subject, or even a specific work, Mrs. Church had always told him exactly where to go.

He walked around the dark wood of the catalogue and stepped into the middle aisle. Sure enough, all of the volumes were gone, only an empty space where they should have been. He quickly scanned the adjoining shelves, on the off chance that the books had been put back incorrectly, then poked his head around the corner of the aisle. "Do you have anything else on vampires?"

"There is general information in encyclopedias and reference books, and we do have a few overviews of the supernatural that would no doubt have information on the subject. Hold on a minute. Let me check. Maybe one of those books has been returned. I haven't looked in the bin this morning."

He walked back around to the front desk, and Mrs.

Church emerged from the back room beaming, four books in her hand. "Here we go. Because of the popularity of this subject right now, I've given these books a three-day checkout time instead of the usual two weeks."

Robert grinned. "You expect me to bring these back in three days?"

"You'll be fined if you don't, Robert Carter."

His grin withered under her stern gaze. "Sorry," he said meekly. "I was just joking."

She smiled. "So was I. You have a two-day grace period." She winked at him. "You think I don't know you by now?"

Robert glanced at the titles of the books: *The Vampire: His Kith and Kin* by Montague Summers; *The Vampire in Legend, Fact and Art* by Basil Copper; *The Book of Vampires* by Dudley Wright; *The Vampire: Monster and Metaphor* by Eugenia deSprague. He handed Mrs. Church his library card. She stamped two date cards, placed them in the pockets of the books, and handed everything back to him. "Is this sudden interest in vampires personal?" she asked. "Or professional?"

"Personal. I guess."

"But it might be both?"

He nodded. "It might be both."

She smiled at him, but there was a hint of worry in her smile this time. "I hope you find what you're looking for."

"I hope so, too," he said.

On his way back to the station, Robert stopped by the newspaper office. Rich was in the pasteup room, carefully placing black border tape around an ad at the bottom of one of the pages.

"Another big issue," Robert said, glancing at the layout, of the front page on the nearest light table.

"Let's hope it's the last." Rich cut the border tape with

an X-acto knife. "Anything new I should know about? We don't put the paper to bed until Wednesday. There's still time to rearrange the front page."

"We'll see what tonight brings." Robert sat down in the metal folding chair next to the waxer. "Who's the babe?"

Rich frowned. "The babe?"

"The Oriental chick at Corrie's desk." Robert leaned back until his head was against the wall and the chair was resting on two legs.

Rich shook his head. "That's Sue Wing. I just hired her on as a production assistant and part-time reporter. Her family owns the Chinese restaurant."

Robert grinned. "Anything going on here that I should know about?"

"I'm not even going to dignify that with a response."

"I just thought that since she'd taken over Corrie's job here at the paper, she might be taking over some of her other duties too."

"Jesus, sometimes you can be a real asshole."

Robert laughed, setting the front legs of his chair back on the ground. "Hit a nerve, huh?"

"No. She's a nice girl, and I don't want you talking behind her back. You're the police chief, for God's sake. Haven't you ever heard of sexual harassment?"

"Heard of it."

"Your neck's getting redder by the day."

Robert stood. "Seriously. Aren't you going to introduce us?"

Rich put down the X-acto knife. "If you can behave yourself and pretend to be a human being."

"I'll try." He followed his brother out into the newsroom. Sue looked up as they approached. She was pretty, Robert thought. In their younger days, they both might've made a play for her.

"Sue?" Rich said. "This is Robert, my brother, our esteemed chief of police."

She smiled shyly. "Hello."

"Hi," Robert said.

"Sue, our reporter-slash-photographer-slash-production assistant, was the lone student in my aborted journalism class."

"Whatever happened with that?" Robert asked. "Did Pueblo ever pay you? What's the deal?"

"We worked out an arrangement. The class was canceled, but technically Sue's still enrolled because she's earning credits for her work experience here. So, technically, I'm still her teacher."

Robert chuckled. "Fill out an application at Taco Bell," he said to Sue. "You'll make a heck of a lot more than you will as a reporter."

She smiled at him. "I'm in it for fame, not fortune."

"You'll get more notice at Taco Bell too. And more respect."

"He's just jealous," Rich told her. "Ignore him." He turned to his brother, motioned toward his desk. "Come on, let her get back to work, have a seat over here."

"I have to get a move on myself." Robert nodded at Sue. "Nice meeting you."

Rich followed his brother around the partition, past Carole's desk, through the front door. "That's what you stopped by for?"

"Actually, I've been getting quite a few complaints the past couple days about Wheeler's church. People there on Arrow say they don't like all that hammering and racket going on all hours of the night."

"That's understandable."

"I talked to the man, gave him a friendly warning, but it was like talking to a wall. He had that damn phony smile plastered on his face, and he kept nodding and agreeing with me, but he didn't listen to a single thing I said."

"What do you want me to do, write an article about it? I'll tell you right now, I'm not taking on a church."

"No, that's not it."

"You want my advice? Get him on noise violations. Throw his butt in jail."

"Rio Verde has no municipal codes coveting noise, hard as that may be to believe. When there's a loud party or something, we usually just issue a warning and things quiet down. If the situation gets too rowdy, we can usually crack down and cite other violations. But Wheeler knows his laws. I suspect he's skirted enough of them in his time to know where the borders lie. He can build all night if he wants to, hammer from dusk to dawn, and he knows it."

"So?"

"So, to tell you the truth, I thought maybe you could get Corrie to talk to him."

"You can forget about that right now."

"He won't listen to her?"

"She won't listen to me."

Robert sighed. "I thought I'd give it a shot. With everything else collapsing around my damn ears, I thought maybe I could take the easy way out and solve the problem with a minimum of hassle. I don't want all those fanatics picketing the station because Jesus told them to build their church, and I told them to keep it quiet after dark."

"Well, I could try to talk to Corrie—"

He shook his head. "Thanks anyway, but don't bother. I'll just try to bully the jerk. Maybe he'll cave."

"I doubt it."

"I doubt it, too."

"Listen, you want to come by for dinner tonight after work?"

"Can't. I'm busy."

"We'll eat late."

Robert looked at his brother. "How come you never come over to my house? How come I always have to go over to yours?"

"Okay, forget it, then."

"No, I'm serious. Why?"

Rich shifted his weight uncomfortably from one foot to the other. "We're closer to town."

"That's not it and you know it."

"You ever thought of getting a dog or a cat? Something to keep you company?"

"Stop changing the subject."

"That is the subject. It' always seems so . . . so lonely out at Mom's place."

"My place."

"Your place. See? Even after all this time, I still think of it as Mom's."

"You two used to come over when Julie was there."

Rich forced himself to smile. "We'll come over sometime this month, all right? We'll have a barbecue."

"I'm not trying to force you."

"Let's not start that crap."

Robert smiled tiredly. "Okay, okay. We'll talk about it later." He opened his car door. "I'd better get back, check in, see who else has been murdered."

"That's not funny."

"No, it's not."

"Have you gone by Billy's garage sale lately?"

"You know I avoid that eyesore like the plague."

"You ought to check out what he's selling."

Robert ran a hand through his hair. Billy Gurdy had had a garage sale every weekend for the past twenty years. The rows of tables set up on the dirt in front of the ramshackle hut he called home were permanent, and although everyone knew that referring to his open-air thrift store as a "garage sale" was just a way to get out of paying for a business license, no one ever called him on it. He was poor enough as it was—and as old as God to boot— and if it made him happy to circumvent county statutes by hawking his wares in front of his house each Saturday and Sunday, well, what was the harm in that?

Rich had always liked Billy, although Robert couldn't stand him. Rich claimed that it was because the old man had caught Robert stealing prickly pears off his cactus back when he was in junior high, and Robert had to admit that there might be something to that.

"I'll bite," Robert said. "What's he selling?"

"Vampire kits."

"Vampire kits?"

"Shoeboxes filled with cloves of garlic and popsicle stick crosses."

"Jesus."

"He told me he's sold over thirty of them already."

"You going to do a story on it?"

"You're the one who thinks there's a monster out there."

"Oh, it's my fault Billy's an opportunistic con artist."

"That's not what I said, and you know it."

"Okay, I'll go by and talk to him."

"I think you should."

Robert got in the cruiser, closed the door, and rolled down the window. He looked up at his brother. "You want to do an editorial for me on unwanted federal intervention in local law enforcement?"

"No, but you're free to write a letter."

"That's what I thought." He started the engine. "Later"

"See you."

He backed out of the newspaper office's parking lot and headed toward the highway.

Thirty-five

Corrie pulled up in front of the church, turned off the ignition, and sat for a moment in the car, watching the other parishioners file in. Rich had refused to let Anna accompany her today, and while she'd been angry and argued with him, a part of her—a deep maternal part of her—was also relieved, and she had not pressed the point as strongly as she could have. She was mad at Rich, but in a roundabout way, she was grateful to him for having taken the responsibility away from her.

She watched as Whit Stasson's family entered the church together. The crowd had thinned from a flood to a trickle, so Corrie exited the car and hurried into the church, afraid that she might be late, that she might miss part of the sermon.

The services were getting more crowded. More people were attending each week.

Maybe the Pastor Dan Wheeler had put the fear of God into them.

Wheeler emerged from the vestibule only seconds after she'd found a seat, and, without preface, he began speaking. As always the smooth oratorical tones of his melodious voice filled the church. Corrie heard the words, understood their meaning, but at the same time was lulled by the voice.

" 'Now could I drink hot blood,' " the pastor quoted. "That's what Jesus said after throwing the moneylenders

Thirty-six

The humidity was going to go up tomorrow. Terry Clifford could feel it in his bad leg. The damn thing hurt like hell, felt like it was a fucking pincushion below the kneecap, and it only did that when they were going to have rain or a real sweatbasket motherhumper of a day.

There were no rain clouds blocking the stars tonight.

When was this unnatural weather going to end?

Terry limped down the kitchen steps and hobbled across the man-made meadow in back of the main building. He heard screams and splashes coming from the pool area. Those young California jocks, no doubt, trying to impress the bimbos they'd brought along on this trip. He crossed the lighted path that led between the buildings and continued in back of the sleeping quarters. From the open window of one of the guest rooms, he heard the sounds of an argument backed by a soundtrack of gunfire from the TV.

Cable, he thought. Now that was a damn brilliant invention. If they'd had cable or satellite TV when he was riding the range, he might've stuck with it. If he could've come back to the bunkhouse after a day of roping and branding and watched some sex and shooting, he might still be back in Wyoming today.

Might.

Probably not.

Truth was, he was never cut out to be a cowboy. Not a

real one. He had the knowledge, he had the skills, he had the talent, but he didn't have the temperament. There was only so much of that lonesome self-sufficient don't-need-nuthin'-but-my-horse crap he could take. It looked ~~great in the~~ movies. When John Wayne and Alan Ladd rode tall in their saddles, afraid of nothing and nobody, he couldn't imagine anyone not wanting to be like them. But the reality of the cowboy life, working ten hours at a stretch, not being able to bathe for days at a time, eating shitty food, sleeping in worn bedrolls on top of rocks and ruts, being bitten alive by bugs, waking up in the middle of the night and listening to the farting of the animals and the sound of other men beating off—that was something else.

He needed people, noise, light, civilization. He liked cowboying, but he had to admit that he was a dude at heart.

That was why he felt so lucky to have gotten in at the Rocking D.

He'd been up in Payson for the rodeo when he'd heard through the grapevine that a dude ranch was opening down in Rio Verde and that the owner was looking for a horseman to manage the stables. He'd never heard of Rio Verde, had never done any stable work or horse maintenance for an animal other than his own, but the promise of a clean bed, a steady paycheck, and access to a hotel-style swimming pool sounded mighty good. The other cowboys laughed off the idea, deriding it as pansy work, but he'd immediately hitched a ride to Globe and then to Rio Verde, where he lied through his teeth to the ranch manager who interviewed him. The manager was a city boy, and though Terry thought the man would catch on to him eventually, he figured he would have a good relaxing few weeks of work before anyone discovered that he wasn't qualified for the position.

Only no one ever discovered it. He knew more about

horses than anyone else who worked at the ranch, more than Hollis or any of his employees, more than any of the guests, and apparently that was good enough. And, of course, in time, he had learned by experience, through trial and error, and actually had become qualified for the job.

Now he was damn good at it, if he did say so himself.

The stables were separated from the rest of the ranch by a short stretch of artificially landscaped desert, a football-field-length section of ground that featured all of Arizona's most famous and photogenic desert shrubs and cacti placed in well-thought-out order. The stables were located away from the eating, sleeping, and recreation areas in order to foster the impression that this was an actual working ranch—and to ensure that guests weren't disturbed by the sounds and smells of horses. They could feel like real ranch hands when they fed the animals, when they saddled up and rode the preexisting trails, but when they returned to their rooms or went to the dining hall or the pool, they needed to be able to leave that all behind. They were paying for fantasy, not reality.

Terry had been thinking a lot about fantasy lately, about ghosts and monsters, legends and rumors. He was supposed to be a rough, tough hombre, and for the most part he played the role well, but he'd become increasingly nervous the past few weeks about these nightly checkup runs. Ordinarily, he enjoyed his last lone visit to the stables each evening, relishing the time spent with the animals. His animals. It was here that he allowed himself to look with pride upon his accomplishments of the day, and it was here he felt most acutely his contribution to the success of the ranch. Since the murder of Manuel Torres, however, that peace of mind had been disintegrating. Each time he went out here now, the desert seemed darker, the stable area more deserted. More than once, he had thought that if something came for him here, no one at the ranch would hear it. His body would not be found until morning.

Terry was not an overly superstitious man. He didn't have the type of imagination that saw aliens in every falling star or creatures in every shadow. But he had seen and heard enough over the years that he did not automatically dismiss such things out of hand. He'd heard tell of cursed Indian ground, haunted stretches of road, ghost towns that were home to actual ghosts. He knew the stories about the Mogollon Monster up in the Rim Country, had heard firsthand about the dangers of staying too long in the Superstitions. He'd also known Manuel Torres, and the old mechanic's death had hit him hard. Manuel had worked on most of the vehicles here at the ranch, had been the one to rebuild the engine on his own pickup, and Terry could not get used to the idea that all of his blood had been sucked out through a bite in his neck. No matter how you looked at it, that just wasn't something that was possible for a human being to do.

That was the work of a vampire.

Vampire talk was all around town, in the feed store, in Basha's, at First Interstate, practically every place he went. Hollis forbade such talk at the ranch, determined to keep his guests out of earshot of local news, but there was talk here too. Ran McGregor, one of the trail guides, had whispered to him the other day that he'd seen a coyote lying off in the brush that looked like all its innards had been sucked out, that looked like a pelt laid over a skeleton.

Maybe he was reading interpretations into things that weren't there, but it seemed to him that the horses had been a bit skittish lately too, and that worried him. He knew that animals were more attuned to changes in their environment than people were, more instinctive in their perceptions, and he couldn't help wondering as he came out here each night if something was out there in the darkness waiting for him.

For the past few weeks, and especially the past week, since the kids' bodies had been found in the river, his nightly rounds had been much less thorough than they usually were.

He reached the back of the stables and grabbed the railing at the side of the building as he slid down the dirt incline to the front. Before him, a long row of horse stalls stretched into the darkness, the identical black squares above the bottom gates through which the heads and necks of the horses usually protruded now empty. He stood there for a moment, not sure if he should proceed or hightail it back to the lighted safety of his quarters. Something was definitely wrong. Ordinarily, when the horses heard him slide down the short slope at the side of the building, they became restless, whinnying and snorting, moving around in their stalls, anticipating the late-night snack he usually fed them. But tonight there was nothing, no snuffling or snorting, no sticking of heads out the open top halves of stalls.

There was something else wrong too, something different, something he couldn't quite put his finger on.

Terry reached over, next to the closed door of the tool room, and turned the metal knob on the outside wall. The knob clicked, and the series of overhanging lights above the stalls winked into existence. There was a stirring in the first stall and Jasper, the ranch's largest sorrel stallion whinnied and poked his head around the edge of the opening.

"Hey, Jasper," Terry said. He walked over and patted the horse's head. The fear he'd felt a moment before was gone, but the sense of unease remained.

Terry looked around. There were shadows outside the stable yard, areas of fuzzy blackness surrounding the saguaros and palo verdes, troughs of darkness in the low ditch running parallel to the riding trail. There was no moon. It would be up in the early morning and would hang there pale and emasculated in the blue light of day until sometime around noon, but for now it was nowhere to be seen, and the world was black, the combined brilliance of billions of stars failing to make even a dent in the dark desert night.

Behind him Jasper whinnied, a quiet sound of fear, the familiar warning noise he made when he could smell something he didn't like but had not yet seen it. The horse shuffled, backing into the wall of his stall, causing the old boards to make a cracking, creaking sound. Other than that, the stable area was quiet. No sounds from the other horses. No faint music from the guest rooms of the ranch. No barking dogs. No cicadas.

No cicadas.

Terry knew now why he had felt so nervous, why something had felt so wrong. The cicadas were silent. Their familiar background chirruping, something he took for granted and usually didn't notice at all, was missing, and it was the absence of that sound which had set him on edge.

What could scare cicadas into silence?

It was a good question, but he did not want to know the answer. He found himself thinking of Manuel lying in the arroyo, of those kids' bodies trapped in cottonwood roots by the edge of the river. Cicadas didn't scare. They just didn't. They could be startled and temporarily hushed, but they got used to situations almost immediately. If a person walked up to a tree in which the insects were roosting, they would shut up for a second, then would start up again, instantly adapting to the person's presence.

But the cicadas had been silent now for over five minutes.

Terry realized that he had not heard a single sound from any of the stalls other than Jasper's, and he limped to the next stall over, peeking in.

Betty, the ranch's cutest filly, was lying crumpled and shrunken on the straw, half in shadow, half in the light. Even in that partial visibility, he could see that her body had been drained of blood and probably a lot of other things as well. Her well-muscled legs were thin straight sticks, and her ribs showed in shadowed slats across her stomach. There was a sickening stench of rot and decay in the small enclosure.

Terry backed up, nearly gagging, and hurried as quickly as he could past Jasper's stall—just as the horse crumpled to the ground.

The vampire!

His leg was hurting like a bastard, but he tried to ignore the pain and pull himself up the incline at the side of the building using the railing.

A black shape loomed out of the darkness above him.

Terry would have fallen had he not been holding the handrail. He stared upward. There was something about the shape that was familiar to him, and he might have thought he'd seen the figure before, as a child, only he knew instinctively that that was impossible because the shape was so old, so very ancient, and he knew that nothing like it had been seen since long before his birth.

It was large, its bulk blotting out the Big Dipper in the sky behind it, and it began to move slowly forward, down the incline toward him. It moved smoothly, as though not propelled by legs or feet. It did not gain clarity as it approached, the details of its face and form were not revealed; it remained as murkily vague as it had at the top of the short slope, but as it drew nearer he could hear it, a sound like liquid, like water.

"Love," the figure whispered, and its voice was low and assured and filled with the confidence of age. Terry heard wind in that whisper, and sand, and years.

Years.

Love?

He wanted to turn, wanted to run, but he couldn't. He was frozen in place, and he realized that even if he had been able to move, his gimp leg would not have enabled him to run fast enough to escape.

A slimy hand pulled his own fingers from the handrail, closing over his fist. Another slipped around his body, lifted him up.

He smelled rot, death.

The figure spoke again, and Terry realized that the word it had spoken before had only sounded like "love."

What the shape had really said was *"blood."*

Thirty-seven

Rich was sitting on top of his desk, notepad on his lap and camera slung over his shoulder, waiting for Sue when she arrived at the newspaper office. He hopped off the desk when she walked into the newsroom. "Thank God you're here," he said. "I'm going to be covering the murders, and I need you to hold down the fort. You'll have to take over the normal news this week. Jim'll help you, but probably not much. He's got another job, and sports is just about all he can handle."

"Murders?" Sue said. "There were more?" She felt weak, almost dizzy, and slightly sick to her stomach. She wondered if she looked as bad as she felt.

Apparently not, because Rich looked straight at her and seemed to see nothing out of the ordinary. He nodded. "The groom at the Rocking D was killed last night. So were all of the ranch's horses."

Sue could not speak. Her mouth was dry, and she could only nod dumbly. There was a dark, empty feeling deep inside her. If she had only talked to Rich or his brother, told them what she knew, maybe this could've been avoided. Maybe the *cup hu girngsi* couldn't have—

But what did she know?

And why would anyone believe her?

And how could she have changed anything?

It didn't matter, she told herself. It was her responsibility to do what she could. If she hadn't wasted her weekend, if she'd talked to her grandmother the way she'd intended to and found out more about the *cup hu girngsi*, if she'd told Rich and his brother, maybe the town could have been alerted, precautions taken.

But the restaurant had been busy, she hadn't really had a chance to talk to her grandmother. Now she had the horrible feeling that time was running out. That if they did not do something, if they did not act *now*, it would be too late.

"It's a vampire," she said.

Rich stared at her. "What?"

"A vampire's killing all these people. We call it a *cup hu girngsi* in Cantonese."

"Not you too."

"My grandmother knows all about it."

"Hold it right there." Rich took a deep breath. "This is going to be a very hectic week. I know there's been a lot of talk about vampires, and that may turn out to be what's occurring here, but right now I need you to help me with the paper. If you can't do that, I'll tell you right now, you're not going to get any credits at the college, and I'll find someone else to do your work. I know this is harsh, and I don't want to sound unreasonable, but this is nearly an emergency situation. I need to be able to count on you."

"You can count on me, but I think we should let people know what's happening."

"That's what we're doing. We're a newspaper. That's our job. But it's not our job to tell people there are vampires murdering people when we don't know if that's the case. Right now, another person has been killed. It is our responsibility to report that death and the circumstances surrounding it, and not to speculate further. At this point, we let people draw their own conclusions. When a cause is discovered, when the murderer is caught, we will report that also."

Sue stared at Rich. She had never seen him this serious before, and she was a little taken aback at his intensity.

He seemed to recognize this himself, because he suddenly smiled. His smile was not as relaxed as it usually was, nor as natural. "Sorry," he said. "Things are a little tense around here today."

Sue nodded. "That's okay. I understand."

"You're going to be doing a lot of writing this week, and I'm going to need you here. Can your parents spare you?"

"I'll work something out."

"Are you sure?"

"Yeah."

Rich's phone rang, and he started to reach for it, but then he motioned for Sue to pick up the line. "Go ahead. You've got to start sometime."

She hurried around his desk, stood behind his empty chair, and grabbed the receiver. "Hello, *Rio Verde Gazette*, this is Mr. Carter's desk."

"You're not my desk," Rich whispered. "And you're not my secretary. Next time, say 'Newsroom.'"

She nodded at him, waved her hand, tried to concentrate on the call. She listened for a few moments, then said, "Wait a minute. I'll ask my editor." She put her hand over the mouthpiece of the phone. "It's a rancher who says his trees are dying. He wants us to do a story on it. What should I do?"

"Tell him we'll do the article, and set up an appointment."

Sue took her hand from the mouthpiece, told the man she would be happy to interview him for a story, and made an appointment for one o'clock. She scrambled around for some scratch paper, Rich handed her a pen, and she wrote down the address and phone number.

"Good job," Rich said after she hung up.

"That didn't sound like a story to me. I thought maybe

we should just refer him to the Forest Service or the Department of Agriculture or someone who could help him."

"This is one of the most important things you need to learn about the newspaper biz. In a town this size, you never turn down stories. No matter how dumb they might be. We have a tough enough time finding new things to write about each week. Sometimes we have to resort to rewriting press releases; sometimes even when we do find a legitimate story, the people involved won't talk. So when you get a guy offering you an interview, you jump on it." He pointed to a handwritten list on top of a pile of papers on the right side of his desk. "That's what you'll be responsible for this week. I'll still be doing all of the layout and most of the pasteup, I'll write most of the articles, but you'll have to take over the columns for me."

Sue licked her lips, wanting, needing to say something, but not knowing what. She felt flustered, thrust into something for which she was totally unprepared.

Rich smiled. "Relax. It's easy. The columns almost write themselves. All you have to do is collect the information when the sources call." He shifted the camera strap over his shoulder. "I'd better be going. You can sit at my desk if you want, use my VDT, but be careful that you don't erase anything. Use your own diskette"

"Wait. Where are you going? When will you be back?"

"The police station. I don't know when."

"What about when I go to the interview? What do I do about the office?"

"Carole will be here." He waved, walked around the partition, and out the front door.

Carole walked back into the newsroom a moment later. "Don't worry, dear." The secretary smiled warmly. "He lives for things like this, and despite what he says, he'll be in here more this week than he usually is. He's just hyper right now."

"But I'm not sure what he wants me to do."

"Just do what you always do. If you have any questions, ask him when he comes back." She looked at her watch, and her smile widened. "By my calculations, that should be an hour or two."

"Are you sure?"

"Positive. Besides, what's he going to do? He'll go out to the scene, talk to some people, talk to his brother, come back and write."

"It sounded like he was going to be gone all week."

"If he is, I'll eat this carpet."

Sue met the old secretary's gaze, and started to laugh. Carole shook her head. "Don't take him too seriously."

Sue suddenly felt much better. She glanced again at Rich's list, then put it back down on top of his pile of papers. From behind the front partition came the sound of the door opening, and, still smiling, Carole walked back out to her desk to see who it was.

Sue sat down in Rich's chair and picked up the phone to call her parents.

LeeAnne was seated behind the receptionist's desk when Rich walked into the police station. He pointed toward Robert's office, she nodded, and he stepped past her through the small gate in the front counter while she pretended to stare down at one of the typewritten pages on her desk.

Rich walked into Robert's office. His brother was on the phone, obviously talking to someone of whom he was not overly fond. He was scowling, trying to speak, but not able to get a word in edgewise. Finally he said, "I'm still the police chief here," and slammed down the phone.

"FBI?" Rich asked.

"That bastard's trying to freeze me out. Pretty soon I

won't be able to scratch my own nuts without asking his permission."

"Talk to his superior."

Robert paced around the room. "I can't think of anyone who isn't superior to that fascist fuckwad."

"I mean talk to his boss, his supervisor."

"I've tried. He's supposed to get back to me. When do you think that'll be? The next decade?"

Rich tapped his notebook on his leg. "I'd like to sit here and chat, but it's getting late. Are you ready to cruise out to the ranch?"

Robert nodded. "Yeah, sure. The body's gone, though. I think the horses are gone, too."

"That's okay. I just want to get a few photos of the site and some quotes from you and a couple of employees. Hollis, if he's available."

"Okay. Just let me make one more phone call, and then we're out of here."

"I have to take a whiz. I'll meet you out front."

Robert picked up the phone receiver, gave the "OK" sign, and started dialing.

Rich walked down the hall, past the tiny locker room, and into the bathroom. He stepped up to the first urinal and, a second later, heard the door open behind him.

Steve Hinkley stepped up to the adjoining urinal. "Nice day," he said.

What was it about cops, Rich wondered, that made them want to talk to you while you were taking a leak? He never had any desire to chat while he was relieving himself, but it seemed that every time he'd been in here and a policeman had walked into the bathroom, the policeman had stepped up to the urinal, unzipped, whipped it out, and started a conversation.

I don't want to talk, he wanted to say, I'm taking a piss. But instead he nodded, smiled, and said nothing.

"You're a writer. Did you ever think about writing for TV or the movies?"

Rich shook his head as he flushed, zipped up, and walked over to the sink.

"I bet you could get a TV movie out of all this vampire shit. You'd make a fortune."

Rich smiled as he wiped his hands on a paper towel and walked out of the bathroom. "I'll keep it in mind."

Robert was already waiting. He straightened up as Rich arrived, and the two of them headed out of the office. "I'll drive," Robert said.

Five minutes later, they were there.

The Rocking D.

As they drove through the entrance, Rich looked up at the logo—the letter "D" resting in the curve of a semi-circle. It had been carved into the sign above the road in such a way that it appeared burned into the wood, like a brand. He shook his head. The idea of a dude ranch in Rio Verde, or, more precisely, a dude resort, since no ranch work was done at the Rocking D, still seemed stupid and inappropriate to him, its artificial extravagance a mockery of the very real accomplishments of the town. As teenagers, he and his friends had referred to the place as the Walking Dick Ranch and to Hollis as the Walking Dick.

It was a sobriquet still used by a lot of those friends as adults.

Robert bypassed the ranch's paved guest road and turned off on the dirt service trail. The cruiser bumped over ruts and chuckholes, and turned off on a side trail that led down to the stables. A brown state police vehicle was already parked in front of the long building, as was a Rio Verde car. Someone was taking photographs inside one of the horse stalls, the flashes, like baby lightning, brightening the interior shadows at irregular intervals.

Robert grimaced as he pulled to a stop. "There may

be fireworks. The state and the FBI are pissed that I authorized Woods to take the body before they'd had time to see it."

"You think that was such a good idea? Maybe—"

"Whose side are you on?"

Rich got out of the car, held up his hands. "I'm staying out of it." He walked around the front of the cruiser and started toward the stall with the flashes.

A state policeman he hadn't seen emerged from behind an open stall door. "Stop right there. Where do you think you're going?"

Rich held up his camera. "Press."

"I'm sorry. This is a—"

"Let him through!" Robert yelled from behind. He pushed past Rich and stepped directly in front of the policeman. "I don't know how things work in Phoenix, but here in Rio Verde, we have a free press. Understand?"

"I have orders—"

"Fuck your orders."

"It's okay," a voice said from inside the stall. "I meant civilians. Keep out civilians."

"I just need a quick picture of the outside of the stables, then I'll get out of your way." Rich nudged his brother with an elbow as he walked past. "I'm on your side. All the way."

Mr. Overbeck was waiting for her on the porch steps in front of his house, and Sue recognized him from the restaurant as he stood up. She'd never known his name until today, but he'd come in quite often for lunch over the past year or so.

He smiled as she got out of the car, obviously recognizing her as well. "I didn't know you worked for the *Gazette*."

"I just started."

"Are you still working at the restaurant?"

"Yes. Both."

"That's great. Your parents must be very proud of you."

"Yes," she said.

"Well, come on in. You want something to drink? Coke? Water?"

"No, thank you. In fact, I'd like to see the trees first, if you don't mind. So I can get an idea of what you're talking about and take a few photos."

"Okay. Let's walk around this way." Overbeck led the way around the side of the house.

Sue looked down at the worn path as she walked. The jagged cracks in the sidewalk looked like horizontal lightning in a gray cement sky. The walkway ended abruptly at the back of the house, and they continued over hard dirt toward a low metal-roofed barn.

"I'm mostly into livestock, but as I told you over the phone, I got myself a little orchard back here. It's not much, I only got a few trees, but it keeps me in lemons, and I usually have some left over to sell. I've even sold some to your old man a couple times." They walked around the side of the barn, past an empty corral. "It's those ones there," he said, pointing toward a stand of citrus trees behind the building. "They just died overnight. Yesterday they was strong and healthy, one of 'em just starting to turn. Now look at 'em."

She saw what he meant. The trees, seven or eight of them, were dead, completely bare, although a circular hill of still-green leaves surrounded the base of each tree. As they moved closer, she could see that the trunks looked shriveled, the bark withered, dry, and peeling.

She felt a wave of cold wash over her, moving from her neck downward. *The trees dried up,* her grandmother had said.

Sue took off the lens cap of the camera, raised the viewfinder to her eye, focused, and snapped a picture. She moved the camera to a vertical position and took another. "Would you mind if I took a closer look?" she asked.

"Go right ahead."

"Do you have any idea what might have caused this?"

Overbeck shook his head. "Disease is gradual, and even bugs can't do this much damage overnight. I did notice a weird kinda notch on the side of one of the trees, though. I don't know if all of 'em have it. I haven't had time to look. I figure that might have some'm to do with it."

Sue's heart was pounding. "Could you show me?"

"Sure." He led the way over to the tree closest to the barn. Up close, Sue could see that underneath the peeling bark, the wood was dull gray and as wrinkled as a dried apple. "It's right here." He pointed just above his head at a large nick on one of the two main branches forking off from the trunk.

No, not a nick.

A bite.

She focused the camera, took a picture. Silently, she walked over to the next tree. Looking up, she saw, at approximately the same spot, another bite. In the pile of leaves at the base of the tree lay two dehydrated lemons.

She cleared her throat, took a deep breath, looked at Overbeck. "I think," she said, "that a vampire killed your trees."

When she returned to the paper, Rich was at his desk, furiously typing on his keyboard. She heard the rapidfire clicking of keys from behind the modular wall as she walked through the front door. Carole nodded knowingly toward the partition, smiled at her. "Good afternoon, sweetie."

"Afternoon," Sue said, smiling back.

Rich looked up as she entered the newsroom. She'd

been pretty shaken by the sight of the decimated orchard, but she'd stopped off at Circle K and made herself a Cherry Suicide—Orange Crush, Hires Root Beer, Dr Pepper, Sprite, and Cherry Coke—and had driven back slowly. That had given her time to compose herself.

"How did it go?" he asked.

"Pretty good," she said. She wasn't sure what she should say to him right now, how much she should tell. She thought it would probably be best to let him read it in the story. She'd felt foolish trying to tell Overbeck that she thought a *cup hu girngsi* had killed his trees, but the rancher had been surprisingly receptive to what she had to say, and though he hadn't wanted to come right out and say so in print, he had agreed to refer to the notches on the trees as "bites" and to state that they had not been there before the trees' deaths.

She did not feel comfortable talking about vampires to Rich, though.

The editor stood. "I was thinking. I may be very busy the next week or so, so I want to show you how to develop film so you can do it yourself. It'll save me some time and help me out quite a bit. Did you take a roll of the trees?"

Sue nodded. "Yes."

"Get the rancher with the trees?"

She shook her head, feeling the hot flush of embarrassment rush up her cheeks. "No. I forgot. I'm sorry. I—"

"No biggie. We may not use a photo with this one anyway. But I will use your roll to show you how to develop film. You have fifteen minutes to spare?"

"Yes."

"Let's do it now then." He turned down the intensity knob on his terminal. "Carole?" he called. "I'm showing Sue how to develop. We'll be in the darkroom. If Jim stops by, have him knock. Anyone else comes by, tell them to wait."

"Yes sir, boss!"

He grinned. "Knock it off."

"Yes sir!"

"Carole . . ."

"Okay, okay."

Rich stood, motioned toward the darkroom. "Shall we?"

Sue took the film out of the camera, put the camera—along with her notebook, purse, and pen—on her desk and followed Rich into the darkroom. He shut the door behind her, and for a brief second they were in complete darkness. He flipped on a red light. The illumination was bright compared to the jet-black of a moment before, and she found that she could actually see.

"When you first take the film out and roll it, you have to do it with no lights on at all, not even this safety bulb. This red light won't hurt prints, but it'll still expose film, so until the negatives are in the can, you have to do everything in total darkness. It'll be tough at first, because you have to do everything by touch, but you'll get used to it.

"All right. This is what's wound up on your roll. In complete darkness, you pop open one side of the roll, feel for the end of the film, and clip it here like so." He placed the end of the film strip in the spool and clamped it with a delicate wire clasp. "Then you roll the film." He wound the strip around the inside of the spool. "You place the whole thing in this can here, and then you're set. You can turn the safety light on."

"Do you have film I can practice on before I use a real roll?"

"Of course."

He started explaining about the chemicals and demonstrated how they were poured into the canister through a light-tight opening in the lid.

Sue glanced around the darkroom. Hanging by a clothespin from a wire strung over the sink, she saw negatives of a woman, a tall woman with dark curly hair. Sue was not close enough to make out facial features, but she assumed the woman was Rich's wife. She continued watching the editor demonstrate the sequence of development while sneaking peeks at the roll of negatives out of the corner of her eye. In the top frame, the woman was outside, in front of a flower garden, pointing at the camera, but in all the other pictures she was wearing sexy black lingerie, positioned in provocative poses on a bare bed.

In the final frame, she was naked.

Sue looked quickly away. Too quickly, she thought. He had to have seen the movement. But, no, he was still concentrating on a plastic container of chemical solution. "Then," he said, "you take the negatives out, wash them in the sink, and, *voila!* they're done."

She nodded her understanding. He probably didn't realize that he'd left the negatives there. She felt guilty for invading his privacy and was thankful that her blush of embarrassment could not be seen in the red glow of the safety bulb.

But she also wished there were negatives of him strung up on the wire.

She realized for the first time how small the darkroom was. And how hot. There was no air movement in here. Even looking away from him, she could feel his closeness, and she was afraid to move for fear that she would accidentally touch him, that her breasts would accidentally rub his back, that her fingers would accidentally brush his buttocks.

What was she thinking about?

There was a knock on the darkroom door, and Rich called out, "Don't open it!"

"Daddy?"

"Just a minute!" He smiled at Sue. "Anna."

"Well, I think that's about all I can absorb for now

anyway. Anything else would be overload. I'd probably forget what I just learned."

"Good enough then. You ready to try developing your new roll?"

"I may still have to ask questions."

"That's why I'm here."

"Daddy!"

"Coming," Rich said. He quickly scanned the darkroom to make sure no light-sensitive film or photo paper was exposed, then opened the door.

Sue stepped out, blinking against the brightness, and saw Anna smiling up at her. "Hi, Sue."

"Hi there." She felt so guilty that she was unable to look into the little girl's face. Nothing had happened, she'd done nothing wrong, but she had the strange feeling that her sophomoric thoughts had somehow been readily apparent to Rich. She glanced back at him, but he was smiling at his daughter and not looking at her at all.

"Did you bring me any fortune cookies?" Anna asked. Sue looked down at the girl, and this time she could meet her eyes. "I forgot. But I'll bring some tomorrow."

"Okay," Anna said. She smiled up at Sue. "I like you better than Mr. Fredricks."

"Anna!" Rich said.

Sue laughed. Feeling better, she walked across the newsroom to her desk. She sat down, opened her notebook, took out a blank piece of paper, and started working on her article.

Thirty-eight

"There's a fax for you, Agent Rossiter."

"Thanks." Gregory Rossiter looked up from the computer screen and forced himself to smile at the intern, a skinny, goofy kid with too-big teeth and too-big ears who would never make agent no matter how hard he tried or how many extra hours he put in.

Some people just didn't have a clue.

He turned back to the information on his screen, moved the cursor to the file number of the next batch of unsolveds, and called up the first case. He scanned the MOD, didn't see what he was looking for, scrolled to the next case.

Three cases later, he found a match.

He pressed the Print key and a hard copy of the information on the screen rolled out of the laser printer attached to his terminal.

Five minutes later, the intern returned. "Agent Rossiter?" The kid shifted his weight uncomfortably from foot to foot.

"What is it now?"

"Chief Engles told me to tell you to pick up your fax."

"I will. Later."

The intern remained in place, unsure of what to do next.

"Leave," Rossiter ordered.

The kid beat a hasty retreat.

Rossiter scowled at his screen. Not only had he been banished to this sinus-sufferers' retirement community that they dared to call a state, but he'd been placed under the command of Frederick Engles, perhaps the most inept administrator he had ever met.

An FBI agent with the name of a Marxist.

That should have said something right there.

Rossiter leaned back in his chair, swiveled slightly to the left, and looked out of the tinted window at the skyline of Phoenix. Outside the federal building, the sky, as always, was blue, clear, and cloudless.

Even the weather got on his nerves here.

He rolled across his cubicle and tore the long sheet of paper from his printer, folding the continuous form along the perforations into pages. He scanned the information again. Six unsolved murders in Roswell, New Mexico, in June, 1984. Cause of death: exsanguination with unusual circumstances. Fifteen deaths in Denver, 1970. Exsanguination. Three murders in Broken Bow, Montana, 1969. Ten in Stewart, Wyoming, 1965. Eight in Cheyenne, 1953. Two in Reno, 1946. Waco, Plains, Mount Juliet; 1937, 1922, 1919.

The MOs and MODs were identical or nearly so in every case, and all were unsolved. The pattern was clear, obvious. Even a rookie could have spotted it.

Rossiter looked up at his screen, at the details of the sixth Roswell murder. He shook his head slowly. This wasn't possible, was it? A connection between crimes that had not been noticed before? A pattern that had not been picked up by any computer program or agent-analyst? He stared at the amber display. Perhaps it had been noticed somewhere at some time by somebody, but the sheer amount of time involved had led them to discount any possible relationship.

He was not so willing to write off any such possibility, no matter how far-fetched.

The question remained, was there a legitimate link between these murders, or were the similarities merely coincidental? It was highly unlikely that they had been committed by the same individual. Such a person, even if he had been a teenager at the time of the Mount Juliet killings, would have to be nearly a hundred years old now. Maybe the murders were the work of some sort of cult or coven that passed on its ritual practices from generation to generation.

Or the work of a vampire.

That was the thought in the back of his mind, and it was hard even for him to keep completely away from it. The appearance of the victims, the fact that the Bureau's experts still had not been able to determine how the physical draining of bodily fluids had been accomplished, the complete lack of witnesses or clues—all of this had the feel of some cartoonish movie or pulp novel, and it was difficult not to think about the case in those terms.

He didn't believe that there was anything supernatural here. But he *did* think that the Rio Verde murders and these other killings were connected.

Rossiter glanced around the edge of his cubicle at Engles's office. The regs said that he was supposed to inform his supervisor at this point, present his facts and ideas in both oral and written form.

But he was not sure he wanted to do that.

Engles was a top-of-the-line, grade-A, number one peckerhead, a softheaded, fat-assed bureaucrat who wouldn't know a crime if it came up and bit him in the crotch. He hadn't left his office for anything more urgent than a trip to McDonald's since J. Edgar Hoover had hung it up, and he certainly didn't have enough ambition to actively pursue a course of action on this. Serial killings or not, Engles's tendency would be to sit, wait everything out, let the locals figure out a solution.

Not him, though. Not Gregory Rossiter.

He had ambition to spare, and if he played his cards right, if he solved this case and successfully tied it to other unsolved cases in other states, this could be his ticket to D.C., his ticket out of Phoenix.

His ticket back to the real world.

The intern came back in, smiling nervously at Rossiter. "Chief Engles told me to tell you to pick up your fax now."

Rossiter grinned, but there was no humor in it. "Tell him to . . ." He trailed off, shook his head. "Never mind. I'm coming." He placed the printout in the top drawer of his desk and turned down the intensity light on his screen.

No, he wouldn't talk to Engles.

Regs or no regs, this one he would keep to himself for a while.

Thirty-nine

Sue wanted to talk to her grandmother following dinner, but immediately after eating the old woman silently left the table and disappeared into her bedroom.

"Is Grandmother feeling all right?" Sue asked.

John shrugged.

Neither of her parents answered.

Sue finished her rice.

In the restaurant, both she and John cleared tables, cleaned, did dishes, but at home such chores were woman's work, and after dinner John followed his father out to the living room to watch TV while she stayed to help her mother. She would have objected to this sort of blatant sexism long ago, but this was really the only time she ever got a chance to talk to her mother one-on-one, and she acquiesced to this unfair division of labor for that reason alone. The truth was, she felt closer to her mother at these times than she did at any other. Doing dishes, working in the kitchen, they were no longer mother and daughter but coworkers, equals. Their roles here were clearly defined—washer and dryer, alternating—and they could talk more freely than they could otherwise, the animosity which sometimes marked their relationship in the presence of others absent.

It was Sue's turn to wash and she grabbed a dishrag from the wooden rack on the side of the cupboard and squeezed Dove into the sink before turning on the water.

Her mother seemed preoccupied, staring silently out the window at nothing, and Sue found herself wondering if her grandmother had said anything to her about the *cup hu girngsi*. She wanted to ask, and she started to say something, but then she looked at her mother and found herself unable to continue.

The sink filled up, soap suds billowing upward like bubble clouds, and Sue dumped the chopsticks and forks in before pushing the faucet over to the other half of the sink for her mothers's rinse water.

They worked in silence for a while.

Sue found herself thinking about her mother, about her father, and she coughed politely. Her mother looked over at her, and she almost backed down, but then she forced herself to go on, to ask the question that she had so often tried to ask before. "Do you love Father?"

Her mother's face registered no response, no surprise at the question. She rinsed a dish and began to towel it dry. "We have a very good marriage."

Sue gathered her courage, pressed on. "But do you love him?"

"Yes, I do." Another dish. Rinse. Dry.

Sue stopped washing, wiping her hands on her jeans, looking over at her mother. "Did you . . . always love him? Did you know when you first met him that you loved him?"

Her mother was silent for a moment, her small hands continuing to towel a dish even though it was already dry. "I grew to love him," she said finally.

"Do you—"

"Wash," her mother said. "I am not in the mood to talk."

Sue nodded. Her mother looked old to her all of a sudden, and that frightened her. She could see her grandmother's face in the patterns of wrinkles beginning to form around her mother's mouth and eyes, and at the same time she could see the bone structure of her own face beneath those wrinkles. Sue realized, in a way she hadn't as the birthdays had come and gone, that her mother was pushing the outer envelope of middle age and that she herself was no longer young.

It was a depressing realization, and it left her feeling strange. She began washing the rice cooker, scraping the sticky rice off the metal side of the container with her fingernail.

Her mother picked up another plate, dried it, and there was something in the slow, deliberate nature of her movements that made her seem frail and vulnerable.

It hit Sue then.

The *cup hu girngsi* could kill her mother.

Or her father. Or John. Or even her grandmother.

None of them were immune.

Sue looked again at her mother and, for the first time, she realized how much she loved her and cared about her. About both her parents. Her whole family.

If this were a scene in a movie or a TV show, this would be the point where she turned to her mother, said "I love you," and hugged, all problems solved, all past conflicts forgotten.

But hers was not one of those fictional families, and Sue handed the rice cooker to her mother without speaking and started scrubbing the chopsticks.

After the dishes were done, Sue sat for a few moments between her father and brother watching *Entertainment Tonight,* then excused herself and walked down the hallway to her grandmother's room.

She opened the door slowly. Her grandmother was lying on the bed, left arm over her face, covering her eyes. The curtains and shades were drawn so that not even a hint of the dying daylight could sneak in, and both lamps were turned off, the only illumination coming from behind Sue in the hallway. The room smelled even more strongly than usual of herbs and Chinese medicine.

"I am tired," her grandmother said, and the old woman's voice, quiet and weak, barely above a whisper, confirmed her words.

A bolt of fear flashed through Sue, a sudden irrational feeling that her grandmother was seriously ill and dying, but she pushed that feeling aside and stepped into the room. She swallowed. "Do you want me to close the door?"

Her grandmother shook her head, not taking the arm away from her face. "It is all right."

"I need to know about the *cup hu girngsi.*"

Now there was movement. From underneath the arm, Sue saw white eyes looking at her. With a soft grunt of exertion, her grandmother sat up, swinging her thin wrinkled legs over the side of the bed. She closed her eyes hard, squeezing them shut, then opened them and looked at Sue. "I am glad you are finally ready."

Sue felt flustered. "I don't know what I'm supposed to be ready for. I don't know if I'm ready for anything. I just want to know about the *cup hu girngsi.*"

"You believe." Her grandmother studied her.

She nodded. "I believe."

"I am tired. I have been thinking on this today, trying to gather my strength, testing myself." She paused, blinked, and Sue noticed for the first time how her grandmother's eyes looked like her own, truly almond shaped, wider than John's or her father's or even her mother's. "I am old, I am weak, and I do not know if I can fight this *tse mor.* I think perhaps that we should leave."

Sue knelt down on the floor in front of her grandmother. "I thought you said it was our responsibility to stop it."

Her grandmother did not respond.

"It is different this time, isn't it?" Sue's voice was as quiet as her grandmother's. She studied the old woman's face. "It is different than it was back in Cuangxun."

Her grandmother sighed, nodded. "The *cup hu girngsi* is no longer afraid. People have forgotten it, people do not believe, people do not know how to fight it. The *cup hu girngsi* is wise or it is foolish or perhaps it is just vain, but it is ready to make its presence known. After all this time, after all these centuries, it has decided that it is tired of hiding in the shadows and living on the outskirts of human society, behaving like a scavenger. It wants to come out in the open."

"What does that mean?" Sue asked. There was a coiled tightness in the pit of her stomach.

"It no longer wants to hunt—it wants to be fed. It wants us to submit to it."

"Us? Who is 'us'? The people in Rio Verde?"

Her grandmother shrugged. "Yes," she said, but Sue could tell from her tone of voice that the old woman did not believe the monster's influence would stop at the boundaries of the town.

Sue licked her lips. "I saw trees today that had been killed by the *cup hu girngsi.*"

Her grandmother sat up straighter. "The land? It is already attacking the land?"

"I . . . I guess."

"Then it is strong already. We must move quickly."

The knot of fear tightened in Sue's stomach. "Should I get Mother and Father? And John?"

"Your parents have asked me not to tell you and your brother about this."

"Why?"

"They do not want to frighten you."

Sue nodded. That made sense. Her parents, her mother in particular, were always trying to protect her and her brother from the vicissitudes of life in the outside world.

They did not seem to realize that she and John were more familiar with the outside world, more conversant in its ways, than they themselves were. At home, her father ruled uncontested. He was the boss, the master of the house, and whatever he said was law. But outside of the house and the restaurant, out in the real world, their roles were reversed. The man who was so sure and strong when dealing with his family was meek, polite, and overly solicitous to strangers, and it was she, and to a lesser extent John, who steered her parents through the rough waters of American society.

"What about John? Have you talked to John?"

"John may have been . . . influenced."

Influenced.

"We must watch him. We must protect him. But we cannot trust him. He cannot help us."

Sue switched positions, unbent her knee, and sat flat on thé floor, stretching her legs out in front of her. "Can the *cup hu girngsi* be stopped?"

"I do not know."

"But there are ways to protect ourselves. The white jade . . ."

"Yes. The jade will protect you. The *tse mor* cannot bite a person wearing the jade. But . . ." Her grandmother grew thoughtful. "But the creature exerts a larger influence than that. It kills its victims, but it also affects others who see it, who are near it, even those who are not directly attacked. It twists their minds. The *cup hu girngsi* is not alive, but it is not dead. It is worse than dead, and it is like a magnet, attracting some people, repelling others, warping both. The jade will protect you from that. But the jade will not protect you from those other people, those who are . . . changed by the *cup hu girngsi.*"

Sue understood. The monster could convince people to do its bidding, convert them. It was a defense mechanism for the *cup hu girngsi,* a survival mechanism, a shield for its weak spot. "We can get people to wear white jade, then."

"White jade? Do you know how rare that is?"

"Is it the only jade that will work?"

Her grandmother shook her head slowly. "It is the strongest, it is the most effective, but even green jade will offer some protection."

"We'll make sure everyone wears some kind of jade, then."

"Not everyone will want to wear jade. Not everyone will believe. And those people will be as lights to a moth for the *cup hu girngsi*. Besides, I do not think that even in the jewelry stores there is much jade in this town."

"What else can we do? What else is good? In American movies, vampires are afraid of crosses and garlic."

"Willow," her grandmother said.

"Willow?"

The old woman nodded.

Sue suddenly understood. "Is that why Father planted those willows in front of the house? For protection?"

"Yes."

"You told him to plant them, didn't you?"

Her grandmother only smiled.

"Father used to tell me about *fung shui*. He said that *fung shui* was harmony between building and land, and I could never understand how he could think that our yard and house were in harmony with this desert.

"*Fung shui* means not only balance between buildings and nature but balance between the material and the spirit worlds. Bad *fung shui* can bring disaster." She shrugged. "Our home is not completely harmonious with the land, but it is harmonious in the most important way. I have made sure that it is safe."

"What else?"

"Running water. The *cup hu girngsi* cannot cross running water."

Sue was silent for a moment. "But those two teenagers were killed in the river. The *cup hu girngsi* killed them *in* running water."

They were both silent now. For the first time, Sue saw doubt on her grandmother's face, and she realized that all of this was academic to her grandmother too. She had learned of these things secondhand—she had never tried them out herself.

All of a sudden, Sue felt much less confident.

Maybe this wasn't a *cup hu girngsi*. Maybe it was something else. Maybe it was something that none of them knew anything about, something that no one knew how to fight.

"It is the *cup hu girngsi*," her grandmother said as if reading her mind.

Sue pulled her legs next to her chest, put her arms around her knees, and looked up at her grandmother. She felt helpless and vulnerable—powerless—knowing that something had to be done but not knowing what it was or how to go about it. "So what are we going to do?"

Her grandmother did not answer.

"I write for the newspaper now. I can warn people. The editor's brother is the police chief. I'm sure he can help us."

The old woman bent forward, reached down, and put her hand on Sue's. The movement was difficult for her, painful, but when she spoke there was renewed strength in her voice. "What do you want to do? What does your heart tell you to do?"

Sue looked into those eyes that were so like her own. "You mean my *Di Lo Ling Gum*?"

Her grandmother smiled, nodded. "Yes."

She felt none of the power within her, but she held her grandmother's gaze. "It tells me to hunt it down and destroy it."

"Then we will." The strength that had temporarily invigorated the old woman disappeared, seemed to visibly seep out of her face, and, grimacing, she leaned back on the bed and lay down again.

"But . . . what do we do? How do we start?"

"We wait. We can do nothing right now. I need to know more. For now, we wait."

"But . . ." Her voice trailed off. People were dying; trees and animals were being killed. A moment ago, her grandmother had admitted that the situation was urgent, had said that they had to act quickly. Now she wanted to lie here and do nothing?

"We are not the architects of events," her grandmother said. "We are merely the construction workers."

What kind of *Kung Fu* crap was that? Sue wondered. "I have to warn people," she said. "Tell them about the *cup hu girngsi.*"

"You can try." But the tone in her grandmother's voice made it clear that she did not think anyone would listen. She sighed. "I am tired. I must rest."

Sue stood, preparing to leave. "What does your *Di Lo Ling Gum* say?"

The old woman shook her head, put her arm over her eyes, refusing to look at her granddaughter, refusing to answer. "I must rest," she repeated.

Sue left the room silently, closing the door behind her, feeling far more frightened than she had before she'd come.

Forty

The Indian summer came to an abrupt end. The temperature dropped sometime after midnight, shifting from summer to winter without even pausing at the intermediate stage of fall.

In the morning, it was cold, and when Robert awoke and walked out to the kitchen, the floorboards beneath his feet felt like frozen steel. He dumped some grounds in his old drip pot, turned on the black-and-white television on the counter, and sat down at the table, waiting. There had never before been an Indian summer in Rio Verde that had lasted this long, and that made him uncomfortable. The cold, too, seemed to be a bad omen, a portent of things to come, and he found himself wondering if anyone had died during the night.

He stared for a moment at the dull gray metal of the coffeepot, then forced himself to stand up and walk out to the living room. He dialed the station, asked Ted if everything was all right, was gratified to hear that it was.

But he still felt uneasy.

He stopped by Rich's house on the way to work, dropping in unannounced. Corrie was already gone, and Rich was in the bathroom shaving, but Anna opened the door and greeted him enthusiastically. "Uncle Robert!" she cried, throwing her arms around him.

Grinning, he picked her up and gave her a loud kiss on the forehead.

She giggled, wiping her forehead with one hand while using the other to check inside his shirt pocket. "Where's my present?" she asked.

He looked puzzled. "Present? What present?"

Anna laughed, hitting his shoulder. "Come on!"

"Hmmm. Let me think." He withdrew a stick of Juicy Fruit from his left front pants pocket, snaked his arm around her head, and pretended to pull the gum from behind her ear. "Why, here's a piece of gum!"

He put her down on the floor, and she ran back through the house toward her bedroom. "Thank you, Uncle Robert!"

He followed her into the hallway. "Rich! You home?"

His brother stuck his head out of the bathroom, small flecks of white shaving cream around his neck. "Yeah. What is it?"

"You busy today?"

"Maybe. Why?"

"I thought I'd go out and see Pee Wee. You want to come along?"

Rich wiped off the excess shaving cream with a towel. "Are you going to be talking about the FBI or vampires?"

"Both."

"Vampires?" Anna yelled from her bedroom.

"Little pitchers," Rich said to his brother. "Get ready for school!" he called to Anna.

"I am!"

Rich turned back to his brother, nodded. "I'll go. But I have to take her to school first. And stop by the paper for a few minutes."

"That's okay." Robert grimaced. "I have some faxing to do."

"Have you talked to Pee Wee at all lately?"

"A little. Just about Rossiter."

"You haven't asked him what he thinks—"

"I was going to ask him today."

Rich nodded. "I'll come by the station, then. Give me an hour."

"You got it."

Pee Wee Nelson lived alone at the far end of Caballo Canyon in a house he'd built himself. He'd started the house in the early 1970s, at the peak of the environmental movement, and had worked on it in his spare time and during vacations until his retirement over a decade later. Made entirely from castoff and recycled materials, the house was known locally as Pee Wee's Pagoda, and that was exactly what the structure resembled. Disdainful of the geodesic domes and submerged earth dwellings popular during the period, he had decided instead to build upward, to showcase rather than hide his home.

The achievement was significant, and the home was still being improved upon long after many other ecologically oriented dwellings had been sold or abandoned. There'd even been an article on Pee Wee and his house in the *Arizona Republic* the week he had retired as police chief.

Of all other respects, Pee Wee was ultraconservative. An ardent NRA member and a Goldwater supporter from way back, he was a past president of the Rio Verde Republicans, and a very vocal right-wing activist. Like many lifelong outdoorsmen, however, he understood nature and valued it in a way that many limousine liberals did not seem capable of.

He was the only man Robert knew who had both NRA and Wilderness Society stickers on the bumper of his pickup truck.

Pee Wee was in his seventies now, but he looked, talked, and acted like a man in his early fifties. He might be a little more stoop-shouldered than he had been in his prime, but at six-foot-five he still towered over everybody else in town and still had the ability to intimidate even the toughest cowboys. He also commanded the respect of nearly everyone in Rio Verde, Rich and Robert included. In recent years, he'd taken to making mirrors to supplement his retirement income, buying the glass wholesale and cutting it into various designs. The venture had proved lucrative, and he more than doubled his retirement earnings selling his "artwork" to tourists from the Rocking D.

Both Robert and Rich had one of Pee Wee's mirrors—gifts—hanging in their respective houses.

It was ten o'clock before they finally left the police station, Robert promising Steve that he would be back before noon, ordering the deputy to stall Rossiter if the FBI agent called.

Robert drove, pulling onto the highway without looking, swerving in front of a refrigerated semi that was already pushing the speed limit. The truck braked, swung into the left lane. The semi's horn blared, but only for a second, the driver obviously realizing that he'd been cut off by a cop car.

"Aah," Robert said, grinning. "The trappings of power."

Rich checked his seat belt. "You're going to get us killed one of these days."

"Pansy."

"You always pull this macho shit when you go to see Pee Wee. You'll probably start spitting when we get there, too. You always do."

They headed out of town, driving north. Robert honked as they passed Jud, hiding in his speed trap behind the bowling alley.

"Would you ever have an affair?" Robert asked.

"Why would you even ask something like that?"

Robert shrugged. "I don't know. It's just that you and Corrie seem . . . well, not exactly all fired up about each other."

"A relationship's not a straight line. There are hills and valleys."

"This is a valley?"

"Maybe a canyon."

"To me, the best part of a relationship seems to be the beginning. You know, when you touch for the first time, kiss for the first time—"

"I don't want to hear where this is going."

"It is, though. It's the best part. It's more exciting when you're first exploring, when her body's new to you—"

"Do we have to talk about this?"

"Just because you're stuck in a rut . . ."

"The longest relationship you've had's been, what, a month?"

"Three years and you know it."

"I wasn't counting Julie."

They were silent for a while.

"Sorry," Rich said finally.

Robert sighed. "You know, sometimes I wish we'd had kids, Julie and me."

"You think that would've changed anything? You think that would've saved the marriage?"

"No. But at least I'd have something to show for it, you know?"

"I've got a newsflash for you. Kids are not trophies. They're people. It might gratify your own vanity if you'd had a child, but think of how tough it would be for the kid, shuffling back and forth between you and Julie—"

Robert groaned. "Lighten up, for Christ's sake. Stop lecturing. I was just talking. You take everything so damn seriously. That's your main problem."

"You weren't just talking; you meant it."

"Give it up."

They were into the desert, the town behind them, and the shoulder at the side of the highway was littered with the discarded husks of blown-out truck tires, their black and twisted forms looking like the charred corpses of unknown animals. The gravel sparkled with the shards of broken beer bottles.

Robert turned down an unmarked dirt road that hit the highway just after the third cattle guard. The car bumped down a low dip, then settled into a rut.

"You know what's depressing?" he said. "I think I'm the only person from my graduating class who's still here. Everyone else has moved out of town, moved onward and upward."

"Yeah, and they're working in windowless offices, breathing smoggy air, driving in horrendous traffic, and living in crowded apartment complexes. You're lucky."

"Knock off the back-to-nature crap."

"You are. I mean, you're well respected, important, in a position of authority. You live in a beautiful area—"

"It's a desert."

"It's a beautiful desert. Look at that sky. Look at those buttes. This is the kind of scenery that photographers make calendars out of. Raw beauty."

"You're so full of shit."

Rich grinned. "You'd better be nice to me. You want me to start trying to talk some sense into Pee Wee again? You want us to get into abortion? Busing? Affirmative Action? The ERA?"

"Don't bait him. He's an old man."

"Answer me, then. Where else would you get to piss off truckers just for the hell of it? And ticket people you don't like?"

Robert nodded. "This is true."

"See? You're not so bad off."

The road curved around a low cactus-covered hill, then headed straight for a narrow opening between two lightly striated cliffs, the western entrance of Caballo Canyon. Nothing was said between them, no words were spoken, but the mood in the car grew palpably more somber as the car fell under the blue shadow of the buttes.

Robert glanced over at his brother. "You still don't think it's a vampire, do you?"

"Not this again."

"Tell me how a human being could suck every last drop of blood and piss and spit and everything else from four people, six horses, and God knows how many other animals through holes in their necks." He shook his head. "You know how you always said you hated horror movies because the people in them were so stupid? They'd hear screams at night and say their house was just settling, or they'd find a friend's body torn apart by a monster and then split up to see if they could find the creature? You always said you hated those movies because the people in them didn't act the way real people would act. Well, you're acting just like one of those people in a monster movie."

He'd expected an argument, had half hoped for an argument, wanting desperately to be wrong and to be proved wrong. But Rich nodded wearily. "You're right."

"I am?"

"I suppose your vampire theory's as good as any other. Probably better than most." The car bumped over a particularly big pothole, bottoming out, and he put a hand on the shaking dashboard to steady himself. "Tell me this. Do you think Pee Wee's going to buy the vampire idea?"

"I have no idea. But I thought, at the very least, that he might be able to tell us something we don't know. Maybe this has happened before, and it was all covered up. Maybe the town was built on burial grounds or something."

Rich shook his head. "What don't we know about this town? We've lived here all our lives. I'm the editor of the paper; you're the police chief. You think there's some deep dark secret that's been hidden from us all these years?"

"I don't know. I'm just throwing out ideas."

"Well, throw that one out for sure. It's stupid."

"We'll see."

The bloom of summer was still visible on the low upward sloping floor of the canyon, the pink cactus flowers and tiny yellow blossoms of brittlebush not yet having gotten word that winter had arrived. The road hugged the southern butte as the canyon opened out, widening into a plain that flattened into desert a few miles eastward. From here they could already see the pointed triangular contours of Pee Wee's home and, next to it, his old metal windmill, silhouetted against the morning sun, tail pointed east, vanes, turning slowly in the nearly nonexistent desert wind.

Robert honked three times and gave a short whoop of the siren to let the old chief know they were coming, although he had no doubt seen the growing dust cloud kicked up by the car. The sound echoed off the rock walls, loud even with the windows up.

"What if he's not home?" Rich said.

"I called. Besides, he's always home."

There was a corral close by the house, a square patch of dry tramped dirt fenced in by four irregular posts and a single strip of barbed wire, and within the corral, a bony horse stood on the hard ground, staring southward. Robert parked the car next to the west side of the corral, and the two of them got out simultaneously. Pee Wee was already walking toward them from the house, grinning hugely. "Glad to see you boys. It's been a while."

"Good to see you, too," Robert said, extending his hand.

Pee Wee shook the proffered palm. "Not a bad grip," he commented. "The job hasn't let you go too far to seed." He nodded to Rich. "Good thing your brother called first instead of just dropping by like he usually does. I was all set to go rabbit hunting this morning."

Robert spat in the dirt. "Out by Dry Beaver Creek?"

"Yeah." Pee Wee chuckled, shook his head. "Dry Beaver Creek. Whoever thought of that name? It had to be a joke."

"Maybe they were thinking of your sister."

"Or your mama."

Rich smiled politely, not joining in. He never had gone in for this sort of macho camaraderie, and he didn't know how to do it. Even witnessing it made him slightly uncomfortable.

"It's chilly out here this morning." Pee Wee nodded toward the house. "Let's go inside, have some coffee, talk."

Robert grinned. "I hear you."

The two of them started walking, Rich following only a few steps behind.

Pee Wee spat. "So the feds're tryin' to horn in on your territory, huh?"

"Not only trying," Robert said. "Succeeding."

"Can't say that ever happened to me. Nothin' big enough ever occurred here in my day to interest the feds."

"But if it had?"

"I woulda fought 'em tooth and nail."

"My approach exactly."

"I hate to bring reality into this," Rich said, catching up and drawing even. "But the important thing is that the murderer get caught, not who catches him. The way you're talking, I can just see you and Rossiter hoarding information, not sharing things with each other, trying to be the first to crack the case."

"Yeah, right," Robert said.

"He has a point," the ex-chief nodded gravely. "Your first duty is to your office, not your ego."

"I know that. But the two aren't mutually exclusive."

They walked into the house. The small narrow entryway opened onto a huge living room with a vaulted ceiling nearly two stories high. One whole wall of the room was an eastward-facing window that offered a truly spectacular view of the open desert past the canyon.

Pee Wee excused himself, went into the kitchen to get the coffee, and Rich and Robert walked silently around the big room, examining the new mirrors hanging on the wall opposite the window. The reflection of the desert in the angular hexagons and parallelograms gave the already oversize room an aura of true vastness, making the house seem as though it were suspended in air high above the sand.

A collection of hunting trophies adorned the stone fireplace to the left of the mirrors, and when the old man returned, carrying mugs of black Yuban, Robert pointed up at the mounted head of a javelina. "Is that new?"

Pee Wee shook his head. "I ain't got nothing new for weeks now. The game source has pretty well dried up around here. I know there's been a drought for the past few years, but this is getting ridiculous. I haven't seen shit but lizards, vultures, and an occasional rabbit for the past month. Even the damn coyotes are playing possum."

Robert and Rich looked at each other.

Robert sipped his coffee, preparing to speak, but before he could say anything Pee Wee cut him off. "All right, what is it? What's up? You two've been pussyfootin' around something ever since you got here. Spill it."

"What would you say if I told you that there was a vampire in Rio Verde?"

"I'd say you were a fool-assed chump and two sandwiches shy of a picnic."

Robert sipped his coffee. Rich nodded.

"A week ago I would've said that," Pee Wee said. "But that was before I saw the body of that wild filly out by the wash. Now I say tell me more."

Robert glanced up. "You believe it?"

"I don't not believe it. That filly was nothing but a

mummified corpse, and two days before she'd been eating my scrub."

"We've found other animals too. And the mechanic and the groom and those two kids were all killed the same way. Drained of blood, emptied."

"Exsanguinated," Pee Wee said.

"Yes."

"Seems to me this is where the feds or the staters'd be some help. What do they say about this?"

Robert shrugged. "I haven't discussed it with them. The FBI agent is in charge of the investigation, but if he has some sort of overall strategy in mind, he's not sharing it. As far as I can tell, he's working on one body at a time. And looking for a human suspect."

"Have you talked to the coroner?"

"He's the one who sprung the vampire theory on me. He's autopsied the bodies and said there's no known way that the blood, urine, and everything could've been sucked out those holes in the necks."

"Necks." Pee Wee nodded, impressed. "Who's coroner these days? Woods?"

"Yeah."

"He knows his stuff." Pee Wee walked over to a wooden rocking chair, sat down. "This is getting interestin'."

Robert sat on the overstuffed couch adjacent to the fireplace. "I'm buying it."

"What about you?" Pee Wee asked, looking over at Rich. "You haven't said much through all this."

"I don't know what to think. I haven't made up my mind yet. But it's definitely open."

The ex-chief nodded. "Let's assume, for the sake of argument, that we are dealing with a real vampire." He looked from Rich to Robert. "How often does he have to feed?"

Robert sighed. "The killings seem to be about a week or two apart."

"So he needs a body every two weeks."

"Plus animals," Rich reminded him.

"Let's just deal with the humans for now. Okay, a body every two weeks. No correspondence with lunar cycles or any of that crap. That's good."

"Why's that good?"

"The less mumbo jumbo we have to deal with, the better. If there are such things as vampires, and if we got one here, we have to figure out how to track him, catch him, and kill him. We have to treat him like an animal, observe his habits and use 'em to our advantage. And the first thing we have to do is separate the myths from the truth."

"The first thing we have to do," Robert said, "is find out how we can protect people from him."

"Or her," Rich said.

"True enough." Robert nodded.

"Let's think about this logically." Pee Wee set his coffee cup down on the floor next to the couch. "If this guy's a vampire, he lives forever, right? He must be a hundred years old. Two hundred, maybe. If that's so, why haven't we heard about him before? Why hasn't he wiped out whole towns? I'll tell you why—because he moves on. It's a big world, and a crowded one, and I bet a vampire could feed a little in one place and then keep moving and no one'd ever know."

"Hell," Robert said. "Maybe he hibernates. Like a bear. Comes out every century, drinks some blood, goes back to sleep."

"Maybe," Rich said doubtfully, and there was silence in the room after he spoke.

Robert picked up his coffee from the floor, drank it, and the three of them stared out of the living room through the huge window into the endless desert beyond.

It was nearly noon when they arrived back in town. Robert radioed over to the station, learned that nothing had happened this morning, and said he would be in after lunch. He turned toward Rich. "You in a big hurry? Let's cruise over to Buford's, grab some chow."

"Okay."

The cruiser slowed for two teenagers crossing the highway in front of the liquor store.

"You know what?" Rich said. "All these years we've been going to Buford's, and I don't even know his last name."

"I thought Buford was his last name."

"I think it's his first."

"We'll check." Robert pulled into the parking lot of the hamburger stand, and they both got out. Robert ordered a half-pound Monstro Burger, large fries, and a large Dr Pepper, and after only a second's deliberation, Rich ordered the same.

Robert grinned. "No willpower." He bent to peek through the order window as Buford pulled two huge hamburger patties from the refrigerator and slapped them on the grill. "I know this is a stupid question," he said to the cook, "but is Buford your first name or your last name?"

"Both."

"Both? Buford Buford?"

"That's what my daddy named me."

Robert glanced over at his brother. "Hear that? I guess we're both right." His smile faded as Rich, frowning, pointed surreptitiously to a hand-lettered sign on the inside of the glass next to the pickup window: "New Hours 11 A.M.–6 P.M."

Robert turned back toward Buford. "You're closing at six now?"

"Yeah." The cook did not elaborate.

"You're going to miss the dinner crowd."

"I changed the hours last week." He paused. "I don't want to work after dark anymore."

Rich and his brother exchanged glances, saying nothing.

The sizzling of the burgers grew louder. "Rumor has it," Buford said, "that you caught your vampire."

"What?"

"Mike Vigil. He went crazy and thought he was a vampire."

"Mike's crazy all right, but he's no vampire. Besides, he was in Florence under observation the other night when Clifford was killed."

"I didn't put no store by it." He flipped over the burgers, pulled a handful of sliced onions from the refrigerator, and dumped them on the grill. He worked the onions with his spatula for a moment. "I think I saw the vampire last week."

Robert tried to peer through the window to judge whether or not Buford was pulling his leg, but all he could see through the dirty rusted screen was the cook's white-aproned chest and clean-shaven bottom jaw.

"I wasn't sure whether I should tell you, but I promised myself that if you came in, I'd bring it up." He pointed his spatula toward Rich. "I don't want none of this in the paper, understand?"

"Off the record," Rich agreed.

"I haven't even told my wife. Don't want to frighten her."

"What happened?"

"I was here late, all alone, and all of a sudden I got . . . kind of a weird feeling. I can't describe it, but it was like I knew something was out there, watching me, waiting for me to leave. Scared the living shit out of me. When I finally did leave and go out to my car, I thought I saw something out of the corner of my eye. A white shape. Big. Kind of fluttering. But then it was gone. I didn't stop to look for it. I just hopped in my car and hauled ass."

"It disappeared?"

"It disappeared into the arroyo," Buford said. "It went into the arroyo."

"The arroyo," Rich said. "It comes back to the arroyo."

Robert shook his head. "We searched it. We didn't find anything but dead bugs and animals. No tracks. Nothing."

"How far did you follow it?"

"Five miles. The damn thing stretches all the way to Rocky Gulch."

"Maybe he uses the washes and gullies and arroyos like trails or tunnels, uses them to get in and out of places. God knows there's a network of them across the desert."

"That's reassuring," Robert said. He sighed. "We'll check it out again. I don't have anything else to go on."

"You could stake this place out, wait and see if he comes back."

"*Steak* it out," Rich said with a wry grin. "I get it."

Robert turned to his brother. "Maybe I'll talk to Rossiter about it. It's about time those guys pulled their weight around here."

"Yeah. I'm sure they're going to assign FBI agents to wait night after night at a hamburger stand for a vampire to show up."

"We have to do something. Do you have any ideas?"

Rich shook his head.

"Neither do I."

A blue Chevy Impala pulled into the burger stand's parking lot. Sunlight glinted off the silver crucifix hanging from the car's rearview mirror.

Buford slid aside the screen on the pickup window and pushed through a tray. "Lunch is served."

Forty-one

Wheeler awoke feeling tired. He had not seen Jesus for over two weeks, and the strain was making him tense, nervous, jumpy. He knew he was doing the Lord's bidding, but he did not feel confident enough in the worthiness of his own thoughts and actions to make decisions without higher approval. What if he were doing something wrong? What if Jesus wanted shakes instead of shingles on the roof of His house? What if Jesus didn't approve of drywall and foam insulation?

There were so many things to consider.

He got out of bed, took a quick shower, and got dressed. The cat Covey had killed yesterday was still lying curled in the basting pan on top of the kitchen counter, its broken dripping eyes staring at nothing, and Wheeler touched a tentative finger to the congealed blood surrounding the animal's body. The blood was sticky, neither cold nor hot, and had the consistency of melted taffy.

The butterflies began flying in his stomach, but Wheeler ignored them and placed two pieces of bread in the toaster. He poured himself some orange juice, took a spoon and knife from the utensil drawer. When the toast was done, he spooned a generous helping of blood onto the bread, spreading it with the knife. It smeared almost as well as jelly.

As always, he gagged when he bit into the blood, but he forced himself to keep chewing, his brain ordering his rebellious tastebuds to ignore the information they were receiving firsthand and concentrate on the importance of getting used to the thick, unnatural flavor.

He was able to eat both slices of toast without spitting out a single bite.

After breakfast, he drove straight to the church. The five men of the morning shift were on top of the newest addition, working on the frame for the second floor, and before he even rounded the corner onto Arrow, he saw the parallel series of black beams they'd put up since yesterday protruding proudly upward from behind the other buildings on the block.

He parked on the south side of the original chapel and got out of the car, waving back to the workers when they waved at him.

The Church of the Living God was taking shape. The contours of the awesome structure placed into his mind by Christ and given material form in Covey's sketches could now be seen in the building itself. The nucleus of the completed church was clearly visible in the existing structure. If work went on at this pace, if construction continued unabated day and night, if they continued to recruit more volunteers, it was quite likely that the church would be completed within the next two weeks.

In time for the Second Coming.

He looked up at the building. The black looked good. It lent the original chapel and its additions a pleasing uniformity.

He waved again to the workers, walked up the front steps, unlocked the door, and stepped inside.

The interior of the church had been transformed.

Wheeler stood for a moment in the vestibule, the door swinging slowly and silently shut behind him.

The pews were gone. The long benches had been disassembled, the wood used to cover all windows in the room and to make crude walkways over the three large holes which now took up most of the chapel's floor space. The cross still hung behind the altar, untouched, but the altar itself was now peopled with the mummified remains of three men, positioned in reclining poses, and a woman who held in her hands a plate on which sat the dehydrated head of a child.

The woman was obviously supposed to be Salome, holding the head of John the Baptist.

It was beautiful.

Wheeler took a tentative step forward, but from within the blackness of the nearest hole there came a sound of wind, a sound of water. A single strong ray of light burst upward from the opening and rising within that light was the Lord Jesus Christ.

Wheeler involuntarily stepped back. Jesus arose from the depths, grinned. His eyes were wide, the brows arched, and His teeth were red, smeared with blood, the divisions between them dark and unusually well defined. His beard was dirty, matted with brown and red, and in His arms was the unmoving body of a goat.

"Truly, truly I say to you, unless you eat flesh and drink blood, you have no life in you." Jesus laughed, almost giggled. "He who eats flesh and drinks blood has eternal life, and I will raise him up at the last day. For flesh is food indeed, and blood is drink indeed."

A slight chill caressed the back of Wheeler's neck. He recognized the verses from the Gospel according to John, but there were words missing, words that altered the meaning of the phrases. Somewhere, a small part of him was saying that Jesus was not supposed to act this way, but Christ looked upon him, held his eyes, and that tiny voice died.

Standing upon the walkway above the hole, Jesus raised the goat to His face. He bit into the animal's neck and placed His mouth over the bite before the blood began to gush. Wheeler watched as the goat's body deflated in-

stantly, shrinking, caving in on itself, the long hair twisting, withering, the skin conforming to the structure of
the skeleton beneath.

Jesus dropped the used carcass into the hole.

And then it was over. He was the Savior again, the
bloody beard and teeth gone, the wild giggling visage replaced by a solemn expression of perfect contentment,
and Wheeler fell to his knees, sobbing with joy, unbearably
happy to be in the presence of this Lord, the Lord he
knew and loved.

"This is my home," Jesus said, his melodious voice
echoing in the pastor's head. "I live here now. And from
this day forward, worship services will be conducted outside. They will no longer be held within the church."

"Yes," Wheeler agreed, nodding.

"Sacrifices acceptable and pleasing to God will be left
in each of the three openings in the earth."

"Yes," Wheeler agreed.

Jesus smiled. "We shall begin the punishment of the
sinners."

Wheeler's pulse quickened, and the excited anticipation which coursed through every fiber of his being was
unlike anything he had ever experienced. "Yes," he said.

Christ's smile was beatific. "They will all die painfully."

"Yes." Wheeler felt a strange stirring in his groin.

Jesus reached out a hand, and the pastor walked across
the small section of floor onto the pew walkway over the
hole. Looking down, he could see that the hole was not
really a hole at all, but a steeply sloping tunnel running
under the south wall of the church. He took Jesus' hand,
and the Savior's eyes twinkled. "I will show you my home.
I will show you my wonders. I will show you fear in a
handful of dust."

That sounded familiar, Wheeler thought. He had heard
that before. Not in the Bible, but somewhere else. He

tried to think, tried to focus, tried to remember, but the connection would not be made.

And then they had jumped from the walkway and were floating down.

Forty-two

"No." Rich shook his head. "I will not."

"I'm not trying to censor you or anything," Hollis said. "I'm just saying play it down, don't sensationalize it, leave it alone for a while."

Rich looked the owner of the dude ranch squarely in the eye. "Play it down? You think I'm making too much of this, blowing it out of proportion? You think Clifford's going to come back to life?"

"That's not what I'm saying. Look, our businesses are interconnected here, and I just think we oughta look out for each other. It's not going to do anyone any good to start a panic. As you know, I'm the largest single employer in Rio Verde. I provide jobs for twenty-five people part time and another twenty full time. If guests get scared away, those people'll be out of jobs. I'll lose money; I won't be able to afford to advertise in your paper; everyone'll get hurt."

Sue watched Rich from the side. She saw his jaw clench, the muscles in his face tightening. "So you want me to pretend that Terry Clifford wasn't murdered, that he's still happily working at your stable and nothing out of the ordinary has occurred."

Hollis smiled. "You're twisting my words, son. All I'm saying is don't blow this out of proportion. Don't give people another excuse to criticize our town. I mean, hell, how do you think it makes your brother look if your paper makes it sound like a damn psycho's running around killing people?"

"And draining their bodies of blood."

"There you go again, talking like a tabloid. All I'm doing is suggesting that you treat Terry's passage with some respect. Inform people that he died, just don't go into the grisly details."

"I didn't go into the grisly details."

"You did from where I stand."

"I'm a reporter. It's my job to tell the truth. If it makes you feel any better, it's October and the tourist season is over and by next summer everyone will have forgotten all about this."

"Oh, no, they won't."

Rich ran an exasperated hand through his hair. "Who reads the paper except locals? They're not the ones coming to your ranch. Jesus, I don't know why I'm even arguing this point. I run a newspaper, crummy as it is, and when news happens I'm going to report it. Period."

Hollis's voice became a little less folksy, the tone hardening. "The First Amendment does not give you the right to damage my business."

"I'm not trying to damage your business. I'm simply reporting the facts. Look, I can get plenty of reliable sources willing to go on record saying that a vampire killed Clifford, Torres, and those two kids. You want me to do that?"

"Reliable sources? Like who? Your dipshit brother?"

Rich stiffened. "Get out of this office," he ordered. "Now."

Hollis started walking. "I'm pulling all of my advertising from this rag."

"Go right ahead." The editor stood unmoving, watching him leave.

Sue tried to return to work on her article, but out of the corner of her eye she saw Rich remain standing in the middle of the newsroom. She looked up, cleared her throat in an effort to get his attention. He turned to face her. "Are you going to be able to keep going?" she asked. "Without his advertising, I mean?"

He waved his hand dismissively. "We'll survive. Hollis has always had an inflated sense of his own importance. The ranch does support a lot of businesses around here, but not us. If Basha's pulled out we'd be in big trouble, but the Rocking D?" He snorted. "Hollis has always been a miser about advertising in *The Gazette*. We'll live without his fifty bucks a week."

"Good."

Rich walked back to his desk. "It just depresses me that the man would even try to tell me what to print and what not to print." He shook his head. "Most people don't believe in freedom of the press. Not really. They think they do, but they don't. People like to hear or read things that they agree with. They want their own views promoted as fact and don't want equal time given to their opposition. They want only their side given. But the presentation of facts is never wrong. Remember that, if you remember nothing else. It is the journalist's responsibility to be objective. When you start printing only one side of a story, when you start limiting people's access to facts, telling them by your presentation and emphasis what to believe, what is truth, then you are not doing your job."

Sue smiled. "Was that going to be a lecture to your class?"

"No. But it should've been."

Their eyes met. It was now or never, she thought. She looked down at the scratch paper on which she'd written her lead. She was nervous, her heart beginning to pound, but the opportunity was here, had presented itself without her having to reach for it, and she forced herself to act. She looked up at him. "It is a vampire," she said. Her voice was meek, barely audible.

"What?"

She licked her lips. She wasn't sure if he didn't believe her or hadn't heard what she said, but she pressed on. "There is a vampire. We call it a *cup hu girngsi.*"

This time he had heard. "*Cup hu girngsi?*"

"It means 'vampire' in Cantonese."

"And these vampires drink the sap of trees, too, I suppose?"

Sue reddened. "You read my story."

"Of course. I copyedited it."

"Then, yes," she said. "As a matter of fact, they do." The editor chewed his lip for a moment, looking at her, thinking. Then he put down his pen and sighed. He stood, walked over to Sue's desk, and pulled up a chair, sitting down next to her. "Okay," he said. "I admit it. I'm not the skeptic I used to be." He crossed his legs. "I guess it's about time I heard this. Tell me about the *cup hu girngsi.*"

She looked at him. "This isn't a joke."

"I know."

Sue nodded. "Thank you," she said quietly.

And she began to talk.

When Sue arrived at the restaurant, both her parents and her grandmother were standing next to the front window, staring out toward the highway. The sight of their faces peering from between the taped signs advertising Egg Roll and Sweet and Sour Pork lunch specials filled her with a sinking feeling. There was none of the dread she associated with *Di Lo Ling Gum,* and she knew that if something truly important had happened, her father would have called her at the paper, but she could still tell that something was wrong, and instead of parking the station wagon in the back, she pulled up to the short sidewalk at the front of the restaurant.

She hurried inside, the bell above the door tinkling as

she pushed the door open. She addressed her father: "What is it? What is wrong?"

"John is late. He was supposed to be here half an hour ago."

There were two diners in the restaurant, eating a late lunch or an early dinner at the far table, and they looked up, frowning, at the sound of the Chinese words.

Her grandmother's voice betrayed no emotion, but her eyes were troubled. "It is not safe today. Not even in the daytime."

Sue looked from her grandmother to her mother and father. "I'll look for him."

"I will go," her father said.

"I want to go too."

Her mother shook her head, but her grandmother nodded. "All right," her father said.

Sue dropped her notebook on the nearest table. "I'm sure he's fine. He probably just stayed after school for something. I don't think anything's happened to him."

Neither her parents nor her grandmother responded.

They pulled out of the parking lot a few minutes later, her father driving, and followed in reverse the path John usually took home from school. They cruised slowly through the parking lot of Basha's, Sue peeking down the trail that led through the vacant land between the shopping center and the restaurant. They even drove past Dairy Queen and the liquor store, in case he'd stopped off to get something to eat or drink. But there was no sign of John, no sign of any students.

Something had happened.

They drove up Ocotillo toward the junior high. The school was hosting an afternoon home game against Globe, and the sound of cheering from the football field carried clearly in the cool desert air. It surprised Sue that real life was still continuing for some people in town, that they knew or cared nothing about the *cup hu girngsi*, and though she knew that ignorance was not really bliss, that not being aware of the situation and failing to take proper precautions was more likely to lead to death than happiness, she could not help envying those people their innocence.

Her father pulled into the school parking lot. There were two dingy buses and some cars parked here, but by no means as many vehicles as usual. The *cup hu girngsi* had had an effect. Could John have gone to the game? She didn't think it likely. He didn't like sports, had never before been to any school activity at all, and if he wanted to go somewhere with friends after school he always called. Still, she mentioned it to her father, who promptly pulled into one of the parking slots. "We will look for him," he said. "Maybe he is here."

There was more wish than conviction in his voice, and that note of nearly desperate hope made everything suddenly hit home. Her brother might really be dead. Or kidnapped, taken to the *cup hu girngsi*'s lair. She might never again see him alive.

She felt not angry, not scared, but drained, tired.

"Sue."

The voice was a whisper, faint but audible. It had come from somewhere close, but if it had been spoken a moment sooner, while the football crowd was cheering, she would not have heard it.

Her father was already walking up the crooked concrete steps that led to the gym and football field. She wanted to call out to him but dared not, for fear of missing the voice if it spoke again. She stood next to the car, unmoving.

"Sue!" The call came again, weak and whispery and somehow familiar.

Frowning, she turned toward the Dumpsters pushed against the low brick wall a few parking spaces away. She thought she saw movement in the shadows between the blue metal sides of the twin bins, and she started cautiously forward.

"Sue!"

It was John. She could see him now, leaning against the side of the closest Dumpster.

"Father!" she called. She did not wait to see if he'd heard her but rushed between the metal bins. John was sitting up but was curled into an almost fetal position, his head nearly touching his knees. His face was purple and red, the skin around his mouth and eyes bruised and swollen, his nose and lips bloody. There was drying blood on his ripped shirt, and his pants were open, the snap torn off. She knelt down next to him, filled with a gut-wrenching hurt that made her want to cry, made her want to hit someone, made her wish this had happened to her instead. She had never before seen any member of her family injured or in serious pain, and the experience made her feel sick inside. "What happened?" she asked.

John's voice was again a whisper, and she realized that he could barely move his puffy lips. "They beat me up. They said God told them to do it. They said God doesn't like . . . Chinese people."

Her father hurried around her, knelt next to John, reached under his arms, and pulled him into a straighter sitting position. "Chink," her father said in English. "They say 'chink.' " It was a statement not a question. John nodded.

Sue thought of Pastor Wheeler and she felt cold. "Who was it?" she asked.

"Kids from my P.E. class. Butch, J.D., Rick, and Marla." He started to cry. "And Russ and Kim and Mr. Peters."

"Your teacher?"

He nodded, wiping his eyes, wincing from the pain as his fingers pressed against his bruises.

The shouts of the football crowd no longer seemed so normal, no longer so benign.

"Do your arms feel broken?" her father, asked in Cantonese. "Are your legs okay? Can you walk?"

John nodded. "Thirsty," he said. "I'm thirsty."

"We'll take you home."

"Maybe we should take him to the hospital," Sue suggested.

"Your grandmother can take care of him. I do not trust the hospital now."

Sue nodded. Her father's paranoid certainty frightened her. Despite all she'd said to her grandmother about wanting the family to open up, communicate, talk more, she found that she longed for the days when her father was an unflappable rock. It reassured her when her parents were calm islands in an otherwise stormy sea. It might not be honest for her parents to keep their knowledge, doubts, and fears from her, but it made her feel more confident when she knew she had solid support at home.

Now they were all adrift. And it scared her.

Her father gave her the keys, told her to drive, and she hurried over to the car, backing it up next to the Dumpsters. Her father helped John into the backseat, sat down next to him, and Sue pulled out of the parking lot.

"Are we going home or to the restaurant?" Sue asked.

"The restaurant," her father said. "We'll pick up your grandmother and then go home."

"I'm cold." John's voice was low, and she had to listen carefully to hear it.

"Roll up the windows," her father ordered.

Sue did so, pressing down on the armrest console that controlled the entire car. She slowed, signaled, pulled onto the highway. "Why did they beat you up?" she asked her brother. "Was there a reason?"

"I told you," he whispered. "They said God didn't like Chinese people."

"That's it? You didn't get into an argument or anything first?"

"Mr. Peters told me to stop wearing jade."

Sue looked at her brother in the rearview mirror. "You didn't—"

"They stole my ring."

Sue's mouth went dry. "We'll find more jade," her father said quickly, as if to reassure himself. "He'll be okay."

They drove the rest of the way in silence, the only sound in the car John's loud, ragged breathing.

There were no customers at the restaurant when they arrived, and both her mother and grandmother were waiting outside, in front of the building. Sue hopped out of the car and opened the door for her father who gently helped John out. "He was beaten up," he said. "They took his jade."

"Leave him there!" her grandmother ordered. "We must get him home. Now. The influence is strong. We must find him jade and cover his window with willow branches for protection."

"He can have my jade," Sue said.

"I'm not wearing a necklace," John croaked.

"I have a piece of jade in my dresser," her grandmother said.

"I'll take an earring."

Sue found herself smiling in spite of the circumstances. "No matter what happened to you, you're still a jerk."

"I'll close the restaurant and put up a sign," her father said.

Sue stared at him. The restaurant had never before closed on a day other than Monday. Not even illness had been able to alter its hours.

Her grandmother nodded. "Let's get him home."

Forty-three

Complaints against the church had reached a fever pitch in the past two days, ever since the three truckloads of new materials had arrived from Globe, and though he'd been dreading it, putting it off, Robert knew that he had to go out to the church this morning and have another talk with Wheeler.

He stopped by the Donut Hut for breakfast, grabbing a glazed and a coffee before heading over to the station.

He pulled into the parking lot the same time as Father Martinez.

"Chief Carter! I need to speak to you!"

Robert slammed the door of the cruiser and swallowed his last bite of doughnut, washing it down with the dregs of the coffee as the Catholic priest hurried toward him across the dirt. He nodded at the clergyman. "What can I do for you, Father?"

The priest was obviously agitated, his face red and sweating, and he had a difficult time catching his breath as he stood before Robert. He put one hand over his chest, held the other up in a wait-a-minute gesture, then bent over to breathe. He stood like that for a moment, then straightened.

"What is it, Father?"

The priest breathed deeply. "The black church."

Robert nodded noncommittally, carefully keeping his expression blank, neutral. He'd been wondering when this would come up. He'd expected the leaders of the traditional denominations to come forth sooner. He'd known that they would have problems with Wheeler's church—religious problems, not noise or nuisance problems—and when he'd seen that black paint being slopped on, he'd expected an outcry.

He was surprised that it was Father Martinez, though, who was standing before him. The Catholic priest was one of the more liberal and tolerant clergymen in town, and he would have thought that the Baptist or Pentecostal preachers would be the ones to object most strongly and be first with their vocal opposition.

Father Martinez looked into his eyes. "This is the work of the devil."

Robert shifted uncomfortably. "Come on, Father. I know this isn't your cup of tea. It's not mine either, for that matter. But Wheeler's got a right to his own beliefs."

"It's not just his beliefs," the priest said. His gaze was unwavering. "I saw him talking to one of the minions of Satan."

"Now, Father . . ."

"I'm not just speaking figuratively or metaphorically. I saw him addressing a demon. Literally. Standing there speaking to one of Satan's brethren." His voice dropped. "And calling it the name of the Lord."

The hair on Robert's arms and the back of his neck bristled, propelled by a rash of goose bumps that were not caused by the chill morning air.

"That black church is a blasphemy," the priest said. "I won't deny it. But I recognize its right to exist. I also understand that Mr. Wheeler has been claiming to have spoken with Jesus Christ; some members of my congregation have even gone over to his church because of this claim. It offends me and angers me, but, again, that is his right. *I* will not be the one to pass judgment on his deeds.

"But a tolerance of the beliefs of others, no matter how

warped or obscene they may be, does not mean that I can sit passively by while the will of Satan is carried out in front of me. It is my duty as a priest, as a Catholic, and as a human being to combat evil."

"What do you think you saw?"

"It is not what I think I saw, it is what I know I saw. I was walking to St. Mary's this morning, before dawn, as I always do, and when I passed by the black church I heard voices. Two of them. Mr. Wheeler's and a strange, whiny voice. The whiny voice said something I couldn't make out, then Mr. Wheeler said, 'You are the way and the light.'

"I couldn't ignore that. I was near the point where the new part of the church comes close to the sidewalk, and I saw a crack of green light escaping from between two sections of wall. I walked over and peeked in.

"The demon was the source of the light. It was bathed in a greenish glow, and Wheeler was kneeling before it, praying to it. He was addressing the demon as 'Jesus,' and there was rapture on his face, but the demon was not even looking at him. It was staring at me, through the crack in the wall, from across the room." Father Martinez shuddered. "And it smiled at me."

"What did it look like?"

"It was greasy. It was short, dwarfish, and horribly deformed. It looked . . . It reminded me of something I used to dream about as a child, a monster from a movie." He shook his head. "I ran all the way to the church—my church, St. Mary's—and locked myself in. I prayed for strength and guidance. I prayed for three straight hours. Then I came here to see you."

Robert nodded understandingly, though he had no idea what he was supposed to be thinking or feeling. He did not believe Father Martinez was lying, but the priest's story did not seem real to him. He felt disassociated from what he had been told, as though he had been listening

to someone recount the plot of a book or a movie, and
he had to force himself to pretend to take the priest seriously. "Look," he said, "I'm going over to talk to
Wheeler this morning. You're welcome to come along and
ask him about this . . . demon."

"Oh, no. I couldn't go back there."

"Well, what do you want me to do then?"

"Kill him."

Robert blinked. "What?"

"Kill Mr. Wheeler. Waste the fucker. Then cut off his
head."

Robert stared at Father Martinez, completely at a loss
for words. He would have thought he'd imagined what he
just heard were it not for the unwavering eyes and the
earnest and deadly serious look on the priest's face.

"You can bring his head to me on a plate."

Robert stiffened. "If this is a joke—"

"The minions of Satan are no joke."

He didn't know what to say, how to reply.

"You can shoot him if you have to. But the most important thing is to cut off his head. You have to cut off
his head."

Robert stared at the priest. "Father, I'm afraid this conversation is over. I don't know whether or not you're serious about this, but if you are, you need help. And not
the kind of help the police can give you."

"You're with him!" the priest yelled, and his voice was
a shocked accusation. "You're part of it! You're consorting
with the devil!"

Robert had started to turn toward the station, but he
suddenly whirled around. "If you don't leave now, I will
be forced to place you under arrest. Do you understand
me? I am going to talk to Pastor Wheeler this morning.
I will ask about your demon if you want. But if no laws
have been broken, there will be no action taken. And
there will certainly be no killing." He glared at Father

Martinez until the priest turned away, then turned and continued across the dirt to the station door.

The Medusa Syndrome.

He would have to call Jacobson, see if the psychiatrist had discovered what Mike Vigil had seen.

And he would have to re-ask Woods's question about the vampire.

Two hours later, Robert pulled up in front of Wheeler's church.

He got out of the car and, hitching up his belt, sauntered over to where permits for the renovation were displayed on a bracketed black post. He scanned the carbon sheets of official paper, shaking his head. Everything appeared to be in order, but he could not figure out how approval from the county planning commission had been granted so quickly. Hell, he'd had a request in for an expansion of the old jail building for two months, and even though the police department was a government agency and its requests were supposedly expedited, the matter had still not come up before the commission.

"God's will."

Robert jerked his head up to see the Pastor Wheeler staring down at him from the church steps. The words, so closely paralleling an answer to his thoughts, made it almost seem as if the preacher were reading his mind.

Wheeler smiled.

That smile made Robert uncomfortable. He had always found the preacher smugly self-satisfied and annoyingly condescending, but there was something else in that smile now. A cruel hardness, a hint of willful malevolence. It was as if Wheeler felt he no longer had to worry about the laws and mores of the material world, as if he was not only convinced that he possessed The Truth but had received concrete assurance that God was acting as his personal bodyguard.

Robert wondered if the preacher really thought he'd spoken to Jesus Christ.

Yes, he thought, looking into Wheeler's face, *he did.*

Robert glanced down the sidewalk, trying to see where the new addition came closest to the edge of the property line—the spot where Martinez claimed to have peeked inside the church and seen the demon.

"May I help you, Chief Carter?"

Robert turned again to face the preacher. Once more, he shifted his belt, reassured by its weight, by the presence of the holster. He nodded a greeting as he walked across the dirty sidewalk to the steps. "As a matter of fact, you can. I've had a few complaints lately from some of your neighbors. As I'm sure you know, some of them don't take kindly to construction going on all hours of the day and night."

Wheeler's smile did not falter. "Go on."

"Well, I just thought you could stop the pounding and sawing after six or seven in the evening as sort of a goodwill gesture. There are some hardworking Christians around here who need their sleep."

"Good Christians? If they were good Christians, they would understand the importance of the Church of the Living Christ. If they were good Christians, they would be volunteering to help with the construction of this glory to God's greatness instead of trying to place obstacles in its path."

That tack had backfired, but Robert kept his voice calm and friendly, maintaining his easy smile. "That may be true, Reverend, but I think it's a fair request—"

"Is it fair to try to stop the will of the Lord?"

"I'm sure your volunteers need rest too."

"They don't like the color either, do they? Those people who complain? They don't like the color the Lord Jesus Christ has chosen to make His church?"

Robert glanced down at the sidewalk. "I wouldn't know about that."

"Black is Christ's favorite color. In Heaven, His rooms are the color of jet. There is a glorious mansion of blackness to house the Lord of hosts."

Robert shook his head. "Look, I'm asking you kindly, as an act of charity so to speak, to cut down on the noise. Your people can still paint, can still do quiet work. Just cut out the sawing and hammering and loud stuff between, say, eight at night and six in the morning."

"No. I am afraid construction of the Lord's home cannot be postponed for the convenience of unbelievers."

"I don't want to fight with you, Reverend."

"Then don't."

"I could charge you with disturbing the peace, you know—if I wanted to get nasty. I hope it doesn't come to that. But the people who live in this neighborhood have rights too. What we need to do here is reach some kind of compromise, find a way to satisfy both sides."

"There is only one side. And if you try to halt construction on this church for even a minute, I will slap you, the police department, and the town with a harassment suit."

Robert started up the steps. "I don't know who you think—"

"You are trespassing on my land," Wheeler said. "Get off my property. You have no warrant."

Robert stared at him in disbelief. "This is a church."

"It is my church. It is not public property."

"Jesus Christ."

The pastor's face turned a deep cranberry red. He turned and walked into the building without speaking, closing the door loudly and firmly shut behind him. Robert waited for a few moments at the bottom of the steps, on the public sidewalk, not on church property, but when it became clear that Wheeler was not going to come out again, he headed back to the cruiser.

If that son of a bitch wanted to play hardball, then hardball it would be.

He did not look back at the church as he peeled out and sped down the street.

Rich came by after four. He'd brought Anna with him, and he left her out in the lobby where LeeAnne and Jud could keep her occupied at the front desk, and walked back to Robert's office alone.

Robert was scanning the index of *The Vampire: His Kith and Kin* when his brother knocked on the door and stepped into the office. He looked up, smiled tiredly, and closed the book. "How's the news biz?"

"Still on a winning streak." Rich nodded toward the pile on his brother's desk as he leaned against the window. "What's with the books?"

"I've been reading up on vampires." Robert smiled wryly, picked up the top volume. "I thought I could learn something, but most of it's a load of crap. I've gotten some history, but mostly it's a lot of English professors talking about the 'metaphor of the vampire,' explaining how sex lies at the root of the vampire's appeal. The reason people have been interested in vampires over the centuries is because they're supposed to be sexy. The vampire represents repressed sexuality, you know."

Rich smiled halfheartedly.

Robert shook his head. "Real vampires aren't sexy, though, are they? The word 'suck' sounds erotic when you read it, but when you come across the body of someone who's been completely drained of all fluids, it's not erotic, just scary as hell." He dropped the book on his desk. "English professors. Literary critics. Who are these people, and why don't they just use a little common sense?

Bloodsucking is erotic? Do these men get boners when they cut themselves shaving? Do these women get all hot and wet when they slice their fingers chopping vegetables? Jesus, what happens when they participate in the blood drive? There must be orgasms galore!" He snorted. "Who perpetuates this shit?"

Rich smiled. "They're talking about vampires in literature. Not real life. They don't know there are vampires in real life."

"Well, there are. That's not a metaphor running around loose out there and draining people of blood." He pushed the pile of books away from him and stood. "We need to kill this fucker, not interpret his meaning. I got more information about vampires from horror flicks than I did from most of these books."

"They're right about one thing," Rich said. "There is an appeal to vampires. But it's not sex. It has nothing to do with eroticism or repressed desire or forbidden love or any of that." He pointed out the window toward the black church, visible over a low row of houses. "It's the same appeal as that, as religion. It's a chance to live forever. A guarantee that your consciousness will survive death."

"What can we do about that place?" Robert walked over to the window to join his brother. "I can't get a search warrant because I have no probable cause. Judge Simons says that the Constitution guarantees freedom of religion and that a preacher can build whatever kind of church he wants. He looked me straight in the eye and told me that a preacher should be able to do that without fear of police harassment."

"He's right."

"I know he is. But it pisses me off." Robert shook his head. "Maybe we should just burn the fucking place down."

Rich smiled. "Do you ever wonder what people would

think if our conversations were bugged? I mean, here we are, the police chief and the editor of the paper, talking about setting fire to a church."

"I wasn't serious."

"I know. But it's still a strange thing for people in our positions to discuss."

"We were brothers before we got our jobs. We were speaking as brothers, not cop and reporter."

"Forget it," Rich said. "It was just an observation. Damn, you're testy today."

"A vampire's out there killing people. What do you expect?"

"You know, I was thinking this afternoon about that old ghost town off the Globe Highway."

Robert frowned. "What ghost town? Those four old shacks by the side of the road?"

"Yeah. I mean, that place has no name. No one knows who used to live there or why they left."

"So?"

"So there are a lot of little ghost towns like that all across the Southwest. Little places that no one knew about and that just disappeared. I was thinking maybe there's a trail of them. A trail of them across the country, leading all the way back to, I don't know, Roanoke."

"Now you're stretching."

"Am I? We've got a vampire here that's who-knows-how-many-centuries old. He's had to feed off something all those hundreds of years. You don't think it's reasonable to assume that he's been traveling around? You think he's been in Rio Verde all this time?"

"All those years." Robert sighed. "Intimidating, isn't it?"

"No kidding."

"Maybe he's not that old. Maybe he was only made recently."

"Then where's the vampire who made him?" Rich

stared out the window. "Either way, there's an old one out there."

"So you think it's a vampire now, too?"

Rich shrugged. "I guess I do. You know, I was talking to Sue Wing, and she told me about Chinese vampires. *Cup hu girngsis,* they call them."

"Cup-who-girng-sees? How do you spell that?"

"I don't know. But, according to the Chinese, vampires aren't afraid of garlic, they're afraid of willow. You keep them away with jade, not crosses."

"I was thinking of having my men wear crosses, just in case."

"Maybe you should have them wear jade, too. It can't hurt."

"How many different vampire legends are there?"

"Who knows? I told Sue to write a feature about vampires, tell people how they can protect themselves according to the English, the Chinese, whatever other cultures she can dig up."

"A vampire story in the paper?"

"It's a feature. It'll be presented like an interesting discussion of foreign customs and beliefs—but I bet there are a lot of people out there who'll be grateful for the information from a practical standpoint. People are worried."

Robert leaned against his desk. "Tell me about it."

Rich paused. "The reason I stopped by is because I think we should bring this up at the town council meeting next Thursday. This is getting too big. I think we need to develop some sort of . . . civil defense plan. I think we need to organize. We're not getting anywhere just waiting around for the vampire to strike again. We need to act, not react. We have to try to do something before someone else is killed."

Robert nodded. "You're right. I've thought that too. Woods told me that over a week ago, but I've been so busy bagging bodies and following up on all the crackpot calls I've been getting, that I haven't even had time to think. I've probably slept a total of ten hours for the past two weeks." He looked at his brother. "You want to put together a presentation?"

"Sure."

"We'll deliver it together. It'll give it more weight." He cleared his throat. "Do you have a cross?"

Rich shook his head. "No. I'm sure Corrie does, though."

Robert walked around the desk, opened the top middle drawer, and drew out a thin gold chain with a crucifix dangling from the end. He threw it to his brother. "Here. Take this. I'll get another one."

"I'm sure Corrie—"

"This one's for you. Get one for Corrie and Anna if they don't have them. Buy some jade while you're at it. Go to Fritz's Jewelry Store. Charge it to me if you can't afford it. Fritz owes me a favor."

Rich stared at his brother, then slowly nodded. "Thanks," he said.

Robert closed the drawer, not meeting Rich's gaze. "Just do it."

Forty-four

What in God's name was she doing here?

Shelly stared out the windshield of the van at Sue's home. There was a small square of light from the bathroom window on the side of the house, but other than that the place was dark. Sue, and the rest of her family, were dead asleep.

Dead.

Asleep.

Shelly shivered.

"What time you got?" Mr. Hillman asked.

There was the sound of shuffling in the back. "Onethirty," Mr. Grimes said.

Shelly turned around, looked at the two men, at the silhouetted forms of the others inside the van. There was an almost palpable sense of excitement within the vehicle, and though she felt it too, though her blood was racing, and she could hardly wait to get outside and get to work, she sensed that they were all a little *too* excited, a little *too* pumped up, that things tonight might go too far.

That scared her.

That scared her a lot.

It had started out innocently enough. She'd gone last Sunday to the Church of the Holy Trinity. She'd heard the rumors, she'd heard the gossip, and she was curious. The service had been held outside, in the vacant lot behind the church, and there had been over a hundred people there, sitting on benches, on folding chairs, on blankets, on boulders. It had been several years since she'd been to any religious service at all, and she was not sure what prompted her to attend this one. She remembered church as being dry and somewhat boring, like a documentary—something you knew was good for you but didn't enjoy.

But she had enjoyed Wheeler's sermon.

Oh, yes, she had enjoyed it immensely.

The preacher told it like it was. His topics were not parables from the past, Bible stories from two thousand years ago. He talked about the present.

And the future.

It was his talk of the world to come that had really held her spellbound; her and all of the other people sitting enthralled in the cold desert air. Pastor Wheeler did not talk in generalities, did not make vague promises about some faraway future. He spoke in specifics, explained how Jesus would wipe the slate clean, would crush the Catholics, bury the Baptists, maul the Methodists. Jesus liked blood, the preacher said, and the taste of human flesh. Christ would feast on the diseased and corrupted bodies of the unrighteous and cleanse the earth. Their discarded bones would line Highway 370, the border of the path of righteousness that would lead through this barren wasteland to the Church of the Living Christ.

The people around her had really gotten into the sermon, shouting "Hallelujah" and "Praise Jesus!" and she had gotten into it, too. It was as if her eyes had been opened, as if she had merely been existing for the past twenty-two years of her life and had now been invited to live. The loose ends of her world, the unconnected bits and pieces that she had learned and absorbed over the years had suddenly fallen into place, like the pieces of a jigsaw puzzle, and she suddenly knew why she had been born, why she was here.

To serve the Lord Jesus Christ.

And Jesus would walk among them next week.

After the sermon, she had hung around, not knowing anyone but wanting to meet everyone. She'd spied Mr. and Mrs. Grimes, whom she recognized from the Ranch Market, and walked over to them. They were talking with a group of five or six other men and women, and all of them had turned toward her when she'd walked up.

"Jesus hates Chinks," Mrs. Grimes said. "The pastor said last week that He hated those slant-eyed heathens."

"Yes," Shelly said, nodding. She did not know why she was agreeing; she only knew that it felt right.

"Do you want to help us smoke 'em out?" another man asked. He grinned, and there was something infectious in his grin, and she found herself smiling back at him. He looked vaguely familiar, and she knew that she'd seen him around town.

Mr. Grimes nodded his approval. "You're in, then."

Shelly had looked around the lot, noticing that most of the congregation had broken into small groups of ten or eleven. All of them seemed to be huddling closer together, becoming more intense, more insular in their discussions.

Were they making similar plans?

It was possible. The Lord worked in mysterious ways.

A short, bald man with a curly gray beard scratched his weathered cheek. "I can get the gasoline," he said. "But what about the kindling?"

"No problem," Mr. Grimes said.

And now they were here.

Once more, Shelly looked out the windshield at Sue's darkened house. She still felt good about what they were going to do. It still felt right to her. She had no second thoughts, no feelings of guilt or pangs of conscience. This might frighten Sue into seeing the error of her ways, into going to church, into realizing, before next week, before it was too late, that Jesus was the truth and the light. And if it did go too far, if something happened and someone got hurt, well, then it was God's will.

But she and Sue had been friends forever. Since second grade, when they'd met in Mrs. Michaels's class. They'd gone through an awful lot together. Grammar school and junior high and high school. Phases and stages: dolls and music and boys. Sue was her best friend in the world.

But Jesus was more than a friend.

And if she expected to be one of The Chosen, one of The Forty, she had to prove herself.

"I think they leave the bathroom light on all night," she said. "I don't think anyone's up."

"I think you're right," Mrs. Grimes said. She opened her door, got out on the driver's side, and walked to the back of the van, opening it. "Be quiet," she said. "And let's do it quickly."

Shelly got out on the passenger side. Her adrenaline was pumping, and she felt ready for anything.

"Jesus wants us to take out those trees," Mr. Hillman said. "The pastor said that's the most important thing."

There were whispers of agreement from the other men and women getting out of the van.

Shelly grabbed one of the Hefty bags filled with the dried leaves they were going to use as fuel for the fire. It felt full and weighty in her grasp, satisfyingly full. Next to her, Hal Newman, the old man with the beard, grabbed his cans of gasoline. "Let's fry us up some chink," he said.

Shelly grinned at him. "Let's do it."

Sue was awakened by the smell of smoke and gasoline.

Her first coherent thought was that the house was burning down. She tried to leap out of bed, but with the partial coordination of the half-awake, she got tangled up in her sheets and fell to the floor, landing loudly on her side.

She didn't know whether it was her fall or the smoke smell that had awakened her parents, but she heard them talking loudly and excitedly in their bedroom, and she caught the muffled words "fire" and "trees." She stood up, untangling herself from the sheets, and saw a thin wisp of smoke drifting through her open window from between the curtains.

She hurried out of her bedroom, down the hall to her parents' bedroom, and through their window she saw an orange-yellow glow in the front yard.

The willows were on fire.

Her father was already dressed and hurrying out of the room, yelling for her to call the fire department, but she stared out the window, transfixed. There were two fires, one at the foot of each tree, and though the blazes were large and growing larger, they had not yet engulfed the trees. They seemed to be burning built-up piles of garbage and debris at the foot of the willows. Across the street, lights were on in the Malverns' and Chapmans' houses, and, silhouetted figures were standing at the windows. There was no sound of sirens, not even from across town, and Sue realized that none of their neighbors had bothered to call the fire department.

"Call!" her father ordered as he ran down the hallway, and she hurried to obey. Her mother was crying, gathering up photos and mementoes, shoving them into her oversize jewelry box.

Sue sped out of the bedroom, down the hall, into the kitchen. She found the list of emergency numbers next to the phone and quickly dialed the Rio Verde Volunteer Fire Department. Chief Simmons answered, "Fire station," he said sleepily.

"There's a fire on our front lawn!" She was practically shouting into the phone, her words all running together. She forced herself to slow down. Behind her, she heard bare feet running across open floor. Her mother, brother, and grandmother. "There's a big fire on our front lawn. My name's Sue Wing. I'm at ten-oh-one East Shadow-bluff."

"East Shadowbluff?" The captain was instantly wide awake.

"Yes."

"We'll be right there."

By the time she ran outside, where her mother, her grandmother, and John were standing on the stoop—her mother desperately clutching the overstuffed jewelry box—she could already hear the sirens. Her father had turned on the hose and was attempting to spray the fire at the foot of the smaller tree, but the water seemed to be having no effect. They had not gotten to the blaze in time. It was spreading, burning out of control.

Sue caught her grandmother's eye. The old woman was tightly holding on to John's hand. He was staring at the fire, the colors of the flames reflected on his face, and he was smiling.

Influenced.

Her grandmother nodded once at Sue, turned her attention back toward the blaze. She understood. The fire had been deliberately set.

The *cup hu girngsi* wanted to destroy the willow trees.

Sue ran back into the house to grab some pots and pitchers they could fill with water.

The fire truck arrived a few moments later. The flames, by this time, were as high as a man and had blackened the first six feet or so of each trunk. Individual branches had also caught on fire and looked like drooping sparklers, the thin willow leaves igniting quickly and in sequence. The fire lit up a full half of the block, and in its glow Sue could see their neighbors standing in front of their own houses, watching, waiting—not volunteering to help.

There was no hydrant nearby, Sue realized as two firemen jumped off the back of the truck, pulling a large canvas hose.

"Stand back!" one of the men ordered. She and her father moved back onto the porch with the rest of the family. Another man ran around the side of the truck, flipped some levers, pushed some buttons, and a powerful jet of water shot out of the hose held by the other two men, drenching the tree on the left and almost instantly dousing the fire.

Three minutes later, both fires were completely out, and the hose was shut off.

A man walked toward them across the scorched grass, and she recognized Mr. Buford from the burger stand. She and her father met him halfway.

"Thank you!" her father said, taking the fireman's hand and pumping it. "Thank you very much for putting out fire!"

Mr. Buford smiled, embarrassed. "That's what we're here for."

"Thank you!"

"Thank *you*. This is the first time we've gotten a chance to try this new pump outside of practice." He looked from her father to the rest of the family. "Are you all okay?"

"We're fine," Sue said. "Thanks."

Chief Simmons walked over. Sue was suddenly embarrassed to be outside and in her pajamas. Neighbors were coming out now, coming by to survey the damage. She saw curiosity on the faces, interest. But no sympathy.

The chief took off his hat, wiped his forehead. "Do you have any idea who might have done this?"

Sue shook her head.

"This was arson, you know."

She nodded. "I know."

"But you don't know who did it? You can't think of anyone who would want to do something like this?"

The *cup hu girngsi*, she wanted to say, but she sensed

that this was neither the time nor place to bring that up. One look toward her grandmother confirmed the rightness of her decision. "I don't know," she said.

"We'll come back in the morning, go over everything, see what we can discover. We're only volunteer, but we're not bad at investigating arson, and we may be able to come up with something. So don't walk out here or touch anything until we go over it first, okay?"

She nodded.

"That goes for your neighbors too."

"No one will touch anything."

"We'll fill out a full report in the morning, too. Your father will have to sign it."

"Then tell him, not me."

The chief looked embarrassed. "I just thought—"

"I understand English," her father said, offended.

"I'm sorry," Chief Simmons said.

"That okay," her father said.

Sue nodded to the chief, to Mr. Buford, left them talking to her father, and walked back toward the porch. Her mother was still clutching the jewelry box, as though she had not yet realized the fire was out and the danger was over, and her grandmother was still holding tightly on to John's hand. John was staring dejectedly toward where the fire had been. She realized that he had not spoken, had not uttered a single word, since he had come outside. Sue moved next to her grandmother. "That was close," she said.

Her grandmother nodded, did not look at her. "Yes," she said. Her voice was flat, completely devoid of emotion. "Yes, it was."

Forty-five

Huell Hinkley had never liked working the lot at night. It wasn't because business was slow at that time, though it was. It wasn't because he would rather be home with Ellie, though he would.

It was because he could never be certain that someone wasn't hiding behind one of the cars.

It was a weird phobia, and not one that should have affected a grown man, but there it was. Although he would never admit it to a living soul, not even to Ellie, that was why he asked Steve to stop by on the nights he worked late. He pretended it was for the company, claiming that he got lonely working at night by himself with no one to talk to, but the truth was that he was scared.

In the daytime, there was no problem. He was king of the car lot. He could be working alone, the whole street could be empty, the whole damn town could be abandoned, and he wouldn't give a rat's ass. But at night it was a different story. At night, he remained a prisoner on the steps of the office, looking over the shiny metal roofs and hoods, peeking through the windshields and windows, trying to detect signs of movement. He would come down from the steps if a browser came by, using the opportunity to look behind whatever vehicles had seemed suspicious to him that evening, and he would do the same thing if Steve stopped by, but otherwise he would remain in the office or on the steps, waiting, worrying.

Hinkley stood on the steps now, wondering if someone had crept between the Nova and the Impala on the northeast corner of the lot while he'd been on the phone a few minutes ago. He stared at the two cars, at the two cars immediately in front of them, but saw nothing, no shadows, no movement.

Did a vampire even have a shadow?

That was what he was worried about. A vampire. The vague fears he'd previously held had coalesced into concrete form within the past week, and had made these past couple of nights a living hell. Once again, he cursed Tanner for making him work evenings.

He glanced to his left, toward the desert. Past the buildings, the sand was purple with dusk, and those sections of hill and butte which had been so clear and so clearly defined only moments before were now little more than hulking amorphous shapes against the darkening sky.

The vampire could be anywhere, he realized. In one of the canyons, in the arroyo, by the river.

Behind one of the cars.

There was a honk from the street, and he jumped, nearly slipping off the step.

"Pop!"

He looked up to see Steve sticking his head out of a police cruiser parked in the middle of the street. "You scared the shit out of me!" he yelled.

"Sorry!" Steve grinned. "I just came by to tell you that I can't stop in tonight! Too many things going on! I'll try to swing by again, though, a little later!"

Hinkley nodded, smiled, and waved, his stomach sinking as his son drove off. His heart was still pounding, and he tried to catch his breath as he scanned the car lot. He had a bad feeling about tonight.

Turning, he walked up the last two steps into the office and closed the door. He switched on the portable black-and-white TV on the desk, and sat there, one eye on the

TV, one on the lot, nervously twisting the jade ring on his right pinkie.

Immediately after stepping outside onto Miss Atwood's porch, Emily knew that it had been a mistake to walk rather than drive. The night air was freezing, more like December than October, but it was not the cold that convinced her she had made a mistake—it was something else, a feeling in the air, a sense that this night was different from others. She had never believed in ESP or premonitions or any of that psychic stuff, but this was not like a vision. It was something she knew, something she felt deep in her gut, and it frightened her.

She buttoned her jacket against the cold and took her daughter's hand. "Come on," she said, "it's freezing. We'd better get home."

Pam turned around and waved to Miss Atwood through the window. The piano teacher waved back.

They lived only three blocks from Miss Atwood, but tonight those three blocks seemed like three miles to Emily. She hurried her daughter along the cracked sidewalk toward home.

"Miss Atwood said that I'm good enough to start in the advanced book next week," Pam said.

Emily smiled, tried to appear interested. "That's great."

Something was definitely the matter. The night was cold, but it was not windy. She could hear wind, however, and water, and the sounds seemed to come from all around them, not from any particular direction. There was something threatening and unnatural about the combined noises, and she wanted to run down the sidewalk, across the street, and around the block all the way home, locking the door behind her and pulling all the curtains. It was only her own high heels and Pam's presence that kept her from doing so.

Pam continued to chatter on about her piano lesson, going aver mistakes she'd made, difficulties she'd mastered, things her teacher had said, but Emily paid attention to none of it. Her eyes were on the night around them, on the houses that looked abandoned, on the saguaros that looked like people, on the bushes that looked like animals. Nothing seemed right tonight, nothing seemed normal. Her perceptions had been altered, heightened, and everywhere she glanced there was danger. The sounds of wind and water increased in intensity.

Then she saw it.

At the end of the block, standing unmoving beneath a weak streetlight, was a large overweight man.

She stopped walking, holding tightly to her daughter's hand. Pam gasped at the force with which her mother held on to her and stopped as well. She'd been talking about how she was looking forward to the advanced piano book because it had more popular songs, but she stopped talking, as she followed her mother's gaze.

"Mom?" she said, her voice frightened.

Emily motioned for her daughter to be quiet. She took a tentative step forward, waiting to see if the figure moved, but the overweight man remained still. She'd been hoping he would step more fully into the light, that she would be able to reassure herself that nothing out of the ordinary was happening here, but her own chills and Pam's voice told her that was not the case. She stared at the unmoving silhouette at the end of the block. Something about the form was familiar but she found that despite the familiarity she was frightened.

"It's Elvis," Pam said softly.

"What?"

"It's Elvis."

So it was. Emily's heart leaped in her chest. She recognized the figure now. Elvis. Elvis Aaron Presley. The King. The King of Rock and Roll.

They stood stock-still, Emily holding tightly to her daughter's hand. Between here and the corner, the sidewalk was a chiaroscuro mosaic, the square sections of cement divided into what looked like huge black-and-white tiles, lightened by porch lights and street lamps, darkened by shadows and night.

She had dreamed of meeting Elvis for most of her life, had faithfully bought every *Enquirer* and *Star* that proclaimed Elvis alive, praying it was true, that he had gone into hiding, become part of the federal witness protection program, that he really had been spotted eating at Burger King.

But she knew now, with that same gut certainty that had earlier told her this night was dangerous, that Elvis was dead and had been since 1977.

And that he was standing at the end of the block.

The figure turned, faced them, and now she could see the white suit, the black hair, the sideburns.

"Mom," Pam said, and there was terror in her voice. "Let's get out of here."

Elvis started toward them, moving through the shadows and light, a labored lumber that would have been comical were it not so frighteningly odd.

"Mom!"

The King lurched toward them, grinning at Pam.

"No!" Emily screamed, jerking her daughter by the hand.

And then Elvis was upon them.

Angelina worked slowly but with purpose. There was no hurry. Her sons, David and Neal, were safely within the padlocked storage shed and there was no way they were going to get out.

She used the wirecutters to snip the strands of clothesline that stretched across the small backyard. Mr. Wheeler was right. If she was ever to get into heaven and save her soul from the eternal torment of hell, she had to abide by the word of God.

And, according to the Bible, if her sons disobeyed her, they were to be put to death. The Lord did not tolerate disrespect to parents.

She heard David crying within the shed, heard Neal yelling, pounding on the door in a desperate effort to get out. She smiled to herself as she snipped the last strand of clothesline and let it fall to the dirt.

She'd called Wheeler this afternoon and told him of her decision to put her sons to death for their transgressions, for David's refusal to brush his teeth after dinner and Neal's unwillingness to make his bed, but the pastor had suggested that she offer her children to the Savior as a sacrifice and let Him decide on their punishment. Her heart had swelled when she'd heard those words. The idea that the Lord Jesus Christ would deign to visit her humble trailer filled her with jubilation, and after she'd locked her sons in the storage shed, she'd set about cleaning the inside of the trailer and sprucing up the surrounding yard.

She threw away everything that belonged to her children, and that made the cleaning much easier.

Now it was night, and she knew that it was time to prepare her sacrifice to the Lord.

She went back inside, took a knife from the drawer in the kitchen, brought along the twine she'd purchased earlier in the day, and walked out to the storage shed. Carefully, not speaking, she unlocked the storage shed door and opened it a crack. As she'd expected, Neal tried to make a run for it, tried to push the door open and flee, but she shoved the knife through the crack, catching him in the cheek. He fell down, screaming, holding his face.

She grabbed David's arm, pulled him out and shut the door, locking it again.

David tried to twist his arm, pull out of her grasp, but she sliced off a chunk of his thigh, the knife easily shaving off a thin piece of skin and muscle, and he went limp in her arms. The blood was flowing, fairly pouring from the wound, but she ignored it and dragged her son across the small backyard.

She tied him to the cross pole of the clothesline, leaving his naked, bleeding body in a reverent position of crucifixion.

For good measure, she wrapped some twine around his testicles and tied it.

She did the same to Neal on the other clothesline pole.

She went back inside, took a shower, put on her pajamas, and crawled into bed to watch an old rerun of *The Bob Newhart Show.*

Outside, David was silent, but Neal continued to howl well into the night.

She turned off the TV and fell asleep to the music of his screams.

She dreamed of Jesus, and in the morning both of her boys were gone.

Forty-six

Emily looked from Robert to Woods and back again. "Elvis killed my daughter."

"The tape is rolling. Tell us again exactly what happened." Robert smiled sympathetically and handed her a Styrofoam cup of coffee. A long time ago he had dated Emily. In those days, before his marriage to Julie, he had even half thought that he and Emily would marry, although he could not imagine himself married to the woman now seated before him. Many times, over the years, he had thought of her, of their short time together, and he wondered if she, too, remembered those old days, or if her time with him had just blurred into a hazy, indistinct past. He wondered what it would have been like had they married. Would he look older now? Would she look younger?

That was what he hated most about living in a small town—the past was always intruding. You could never get a clean start if your history was a part of your present.

Emily sipped the coffee, looked up. Her voice was surprisingly calm, eerily devoid of emotion. "Elvis Presley killed Pam. We were walking home from her piano lesson, and we saw him waiting under a streetlight at the corner of Ocotillo and Indian Hill. Pam recognized him first. Then he ran toward us, and I thought he was going to tackle us both, but I just felt a . . . a rush of air, and then both of them were gone."

"Elvis and Pam?"

"Yes." Emily leaned forward in her chair, and around her neck Robert saw a gold chain and a square of green. A jade pendant.

He stared at the chain around her neck. "May I see that?" he asked.

She frowned, fingering the necklace nervously. "This? What for? Pam gave that to me last Christmas."

"Humor me."

She unhooked the necklace, handed it to him.

"What did Elvis look like?" Woods asked. "Did he look like he was dead? Did he look like a ghost? Do you think it might have been an Elvis impersonator, someone dressed up to look like—"

"It was Elvis, and he was dead, and he looked like he did the day he died."

Robert was examining the jade. It was a simple square with some sort of Chinese character carved on it. He handed it back to her. "All right," he said. "We've searched that area of the town, and my men are combing the rest of Rio Verde with Pam's picture. We'll get a posse together and search the surrounding desert if we have to, but we need as much information as you can give us."

"That's it. That's all there is."

"Let's go through it step-by-step, from the moment you left your house to take Pam to her lesson."

An hour later, they were all exhausted, Emily was crying, and they still had no new information. Robert dismissed Emily, thanking her, promising they would keep her informed, and dispatched Ted to take her home. Robert sighed, popping out the tape and carrying it out to LeeAnne. "Type up a transcript and fax it to Rossiter, okay?"

She nodded. "Okay."

Stu walked in, limping.

"What happened to you?"

"Nothing." He moved behind the counter and sat down at his desk, painfully grimacing as he stretched his right leg out in front of him. "Charley horse."

"Great. People are dying and Elvis has come back to life and my officers are incapacitated by charley horses."

"I'm not incapacitated." He frowned. "Elvis?"

Robert waved tiredly. "Have LeeAnne explain it to you while she types. We have a missing person. You're going to be out there searching next shift."

He walked back to his office. Woods was seated at his desk, contorting his face. "My mouth tastes like I've been gargling with sewer water."

"Really? That's nice. Get out of my chair."

The coroner stood. "Medusa Syndrome," he said. "I'd bet money on it. She saw the vampire kill her daughter, or abduct her daughter, and the shock was too great. Now she thinks she saw Elvis."

"You never heard of the Medusa Syndrome a month ago. Now you're an expert?' "

"Let's call in Jacobson, have him look at her."

"He still hasn't gotten through to Vigil."

Woods took a cigarette out of his pocket, looked at it. "The only thing I can't figure out is how come the vampire didn't take her down, too. Why just the daughter?"

"The jade."

"What was all that about? I was wondering why you wanted a peek at that necklace."

"According to the Chinese, jade scares vampires away. Works like a cross is supposed to."

"So we have ourselves a Chinese vampire here?"

Robert shrugged. "I don't know. Could be."

Woods put the unlit cigarette in his mouth. "Clifford and the horses were cremated Monday. They won't be coming back."

"Good."

The two of them were silent for a moment. "I think people are missing," Woods said finally.

Robert didn't respond right away. He kicked his shoe against the floor, trying to dislodge a small rock pressing against the sole of his foot. "What people?"

"I don't know. It just seems to me that there are fewer people around town than there's supposed to be. I went into the pharmacy yesterday, and while it's never the most happening place in town, it seemed downright deserted. Even the Basha's parking lot looked kind of empty."

It was true. Robert had not wanted to admit it, might not have even noticed it on a conscious level until Woods had brought it up, but now that he considered it, Rio Verde had seemed unusually quiet since the weekend. With the absence of the recreationers and the coming of the cold weather, it was as if the town had emptied out, leaving only a skeleton crew of citizens.

"Maybe people are scared. Maybe they're leaving."

"Maybe," Woods said doubtfully.

"What's that supposed to mean?"

"It means most people around here have a tough time just making their car payments. You think they can suddenly decide to take a few weeks off work and stay at a hotel in Scottsdale because they're scared of a vampire? You think they're packing all their belongings, calling moving vans, and heading off for California?" The coroner shook his head. "That looks great in movies, but real life economics ensures that that won't happen here."

"What's your explanation, then?"

"People are staying home, not going out. They're frightened. Many of them might not even know why. But they're scared. It's in the air now, Robert. It's not working behind the scenes anymore. It's out in the open." He took the cigarette out of his mouth. "And I think some people have . . . disappeared. Like Pam Frye."

Robert stared at him. "But people would report that.

Wives, husbands, parents, kids. Someone would call that in."

"Maybe."

There was a knock on the door frame, and Robert turned to see Jud and Steve standing in the hallway outside the office. "What is it?"

"We found a girl's shoe in the drainage ditch behind Basha's," Jud said. "We think it may be Pam Frye's."

"Why are you here then? Why aren't you searching?"

"We found it an hour ago," Steve explained. "We've been searching the ditch and the area behind the store since then and haven't found a thing."

"Where's the shoe?"

"Tagged in an evidence bag. We thought you might want to call in the mom, have her look at it before we devote any more time to that area."

Robert nodded. "Good thinking. If it is hers, we'll focus on that sector. If not, we can move on." He looked at Woods, then back at the two officers. He cleared his throat. "I know you may be thinking this already, but I just wanted to make it official: We're dealing with a vampire here. That's what we're looking for now."

Steve nodded. "What does Agent Rossiter say about that?"

"Who gives a fuck what he says?"

"Yes, sir."

"I haven't told Rossiter yet. But I will."

"It's punishment," Jud said. "Those people who died were punished for their wickedness and their sin. Maybe Pam Frye's been punished, too. Maybe the whole town's being punished."

Robert turned to face him. "Where did you hear that crap?"

The policeman looked embarrassed. "Pastor Wheeler. He says this is the work of God."

"The work of God? And you believe that shit?"

"I believe in God more than I believe in vampires."

Robert shook his head disgustedly. "I can't believe you're stupid enough to fall for that."

Jud's face reddened again, but this time from anger. "We have freedom of religion in this country, sir, and I can go to whatever church I want without having to get my boss's permission. You can tell me what to do on the job, but no one tells me what to do in my real life."

"You're right," Robert said. "Sorry." He glanced again at Woods, who raised his eyebrows questioningly. "Call Mrs. Frye," he told the policemen. "Have her come down and identify the shoe. Have LeeAnne ring me when she's here."

Steve nodded. "Yes, sir." Both he and Jud headed back down the hall.

Robert closed the door. "What do you make of that?"

"Is that officer a religious man?"

"Didn't used to be."

Woods put the unlit cigarette in his mouth. "Wrath of God. That scares me."

"You buy it?"

"No. But it scares me that other people do." He examined the map of Rio Verde on the wall opposite the window. "It scares me a lot."

Forty-seven

Sue stood uncomfortably in the middle of Janine's living room, waiting for her friend to get out of the bathroom, acutely conscious of Janine's mother lying passed out on the couch.

"One more minute!" Janine called.

Sue did not answer, not wanting to wake the snoring woman. She glanced slowly around the room. The interior of Janine's house looked like the office of a cut-rate travel agency, the paneled walls decorated with posters advertising the sightseeing attributes of various countries, the posters tacked up at off-center angles that were supposed to be artistic but instead looked sad. "Early white trash," Shelly called the decor. Sue could not bring herself to be quite that harsh, but she had to agree that Janine's mother would not win any awards for interior decorating.

Janine walked in from the hallway, adjusting her tasseled cowgirl jacket. "Thanks for coming. I don't know what I'd do without you."

"That's what friends are for," Sue whispered.

"So says the song." Janine nodded toward her mother. "And you don't have to whisper. She's out like a light."

"We'd better get going. I have a busy day ahead of me. I have to drop the car off for my father. I work at the newspaper in the morning and the restaurant in the afternoon. What time do you want me to pick you up tonight?"

"I'll get a ride." Janine straightened her hat. "God, I hate car problems."

"Who doesn't?"

"They're talking about laying people off at the ranch, you know. That's why I'm filling in today, to earn some brownie points."

"Laying people off?"

"They said it's because of the stories in your paper."

Sue bristled. "That's stupid. The paper printed an article about a murder, and now the Rocking D's immediately going to start firing people because the bad publicity *might* scare some people away next summer? That doesn't make sense."

"No," Janine admitted. "But it sounded logical when Hollis talked to us. I mean, he has a point. Why does the paper always focus on bad and negative things? Why doesn't it ever show some of the positive aspects of our town?"

"The paper focuses on bad things? Since when? All the *Gazette*'s ever had in it are ads and fluff stories about old people. You've said so yourself. Now people are being murdered, the paper's reporting it, and you think the coverage is too negative?"

"You're getting awfully fired up about the responsibilities of the newspaper lately."

"Yeah, well." Sue felt her face flush. She looked at her watch. "We'd better get going. Or else we'll both be late."

Janine followed Sue out the door, closing it and locking it behind her. She put the keys in her right front pocket, and there was a clanking rattle as they fell through a hole in the pocket and down her pants leg onto the ground. She picked the keys up, putting them into her other pocket. "So what are you going to do with the extra money you're making at the paper?"

"I'm saving it for college."

"Still?"

"It's expensive."

"Why don't you break down and do something fun for a change? Celebrate. All you have is that old record player. Why don't you buy a new stereo? Put a CD player on layaway at Radio Shack."

"Radio Shack? You expect me to trust that place? It's an electronics store, and they don't even know how to use a cash register. They still write everything out by hand."

"I'm just saying do something fun for once. At least with your first paycheck."

Sue shook her head. "I'm not getting any younger."

Janine nodded slowly as they walked out to the car. "That's true. Neither of us are."

There was a resigned sadness in her friend's voice that made Sue think of the unborn baby, and she found herself surreptitiously glancing at the other girl's abdomen. Had she made a decision yet? Had she told her mother?

Maybe that's why her mother had gotten drunk last night and passed out on the couch.

Sue unlocked the passenger door, walked around the front of the station wagon. From down the street came the sound of a souped-up engine, roaring, growing louder. A red Mustang sped by.

"Go back to China!" a male voice yelled.

There were hoots of encouraging laughter, and then the Mustang squealed around the curve of the road and was gone.

"Assholes," Janine said.

"Who was that?"

"It looked like Bryant Taylor's car."

"God, he's twenty years old, and he's still cruising around yelling insults at people?" Sue shook her head. "When's he going to grow up?"

"He and his buddies are probably looking for a high school couple walking to school now, so they can yell, 'Fuck her! I did!' "

Sue laughed. "I remember that one."

The two of them got in the car, and Sue started the engine, put the car into gear, and made a U-turn in the middle of the street.

Janine pulled down the sun visor to examine her face in the small makeup mirror. "Have you talked to Shelly lately?"

Sue shook her head. "Not since last week. She never seems to be home when I call. Why?"

"She's never home when I call either, but I saw her yesterday at Circle K. I'm worried about her. She's . . . I don't know. I think she's losing it."

"Losing it?"

"I went over to talk to her, and she started giving me all this church talk, all this stuff about blood and death and Jesus and I don't know what all. It was creepy."

"Shelly?" Sue said, surprised.

Janine nodded. "Shelly. And, I don't know how to put this delicately, but she smelled. Bad. Like she hadn't bathed for a long time, you know? It's hard to describe, but you'd understand if you were there. It was weird. Scary. The way she looked and the way she was talking, I kept thinking—I know this is cold, but I kept imagining her mom, dead, in the kitchen or something, stabbed. Shelly hates her mom, you know."

"I don't think she hates her."

"I think she does, and the way she was acting yesterday . . ." Janine shivered. "I don't even want to think about it."

"A lot of strange things have been going on lately."

"You can say that again."

Sue drove for a moment in silence. "What would you say," she said finally, "if I told you there was a vampire in Rio Verde?"

"I'd say I've heard that one before."

Sue did not take her eyes off the road, but she reached

into the open purse next to her. Her fingers found what
she was looking for—one of the small jade stones that her
grandmother had given her—and she offered it to Janine,
opening her palm. "Here. This is for you."

Janine took the stone. "What is it?"

"Jade. It'll protect you from vampires."

"I thought crosses did that."

"Not according to my culture."

Janine said nothing, looked at the jade. "You're serious
about this, aren't you?"

Sue nodded, feeling a little embarrassed but not as
much as she'd expected. "These people who were killed,
the man at the Rocking D, they were killed by a vampire,
or what we call a *cup hu girngsi.*"

Janine licked her lips. "One of the maids said she saw
a vampire," she admitted.

"What did she say he looked like?"

"A she."

"The vampire was a woman?"

"Yeah. La Verona."

The flesh prickled on Sue's arms. La Verona, the wail-
ing woman of the canals, was an Arizona legend that had
been used by more than one mother to ensure that her
child did not venture too close to open waterways. In the
version Sue had heard, La Verona had been tall and
wraith-thin, with white skin and long black hair. In Sue's
mind, La Verona had always had vaguely Asian features,
and it was that image that chilled her now, made her feel
so frightened.

"Where did she see the vampire?" Sue asked.

"By the river."

She pulled onto the dirt road that led to the Rocking
D. "Keep that jade with you, okay? No matter what happens. And tell other people, anyone you can. Get one for
your mother."

"A jade rock?"

"Anything made out of jade. White jade's the best, the most powerful."

Janine looked at her suspiciously. "How come you're such an expert in all of this?"

"It's a long story. Remind me to tell you sometime. After it's all over."

"After what's all over?"

"After the *cup hu girngsi* is dead."

Rich was pasting up the paper in the back room, his tape player cranked up, playing an old Yes cassette. Jim Fredricks was with him, cutting halftones to size and running them through the waxer before slapping them down on the sports page.

Rich glanced at Sue as she entered the room. "Hey," he said, "what's up?"

"I was going to ask you." She nodded to Fredricks. "Hi."

The sports reporter nodded back.

"So," she said, "any new developments?"

Rich critically eyed the column of type he'd just pressed down on the page dummy. He pulled up the wax paper and repositioned it. "Woman claims Elvis stole her daughter."

Sue sucked in her breath. "The *cup hu girngsi.*"

"What?" Fredricks said, turning around to look at her.

"Vampire," Rich explained.

The sportswriter looked from Sue to the editor and back again, trying to determine if they were pulling his leg. Apparently deciding that they were serious, he quickly turned his back and returned to his sports photos.

Sue stared at Rich. "Why are you here, then? Why aren't you helping your brother?"

"Help him do what?" The editor shook his head. "I

can't spend all my time running around. I have a paper to put out."

"But—"

"No buts. I can't do anything by following my brother around. What I can do is make sure that the paper comes out on time, like it always does. We can reach more people that way than any other."

She nodded. "Are you going to run my feature?"

"Did you write it?"

"Sort of."

"Sort of?"

"It's not typed yet, but I've written it." She reached into her notebook and withdrew several folded pages, unfolding them and handing them to him. "Here."

Rich scanned the first page, the second, the third. He looked up at her. "There's no attribution here."

"I didn't have time to talk to anyone."

"This isn't an article. It's a report. And it's only about Chinese vampires."

"That's what we have here, a *cup hu girngsi.*"

"We don't know that."

"I know it."

He looked at her, met her eyes, then turned away, nodding. "All right. Type it up. Bring me your disk when you're through. I need it within the hour."

"I will." She took the pages from him and hurried off to her desk, where she grabbed her floppy disk from the middle drawer. She pulled her chair up to his VDT, turned on the machine, and after loading her disk began to type.

She was nearly finished with the article when she heard voices from behind the dividers in the front of the office. Male voices. Two of them. She heard Carole tell them that Rich was in the back, pasting up, and then the men—Rich's brother Robert and what had to be the tallest man she'd ever seen—were rounding the corner into the newsroom.

Robert nodded at her. His eyes looked tired, and it appeared as though he hadn't shaved; there was brown and black stubble on his chin. "Hi there," he said.

"Hi."

Rich emerged from pasteup, an X-acto knife in his hand. "I thought I heard your voice," he said to his brother. He smiled at the big man. "Hey, Pee Wee."

Pee Wee nodded absently to the editor, but he was staring at Sue, studying her. There was nothing sexual in his gaze, nothing sleazy or secretive or even remotely salacious, only an open, honest interest, and although he did not take his eyes off her, she found that she didn't mind the attention. "Aren't you going to introduce us?" he asked Rich.

The editor shook his head. "My manners again. I guess I should have gone to finishing school. Pee Wee, this is Sue Wing, the newest addition to our newspaper family. Sue, this is Pee Wee Nelson. I don't know if you remember, but he used to be police chief before Robert."

The big man smiled at her. "Pleased to meet you, little lady."

There was something about Pee Wee that put her at ease, that made her feel comfortable in his presence. She smiled back at him. "Hello."

"He's retired now," Rich explained. "Lives alone in the desert, spending his time living off the land and making mirrors like some leftover overage hippie."

Pee Wee laughed.

"He's very talented, though," Rich said. "And a great feature story. I think we tap him for an interview and photo essay at least once a year."

The big man squinted at Sue. "You know, you look familiar to me. I don't know how, but it seems like I met you before somewhere."

"I don't think so," she said politely.

"Maybe I'm just getting senile."

"Sue's writing an article on Chinese vampires," Rich said. He cleared his throat. "She thinks that's what we have here in Rio Verde."

There was silence. Spoken at a different time, in a different tone of voice, those words would have been cruelly mocking, dismissively condescending, but Rich had said them straight, seriously, with respect, and that was how they were taken by the other two men. She was acutely aware of the fact that she was not embarrassed by the revelation, but proud.

"She's the one who told me about the jade," he explained.

"I was doing some reading yesterday," Robert said, "and in the Basil Copper book I checked out of the library it talks a little bit about Chinese vampire legends. It didn't say anything about using jade for protection."

Sue turned to him. "So?"

"Well, are you sure you got your story straight on this?"

Sue's jaw muscles tightened. "Are you going to believe a paragraph in some book about vampire *legends* or my grandmother, who's had firsthand experience with the *cup hu girngsi?*"

"Just calm down there, hon."

"My name's not 'Hon.' My name's Sue."

Rich grinned.

"I didn't mean—"

"Believe it or not, there are things that weren't told to Western writers about the *cup hu girngsi.* Western scholars don't know everything there is to know about my culture. I know a little something about it myself."

"I was just asking," Robert said humbly. "I believe you." He held out his right hand. "I'm wearing a jade ring, see?"

Pee Wee laughed. "I like her," he said to Rich.

The editor grinned. "I'm just glad she's on our side."

There was silence among them for a moment. Robert

scratched his stubbled chin. "Have you asked your grandmother where she thinks the vampire might be? I assume Chinese vampires hide during the day like American vampires. He has to have a place somewhere."

"There are no 'Chinese vampires' or 'American vampires.' Those are only different ways of looking at the same creature, the *cup hu girngsi.*"

"Whatever. Do you know where he is?"

Sue paused. "I felt it at the school," she said. "The high school." She looked at Rich. "The night I tried to sign up for your class."

He licked his lips. "At the school?"

She nodded.

"Did you notice anything about it?" Robert asked. "What did it look like?"

"It's old," she said quietly. "That's what stood out the most to me. It's very, very old."

"Where did you see it?"

"I didn't see it, exactly. I felt it. I sensed its presence. It was like . . . I don't know. I just knew that it was there. And I knew it was ancient." She met the police chief's gaze. "It was by the lockers, at the end of the main corridor."

"That's a place to start."

Rich stared at the blade of his X-acto knife, turning the knife in his hands. "What if it is as old as you think? What if it is centuries old? How can we fight something like that? Our little lives pass by in a blink of its eye. We're nothing to it; we're no threat."

"My grandmother is."

Pee Wee shook his head. "If it's always been here, how come it didn't start killing until now? I don't buy this invincible stuff. That's crap." He nodded toward Sue, smiled at her. "I'm with Sue here. I think we can fight it."

"I hope so," Rich said.

Robert nodded. "Me, too."

* * *

Robert and Pee Wee went into the pasteup room with Rich, while Sue finished typing her article. Robert and Pee Wee left soon after, and she went into the back to help Rich and Fredricks put the paper to bed.

Robert returned alone a little after noon. Fredricks had gone home nearly an hour before, and she and Rich were alone in the back room. It was Rich's turn to pick up Anna from school, and Robert offered to accompany his brother on the trip. It was obvious to Sue that the police chief had something he wanted to say to Rich alone, so she declined Rich's invitation to join them. The editor promised before they left that he would bring back tacos and a Coke for her lunch, and she gratefully and hungrily accepted.

They'd been gone only a few minutes, and she was still looking through her desk drawer for a blue correcting pencil with which to go over the pages, when the front door to the office opened and she heard Carole's cheerful greeting. "Good afternoon, sir. May I help you?"

The visitor had the pained, gruff voice of an older man. "I need to talk to Rich."

"What does this concern?" the secretary asked.

"I have an item to put in the 'Upcoming Events' column."

"Then you need to speak to Miss Wing. She's out of the office right now."

"Who's Miss Wing?"

"The chink that Rich hired."

Sue felt her stomach drop and her chest tighten. She had to remind herself to breathe. The secretary's voice was just as saccharine sweet as always as she continued to talk to the man, but Sue heard only the tone, not the substance. The word—*that* word—was still echoing in her mind.

Chink.

It was the fact that Carole knew her personally and still chose to refer to her in such a degradingly depersonalized way that hurt her the most. In that telltale moment, she had been granted a glimpse behind the facade, and she knew now that Carole's grandmotherly niceness was only a show, a front.

It felt to Sue as though the ground had been pulled out from underneath her. A moment ago, this newsroom had been her home, a place as known and comfortable to her as the restaurant, but now she felt like an intruder, her surroundings suddenly alien.

In high school, she'd never encountered any overt racism, but she'd heard the jokes out of the corner of her ear. "Her pussy's sideways, too," Bill Catfield had said once to his friends. She'd wanted to tell him that her eyes weren't "sideways," that her mouth wasn't "sideways," and that even a pinhead could deduce from that that her vagina would not be "sideways" either, but she'd walked by and pretended not to hear, trying to ignore the snickers of Bill and his friends.

She'd done a lot of ignoring over the years. And she'd thought all that was done with.

But apparently not.

She closed her drawer, walked over to Rich's desk and looked through it, and went back to pasteup before realizing that if she was going to find a blue pencil, she would have to get one from Carole.

She didn't want to face the secretary, was afraid to face her. Her hands were shaking slightly, and for some absurd reason she felt guilty, as though she had done something wrong, but she forced herself to walk around the partition to the front office.

Carole smiled sweetly at her. "Oh, hello, hon. I didn't know you were here."

"I, uh, was in the back," Sue lied. "Pasting up. I was

wondering if you have a blue correction pencil I could use."

"Why sure." Carole opened her middle drawer, took out a pencil, and handed it to Sue, who took it with trembling fingers. "By the way, a man stopped by with an item for 'Upcoming Events.' " She handed Sue a pink "While You Were Out" note. "He said to give him a call."

Sue nodded. "Thanks." She walked quickly back behind the modular wall into the newsroom. She vowed to herself that she would not be intimidated by the secretary's bigotry, that she would not allow the old woman's attitude to dictate her actions or affect her in any way.

But she was still shaking as she went into the back room and started to proof the front page.

Sue felt drained by the time she arrived at the restaurant. She wanted to go into the back and talk to her grandmother, but before she even reached the cash register her mother was walking toward her, motioning toward the table where John was busily writing on a mimeographed worksheet. "I want you to help your brother with his homework."

Sue did not even feel like arguing. She dropped her notebook on the table. "Fine," she said in English.

She pulled up a chair and sat down. John, seated opposite her, papers fanned out before him, textbooks piled near his elbow, looked up. "I don't need your help," he said.

"Mother wants me to help you. I don't want to."

"Why do I have to do homework today anyway? It's Friday. Why can't I just do it Sunday and take today and tomorrow off?"

"Talk to them."

"They don't understand anything."

"Tough." Sue leaned forward to look at his worksheet. "What do you need help with?"

"I told you. Nothing."

"Then why did Mother tell me to help you?"

"Because they're fighting and they don't want you to go back there. We're not supposed to know."

Sue listened. Sure enough, she could hear the low, angry tones of a hushed argument coming from the kitchen. "What are they fighting about?" she asked.

"The menus."

"What about the menus?"

"Who knows? Who cares?"

Sue sighed, leaning back in her chair. She wished sometimes that she and John were closer. She wished she could talk to him, seriously talk to him. But they'd never had that sort of relationship; she'd never been the patient, understanding older sister, he'd never been the adoring younger brother, and it was too late for them to change now. Their roles were set, the confines of their relationship clear.

Had he been acting differently lately? That was something she had not been able to determine. Her grandmother and parents had been closely watching him also, she knew, and although none of them had discussed it, all of them had been tiptoeing around him, treating him as they would someone with a fatal disease. Maybe he sensed it, maybe he could tell. Maybe that's why he was so angry.

Influenced.

John pushed his paper across the table toward her, spinning it around. "Okay," he said. "Number five. See if you can figure it out."

Sue looked down at the worksheet, read the question, a simple geometry problem, and turned the paper sideways between them so they could both look at it. She leaned forward over the table and explained to him how to figure it out.

He sat back in his chair, frowned at her. *"Ya tsa may,"* he said.

She hit his shoulder. "Shut up. Your breath's worse than mine."

"He won't want to kiss you."

"Who?"

"The editor."

She shook her head. "Don't be stupid."

John grinned. "You like him, huh?"

Sue reddened. "Knock it off."

"I'm telling Father."

"Telling him what?"

"That you like that old guy."

"He's not that old."

"See? I'm telling."

She pushed the paper across the table at him. "Fine. Do your own homework. I hope you fail."

"I didn't want your help anyway."

She walked around the register, into the kitchen. Her parents were still arguing, but they shut up the second she came through the door. She opened the refrigerator, grabbed a can of Coke, and continued through the kitchen into the back room, where her grandmother was plucking a chicken. "Hello, Grandmother," she said.

The old woman turned down the volume on the cassette player next to her, atonal Chinese music fading into a pleasant muted tinkle. Her fingers continued to pull feathers from the chicken as she looked up at Sue. "More have died," she said.

Sue looked at her grandmother, confused, not knowing if that was a statement or a question. "I don't know," she said, a response that applied either way.

"More will die."

Sue sat down on an overturned vegetable crate next to

her grandmother. "Why will more people die? If we are going to fight the *cup hu girngsi*, why don't we fight it now? Why are we waiting? Can't you find out where it is hiding? Can't we go there and destroy it?"

Her grandmother did not answer. "I dreamed last night of a mirror man. A giant who makes mirrors."

"A real giant?" Sue asked. "Or a tall man?"

"A tall man."

"Pee Wee Nelson."

"Do you know him?" Her grandmother did not sound surprised.

"I just met him today. He used to be the police chief. He is a friend of my editor and his brother, the current police chief."

The old woman nodded, as if this was what she had expected to hear. "We must talk to this tall man. We will need a mirror to use against the *cup hu girngsi.*"

"A mirror?"

"Baht gwa. The mirror with eight sides." The old fingers moved away from the chicken, traced a delicate octagon in the air. "It will reflect and frighten the *cup hu girngsi.* Even *tse mor* are afraid of their own appearance."

"But what are we going to do? Are we going to wait for the *cup hu girngsi* to come to us and attack?"

"No," her grandmother replied, resuming her plucking of the chicken. "We will go to its lair and confront it there."

"Where is that?"

"I do not know."

"How will we find out where it is?"

"Di Lo Ling Gum."

Sue shook her head, frustrated. "Well, when will we find out?"

"When it is time."

"What if we find out too late? What will we do then?"

The old woman's voice was low and filled with an emotion Sue had never before associated with her grandmother—fear. "I do not know," she said quietly. "I don't know."

Forty-eight

He stared at the figure in disbelief.

Fifteen thousand.

Fifteen thousand people had died of exsanguination in the United States since the FBI had begun keeping statistics. And that only included the information that had been entered into the computer. Who knew how many more cases were sitting in files that had not yet been input? The pre-1920 backlog was not a high priority, and updating of the computer files was being done piecemeal.

Fifteen thousand.

Rossiter turned down the intensity knob on the screen, the amber numbers fading into black. A pattern had emerged here, but it was not a pattern that made any sense. With few exceptions, the murders recorded had traced a recognizable path across the country that corresponded to a very definite time line. It was as if the murderer or murderers had crisscrossed the nation for the past six decades, killing as they went, draining the blood of people from the West Coast, the Midwest, the East Coast, the South, and the West.

The amazing thing was that there was nothing more to go on, no other tie-ins, not even an increase in other crimes along those routes. In a few cases, there had been arrests, but no convictions, the individual trials obviously attempts by the politically ambitious to prove to the voting public their criminal-catching credentials despite the obvious lack of evidence.

If these deaths really were connected, how had the killers survived in their travels? They hadn't robbed stores or houses along the way, apparently they had not even stolen from the victims. Had they taken ordinary day jobs to earn money while they went on their cross-country killing spree? Were they now working as clerks at the drugstore in Rio Verde? Attendants at the gas station? It just didn't jibe. Some of the murders were too far apart in too short a period of time. There had to be pieces of the puzzle still missing. From the facts available to him now, it could reasonably be deduced that the murderers had not had to eat, buy gas, or find places to stay, that the killings themselves had been sustenance enough—and he knew that could not be the case.

Sustenance.

It was still in the back of his mind, though he didn't want to admit it.

Vampires.

Rossiter closed his eyes, massaged his temples. He was not an overly imaginative man. Even as a child, he had never been afraid of ghosts or monsters or the dark. His fears had always been more concrete: accidents, adults, the tangible dangers of the real world.

But he had not been able to shake this vampire fixation, and when he tried to rationally analyze each new piece of information he uncovered, his mind kept drifting back to thoughts of the undead. He'd considered pulling in another agent to look at the data, maybe Buetell or Hammon, who were assigned to the case anyway, but he didn't want to give up his baby just yet. The more of a hot dog he was, the more he brought in on his own, the greater the reward would be careerwise. Before he started adding others onto the bandwagon, he had to be sure that his contribution was definitive and documented, that it would be clear to everyone that this was his idea and that the essential work had been done by him.

One interesting thing he'd discovered was that the Bureau did maintain quite a bit of information on vampires. He'd checked out several books and articles from the Bureau's library, three of which had to be sent from D.C., and he'd accessed two studies on the subject that had been conducted by operatives in the late 1960s and early 1970s. Of course, the existence of such information didn't mean much—the Bureau had files on anything and everything even remotely related to murder and death—but if he ever decided to pursue the vampirism angle, he at least knew he had Bureau sources he could quote for backup.

Not that he would ever consider ascribing a series of murders to vampires.

Unless . . .

Unless he could prove the existence of multigenerational medical vampirism within a specific family.

A family of medical vampires that had killed fifteen thousand people?

He had to stop thinking about this. He had to put it out of his mind.

He opened his eyes, stared at his darkened computer screen. One of the reasons his brain was running along this track was the last series of faxes he'd received from that hick police chief in Rio Verde. Apparently, a housewife claimed that her daughter had been abducted by Elvis. Ordinarily, he would have assumed that the woman was in shock because her daughter was missing or that she was already planning her insanity defense in case her daughter's body was found and she'd done a poor job of hiding her involvement. But the fact that the police had not ordered any psychological tests for the woman and were apparently treating this as an ordinary missing persons case, and the fact that this incident, bizarre as it was, fit cozily into the mainstream of current events in Rio Verde, made Rossiter take it a little more seriously himself.

Could Elvis be a vampire?

That was just too far out to even consider.

He needed to get out of Phoenix, get back over to Rio Verde, and check things out for himself. He'd made a big deal of his jurisdictional authority on his last trip there, but he hadn't been back since. He'd been so absorbed in this computer search that he'd virtually abandoned leg-work the past week or so and had given the case back to Captain Hick by default.

He was turning into a petty bureaucrat.

He was turning into Engles.

Working here could do that to an agent.

Rossiter reached into his pocket, took out his key ring, and found the key to the computer. He shut off the monitor, locked the keyboard, but kept the computer on to retain the information he'd accessed. He stood, pocketed his keys, then walked over to the elevators. He was going stir-crazy in here.

Outside, the day was overcast, a patchwork of light gray and white clouds covering the sky over Phoenix, a wall of black storm clouds massing above the desert to the north. Across the street, a small group of cowboy-hatted Indians stood blocking the doorway of a bar, talking among them-selves. Next door, a team of well-dressed lawyers were posed on the courthouse steps, addressing a news crew from Channel 10. In the real world, it was business as usual.

But in Rio Verde, people and animals and insects were having the bodily fluids sucked out of them through holes in their necks, and Elvis Presley was kidnapping little girls.

What would J. Edgar do in a situation like this?

Go home crying to mama, a small mean part of him said.

He reached into his jacket pocket, pulled a cigarette out of the pack, put it in his mouth, and lit it. He stared up at the sky and wondered if it was going to rain.

Forty-nine

It was raining outside, a light drizzle, and though she couldn't hear it on the roof, she could see the mist on the stained glass windows and could feel the cool dampness in the air. Sitting at her desk, opening today's mail, Corrie glanced over at the Pastor Dan Wheeler. He was at his own desk, leaning back in his chair and smiling at her. She smiled back.

For the past week, the pastor had kept her busy doing menial paperwork, filing old invoices, paying bills, reading and answering all mail, even the form letters. He had remained with her at all times, had been so omnipresent as to be suspicious. She began to wonder if he suspected her of something. He definitely seemed to be watching her, keeping an eye on her.

She took the electric bill out of its envelope and put it in her in-box. She hazarded another glance at the pastor.

He was still smiling at her.

She felt happy being here, content in the presence of the pastor, but she was starting to worry about her position in the church. For the past week, the chapel and all other rooms within the complex had been sealed off from the outside, the doors padlocked, and she was confined to the office. If she had to go to the bathroom, the pastor made her use one of the porta-potties set up outside for the construction workers and volunteers. Out of all of the rooms in the growing church, she was allowed only in this one.

All that had been strange enough, but today things were even stranger. It was nothing that had happened, nothing she could pinpoint. It was a feeling. Things were different today.

She suddenly wished she'd worn the jade necklace. Last week, Rich had tried to bully her into wearing it, telling her that he'd bought it in order to protect her from vampires, but she'd responded that her faith in Jesus was the only protection she needed. She'd made a show of leaving the necklace at home, on her dresser.

Now she wished that she'd worn it. Something within her sensed that the necklace should have been worn today, that it would have helped her, would have . . . protected her. From what she did not know, but her neck felt bare and naked, like her finger had the time she'd lost her wedding ring.

"Corrie," the pastor said.

"Yes?" She looked up. In person, in a one-to-one setting, Wheeler's voice did not have the authority that it had on the pulpit, but what it lost in strength it gained in intimacy, and in many ways that was even more powerful.

"Jesus wants to meet you."

A thrill of excitement shot through her, but she was aware of another feeling, a feeling of apprehension somewhere deep inside her.

The necklace suddenly seemed very important.

"He wants you to deliver the sacrifice."

Corrie's hands were trembling, and her mouth was dry. "He wants me to deliver the sacrifice?"

The preacher stood. "Yes."

"I'm honored," she said.

"Follow me."

Corrie followed him outside into the drizzle, around

the side of the building to the locked door of the first addition. Wheeler withdrew a key from his pocket and unlocked the door, pulling it open.

They walked into the addition. Like the outside, the inside of the building was painted black. She would have thought that extra lights would be installed to compensate for the darkness, but the illumination in here was purposefully dim, the primitive bulbs a soft yellowish white. In the murky shadowed corner, she saw figures moving, and she heard the sound of sawing. Construction, as always, was continuing.

She followed the preacher through another set of doors and down an unlit hallway. There were windows here, but they were of the darkest stained glass—navy blue and crimson—and let in very little light.

Then they were in the chapel.

Corrie had wondered why sermons had been held outside for the past two Sundays, and she'd assumed that it was because of the construction and remodeling that were taking place in the chapel.

She saw now that that was not the reason at all.

Wheeler stood just inside the doorway, beaming proudly, staring at her, gauging her reaction. Corrie looked into the chapel, awed, impressed, and, above all, enraptured. The church she had known was gone. There was no floor, only board paths over dirt that led toward three huge holes in the ground. Each hole was approximately the size of her bedroom and partially ringed by a small group of men and women. Piles of trash stood behind each group. Wooden bridges, apparently made from the backs of pews, stretched over the tops of the holes. The altar was still in place, but there were bodies lying atop it, leaning against the pulpit, placed in the choir cubicles. The bodies were all mummified, and although they appeared to be ancient, she thought she recognized some of the faces. The windows had all been painted black.

And it was beautiful.

"Come with me," Wheeler said, and she followed him into the chapel.

She stared at the people standing next to the openings in the earth. These, she assumed, were part of the church's inner circle, those parishioners who had been with the preacher from the beginning and whom he knew to be loyal. Among the first group she recognized Bill Covey. And Tammette Walker from the bank. Some of the others looked familiar—she'd seen them in church or around town—but she could not put names to the faces.

She wondered when these people had come in here. And how. She'd been in the office since eight this morning and had heard or seen nothing, no one going in or out.

They reached the first hole, and she saw that what she had at first taken for trash was actually a collection of small trees and shrubs. Next to the shrubs were coffee cans, filled with what looked like ultra-black and unusually large coffee beans.

Wheeler noticed the direction of her gaze. "Insects," he explained. "Snacks for the Savior."

She nodded, looked toward the other openings. Dead animals—cats and dogs and mice and rabbits—were piled next to the second hole.

The nude, unmoving forms of two women, a man, and a child were lying behind the third group of people, the child lying lengthwise across the buttocks of the women.

Corrie returned her attention to the first hole. It was the bugs and plants that struck her as the most peculiar, and although she knew that she should be shocked by all of this, particularly by the people, she was acutely aware of the fact that she was not. Her thoughts felt strangely slow, her brain numb.

Covey smiled at her. "We proffer our offerings to the Lord, and He looks upon us with favor. Are you to deliver the sacrifice today?"

"Yes," Wheeler answered for her. "Where is the infant?" Corrie looked into the opening. The hole did not continue straight down, as she'd assumed, but sloped, curved, turned into a tunnel some fifteen feet below the rim. It was dark but not black; there was a hazy glow coming from somewhere beneath the earth.

One of the women from the group by the third hole, an old lady Corrie did not know, brought forth a baby and handed it to the preacher. The baby was dead, its tiny eyes staring blindly at nothing as its head flopped from side to side on its too small neck. It had been a boy before the castration.

Covey and another man walked into the gloom beyond the other side of the opening. They returned with a heavy retractable metal construction ladder. Holding the ladder by the top rung, they placed it over the hole. The other sections scoped downward, clanking into place as the ladder expanded. The bottom of the ladder reached the bottom of the hole, or the point where the hole began to curve, and the two men leaned the top of the ladder against the side of the dirt.

"Go down," Wheeler said.

Corrie had always been afraid of heights, had never even liked stairways with gaps between the steps, let alone ladders, but now she had no fear and walked around to the opposite side of the hole, accepting Covey's hand as he assisted her onto the top rung.

She climbed quickly down.

Wheeler came after her, clutching the dead baby in his right hand, holding onto the ladder with his left.

The roof of the tunnel was high, Corrie noticed, and rounded, as though it had been created by the passage of a giant earthworm. The dirt on the floor and roof and sides was smooth. Looking up the way she had come, she could see, around the rim, a ring of joyous faces. They were singing. A hymn. "Shall We Gather At The River," it sounded like, although those words did not seem to correspond to what was being sung.

Wheeler reached the bottom and immediately moved away from the ladder. There was excitement in his step and also fear. "Jesus is waiting," he said. He did not even look at Corrie but began walking down the tunnel toward the far end, where a pink glow pulsed faintly.

Corrie followed him. That numb sense of emotional disassociation was still with her, but there was a pleasant glow beneath the numbness, a contentment spreading outward from somewhere deep within her being.

Wheeler turned to look at her, and there was joy in his face, rapture in his eyes. "Jesus walks these halls," he said wonderingly. "He lives here now."

He lives here now.

The words made her feel warm and tingly inside.

They stopped walking. Corrie estimated that they were now under the building next door to the church. The preacher handed her the dead baby. She took it from him, entranced by the cold rubbery feel of its skin, by the inert heaviness of its form.

Wheeler cleared his throat, and when he spoke it was in the strong oratorical tone of his sermons: "We have come to praise Thee, oh Jesus. We have come to pay tribute to the Lord of Hosts."

There was the sound of wind, but there was no wind, the sound of water but no water, and then, out of the pink glow before them, came Jesus. He glided rather than walked, moving with a fluid smoothness, and His presence was as awesome as Wheeler had said. More so. He was perfection, divinity in human form, the living embodiment of God.

Corrie fell instinctively to her knees, as did Pastor

Wheeler. Tears of joy slid down her face, but she did not wipe them away, she did not want them to stop. She held forth the body of the infant. Jesus stepped up to her and, with tender fingers, took the baby.

She was nearly blinded by His beauty, by the elegance of His being, nearly stunned into silence, but she managed to whisper, "For you."

Jesus nodded graciously. He held the baby to His lips, bit carefully into it and, with kneading fingers, began to drink.

"Welcome," Wheeler said, "to the Kingdom of God."

Fifty

Robert walked into his office, tossed his hat at the rack, and missed. He did not bother to pick it up but sat down, slumping tiredly in his chair.

It was then that he noticed what had been left on his desk: a gun, a badge, an ID card, and one sentence on a sheet of yellow legal paper: "I cannot serve both God and mammon."

It was signed by Jud and dated yesterday.

Robert stormed out of his office, clutching the note in his hand. "What is this shit?" He strode over to LeeAnne's desk, waved the paper at her. "Did you see him do this?"

She looked up at him, confused. "Who?"

"Jud." He dropped the note on her desk, watching as she read it. "Did he talk to you about this?"

"No," she said.

"Stu?" He turned toward the other officer. "Were you here when Jud put this on my desk?"

Stu shook his head.

"Shit." Robert reached down, grabbed LeeAnne's phone, and dialed Jud's number. The line was busy, and he slammed the receiver in its cradle. "Get him for me," he ordered the secretary. "Keep trying until he answers and patch him through. I want to talk to him."

"Yes, sir."

Robert strode angrily back to his office, telling himself to calm down, not to overreact. He walked over to the window, stared out at the highway, trying to figure out why Jud would just quit like this without first talking to him. The two of them had been friends for years, since they'd both been patrolmen, and they'd never, to Robert's knowledge, had a serious falling out. Even if he made up his mind to quit, Jud still should have talked to him.

What the hell was he going to do with one less man and all this crap going down?

Robert glanced toward the fax machine, grateful for once for its presence. The machine, until now an annoyance and a reminder of the FBI's unwanted interference, suddenly represented a link with the outside world, an anchor to reason and reality.

He needed that right now.

He looked out the window again, noticed how few cars were on the highway. Complaints about the church had tapered off the past two days. Complaints about everything had tapered off. He didn't like that. It wasn't natural. There were bound to be fights somewhere in town, noisy neighbors, illegally parked cars blocking driveways. Something. But here at the station, normally command central for all town trouble, it seemed as if Rio Verde was deserted. No phones rang; no people came in.

LeeAnne had noticed it too, he knew. As had Stu. Both of them were less talkative than usual, jumpier, more on edge. Stu was on desk duty and was catching up with his paperwork, but there was a strange, almost desperate quality to his typing, Robert thought. LeeAnne had spent half the morning staring at a single article in *People* magazine.

He was not feeling so hot himself. Last night, he had been awakened long after midnight by the sound of low laughing, a sound that grew quickly in power and volume. He had recognized the distinctive tone and pitch of the laughter and had immediately pulled open his bedroom shades, and he'd seen, standing out in the desert in the moonlight, beneath the thin leafless branches of a palo verde tree, what he was afraid he would see. The Laughing Man.

The figure disappeared the second he laid eyes on it, fading back into the blackness, the laughter dissipating into the sound of a light breeze, but the feeling that the Laughing Man was still out there, watching the house—waiting—made Robert unable to fall back asleep, and he spent the rest of the night watching old Westerns on TNT, his loaded pistol and a clip of extra ammunition on the end table next to him.

Tonight he was going to have two officers stake out the house, armed with guns and jade, holy water and crucifixes.

Maybe then he would be able to get some sleep.

The phone rang, an inside call. He hurried over to his desk, picked up the receiver. "Yes?"

It was LeeAnne. "Jud's line isn't busy anymore, but he's not answering. Do you want me to keep trying?"

"Keep trying until you get him."

"Gotcha."

Robert hung up the phone. He sat down in his chair, picked up Jud's badge, hefted it in his hand, then threw it against the wall, where it hit with a disconcertingly tiny thump.

Rich stopped by at lunch to deliver copies of the newspaper, laying a stack on the front counter next to the March of Dimes donation can, and bringing one back to Robert's office. He dropped the paper on the desk and pointed to Sue's story beneath the fold on the front page, to the two-deck headline "Vampires Can Be Killed, Chinese Experts Say."

Robert smiled wanly. "Chinese experts?"

"People believe authority. And I think Sue's grandma qualifies."

"So when do we get to meet this old woman? We're supposed to be following her lead, taking her word as gospel, and we've never even met her. I don't feel right placing my trust in someone I don't know. It doesn't sit well with me."

"I thought we could go over to the restaurant for lunch, meet her now. I have some things I want to talk to her about, too."

"Now?" Robert shook his head. "I have to wait for Joe Cash from the state police to call."

"About what?"

"Pam Frye. I told him she was kidnapped here in town, in front of her mother, that we found her shoes in a ditch, but the Elvis bit threw him off, and he's insisting that we expand the search statewide."

"What about the FBI? Do they know?"

"They know and they don't care."

Rich shrugged. "I don't suppose we can talk to them about vampires, can we?"

"I'm not bringing it up."

Rich sat down in the chair in front of his brother's desk, turning his body sideways and draping his legs over the chair arms. "We'll have a late lunch, then. We'll go after he calls. Sue said they'd be there all afternoon."

"The old lady knows we're coming?"

"I guess."

Robert leaned back in his chair, tapped a pencil on his knee. "I was thinking. Maybe Wheeler's on to something. Maybe this is the Second Coming."

"What is this horseshit?"

"Things are supposed to get bad before Jesus returns. Read your Revelations."

"Come on. You're no churchgoer and neither am I."

Robert shifted uncomfortably in his seat. "I'm not saying I believe it. But one of my officers pointed it out to me the other day. He goes to Wheeler's church."

"Jesus—"

"Exactly."

Rich looked at his brother and both of them laughed, the spell broken.

"Okay, I don't believe it," Robert admitted. "But I can't help thinking that these two things are connected, the vampire and Wheeler's Second Coming. Who knows? Maybe Wheeler does know something we don't."

"Shit."

"People are seeing dead rock stars and dead child molesters and vampires. That's not the normal course of events."

"Wheeler doesn't know his ass from a porkpie hat. Even though I don't go to church, I think there is something after we die. Some sort of afterlife. But I don't think it can be understood by us. And the idea that the nature of God can be fully understood by a semiliterate Neanderthal like Wheeler . . . I just don't buy it."

"Oh, but you think your part-time employee's grandma does possess the secrets of the universe."

"What is it with you? What do you have against Sue?"

"Nothing."

"It doesn't seem that way to me."

"That's just because you want to pork her."

Rich swung his legs off the chair and stood. "I don't have to listen to this."

"Oh, get off your high horse. Can't you even take a joke?"

"That wasn't a joke."

"Okay, I'm sorry."

"Yeah. Right."

Robert stared at his brother for a moment, then nervously cleared his throat. "I heard laughing last night, Rich."

Rich glanced toward the window, not responding.

"I heard the Laughing Man."

"No, you didn't." Rich shifted in his chair, looked at his brother. "I know this is some pretty scary shit, but . . ."

"But what?"

"Look, there's no such thing as the Laughing Man, okay? Just drop it. That's kid stuff. And it's not going to help us out here."

"Kid stuff? You saw him too, Richie. You saw him when Mom died. You heard him."

"No, I didn't."

"The hell you didn't. Who was that then, huh? Who did we see out there?"

"Look, we were both under a lot of stress."

"We saw the Laughing Man. You know it and I know it." Robert stood. "And I heard him again last night."

"Bullshit."

"Oh. You believe in vampires, but you don't believe in the Laughing Man. You're picking and choosing your monsters, huh?"

"We have bodies that have been drained of blood. We have no proof of the Laughing Man."

"We have me. I saw him. I heard him."

"Medusa Syndrome," Rich said, looking straight at his brother.

"That's not it."

"No? It was when Emily saw Elvis steal her daughter. It was when Mike was living in a septic tank. It was when Sophocles Johnson was making underwear clothes."

"It's not the same."

"It's exactly the same."

"Fuck you." The phone rang, two rings, an outside call, and Robert reached over and picked up the receiver. "Carter." He glared at Rich. "Yes," he said. "Yes." He put his hand over the mouthpiece. "It's Cash."

Rich nodded disgustedly. "Fine." He walked outside to wait in the hall.

The old lady was nothing like he thought she would be. Robert didn't know what he'd expected—a wise, saintly Buddha-esque guru, he supposed, or maybe a smug condescending know-it-all—but he had definitely not been prepared for this mild old woman who sat on an overturned plastic bucket shelling peas.

She looked like a turtle, he thought. Her face was wrinkled, her almond-shaped eyes unblinking, and her small fragile head looked as though it could be recessed into her body on its retractable neck. She spoke no English at all beyond the word "Hi," and all communication was directed through Sue, who translated for both sides, but Robert was surprised at how much respect he immediately had for this old lady. There was something in her soft, almost musical voice, in the matter-of-fact way in which she continued to shell the peas as she spoke, that gave him a feeling of confidence in her. When he looked over at Rich, he could tell from his brother's expression that he felt the same way.

Sue's parents had ignored them as they'd walked through the kitchen to the back of the restaurant, continuing their cooking chores as though nothing out of the ordinary was happening, as though this sort of thing occurred all the time. Robert found himself wondering if they knew about the vampire at all, or if this was something between grandmother and granddaughter.

Rich did most of the talking, asking questions and writing down the answers in his little notebook, but finally the old lady turned to face him. She said something to Sue, and the young woman translated. "She wants to know why Pee Wee Nelson is not with you. She calls him the 'tall man.' "

Robert shrugged. "Should he be here?"

"My grandmother wants him to make *baht gwa,* a mirror. She says we need it to fight the *cup hu girngsi.*" Sue paused. "She dreamed of Pee Wee the other night."

Robert didn't know what dreaming about Pee Wee had

to do with anything, but he knew enough not to say so. "What kind of mirror is it?" he asked.

"A mirror with eight sides." Sue spoke rapidly in Chinese, and the old lady nodded, tracing an octagon in the air.

"You want us to bring him over here?"

Sue spoke again in Chinese; again the old lady nodded. "Yes."

"Does she know where the vampire is? Does she want to . . . ride around with us? We can take her to the spots where he struck, where he killed people. Maybe she can get some vibes or something from that."

Sue translated, and the grandmother smiled, revealing small stained teeth. She spoke rapidly to her granddaughter, and at length. "It does not work that way," Sue explained. "*Di Lo Ling Gum* does not depend on the material world. It does not matter where she is. She can learn as much sitting here as she can seeing the bodies of the dead. When she is to know the *cup hu girngsi*'s lair, it will be revealed to her."

"Isn't there any way to . . . push it along?"

Sue shook her head. "I already asked her that. She says no."

"So more people could die?"

"More people *will* die."

"And there's nothing we can do?"

"Tell them to protect themselves. Tell them to wear jade. Tell them to place willow branches on their doors and windows."

"But there's no way to know where he will strike again?"

Sue translated, her grandmother answered, and she shook her head. "No."

"Will you come with us to the town council meeting on Thursday?" Rich asked. "Will you tell this to the council, so we can come up with some type of civil defense measures?"

This time, Sue did not even have to ask her grandmother. "Yes," she said. "We'll come."

Fifty-one

Corrie sat in her car across the street from Taco Bell, looking through the front windows at Rich and that slut, sitting across from each other at one of the tables and eating. Jesus had been right. Rich was slipping it to that Oriental whore. No wonder he'd been so eager to get rid of her, to pack her off to a new job so he could set up his little teaching scam and pick up a young bimbo.

Of course Jesus had been right, she told herself. Could Jesus ever be wrong?

No.

She knew that now.

But there had been some doubt. What interest could the Son of God possibly have in the minutiae of ordinary lives like hers and Rich's? Why would He spend His valuable time playing fortune-teller for her when He could be ending world hunger and revealing the cure for cancer?

It was blasphemy to think that way.

She stared at the Taco Bell window. Behind the hot pink words painted on the glass that advertised the "Fiesta Deal," she saw Rich laugh, nod. In her mind, she saw him going down on her, burying his face between her legs and licking her wet pussy while the slut moaned and thrashed beneath him, her slitty eyes closed in ecstasy.

He would pay for his adultery.

And she would *definitely* pay. Jesus hated chinks. He had reserved a special place in hell for those slant-eyed heathens. And there was no way the Son of God would tolerate this sort of harlotry in the town of His rebirth.

Corrie smiled to herself. A month ago, a week ago even, if she had learned of her husband's unfaithfulness, it would have devastated her. But she was stronger now. The Lord had given her strength.

Let them do what they wanted. Let them consort in public. Let them fuck in the middle of the street for all she cared.

She would have the last laugh.

Jesus would see to that.

She took her hands off the steering wheel, pressed them together, closed her eyes, and began to pray.

Fifty-two

The Rio Verde Town Council met on the third Thursday of every month. More than one council member over the past few years had tried to get the meeting day switched from Thursday to Tuesday since Thursday was a good night for TV. But the mayor, who owned Desert Access Cable, and Councilman Jones, who was the manager of Radio Shack, had always successfully defeated such efforts, citing tradition and stating that if an individual believed that television was more important than town business, then that person did not belong on the council.

The two men also mentioned at each of these junctures that, if desired, shows could be videotaped and watched at a more convenient time.

With VCRs and blank tapes purchased from Radio Shack, Rich had always thought, and though he'd never said a word about it, he had stored that idea away as the basis for a future editorial.

Tonight, though, the meeting concerned nothing so frivolous.

Tonight they were here to talk about vampires.

For the first time since the water-rate increase controversy two years back, the council chambers were filled, although this time the mood was tense, the room overflowing with frightened people who ordinarily had no interest in civic affairs. Townspeople filled all of the extra seats, and the crowd spilled outside to the front of the building where a large group had gathered to listen to the proceedings through the door. Most of the people, Rich noticed, looked tired, nervous, on edge. He saw homemade crosses hanging around necks, smelled garlic mixed with sweat.

In addition to the mayor, council, and town manager, the leaders of most of the churches were here, as were most of the members of the Chamber of Commerce, including Hollis and several of his cronies. Rich sat between Robert and Sue, who was seated next to her father and grandmother. In the audience he could see the FBI agent and the guy from the state police.

"I should've prepared something," Sue said. "I hate talking in front of crowds. I'm going to freeze up."

"You may not even have to talk at all," Rich told her. "We'll see how things go. Robert has some prepared statements, so do I, if we need them, and if that's not enough to convince people, we may ask your grandmother some questions so they can get it from the horse's mouth. Basically, you'll just be a translator."

Robert leaned behind his brother and addressed Sue. "Don't forget, we already have a head start. People read your story in the paper. That already gives us some legitimacy."

Sue nodded and said nothing.

The meeting was called to order, and in a frayed and worried voice Mayor Tillis announced that the usual reading of the minutes would not take place today so that they could proceed directly to the matter at hand.

He looks old, Rich thought. Old and scared.

"We're here to talk about vampires," the mayor said. He scanned the room, waiting and prepared for a reaction, but there was none. No one smiled, no one laughed, no one spoke. There was only a hushed and fearful silence. "We will hear from our police chief," the mayor said. "Robert Carter."

Robert stood. "Thank you."

He began with the discovery of Manuel Torres's body and Donna Sandoval's assertion that she saw Torres walking with Caldwell Burke, and continued through to the abduction of Pam Frye, spelling out the events clearly and chronologically. He mentioned the expert opinion of Woods, who nodded in agreement, and went into just enough detail on the murders to let people know what they were dealing with.

Rich glanced over at the FBI agent and the state policeman, to see how they were reacting to this. Both had been invited by Robert to the meeting, but neither had been told in advance what exactly was going to be discussed. The state policeman was openly smirking, feeling smugly superior to the rural bumpkins surrounding him, but the FBI agent had no smile on his face. He appeared to be genuinely interested in what was being said.

Rich filed that in his mind for later.

Robert put down the paper from which he'd been reading. "Hard as it may be for us to believe, we have a vampire here in Rio Verde. I know such things aren't supposed to exist, and two months ago I would've bet my bottom dollar that they didn't, but I believe now that they do. And that's why I wanted to speak today. One is here. And it is killing people. Our people. I think we need to figure out a strategy for dealing with this creature, for protecting ourselves from it and killing it."

Matt Calderon raised his hand and began speaking in a too-high voice even before the mayor nodded toward him. "Why don't we feed him someone with AIDS?" Calderon asked. "We could test everyone, maybe find someone staying at the ranch, and when he bites into that AIDS blood, that'll be the end of him."

"Vampires don't get diseases," the mayor said. "They're already dead. That's a nitwit idea."

Hollis stood and began to speak, though he had not

been recognized. "There are no such things as vampires," he said. "I wish you'd all stop—"

He was drowned out by the loud sound of angry disagreement from the assembled crowd. "If there's no vampires, who killed Terry Clifford?" someone asked.

"I saw one!" Buford exclaimed from the back.

"Me too!" someone else echoed.

The mayor pointed at Hollis. "Sit down," he said. "We're not here to debate the existence of vampires. That's something all of us except you seem to agree on. We're here to decide how to protect ourselves against them. How to kill them, if possible."

The questions came fast and furious. Where did the vampire live? What did it look like? How old was it? Had any of the victims become vampires themselves? Robert answered as best he could.

"How are we going to kill him?" Buford asked. "That's the main thing we need to know. Silver bullet? Stake?"

"Yeah!" someone said. "Stake him!"

Robert glanced over at Sue. She took a deep breath, nodded. "I'll let Sue Wing tell you about that," he said.

Sue stood. She was visibly nervous, her hands trembling, but she nodded to the mayor and the council, then turned to face Buford. "What you call a vampire, we call a *cup hu girngsi* in my culture. It's basically the same thing, but the difference is that we do not believe that the *cup hu girngsi* has anything to do with Christianity. It is not a monster that preys only on the members of one religion. It kills anyone. It kills animals. It even kills plants. It exists and it has always existed, and that's why the symbols of Christianity won't stop it. You can't use holy water or crosses like you can in the movies. Jade—"

A tall cowboy standing next to the door smiled patronizingly at Sue. "I read that article too, and, no offense, babe, but what we got here's an *American* vampire."

Lee Hillman nodded. "This thing's a bloodsucker, not a rice eater."

There was a chorus of good-natured chuckles.

Sue felt the blood rush to her face, her cheeks burning with anger. "Listen, you ignorant rednecks—"

"There's no call to use language like that," the mayor said sternly.

"This isn't a game!" Sue said. "Don't you realize that?"

"I don't know who you think you are—" Councilman Walters began.

Pee Wee stood, his frame dwarfing all those around him. "Let her speak," he said, and the argument quieted down. He nodded toward Sue. "Go on."

"What you've seen in the movies is wrong. The *cup hu girngsi* doesn't care about Christian symbols. It was around long before Christianity. But it is afraid of jade. It can be hurt by the wood of the willow tree. It can be turned back with the *baht gwa*, a mirror with eight sides. These are what you need to be arming yourselves with." She looked around the room, saw hostility on some faces, indifference on others, interest on only a few. "We can kill it," she said, and she purposely made her voice softer, more sympathetic. "But until we do, you need to protect yourselves and your loved ones. My parents have a willow tree. I think a few of you ranchers have some too. Use the branches to make spears. Wear jade or carry it with you. Do not go out at night."

Rich nodded. "If we just behave sensibly, if we just act on what we know, we can get through this thing."

"How did a Chinese vampire get all the way over here in America?" Councilman Jones asked suspiciously.

"They brought him!" a woman yelled. "Her family brought him with them!"

"There's no such thing as a 'Chinese' vampire," Sue said. "There are only *cup hu girngsis*. They're the same everywhere."

"Then how come your stuff works against him, and ours doesn't?" a man called out.

"I don't know," Sue said patiently. "Information gets changed over the years, over the miles. Somehow you got the information wrong. It's like that kid's game where you start a message at one end of a room and whisper it to the person next to you, and by the time it gets to the other end of the room, it's screwed up." She looked down at her grandmother, placed a hand on the old woman's shoulder. "We know about these things because our culture is thousands of years old. And continuous. We've learned a few things over the centuries. America is only a couple of hundred years old—"

"Maybe we could burn the vampire," Mayor Tillis interrupted. "Find out where he lives and torch it. Or we could douse him with liquid nitrogen, freeze him."

"You're thinking of scientific solutions," Rich said, looking exasperatedly at Sue. "Listen to what she is saying. This is not something that obeys the laws of science. This thing has nothing to do with logic or reason. We need . . . I don't know, magic to fight him. Sue just told you what you need to do to protect yourselves—"

"We can just drag him out into sunlight," a young man said. "Let him fry and turn to dust."

"Whatever we do, we need to catch him first!" Will Overbeck shouted. "I think we should set a trap. I'll donate a cow, Lem could kick in a goat, maybe some of the other ranchers would be willing to fork over some chickens. We could slaughter them all, spread the blood around, like they do for sharks, and then wait. When he comes to eat—Pow!—we've got him."

Robert looked over Rich's shoulder at Sue, shook his head disgustedly.

"They're not listening to us," Rich whispered.

Dozens of people were speaking at once now, their competing voices worriedly anxious and, at the same time, defensively belligerent.

"This demon can only be fought with prayer," Pastor Wilkerson from the Lutheran Church was saying from his seat.

Mrs. Church, the librarian, vehemently shook her head. "I cannot sit idly by, praying for God to do something when I can do it myself. God gave us brains and free will so we could make our own decisions, so we could fight our own fights. The Chinese girl said the vampire's afraid of jade instead of crosses, and I believe her. God has allowed this information to be placed in front of us; now he is waiting to see what we do with it."

"Exactly," Robert said.

The mayor banged on his desk with a gavel. He stood and continued to bang until the room was silent. He looked slowly around the room. "I don't know if we've succeeded in reaching an agreement on anything yet, but I do suggest that we proceed in a logical and orderly fashion. I am proposing that we adopt an emergency curfew, that we ban all children and adults from being on the street after dark until such time as this situation is resolved. Once the proposal is seconded, I will open the floor for discussion."

"Basha's is open twenty-four hours," Jim Kness, the manager of the grocery store said. "That's corporate policy. I can't change that. I'm going to be arrested for doing my job and keeping the store open?"

"What about the movie theater?" someone said.

"I can't go shopping until after I get off work, and I don't get off until it's dark."

Robert raised his hands for silence. "We won't enforce any curfew." He looked over at the mayor. "Sorry, Al. But we do need to decide how we're going to deal with this."

Tom Moore, the Baptist preacher, jumped up from his seat and rushed into the center of the council chambers.

"Vampires," Moore announced loudly, "are the spawn of Satan. They are among us because we asked them here with our wickedness and our sinfulness. But Jesus Christ, our Lord and Saviour, has returned to protect us, has offered us sanctuary from the adversary if only we dedicate ourselves to obeying the word of God." He turned slowly on his heel and raised his arm until he was pointing at Sue. "This heathen has asked us to adopt the ways of evil, to forsake the holy word of God—"

"Shut up," Robert said, facing Moore. "Just shut the hell up. This isn't your church, this is a town council meeting. We're here as citizens of Rio Verde, not as individuals. We're here to draft a civil defense plan for our town, not to promote our own interests. If you have nothing to contribute beyond your racist bullshit, then stop taking up our time. We have work to do."

There was the sound of two hands clapping from the back of the now silent audience, and Buford stood, grinning hugely, hands high over his head, applauding. To the side of him, someone else began to clap. The applause grew. It by no means included most of the assembled people, but it was definitely close to half, and Rich felt proud as he looked at his brother, standing tall and proud against the preacher.

Moore turned without a word and walked out of the room, the crowd parting before him to let him through. Some people watched his departure with concern, still others hurried to join him, but most remained where they were.

Robert did not even wait until the preacher left the chambers. "We don't have time to play games here tonight," he said. He looked around the room, and to Rich it seemed as though he had gained a stature he hadn't had a few moments before.

What a difference the perception of power made.

"The important thing right now is that we get the word

out and make people aware that there's a vampire loose
in Rio Verde. He's already killed four people, maybe
more, and God knows how many animals. He'll kill again.
You can believe in the Chinese stuff or not, but make sure
that you and your families and your friends and your coworkers stay indoors after dark. If you have to go someplace, run *to* your car, run *from* your car, stay inside locked
buildings as much as possible. All of the murders so far
have taken place outside, In the open air. I don't know if
it's true that a vampire has to be invited before he can
come in"—he looked at Sue, who shook her head—"but
he's not going into people's homes or places of business.
So far. If we take precautions and don't act stupidly, we'll
get through this."

The questions were again shouted chaotically, but they
were more serious, more thoughtful, more specific. Many
of them were addressed to Sue, and she and her father
tried to answer them carefully and thoroughly.

"I am going to need volunteers!" Robert announced.
"I want to establish patrol teams to watch for the vampire
each night, and I don't have the manpower for it. You'll
be in pairs, either patrolling the streets or stationed in
appropriate locations, and you'll be outfitted with two-way
communications devices. If that thing makes a move
against anyone in this town, I want to know about it. We'll
be on him so fast, he won't know what hit him. If anyone's
interested, come up to me afterward. I have a sign-up
sheet here, and I'd be glad to have you aboard."

This time the applause was unanimous, erupting simultaneously throughout the members of the crowd.

"We got to them," Rich said to Sue. "They heard us."

"Maybe."

"Maybe?"

She frowned. "Your brother made it sound as though
jade is an option, like they can use jade or a cross; that it
doesn't matter as long as they believe in the *cup hu girngsi*'s

existence. But the creature doesn't care whether you believe in it or not. It exists, and jade and willow can ward it off. Crosses and garlic and the rest of those movie things do nothing."

"But they know that now. They heard you. They listened."

"Maybe," she said again.

Robert had moved to the center of the council chambers and was surrounded by a clamoring group of men and women trying to talk to him. Rich could see that a clipboard was being passed around. Apparently, there was no shortage of volunteers.

It was late, and it was dark outside—a fact that seemed to be just below the surface of everyone's mind. People kept glancing toward the door, toward the blackness beyond the exterior lights of the building. The crowd outside had virtually disappeared, and it was not too long before the inside crowd began to thin out. Rich sidled up next to his brother. He saw the FBI agent, who had remained unmoving in his seat until now, stand and approach. Rossiter stopped in front of Robert. "I need to talk to you," he said.

"Where's Cash?"

"Cash is an asshole."

"You're not?"

"I believe you about the vampire," Rossiter said. "I'm willing to support you on this. The FBI's behind you." He looked toward Sue, her father, and grandmother. "I'd like to talk to the Chinese girl."

"Sue Wing," Robert said.

"What?"

"She has a name. Her name is Sue Wing."

"Right." Rossiter looked at his watch. "Finish this up and meet me in your office in ten minutes." He turned to leave without waiting for a response.

"Make it twenty," Robert said.

Rossiter did not turn, did not seem to have heard him but continued walking.

Rich grinned. "I guess he'll just have to wait an extra ten minutes."

Robert grinned back. "I have a sneaking suspicion it'll be closer to fifteen." He turned back to the excited men and women in front of him.

Rich leaned against the front counter next to Woods. The coroner was tired, and more than once had announced he was going home, but he continued to tough it out.

This was too important to miss.

Sue sat at LeeAnne's desk, her father and grandmother in borrowed chairs next to her. Robert and Rossiter leaned against the desk opposite them. The FBI had been asking questions for over an hour, of all of them, but mostly of Sue and her grandmother.

"How much firepower are you going to need?" he asked Sue. "How many men should I have assigned to this case?"

She shook her head. "I told you. We don't need any of that."

"It can't hurt."

"Human weapons are of no use against the *cup hu girngsi*. And, yes, it can hurt. We need seven men. Seven men to be chosen by my grandmother."

"Because seven is a lucky number."

"Right."

"But it just seems to me that it would be prudent to have some backup."

"Do you understand what I'm telling you? You can have nuclear weapons, and it won't make any difference."

A flicker of interest crossed the agent's features. "Now that would be interesting."

"Jesus."

"I think we've had enough here tonight," Robert said. "We're all tired; we're all a little cranky. Let's just go home and get some sleep."

"No," Rossiter said. "I'm not finished here."

"We are." Sue stood. She said something in Cantonese to her grandmother and father, and the three of them rose. They walked around the desk and toward the gate in the front counter. She turned, looking over her shoulder, and smiled at the agent. "Keep in touch."

Rich grinned at her as she passed by on her way out.

Fifty-three

Pastor Wheeler looked at his watch. It was midnight. Exactly. He walked onto the makeshift platform and faced his congregation. They were seated before him on chairs, benches, boulders, and the hard ground of the vacant lot. Behind them, in its exquisite blackness, was the Church of the Living Christ.

In three days it would be completed.

In three days, the Second Coming would be upon them.

Wheeler looked out upon his flock. There were easily two hundred people here tonight. In the first row, he saw Bill Covey seated next to the Methodist pastor.

They were all coming around. Just as Jesus had said they would.

It was too bad that only forty of them would be chosen by the Lord to live, but, as the Savior liked to say, those were the rules of the room, love 'em or leave 'em. And, of course, those of the faithful who voluntarily sacrificed themselves on the altar or in the pits would be rewarded in Heaven and would not perish but would have everlasting life. The rest . . .

The rest would get what they deserved.

He felt exhilarated, and he breathed deeply, taking in the cold desert air. After Jesus' rebirth, the Word would spread, and soon people from all over the state, all over the country, all over the world, would come to pay homage to the Living Christ. And Jesus would pass judgment on them.

The preacher smiled upon his congregation. He began to speak. He spoke of the wickedness of the world and the goodness of God, and then he said what Jesus had told him to say. "Chinks!" he said, grinning fiercely. "The heathen Chinee! The Lord Jesus Christ has foreseen that the yellow race will try to prevent Him from accomplishing His goals and bringing to light a brave new world! It is up to us, the servants of God, the Christian soldiers, to prove our love for Him by stopping this pagan plot!"

Wheeler looked upon the sea of rapt faces before him, pale blurs in the night. He lowered his voice, but it could still be heard clearly in the hushed stillness. "They will try to attack the church. They must be stopped. Go home tonight and get your guns, your knives, your axes, your hatchets. Anything that can be used to defend the house of the Lord. Bring them here to me." He grinned. "When they attack, we will be ready. And we shall overcome. We will hurt them and torture them and feed their bleeding yellow bodies to Jesus, and He will pick his teeth with their bones."

Heartfelt murmurs of "Amen" echoed throughout the crowd of men and women gathered in the darkness.

The preacher looked toward the church where, faintly, he could hear the sound of hammering.

Three more days.

It was going to be glorious.

Fifty-four

Sue sat on the floor of her grandmother's room, her nostrils filled with the mingled scents of ginseng and chrysanthemum. It was nearly dawn. John and her parents would be up soon. Although she and her grandmother had been talking since they'd returned from the police station, Sue did not feel the least bit tired. In many ways, she felt more awake than she ever had.

She'd learned a lot this night. Legends and facts and the connective bridges between the two. The tales and truths her grandmother told her she would have dismissed two months ago, cringing with embarrassment at the old woman's uneducated backwardness. But, since then, her attitudes had changed, her mind was not as closed as it had been, and she knew that there was nothing her grandmother could say that she would not believe.

For the past two hours, the old woman had been lying on her bed, eyes closed, but now she sat up, turning to look at Sue. "Are you a virgin?" she asked.

Sue stared at the carpet, at her toes, anywhere but into the eyes of her grandmother. Her face burned with the heat of embarrassment, and she found that she could not answer the question.

"Have you had sex?" her grandmother asked gently.

Sue knew her answer must be important, knew that it had to have some relevance to the *cup hu girngsi,* but still she could not meet her grandmother's eyes. "Not really," she said.

"You have not accepted or tasted the seed of a male?"

Tasted? Was this her grandmother speaking? Sue shook her head quickly, not looking up, wishing she was anywhere but here.

"Good," her grandmother said, touching her head. "You are the second of the seven."

"Who is the first?" Sue asked.

"I am."

"And the others?"

"I do not know. Perhaps the mirror man, perhaps the policeman."

"Pee Wee and Robert? What about Rich, my editor?"

Her grandmother's gaze darkened. "No."

A wave of cold washed over her. Sue nodded, wanting to ask why but not daring to question her grandmother's wisdom. "What about Father?" she asked. She felt guilty for the way her parents, her father in particular, had been pushed aside during this whole affair. It did not seem right, and she felt that despite the communication problems her parents had, both in their family and among other people, it was only right that they should share center stage with her grandmother and herself.

"No," her grandmother said.

Sue stared again at her feet, licked her lips. "Why is it important that I am . . . a virgin?" She had a tough time even saying the word. "What if I had not been?"

"It would make no difference."

Now Sue looked up at her. "Then why did you ask?"

Her grandmother smiled slightly. "I just wanted to know."

Sue blinked dumbly, then started to grin. *Tasted?* In the midst of all the horror, in the middle of the craziness, this struck her as funny. And for the first time since the beginning of this long, long night, she began to laugh.

Fifty-five

Rich awoke to feel a hand on his penis, fingers firmly grasping his shaft as a thumb rubbed the sensitive area directly below the tip, trying to stimulate him. He opened his eyes, looked at Corrie, pulled away, out of her grasp. "Not this morning," he said. "I don't feel up to it."

"Why?"

He shrugged. "I just don't. I'm not in the mood."

Corrie glared at him. "Who're you getting it from then, that Oriental slut?"

"What?"

"Has she been servicing you, your big white studliness?"

"What the hell are you talking about? You're the one who never wants to do it anymore. You're the one who's been acting for a month like sex is something good Christians don't do."

"Yeah? Well, I want it now."

"Well, I don't."

"Why? Aren't you man enough?"

He rolled over, faced away from her. "I'm not going to listen to—"

"Or did little Miss Hong Kong Whore suck it all out of you last night?"

He sat up. "That's it. I've had enough of your bullshit."

"The truth hurts, doesn't it?" There was a malicious smile on her face, cruel derision in her eyes, and he thought to himself that this was not Corrie, this was a person he did not know.

Anna was already awake and watching cartoons, and he forced himself to put on a cheerful front as he made breakfast. Corrie came out, already dressed for work, as he was wiping egg yolk from Anna's face with a washcloth.

"Hi, Mommy," Anna said. There was a formality to her voice that seemed unusual, and Rich looked at her.

Corrie smiled at her daughter, pulled back her hair, kissed her forehead. "Morning, cutie"

Anna wiped off the kiss, frowned.

"I'll take you to school, but Daddy'll have to pick you up, okay?"

"I want to go with Daddy," Anna said.

"You go with your mother," Rich told her.

Anna said nothing.

Corrie straightened, fixed Rich with a flat gaze. "I may be late tonight. Don't wait up."

Rich tossed the washcloth in the sink. He looked at her, frowned. "I want you to be careful."

She appraised him coolly. "You don't think I can take care of myself?"

"It's not that."

"What is it, then?"

"I'm worried about you. I care. I'm concerned."

"Oh. So dictating what I do shows concern."

"I just said be careful."

"I can take care of myself. I'm in better shape than you are. At least I get out and exercise. All you do is sit in front of that damn computer all day."

"You're not in better shape than Manual Torres or Terry Clifford."

She turned away from him. "Fine."

Rich turned to Anna. He bent down, gave her a light tap on the rear. "Go brush your teeth," he said. "Mommy's getting ready to go." Anna hurried down the hall, and he again faced Corrie. "Why are we even fighting?"

"Because I don't like the way you treat me."

"The way I treat you? There've been all these murders here, so I tell you to be careful, and you jump down my throat."

"I don't like your condescending attitude."

"Go to hell." He walked into the kitchen, grabbed his and Anna's plates from the counter, and placed them in the sink.

Corrie started down the hall. "Don't take it out on me because you can't perform your manly duties," she said sweetly. She smiled daintily at him as she went to get Anna.

Things were different at the paper. Especially in the early afternoon. As he sat at his desk, proofreading the account of the council meeting he'd written, he glanced over at Anna and Sue, talking together at the far desk, and smiled. Being here with them, it felt almost as though they were a family. There was that same sort of easy naturalness, that comfortable familiarity. It was a very different feeling than the one he experienced with Corrie. When he, Corrie, and Anna were together, it was like the meeting of two single parents sharing joint custody of their child. There was none of the sense of togetherness that had once marked their relationship or which now characterized his relationship with Sue.

Maybe Corrie was right. Maybe they should have left, gotten out of town, blown this burg. Maybe they would have had a chance someplace else.

Were his loyalties to this town, to this newspaper, really more important to him than his marriage?

He didn't know. That was the truth: he didn't know. He wished he could come to the revelation that always came to movie protagonists, realizing in one clear thinking instant that it was family that was really important; everything else in life was superfluous.

But he could not make such an assumption. For him, it did not seem to be true.

Could they really save their marriage if they moved somewhere else? If so, why couldn't they save their marriage if they stayed here?

He looked over at Sue, brushing her hair back from her forehead. He had never really noticed, before Robert had commented on the matter and Corrie had made her wild accusations, how pretty Sue was. Well, he *had* noticed, but it had been a distanced intellectual recognition. He had seen her only as a student, as an employee. But he saw now that she was pretty. Very pretty. Sexy.

The thought made him uncomfortable, and he tried to push it from his mind, knowing he was edging dangerously close to sexual harassment territory. How many bosses or supervisors had felt themselves attracted to one of their employees, had subtly used the power of their positions to exploit that situation?

What was wrong with him? He was married, for Christ's sake. With a daughter.

He remembered when he and Corrie had been Sue's age. It seemed like only yesterday, but it had been what? Nine years? A decade? More? He recalled, when he was twenty, how old he had considered people in their thirties. Did he seem that old to Sue? It was hard to believe. He still felt young, still thought of himself as young, still identified more with people her age than with other middle-aged adults.

Other.

Middle-aged.

Adults.

Was that what he was? He felt depressed all of a sudden, but then Anna ran over, a crayon picture of Big Bird in her hand, and his spirits instantly rose again. He praised her work, then made a big show of proudly tacking it on the cork bulletin board next to his desk. He rewarded Anna with a big kiss.

She ran off to see Carole in the front, and he swiveled in his chair to face Sue. "So who's going to be in this party of seven besides me and Robert? Does your grandma know yet? How about Rossiter? I think he wants in on the action."

"Maybe," Sue said evasively.

Something about her answer sounded suspicious to him. "Sue?" he said.

"I don't know yet who she wants."

"You don't even know about me or Robert?"

"Your brother will be part of the group."

He looked at her. "And me?"

"She says she wants someone else," Sue admitted, not looking at him.

Rich's face hardened. "I don't care what she says. I'm in. I may not be Joe Macho, but I can take care of myself—"

"That's not it," Sue said. "There's more to it than that."

"What?"

"I have to talk to her some more."

"Talk to her, then. But I'm in. Tell her that. I'm in."

"I'll try," Sue said.

After work, he and Anna came home to a dark house. He knew Corrie had said she was going to be late, but the sight of that dark house disturbed him, and though he pretended for Anna's sake that everything was fine, as soon as he turned on the lights and the television, he went into the bedroom and dialed the number of Wheeler's office.

He let the phone ring ten times before hanging up.

He walked back into the living room and was about to suggest to Anna that they grab some Taco Bell food and cruise by the church on the way back—

the black church
—when Corrie walked in, tired, angry, but obviously alive and all right.

He was grateful, but he said nothing, only sat down on the couch, pretending he'd come in to watch the news.

Corrie made dinner, Cajun chicken. It was the same old game: he did not talk to her, she did not talk to him, but they both talked endlessly to Anna.

Everyone went to bed early.

Rich was awakened by a small hand pressing against his shoulder.

"Daddy?"

He opened one eye, saw Anna standing next to the bed in the dark. "What is it, honey?"

"There's a man outside my window."

He was instantly alert and pushing off the covers. "A man?" He swung his feet onto the floor and grabbed the baseball bat from under the bed.

"Yeah. And he keeps laughing at me."

Rich felt his body grow cold.

No. Jesus, no.

"I don't like the way he laughs, Daddy."

"I'll take care of it, sugar." Rich tried to smile at his daughter, though he was not sure how well he succeeded. His smile felt faint and plastic on his face. "You wait in bed here with Mommy."

"I'm afraid."

"I'll take care of it. I'll make sure no one's there, and when it's all safe, I'll come and get you and tuck you into bed, okay? How does that sound?"

"Okay," Anna said uncertainly.

Rich walked slowly down the hall to his daughter's bedroom. Robert had said he'd seen the Laughing Man. Was that what the vampire looked like? The Laughing Man? That was one thing Sue's grandmother was always vague on—the way the vampire looked. She made it sound as though its appearance varied, changed. Could it assume the shape of other monsters? Of fears?

If it was the vampire, they were safe. There were willow garlands around all the doors and windows. Sue's family had spent the past few days making them from what remained of the willow trees after the fire, and she'd brought some into work. He had availed himself of the Wings' generosity, picking up two long garlands and cutting them to fit, placing them around the doors and windows after dinner.

Anna's door was open, her light on. He walked into the room and turned off the light. Her curtains were closed, but when he opened them he wanted to be able to see. The light would make the world outside as black as pitch, and he wouldn't be able to see a thing other than his own reflection.

He walked slowly across the floor, bat in hand, almost as though he expected to find someone hiding in the curtains. Winnie-the-Pooh stared at him blankly from the baby chair in the corner of the room. He stepped over Anna's Ping-Pong paddles.

He stopped.

He could hear it from here, through the glass, through the curtain, and the hackles rose on the back of his neck. He had heard it before and he recognized it. That familiar throaty chuckle, that low, quiet laugh that would not stop but would continue without pause and grow slowly into loud, wild guffaws.

He forced himself to walk forward, push aside the curtains and look into the side yard.

And there he was.

The Laughing Man.

Rich was frozen in place, unable to move, unable even to think. He was suddenly confronted with his worst nightmare, and though he'd known what to expect, had been halfway prepared for it, he had not anticipated the incapacitating terror that had taken hold of him.

The Laughing Man looked at Rich from beneath his brown derby and chuckled. He was standing next to the storage shed not five feet away, hands clasped primly before him, wearing the same dark brown suit he had always worn, and he was laughing. Rich had never seen the Man this close before, and for the first time he noticed the complete absence of lines or character on that mirth-struck face, the one-dimensional unreality of the perpetually smiling eyes.

The chuckle grew, increased in intensity, became a chortle, a cackle, a laugh, and there was no gap, no pause for air, only that inhuman unstoppable laughing.

"Daddy?" Anna said behind him.

He turned, the spell broken, to see his daughter's frightened face looking in at him from the hallway. He let the curtain fall. "I'll be there in a minute," he said, and his voice sounded surprisingly normal to his own ears. He waited for her to leave, go back down the hall, dimly aware that the laughing had stopped. When he was sure she was gone, he opened the curtain again.

The side yard was empty.

He let the curtain fall once again and, still with a death-grip on the bat, walked out of the room, closing the door behind him. He returned to his bedroom, where Anna was lying on his side of the bed, and Corrie was looking at her through mostly closed eyes.

"Is he gone, Daddy? Is the man gone?"

"What man?" Corrie said sleepily.

"Yes," he whispered to Anna. "He's gone. But I think you should stay with Mommy and Daddy tonight."

She nodded, and he saw the relief in her eyes. "Okay."

He crawled into bed next to her, pulled the covers over both of them. "Let's go to sleep now," he said.

"All right."

He smiled. "Sleep tight."

"Don't let the bed bugs bite." Anna smiled.

She was still smiling two minutes later when she fell asleep.

Fifty-six

Corrie waited until after Rich left for the office to tell Anna that she would not be going to school today. Her daughter had not yet learned that school was something to be hated and avoided—she still enjoyed going to kindergarten each day—and she looked crestfallen when Corrie told her that today they were going to do something different.

"But Jenny said I could play with her on the teeter-totter," Anna whined. "She never lets me play on the teeter-totter."

"You can play with Jenny tomorrow. Today we're going to do something extra special!"

"What?"

"I can't tell you yet. But I'll give you a hint—it's even better than ice cream!"

Anna should have been thrilled. Should have. But was not. There was reluctance in the way she nodded, apprehension in the way she followed her mother into the bedroom. Corrie ignored her daughter's mood. She dressed Anna in her best pink outfit, clipped the matching pink barrettes in her hair, and gave her the little pink purse to hold. The two of them walked outside together. Corrie unlocked the car, opened it, but Anna backed up.

"Come on," Corrie said. "Get in."

Anna shook her head. Her daughter was afraid of her, Corrie realized. She knew that should make her sad, but somehow it didn't. It made her angry. "Get in the car!" she ordered.

No daughter of hers was going to go against the word of the Lord Jesus Christ.

Anna reluctantly got into the car. Corrie slammed her door, walked around, and got in on the driver's side. She found and put in the Beach Boys' "Endless Summer," Anna's favorite tape, while Anna buckled her shoulder harness belt, but it made no difference in her daughter's attitude.

Corrie only half listened to the music as she pulled out of the driveway onto the street. She found herself thinking about Rich. He had seemed strange last night. Nervous. He had not said why he'd asked Anna to sleep with them, and she wondered if he'd heard the voice of Christ. She had heard the voice. She'd heard it clearly.

And it had told her to bring her daughter to the church.

The morning was clear, but there were clouds in the west, a light band of gray that stretched across the horizon, dividing the sky. She felt good as she drove, content to the core of her being, happy and grateful that she had been chosen to do the Lord's bidding. Her contentment grew the closer she drove to the church, Jesus' home.

He lives here now.

Corrie pulled to a stop in front of the interconnected black buildings, unbuckling her shoulder harness. Anna did not do the same, as she usually did, but instead remained tightly buckled in place. She was tense, her little neck stiff, her eyes wide as she stared at the church. "I want to go to school," Anna said.

"You're not going to school today," Corrie said.

"I want to go home."

"You're going to church."

"Daddy doesn't want me to go to church." Anna was clearly frightened.

"I don't care what Daddy wants. Mommy wants you to go to church."

Anna reached instinctively for the thin bracelet around her wrist, holding it tightly, her fingers pressing against the small piece of jade.

"And you don't need that," Corrie said, reaching over and ripping the bracelet off her daughter's wrist. She threw the bracelet out the car window. It landed in the gutter on a bed of dead leaves.

"No!" Anna cried.

"Shut up," Corrie said, and there was enough seriousness in her tone of voice that Anna was cowed into silence.

"It's time to meet Jesus" Corrie said.

Anna burst into tears. There was none of the usual sniffling and blinking, the attention-grabbing preliminaries that gradually grew into a full-fledged cry, there was only this sudden onslaught of fullblown emotion, and Corrie was momentarily taken aback, unprepared for this response. Anna had not behaved like this for over two years, since her Terrible Temper Tantrum days, and Corrie was brought back to herself by the ferocity of her daughter's reaction. Anna was frightened. No, not just frightened. *Terrified.* And it was her responsibility as a mother to comfort and reassure her daughter.

She reached instinctively for Anna, ready to give her a warm hug and tell her everything was okay, when a more reasonable, less emotional voice within her said that Jesus would not like this. This was not what He wanted.

Instead of hugging Anna, she slapped the girl across the face. Hard. "Shut up," she said. "The Lord Jesus Christ is waiting for us."

Anna did not shut up. Her crying grew louder, wilder, and when Corrie unbuckled her shoulder harness and tried to drag her across the car seat toward her, Anna put up a fight, kicking and lashing out with her small fists.

"I'll help you."

Corrie looked through her window to see Pastor Wheeler smiling in at her. Her heart gave a quick involuntary leap in her chest, then she was opening the door and climbing out. "I'll get her," she said. "She's my daughter." Corrie walked around the front of the car and opened the passenger door, grabbing Anna by the arm and yanking. There was a muffled crack, the sound of a twig snapping under a blanket, and then Anna was not crying but screaming, a single long sustained note that sounded louder than an air raid siren in the morning stillness.

Corrie knew that she had broken her daughter's arm, but the feeling that rushed through her now was anger, not sympathy, and she did not let go, pulling harder until Anna was all the way out of the car.

Wheeler took the girl's other arm, put a hand over her mouth, and between the two of them, they dragged the girl into the church.

The church.

It had changed, even since Tuesday, the last time she'd been here. The empty shells of the Savior's sacrifices were arranged around the perimeter of the chapel in staged scenes from the scriptures, and they were beautiful: the resurrection of Lazarus, the death of John the Baptist, the confrontation between David and Goliath. The bodies were positioned in amazingly lifelike poses, their forms sculpted into Art by the hand of Jesus.

She let go of Anna, leaving her in the pastor's hands and walking slowly around the openings in the floor, following the walls of the chapel. She stared, mesmerized, at the sculptures, awed and overwhelmed by the divine inspiration that had created wonderment from such uninspired material. Tears of joy rolled down her face as she recognized the mortal coils of several of the people who had volunteered their lives for the glory of Christ, and she thought that this would indeed be a glorious way to slough off the burden of life.

She reached the front of the chapel and stood there for a moment, staring upward. On the raised pulpit was an oversize throne made from the bones of men and the heads of jackals.

The Throne of God.

A thrill of fear and excitement, exquisitely mingled, ran through her as she eyed the magnificent chair.

"Jesus is waiting," the preacher reminded her.

The sound of his voice broke the spell, and she turned to face him. He was on the other side of the first hole, both arms locked around Anna.

She nodded and started around the hole toward him. It should have smelled horribly here, she thought, surrounded by the castoff vessels of those who had ascended to heaven, but Jesus had somehow metamorphosed the odor of the dead bodies into a scent more lovely than that of the most fragrant and beautiful bouquet, and she breathed deeply as she walked, inhaling the perfumed air. She reached the other side and held her arms out for her daughter, but Wheeler pulled away.

"He is come," he said.

There was coldness in the air, the coldness of the grave. It lasted only for a fraction of a second, but it was enough to cast doubt on everything she'd experienced here, everything she saw before her. She suddenly thought that she should take Anna to the Emergency Room and get her arm set.

And then those thoughts fled.

Jesus arose from the opening in the earth on a beam of light, His radiance illuminating the interior of the chapel, brightening even the dark corners of the pulpit. Corrie fell to her knees, her heart hammering crazily, the accelerated pulse thumping in her head and chest and stomach, echoing between her legs in a sensuous throbbing.

"I have brought them," the preacher said.

"Yes." The Savior's voice was like golden chimes in clear spring air.

I love you, Corrie wanted to say, but her lips would not move, no words would come.

Jesus smiled upon her. "I know." He touched her head gently, tilted it.

Bit into her neck.

Corrie died screaming, thrashing in agony, the substance of her form withering, shrinking as the liquid drained out of it and into the hungry open mouth of Jesus Christ.

Five feet away, trembling with terror, Wheeler watched. At one time, he would have looked away, would not have been able to stomach the final minute, but now his gaze was riveted, and he licked his lips with a dry tongue, a thirst growing within him.

Bloodthirst.

Jesus turned, still holding Corrie's shrunken head, and fixed him with eyes of deep solid crimson. The Savior's gaze moved to Anna. He nodded.

With trembling fingers, Wheeler pushed the girl forward. She was whimpering, a quiet, almost inaudible sound released reluctantly from between tightly closed lips. She was not moving, obviously in shock, her eyes fixed and glassy, and she did not react as Jesus touched her shoulder and drew her to Him.

Jesus bent her head to the side, pushed her hair out of the way, bared her neck. He bit down, but only slightly. A streaming wash of dark blood spilled over her white neck, coursing down her pink dress.

"This is her blood," Jesus said. "Drink of it."

Wheeler hurried forward, put his mouth to the wound. He did not even have to suck. The liquid was drawn into his mouth automatically, a hot, sourly bitter substance, thick and viscous and intermittently chunky.

And it was good.

Fifty-seven

Across the desert, the radio picked up only middle-of-the-road stations that seemed to play exclusively hits from the sixties and early seventies. Glen Campbell. The Carpenters. The Fifth Dimension. Melanie. Joe South.

The songs made Robert feel slightly sad. Nostalgia, he supposed. The first sign of encroaching old age. He didn't know whether his life had been less complicated then or whether the world had been less complicated, but it had been a happier time, a more innocent time, and both he and the world had since moved on.

He had been to Phoenix, had spent the morning at the federal building with Rossiter, and what he had been shown had been enough to curl his hair. After that prima donna shit the agent had been pulling for the past month, it was strange to see him open and cooperative, offering help and information. Robert was shocked to find that Rossiter had an entire vampire file, a massive list of people over the past several decades who'd had the blood sucked out of them. Neither he nor the agent knew whether this was the work of many vampires or if their vampire had simply been traveling around, but Rossiter wanted him to ask Sue and her grandmother about it.

Robert felt good that he had finally been let into the agent's confidence, that he was finally being treated as though he was an equal, but he knew that it was only occurring because Rossiter thought he could be of some use to his career. The agent was no longer rude and dismissive toward him, but he was toward his own people. He'd been curt to one of his fellow agents, downright nasty to an assistant, and Robert realized that this selfish arrogance was a fundamental part of Rossiter's personality. Perhaps it was what made him a good law enforcement officer. Perhaps it was why he was Robert's age and so much more successful in their field. But if that's what it took to get to the top, Robert thought, he didn't want it. Rich was right. Rio Verde really wasn't such a bad place to be.

Rossiter also appeared to be acting somewhat secretive about the existence of the vampire. When he'd asked Robert to accompany him to Phoenix, to the FBI offices, Robert had envisioned a meeting with a task force, a conference with business-suited experts who would map out a quick coherent strategy to deal with the problem. Instead, they'd walked unnoticed to the little cubicle Rossiter called an office and had not discussed anything with anybody. Instead of world-class minds addressing themselves to the situation in Rio Verde, he was presented with xeroxed copies of declassified information and was asked to consult Sue's family.

It seemed strange to him, and he said as much to Rossiter, but the agent assured him that, within the next few days, the big guns would be called in. "This is a bureaucracy," he explained. "We work differently here than you do on your little police force."

Robert left around noon. Rossiter said he had to check in with his supervisors, make a report or something, and he would be following later. He wanted to meet again with Sue and her grandmother and plan a specific strategy for tracking down and disposing of the vampire.

The vampire.

It was amazing to Robert how quickly he, and everyone else, had accepted the existence of a vampire in their midst. Even Rich had come around. The supernatural was supposed to be fodder for B-movies and pulp fiction, believed in the real world only by the ignorant and uneducated, an embarrassing reminder of a more superstitious past. But apparently those roots were not buried as far as people liked to pretend. Or perhaps all of those books and movies somehow sustained a tolerance for such ideas. Whatever the reason, the revelation that vampires were not the figment of some author's imagination but were honest-to-God beings had not thrown everyone for a loop. There were those few Medusas, but other than that, people were willing to confront the problem with the new information at their disposal.

That gave him hope.

He drove into town on 370. He hadn't realized how much the black church had grown until he saw it from the perspective of the highway. It was now the dominant structure in Rio Verde, its black hulking shape visually overriding even the formerly prominent mine. The church was the most visible object when Robert rounded the curve of the first foothill, thrust into prominence by the stark contrast of its blackness with the pale tones of the earth, rock, and surrounding buildings. It looked to him like a shadow, a shadow that was growing, spreading, and would eventually encompass the whole town.

That was a strange thing to think, Robert told himself.

Strange but appropriate. He found his attention focused on the church as he passed the first few shabby shacks and trailers on the outskirts of town, and he still saw its shape, imprinted on his mind, as he pulled into the parking lot of the station.

People were missing. It was now confirmed. No one had called, no reports had been made, but he had instructed Ted, Steve, Ben, and Stu to canvas the town, to look for anything suspicious, to try to determine whether anything out of the ordinary was occurring. They'd found two abandoned cars, several empty houses with open front and garage doors, and more than a few dead dogs and cats. Throughout the town, businesses were closed. Traffic was nonexistent.

Robert took the list from Ted. Whether people were missing because they'd been frightened off and had left voluntarily, or whether they'd been . . . taken, this news was disturbing.

Rossiter arrived just after five, a few moments after Woods, and the three of them met Rich at the paper. They waited several minutes for Pee Wee, called his house and got no answer, then left a note for him and went to Sue's.

The meeting was short and maddeningly uninformative. The old woman had apparently said she was tired, had gone to her room, and would not come out. Sue and her parents seemed to accept this as a matter of course, but Rich and Woods and Rossiter also seemed to accept this as SOP, and that made Robert angry. They placidly accepted the news that nothing was going to be accomplished tonight, and spent fifteen or twenty minutes rehashing information that they'd already gone over twenty times.

Didn't they realize that lives were at stake here?

Robert left alone—angry, tired, and frustrated. He'd come with Rossiter, but there was room in Woods's car for the FBI agent, and he decided to let the coroner take Rossiter to his motel. He wasn't in the mood for companionship tonight.

He sped toward home. It was cold outside, all trace of Indian summer long since gone, but he felt warm, sweaty, and he drove with the windows open, Lynyrd Skynyrd cranked up on the stereo. He wiped the sweat from his forehead. Maybe he was getting a fever. Maybe he had the flu.

Or maybe it was stress.

He gunned the car as the asphalt changed to dirt. Ronnie was singing "I'm on the Hunt," and Robert sang along at the top of his voice. It felt good to scream out some rock and roll, cleansing.

The rocks and cacti on the side of the road were black amorphous shapes, but on the hill beyond his house was a strange white object that stood in sharp contrast to the otherwise uniform darkness. He slowed the car as he neared his drive, finally pressing the brake pedal all the way down. At the top of the hill, clearly visible by the light of the half moon, was something bright and fluttering. It had no distinct shape but grew and contracted in rhythmic billows, segments reaching out and retracting, twisting and turning, dancing with the cold desert wind.

The sight sent shivers down Robert's back, and he thought he heard whispers on the breeze. The fluttering thing on the hill was unknown, yet somehow familiar, like something half-remembered from a long-ago nightmare, and the agitated mutability of its shape struck a chord within him.

He put the car into gear, turned onto the driveway, and sped through the darkness, maneuvering the tricky bumps and ruts by instinct. He slowed as the drive opened onto the front of his house and slammed on the brakes.

Pee Wee's pickup was parked in his carport.

Robert got out of the car and hurried across the dirt, heart thumping. Pee Wee's passenger door was open, the overhead light on, but the big man was nowhere to be seen. Robert called out his friend's name, yelled it more loudly, then walked backward out of the carport. He would have sped inside the house, checked to see if Pee Wee was there, but the front door was locked and his friend could not have gotten in.

The burning overhead light worried him.

Pee Wee never wasted energy.

He continued to call the big man's name. Could Pee

Wee have tried the back door? Was the back door open? Robert hurried around the side of the house.

And stopped dead in his tracks.

The tall saguaro next to the kitchen window, the one his father had specifically told the home builders to save when constructing the house, was now thin and anemic instead of thick and healthy. He could see that much even in this weak light. The huge cactus was a skeleton of its former self, and as Robert moved closer he saw exaggerated ridges beneath the dry wrinkled skin and drooping needles.

He'd been here.

The vampire.

Robert reached into his pockets for his crucifix, his jade. Had Pee Wee been killed by the vampire or simply . . . taken? He looked quickly around. He saw no corpse, but every boulder, every cactus, every shrub, was suddenly the location of a potential ambush. The desert was silent. Completely silent. There was not even the whisking sound of nocturnal animal scuttlings.

He glanced to the right, toward the thing on the hill. There was something threatening in its unnatural fluttering, and Robert's grip on the jade tightened. He let go of the crucifix, allowing it to fall limply back to the bottom of his pocket. He knew he should go into the house, call the station, at the very least pick up a flashlight, but instead he began walking across the rocky ground toward the hill.

The wind increased in intensity as he reached the bottom of the slope, coldness whipping his hair, stinging his face, but he did not stop, did not even slow down. All of the saguaros here had been drained. In the pale moonlight, the once formidable army of cacti that stretched up the incline looked now like a regiment of stick figures. The destruction was crude and obvious, like a trail left deliberately by the monster, a swath of drained life that cut through the living desert.

He reached the summit, panting and out of breath. He stared at the figure before him. It was Pee Wee—although he'd already known that—and somehow the inevitability of this outcome scared him more than its actuality. The big man was wrapped in whitish clear plastic, a tarp of some sort, no doubt taken from the back of his pickup. Beneath the wind-tossed, still-fluttering plastic, Robert could see the dead, dried body of his old friend and mentor, shoved flat against a spiny saguaro, wrinkled face caved in on itself, the shape of the body conforming to the skeleton.

The vampire was not here. He knew that, too, but he kept his fingers pressed tightly against the jade anyway. From this vantage point, he could see below him an intermittent trail of house lights leading into the larger pool of lights that was Rio Verde. Moonlight glittered on the moving water of the partially visible river. The town was small, he saw from up here. Small and helpless. A tiny oasis of light in a desert of blackness.

The smell of blood reached his nostrils, and he turned to face the impaled corpse of his friend, but there was no blood. Even the plastic was spotless.

"Pee Wee," he said softly. "Pee Wee."

And the first tear spilled from his eye onto his cold cheek.

Fifty-eight

They were gathered in the chapel, over forty of them, and Shelly felt thrilled and honored to have been chosen as part of such an elite group.

"He is a glutton and a sloth," Pastor Wheeler said. "And according to the mandate of the Holy Scriptures, the written word of God, he must be stoned to death for his sins."

Shelly's gaze turned toward the young boy standing at the edge of the hole next to the pew bridge. He was eight or nine, with short brown hair and a face that would have been cute were it not so distorted by fear. The boy tried again to bolt, but instead of a mad dash, there was only a frustrated twitch. His mother and father held him fast while Wheeler tied his hands behind his back. The boy stood trembling before them.

"You disobeyed your parents," Wheeler said.

"I didn't want carrots!" the boy's voice was filled with panicked terror.

"You disobeyed the word of God."

"I don't like vegetables!"

The preacher unfastened and removed the boy's belt, ripped open and yanked down his pants. His jeans and underwear gathered around his ankles. "Walk," the preacher commanded.

"No!"

"Walk!" The boy's father pushed his son onto the pew bridge above the hole.

The boy began hobbling across the bridge toward the other side, looking fearfully over his shoulder.

Wheeler picked up a stone from the pile at the edge of the hole and threw it as hard as he could. It hit the boy's shoulder, and he screamed, whirled around, nearly losing his balance on the bridge. The fear on his face gave way to pain for a second, then fear resumed its dominance.

Other people picked up rocks, began throwing.

The boy's mother hit him on the side of the head, bloodying his ear.

His father hit him in the stomach.

One woman hit the boy in the eye, and there was a quick miniexplosion of blood, a jetlike stream that erupted from his socket.

This felt good, Shelly thought. It felt right. The boy was screaming at the top of his lungs, trying vainly to dodge the increasing number of rocks thrown at him while maintaining his balance on the bridge. Shelly bent down and picked up from the pile a small flat hand-sized chunk of sandstone. She heaved it at the boy and was gratified to see it fly into his small dangling testicles. The boy fell, writhing, drawing up his legs, causing the bridge to tilt.

From inside of the hole came a pulsing glow, a divine whiteness.

The boy tried to stand again, but his hands were tied, his pants were around his ankles and he could get no purchase. The bridge tilted again, in the opposite direction, and with a primal yell, the boy fell.

Shelly moved to the edge of the hole with everyone else. She looked down into the opening and smiled.

Jesus fed.

Fifty-nine

Corrie's car was not parked in the driveway, and the house was dark when Rich came home. He looked at his watch. It was after eight. Corrie had promised him before he left this morning that she would pick up Anna at lunch and take her home. This was supposed to be a day off for her. Pastor Wheeler in his infinite magnanimity had been so pleased with Corrie's work that he had graciously condescended to give her a day off with pay.

So why wasn't she home?

And where was Anna?

The thought occurred to him that they were at the church, and he cursed himself for being so selfish and stupid. He'd been so wrapped up in getting the word out to the general public, trying to play hero and save the damn town, that he had taken Corrie at her word and had not bothered to check up on her.

He should have known better than that. He should have called at noon. And at one. And at two. Corrie had not been herself lately, and it was more than possible that she had taken their daughter to church in an effort to indoctrinate her.

Why was he thinking of Corrie as the enemy? Had their relationship really deteriorated to that extent?

He went inside, looked on the refrigerator to see if Corrie had left him a note. She hadn't, but he saw something in the kitchen that made his blood run cold.

The milk and bread and butter from breakfast were still out on the counter, the butter melted.

Corrie never left perishables out for more than ten minutes at a time. On those rare occasions when she awoke earlier than he did and made herself breakfast, she put the refrigerated food away, making him take it out again when he made his own meal.

The bread and butter and milk had been left out all day.

Something had happened to her and Anna. He knew it as surely as he knew that tomorrow was Saturday. He ran into the bedroom. As he'd known, as he'd feared, Corrie's jade necklace was lying on top of the dresser.

Anna was wearing her jade, though. He knew that. Would it be enough to protect both of them?

He felt himself slipping, his thought processes not reasoning as clearly as they should be, worry and panic distracting him, injecting emotional responses where there should be none.

Robert. He needed to call Robert.

No. The church. He should call Wheeler first, see if they were there.

He dug through the notes and scraps of paper underneath the telephone that served as Corrie's address book, found the number of the church, and called it. He got an answering machine, Wheeler telling him in the slow placating tones usually reserved for obstinate children that he was not in right now, but he cared about what you had to say; you could leave a message at the beep. Rich left a message, then found Wheeler's home phone number and dialed it. No answer.

Corrie had no real friends in Rio Verde. Acquaintances maybe, but no friends, no one she saw socially after dark. Still, he called the women she did know—Marge and Peggy and Winnie—but, as he'd known, they had no idea where she was.

Maybe she was paying him back for the pizza night. Maybe she'd just taken Anna out for dinner.

But she didn't believe in wasting money on eating out.

He called Robert at home, let the phone ring fifteen times, in case he was in the shower or going to the bathroom, then dialed the station. His brother wasn't there, but Rich talked to Ted, told him the problem, and the officer promised to let Robert know the second he came in.

"You want me to have Steve swing by the church on his patrol?" Ted asked. "See if anyone there can tell him anything? Those construction volunteers are still working all night."

"Yeah," Rich said. "If you would. I'll make some more calls. I'll buzz you back in a few minutes."

"Make it ten."

Rich hung up. Underneath the end table on which the phone sat, he saw the peachy pink legs of a half-dressed doll. He was filled with a sudden, aching sense of loss. He'd been about to try dialing the number of one of Anna's friend's parents, but he found that he had to put down the phone. He was shaking, and it was difficult for him to breathe. He hadn't realized until this moment how much he had taken for granted the notion that none of this would touch his family. He had made them take precautions, sure. He had done everything he could or was supposed to do. But deep down, on that bedrock emotional level that set the tone for the thoughts that came after it, he had not thought that he or Robert or Corrie or Anna would be touched by this. Not even last night, when he'd seen the Laughing Man. He'd been terrified, but he had not, in his heart of hearts, thought that he or his family could be killed or even hurt. They were the good guys. The injuries would happen to other people, people he didn't know that well, peripheral people.

He knew now how wrong he was.

He reached out and picked up the doll. Maybe this morning, maybe yesterday, Anna had been playing with this toy, pretending it was another person, making believe that she was its mommy.

What would he do if something happened to Anna? Since the day she was born, he had not conceived of a future without her. His mind had concocted a million scenarios. She'd been everything from the first woman president to a runaway hooker, and he had mentally prepared himself for all eventualities, deciding ahead of time how he would react to each situation.

But he had never imagined her death.

That was something he had never planned for.

He took a deep breath. They weren't dead. They couldn't be dead. At the very worst, they were being held hostage, and he and Robert and Sue and their team would rescue them at the last minute. Probably it was not even that bad. Probably the car had gotten a flat, or they were at Basha's or Dairy Queen.

Maybe.

Hopefully.

His hands were still shaking, he was still having a tough time catching his breath, but he forced himself to pick up the phone and start dialing.

Sixty

They were in the living room of Sue's house: Rich and Robert, Rossiter and Woods. Rich and the coroner sat on the couch across from Sue and her parents. Rich's eyes were bloodshot. He had obviously not slept at all last night, and his head kept falling forward and snapping back as he began dozing and then suddenly jerked awake. Robert and the FBI agent stood, Robert pacing agitatedly back and forth in front of the silent television.

"This is bullshit!" Robert said. "How long are we going to wait here and do nothing? I'm starting to think you guys don't know as much as you pretend." He addressed Sue but pointed at her grandmother. "How many people have to die before that old woman gets off her wrinkled ass and starts helping us here?"

"Robert," Woods warned.

"It's okay." Sue faced the police chief. "You can't hurry *laht sic.*"

"Lot sick?"

"Fate."

Sue's father nodded. "World not follow your timetable," he said. "You follow world timetable."

"Exactly. Just because you want something to happen at a certain time doesn't mean it will. Even my grandmother cannot hurry *laht sic.* Things will be revealed in their own time."

"It just seems to me that you're all being way too calm and inscrutable about this."

"The old woman knows what she's talking about," Rossiter said.

Sue fixed him with her gaze. "Her name is May Ling, not Old Woman."

"I'm sorry. I apologize."

"Okay." Sue looked toward Rich. He had been in bad shape when he'd first come over, and though he looked a little better now, she was still worried about him. He had been hoarse and despondently slump-shouldered when she'd opened the front door, and the first thing he'd said was, "Corrie and Anna are gone."

Her grandmother had spoken up immediately, before she'd even had time to tell her what he'd said. "Tell him he is now one of the seven."

"But I thought you said—"

Her grandmother frowned. "Things have changed."

"He says his wife and daughter are missing."

"I know. Tell him this . . ."

"Your wife and daughter are fine," Sue translated, and though she sensed the falsity in her grandmother's words, she tried not to convey that in her speech to him. "She said she does not know where they are, but they are safe. They sensed danger and protected themselves from it, going into hiding, and they are afraid to show themselves. They will be okay."

The look of relief on Rich's face told her that he had believed her, and as she looked at him, she understood how people came to believe in fortune-tellers and palm readers. They believed because they wanted to believe. It was easier to accept the reassuring words of others than face the truth yourself.

She'd wanted to ask her grandmother what she knew about Corrie and Anna, and how she knew, but she did not. It was one thing to translate. It was quite another to knowingly lie.

There was pain in her own chest now as she thought of Rich's daughter. Had something happened to the girl? She hoped with all of her heart that nothing had. She'd only known Anna for a short time, but she liked her and cared for her, felt almost as though she was a baby sister. She stared at Rich. She knew what he was going through. She recalled how she'd felt the other day when they'd been searching for John, when she'd thought the *cup hu girngsi* might have taken him.

She hoped both Anna and Corrie were all right.

Rich looked up from the couch, met her eyes, and she looked quickly away.

She thought John should be at this meeting too, but for once her grandmother had sided with her parents and said no. He was too weak, too young. As far as she was concerned, his trial by fire had earned him a place here, but her grandmother had not agreed.

Influenced.

The word scared her.

"We went out to Pee Wee's today," Robert said slowly. "Went through his stuff."

Pee Wee. Another empty spot within her. There had been so many deaths lately. She wondered if at some point she would not be able to deal with any more of them, if an emotional wall would go up to protect her and keep her from feeling each loss so profoundly. Or if her emotions would just keep on taking hits as her battered psyche spiraled downward.

"Did he finish the *baht gwa*?" her grandmother asked.

Sue translated.

"One of them," Robert said. "The other's halfway done. They're both out in my car."

Sue translated again, and the look that fell over her grandmother's face caused them all to fall silent. The old

woman did not speak for a moment. "Tell them to bring
the *baht gwa* inside," she finally said to Sue. Her voice was
not as strong as before, and there was a slight quaver in
it, though she was obviously trying to pretend as though
nothing had changed. "You and your father get the
spears."

Sue and her father walked through the kitchen and
into the laundry room to gather up the willow branches
they'd sharpened earlier, while Robert and Woods went
outside and brought in two oversize mirrors wrapped in
blankets. The two men unwrapped the blankets on the
floor, revealing one octagon mirror the size of a small
coffee table and another mirror, slightly larger, that was
something between a pentagon and a hexagon.

Her grandmother looked at the *baht gwa,* said nothing.
She took the spears and gave one to Robert, one to Rich,
one to the coroner, one to the FBI agent.

"Hold on to these," Sue translated. "Until tomorrow."

"Tomorrow?"

Sue's pulse sped up as she translated her grandmother's
words into English. "Tomorrow we will know."

"She said there were supposed to be seven of us. Who
are the other three?"

Sue repeated the question, and her grandmother responded with only a few terse syllables. "She is," Sue said.
"And me. And Mr. Buford."

Robert frowned. "Buford?"

"That's what she says."

"I must go also," her father suddenly announced in
Cantonese. "I must fight the *cup hu girngsi.*"

"You cannot," her grandmother replied. "You must remain here and protect your family."

"I cannot let women go out and do men's work while
I stay here and do woman's work."

"It's the twentieth century," Sue told him.

Her grandmother turned to face him. "There are to

be seven of us. If you go, there will be eight. Someone will die. We may die anyway, but if there are eight it will be certain. Is saving face worth the cost of a life?"

"No," he admitted.

"John needs you here. You must protect him."

During this exchange, the other men watched them, uncertain of what was being said, not knowing if it was a conference or an argument. Now her grandmother handed Robert the final spear.

"For Mr. Buford," Sue translated.

Robert looked at the sharpened sticks. "Will we succeed?" he asked Sue. "Does she know that? Can she tell us if we'll get the . . . *cup hu girngsi?*"

"We will succeed," her grandmother said, and chills raced down Sue's arms. Her grandmother was lying.

She felt it. She *knew* it.

Di Lo Ling Gum.

She looked into the old woman's eyes, looked away, frightened.

"We will succeed," Sue said. She tried to make her voice strong, enthusiastic, but she was not sure if any of the men believed her.

They nodded.

But they were silent as they left the house.

After everyone was gone and the house locked up, Sue took a shower. She felt dirty. Unclean and uncomfortable. And the water on her skin felt soothing and good. She got out of the shower, dried herself, then put on a maxi-pad and panties before pulling on her pajamas.

God, she hated having her period. She'd read somewhere that women were luckier than men because they were multiorgasmic, but she thought she would gladly give that up if she didn't have to suffer each month. Men were really the lucky ones; they didn't have to go through this.

She had never gotten a sex lecture from her mother. Or from her father, for that matter. It was simply something that was not discussed by the family. If she hadn't seen *Carrie* and hadn't talked about it with her friends, she would not even have known what to expect, she would not have been prepared for her period. She would have thought she was suffering from internal bleeding or something the first time it came.

Well, that wasn't precisely true. Menstruation had been discussed in seventh grade health class. But the discussions in class about menstruation and sex had been so technical and scientific, so vague in practical applications, that she'd really learned nothing from them. The real facts of sex, the physical, bodily part of it, she'd had to learn from her friends and, later, from the books she surreptitiously read in the library.

She opened the bathroom door, and a cloud of steam escaped into the hallway. She glanced toward her parents' room at the end of the hall, saw her mother sitting on top of the bed, brushing her hair.

Why would her grandmother lie?

That bothered her. She had been so sure of everything until now, so certain that her grandmother would tell them exactly what to do, they would do it, the *cup hu girngsi* would be destroyed, and everyone would live happily ever after. But she recalled now that her grandmother's only other encounter with a *cup hu girngsi* had been as a small child, and that everything she might have learned about *sun-sun gwaigwai*, the supernatural, in Canton was probably only theoretical. For all Sue knew, she might be making this up as she went along, acting entirely on instinct.

She remembered that the *cup hu girngsi* couldn't cross running water.

But had killed Aaron and Cheri in the river.

She reached her bedroom. The door was closed. She

distinctly remembered having left it open before going in to take her shower. She frowned, turned the knob, pushed the door open.

And stopped.

John was naked and kneeling before her bed. He had thrown the bedspread and the blankets onto the floor, and on the flat sheet in front of him were four or five used maxi-pads. Her maxi-pads. He turned toward her, and she saw weak red smears on his chest and cheeks and forehead, blood on his lips and nostrils.

"What are you doing?" She stared at him, shocked, frightened, and filled with a deep humiliating shame.

Influenced.

He grinned, and there was red on his teeth, on his tongue. "I love your blood," he said.

She grimaced in disgust, overcome with revulsion. The saliva in her mouth suddenly tasted putrid, and she felt like throwing up.

He picked up a maxi-pad, pressed it against his mouth and nose like a surgical mask, breathed deeply. He turned toward her, grinning. "I can smell you in the blood," he said. "I can smell your ripe pussy."

She backed away. "I'm telling Father. I'm telling Grandmother."

"Have you ever been fucked? I could do it to you if you let me in your bed tonight."

She turned, ran down the hall. "Father!" she called. "Father!"

There was the sound of shattering glass from behind her, from within her room. She stopped running. Her parents and grandmother were already emerging from their respective rooms, her father tying the belt on his bathrobe, her mother and grandmother holding shut the tops of their nightgowns as they ran.

She hurried back to her room, reached it the same time as her father. John had punched a hole through the window and was now trying to clear out the shards of broken glass still embedded in the window frame. Blood was flowing down his arm in huge streams, and the remaining pieces of window looked like a pop art project, drops and droplets of red spread out centrifugally.

Her father ran past her, into the room, and grabbed John's shoulders, spinning him around, away from the window. John hit him across the face, a wet, sickening slap, and then her grandmother was in the room. The old woman held her hands in the air and began chanting in a strange musical dialect with which Sue was not familiar.

Yet, already the chanting was having an effect on John. His arms were falling to his sides, the tension and aggressiveness leaving his muscles. Sue looked over at her mother, who seemed as confused as she herself felt.

Her grandmother wasn't a witch?

Then what was this?

John's eyes were fluttering, starting to close, his body beginning to go limp. Sue tried to listen to the low words her grandmother was speaking and thought she made out the Cantonese phrases for "evil" and "mother" and "moon."

John collapsed into his father's arms, and her grandmother stopped chanting. "Get him into the bathroom," she said. "I will treat his wounds."

"Will he be all right?" her mother asked worriedly.

"He will be fine. He will sleep for a day, and then it will be as if this never happened."

Her mother hurried across the room to help her father with John.

"Can you do that to the *cup hu girngsi?*" Sue asked. "Talk to it and put it to sleep?"

Her grandmother smiled. "I wish I could. But I cannot."

"Sue," her father said, as he pushed past her, John's

bleeding body in his arms, "you sleep in our room tonight."

"No," her grandmother said firmly. "She will sleep with me."

Sue stood in place as they moved into the hall behind her, took John into the bathroom. She faced the broken window, a cold breeze ruffling her hair, and stared unblinkingly into the darkness of the night.

Sixty-one

Pastor Wheeler knelt in the empty church and prayed, his elbows resting on the soft rise of Bill Covey's stomach. The old fuck had died happily, voluntarily, and though he'd thought that would admit him to the kingdom of Heaven, it would not. Oh, no. Wheeler knew that now. There was room in Heaven for only forty more, and Jesus had come to earth to personally select those forty. He was separating not only the wheat from the chaff, but the good wheat from the bad wheat.

Wheeler heard the sound of muffled hammering from far away.

Tomorrow.

The Second Coming was tomorrow.

An electric tingle coursed through his body, causing his penis to stiffen. It would not be long now.

Wheeler closed his eyes. "Now I lay me down to sleep, with the girl across the street. If I should die before I wake, please, dear Lord, don't let me bake." He squeezed his hands more tightly together, prepared for the big send-off. "Amen."

He opened his eyes, unclasped his hands. He pressed his fingers against Covey's naked body, felt the cold, bloated stomach, the white-haired chest. His mouth felt dry, and he knew what Jesus wanted him to do.

He took a deep breath, bent over, bit into Covey's neck, and as the cool blood spilled, pooled, he began to lick.

Sixty-two

Mayor Tillis was cold. He had wrapped himself up like a mummy while asleep, rolling around in his blankets until every square inch of his body was covered, but the freezing air had penetrated his defenses, and now he lay shivering beneath his comforter. His breath was visible, white in the darkened room.

The darkened room?

He had fallen asleep with the light on.

The mayor sat up in bed, the movement awkward due to the bulky and closely wrapped blankets. He twisted his arms free, and reached to the left, his fingers finding and turning the black plastic knob just below the bulb on the nightstand lamp. Nothing. The light did not go on. Then he remembered. He had been watching TV when he fell asleep also, a rerun of *M*A*S*H*.

Blackout. It had to be a blackout. He felt around the top of the nightstand for his glasses, found them, and put them on. The fuzzy monochromatic blackness was differentiated into shades and gradations, and he saw the outline of his dresser, desk, file cabinet. There was nothing out of the ordinary in the room, nothing there that shouldn't be, no unaccounted-for pools of shadow, but he still felt nervous.

As though there was someone in the room with him.

Or some*thing.*

Through the top of his pajamas, his fingers found the

silver crucifix on the thin chain around his neck. He felt reassured just touching it, but the feeling that he was not alone did not go away. He extracted the rest of his body from the tangled blanket and swung his legs off the mattress.

A cold breeze blew against the skin of his feet from underneath the bed.

Instinctively, without thinking, he jumped, pushing off from the floor, leaping away from the bed. He sprang toward the bathroom and caught himself, his fingers grabbing both sides of the doorjamb.

Something moved within the bathroom, doubled by the mirror.

The vampire!

The monster loomed out of the darkness before him.

He was tall and aristocratic, vaguely European. In life, he must have cut an impressive figure. In death, he was truly terrifying. His skin was the bluish white of an untouched corpse, and a palpable sense of coldness radiated outward from his form. There was no expression on the impassive face, only an all-consuming hunger in the red-rimmed eyes and a glimpse of white fang between partially parted lips.

The mayor wanted to run but could not, wanted to scream but was unable.

The vampire smiled. Blood filled the thin, gummed spaces between his teeth.

No! The mayor fumbled with the top of his pajamas, then tore the top open and held forth his crucifix. The vampire chuckled, an evil inhuman sound that seemed more like an expression of disdain than mirth, and snatched the crucifix from the mayor's fingers. The mayor's skin burned where the vampire touched it, as though it had been seared with a branding iron, and he watched as the white fist clenched, grinding the silver crucifix into a dusty powder that slipped through the long, tapered fingers.

The burning pain awakened him, enabling him to throw off the shocked lethargy that had settled over his mind, and he quickly backed away from the bathroom. Taking a chance, knowing he had nothing to lose, that this was the only way he could even hope to escape, he turned his back on the vampire and ran out of the bedroom into the hallway. He raced down the hall to the front door, running as fast as he could, his heart pounding painfully in his chest. As he fumbled with the doorknob, he turned to look behind him and saw the vampire gliding smoothly and effortlessly in his direction. The monster was grinning, and his fangs glinted in the weak moonlight that shone through the open doorways of the den and bedrooms.

The door was locked, and the mayor tried desperately to turn the small piece of metal that would throw the deadbolt, but his sweaty fingers slipped on the catch.

And then a huge freezing hand grabbed the top of his head, palming it like a basketball, and turned him around. He was staring into the most ancient and evil eyes he had ever seen, and then his head was being bent, his neck exposed.

He felt himself die, and it was not at all the way he'd thought it would be. There was no floating sense of peace, no drifting off into a pleasant sleep. There was the sharp, shocking pain of skin being ripped open, blood gushing out, the vampire biting harder, clamping down, teeth tearing through veins into muscle. Then he felt a sudden slashing agony that jerked his entire body, burning through his innards like acid. Spasms of torment ripping simultaneously through individual parts of his body that had never before experienced sense: spleen, appendix, liver. He would have doubled over from the powerfully wrenching cramps, but the vampire was still holding him up. He felt his bowel and bladder muscles give way, but nothing came out, and he knew that all of the fluids in his body were being vacuumed out through his neck.

His last coherent thought was uncharacteristically unselfish: I hope they cremate my body. I hope they don't let me come back.

Sixty-three

It wasn't just chilly, it was downright cold, and Janine wished she'd brought a jacket. Her breath escaped from between her lips in visible puffs of white, and she tucked her hands under her armpits for warmth as she hurried across the open area between the buildings. It was quiet tonight: no fighting cats, no howling dogs, no cawing birds, not even the whisklike scuttling of nocturnal bugs and lizards. No natural noises at all. There was only the muffled rhythmic sound of machinery—the dishwashers in the kitchen, the heaters on the roof—and, from the rooms, occasional human voices and the fake, flat sounds of television.

She didn't like walking alone across the ranch, not since Terry Clifford's murder, but it was the beginning of the off-season, she was pulling double duty, and she knew that if she balked or complained, her hours would be cut. Or worse. Hollis seemed to be on a rampage, punishing anyone who even appeared to believe in the existence of vampires.

Vampires.

She looked toward the flat boxlike structure at the north end of the ranch. The stables.

She walked faster.

And the lights went out.

They went off first in the main building, then around the pool, then in the guest lodges. The recessed bulbs along the pathway faded away into nothing. She was unable to see even the path beneath her feet, and was forced to slow down, staying on track only by the feel of the concrete walk. She wanted to run, but she was afraid she would trip and fall, and she definitely didn't want that to happen.

She swallowed hard, forced herself to walk slowly forward, one step at a time, though a feeling of panic was growing within her. Something was wrong. The ranch's backup generators weren't kicking in the way they were supposed to. The lights weren't coming back on.

She stepped on something. Something hard and brittle that cracked beneath her boot and felt like neither rock nor branch. She stopped, crouched down, looked.

It was a jackrabbit.

A jackrabbit that had been drained of blood.

Oh, God. She stood, wishing suddenly that she hadn't lost the piece of jade Sue had given her, wishing that she hadn't been too embarrassed to tell Sue she'd lost the jade and wanted another.

But the time for wishing was past.

The vampire was here.

She heard shouting from somewhere. It sounded as though it was coming from her left, from one of the guest lodges, but she couldn't be sure. The darkness seemed to do something to the acoustics, to warp the directional capabilities of her hearing. She ran to her right, breaking away from the path and speeding through the sand toward the nearest building, navigating by instinct. The laundry room was in here. Assuming the vampire wasn't in the laundry room—and why would he be with so much fresh meat elsewhere?—she could lock herself inside and wait it out until morning. The laundry room's door and walls were especially thick, to muffle the sounds of the washing machines, and there were no windows. It was probably the safest place in the whole ranch.

Her right boot sank into the sand, and she slipped, nearly twisting her ankle, before quickly righting herself. Her heart was pounding crazily, and she wondered if the vampire could hear it. She thought, absurdly, that the sound of a beating heart was probably like a dinner bell to a vampire, calling him, like an amplified tom-tom in his head.

She ran faster.

She finally reached the building's double side doors, yanking open the left door and running inside.

Ramon and Jose were lying in the hall, outside the laundry room.

It was dark in the hallway, but there was a flashlight lying between the sprawled corpses on the floor, the beam shining through cracked glass onto a portion of Ramon's hand and Jose's shoulder.

Flashlight?

Her mouth felt dry. They had to have gotten the flashlight out after the blackout hit. That was three minutes ago, four at the most.

Which meant that the vampire was probably still in the building.

She ran over, picked up the flashlight. She shone the beam down the hallway. To the left, to the right. The hallway was empty. She saw no other bodies. And no vampire.

She ran. Her boots echoed on the wood floor. The sound was loud in the stillness, would alert anyone—

anything

—in the building to the fact that she was here, but there was nothing she could do about it, and she forced her legs to pump harder. The door at the other end of the hall opened onto the parking lot. If she could make it out of here, she could run straight to her car, take off and go to the police, tell them what was happening.

She reached the door, shoved it open.

And the vampire was right in front of her.

She stopped, nearly fell, but she grabbed onto the side of the closing door and only by luck regained her balance. The vampire was bending over a boy lying dead or unconscious on the sidewalk next to the parking lot.

He did not look like a vampire. He looked like a zombie, movie zombie, one of those poorly made up zombies from *Night of the Living Dead*. If she had seen this in a fright flick, she would have laughed. But the fact that the vampire in real life was not a sophisticated special effect but a B-movie monster with a bad makeup job was somehow much more frightening than anything else could have been.

The vampire bent over the boy. His head did not touch the child's neck but hovered about an inch above. She saw the boy's bodily fluids sucked up, vacuumed into the monster's mouth, a sickening mixture of red and green and brown and yellow that was simultaneously thick and thin, a torrent of combined liquids that spewed forth from the neck as the body visibly withered.

She'd been standing in the doorway for no more than three seconds, but the intensity of the scene before her was so great that every aspect of it was burned permanently onto her memory. She let go of the door, and the vampire looked up. She saw lust in those black-ringed zombie eyes.

She thought of the fetus inside her.

Her baby.

The monster grinned.

She broke, ran screaming toward the parking lot. There were other people screaming now: women, children, and most frighteningly, men. There was not just one vampire, she thought. There were many. An army of the undead. They were here, and they were hungry, and they were taking over.

She turned and looked over her shoulder, but the vampire was not following. He had found another victim.

Ahead, she saw Sally Mae crying, leaning despairingly against the hood of a pickup truck, snot running out from her nose and over her lips. Sally Mae did not seem to know where she was or what was happening, and her eyes registered no recognition as they looked into Janine's.

Janine grabbed the other woman by the arm, pulling her through the parking lot. "Come on!" She had already taken out her keys, and when she reached her car she quickly unlocked the driver's door. "Get in!" she said.

Sally Mae looked at her uncomprehendingly.

"Get in the car!" Janine screamed. She shoved the other woman onto the seat, pushed her past the steering wheel to the passenger side, and hopped in herself, slamming the door and locking it. She started the car, floored the gas pedal, and peeled out, speeding toward the highway.

"What in cow's ass heaven is that?"

Hal, the friendlier guide, stood and walked over to where his partner stood looking toward the ranch. "What?"

Tracy looked quizzically at her husband over the campfire. Ralph only shrugged.

"Listen. Don't you hear it?"

Hal shook his head. "No . . ." His eyes widened. "Yes!"

"What is it?" Tracy asked.

Hal walked over, threw another branch onto the blaze. "You two stay here by the campfire. We'll be back in two shakes of a lamb's tail."

Two shakes of a lamb's tail? Did they really talk like that, Tracy wondered, or was this something they just put on for tourists? "Where are you going?" she asked.

"Back to the ranch to see what's happening."

Ralph stood. "We might as well go, too. It's getting cold

out here, and I'm sure we'd be much more comfortable in our rooms than we would out in these sleeping bags."

"We're camping," Tracy said firmly, fixing him with a determined stare.

Ralph sighed, sat down. "Whatever you say."

"What's the point of going to a dude ranch if you're just going to treat it like a hotel? Why did we come all the way out here if we weren't going to take advantage of it?"

"I said okay."

"We'll be back," Hal said, nodding at them. The other guide had already mounted his horse, and Hal followed, slipping his foot easily into the stirrup and swinging his leg over the saddle. With a "Hey!" and a couple of clicks, the two cowboys were off, riding into the desert night.

Tracy leaned back on her sleeping bag, staring up at the stars. It was cold out here, but it was invigorating, and she felt—

"Trace!"

She turned her head toward Ralph. "Yeah?"

"Look!"

She sat up, followed his pointing finger.

A bird was hovering in the air above the desert at approximately the spot where the ranch was located.

"It's a phoenix," Ralph said, his voice quiet and filled with awe.

It was.

Tracy stared at the bird. It was huge, the size of a small plane, and totally unlike anything she had ever seen. It seemed to glow from within, radiating a diffused white light that brought into extraordinarily vivid clarity every feather, every talon, every detail of the creature's majestic body. The bird looked more real than real, a three-dimensional being in a two-dimensional world. There were colors in its plumage that she had never seen before, that were not variations

on black or white or blue or yellow or red, colors that were
not part of the known spectrum.

"Are they having some kind of laser show?" Ralph
asked. "Is that what this is? I don't remember reading
anything about it in the list of events."

She ignored him. It wasn't a laser show. It was a bird.
A real bird. An honest-to-God phoenix. She reached
across her sleeping bag and grabbed the strap of her camcorder case. She unzipped the vinyl bag and took out the
camera. She wasn't sure there was enough light for her
to shoot, and she knew instinctively that there was no way
this magnificence could ever translate to videotape, but
she had to try.

She aimed the camcorder at the bird, pressed down on
the "Record" button, and began to speak for the benefit
of the multidirectional microphone. "It is about nine-
thirty, and we're in the desert outside the Rocking D
Ranch in Rio Verde . . ."

Janine sped down the narrow dirt road that led to the
highway, refusing to look in the rearview mirror, concentrating solely on the portion of the road before them that
was illuminated by the headlights. Sally Mae lay huddled
against the passenger door, not moving, not speaking, not
even whimpering.

They had passed no other vehicles, had seen no taillights or headlights, and Janine wondered if they were the
only ones to have escaped. How many people were at the
ranch right now? Fifteen employees, maybe. About twenty-
five guests.

Could the vampires have killed forty people?

She pressed down harder on the gas pedal, but the car
was just heading into a turn and the vehicle fishtailed
wildly in the dirt as the road curved. Janine held hard on

to the wheel, struggling to maintain control, straightening out only after almost swerving into the adjoining ditch.

Ahead, her high beams reflected off the bullet-riddled face of the stop sign that stood at the edge of the highway.

They'd made it!

She slowed down, the car bumping over the serrated steel of the cattle guard that separated the dirt from the asphalt.

And the car stalled.

Died.

No! Janine pumped the gas pedal, trying to will the car back to life, but there was no response, and the vehicle rolled back a few feet on the slight incline.

"Start, you piece of shit!" Janine was screaming at the car and crying at the same time, tears blurring her vision as she turned the key in the ignition and heard only a series of impotent clicks. Sally Mae, still huddled in the corner, made a low, incoherent sound of abject terror. "Shut up!" Janine yelled at her. She turned, slapped the woman hard across the face.

And saw movement through the passenger window.

"Help!" The windows were closed, there were no lights on the empty highway, no cars, no trucks, but she screamed anyway, a raw panicked shriek that threatened to permanently damage her vocal cords. "Help!" She pumped desperately on the gas, turned the key.

The monster was coming.

He lurched toward them out of the darkness, an over-tall man in a frayed out-of-date suit, face rotting from the inside out, decay pushing through the thin layer of skin on the forehead, cheeks, and chin. He staggered around the front of the car, through the twin beams of the head-lights, and around to the driver's side as Janine continued to frantically turn the ignition key. He grinned, revealing dirty bloody teeth. His bulging eyes looked downward from her face to her abdomen.

He knew she was pregnant. He could sense it.

He would eat the fetus.

"Don't move!" Janine screamed, though Sally Mae had not moved at all. "Stay in here! The door's locked! He can't get in!"

A fist punched through the window, shattering the glass.

She did not even have time to cry out as strong fingers closed around her neck and yanked her outside, through the broken window, into the cold air of the night.

Sixty-four

The hotel room was shitty. It was supposedly the best this town had to offer, but despite the bland pleasant cleanliness of the accommodations and the reassuring presence of HBO and CNN on the television, there was something second-rate about the room, as though it was straddling the line between adequate and shabby and was leaning clearly toward the latter.

But Rossiter didn't care. He felt good, charged, more alive than at any time since he'd left the Academy and happier than he'd been since he'd come to this hellish state.

This was big.

He'd known it in the back of his mind when he'd correlated the figures on the computer, but it had been confirmed when he'd met the Oriental girl and her grandmother. This was big, not in a pulp-novel Melvin Purvis G-man way, but in a manner that was far more profound.

He was not just catching criminals.

He was fighting the forces of evil.

He had not talked with Engles when he'd told Robert he would—he'd spent that time severing ties with the state police and kicking those dipshit lazy-assed bastards off the case—but he had called his supervisor and left a brief message on his answering machine, providing just enough description to keep him out of trouble with protocol. He'd then immediately called Washington and, after some necessary phone bullying that led him quickly up the chain of command, had made a full report to James F. Watley, head of the Bureau's Western Division. It was foolhardy, perhaps—he knew how crazy all this sounded. But he'd written his speech out beforehand, and he was an old hand at making the implausible plausible, and he believed he had successfully demystified the more fantastic aspects of this situation until it fit foursquare into the Bureau mold.

Nevertheless, he was surprised that Watley did not nail him on several points, and he wondered if perhaps another department or team within the Bureau was working on a connected project. Or if a think tank somewhere had already postulated the existence of vampires.

Or if the director was simply writing him off as a loon.

Whatever the reason, Watley's low key and reasonable reaction to his unreasonable hypothesis caused him to change his plans. He had intended to ask for backup, but had decided against it then and there. It was a dangerous decision, and an obvious violation of regulations, but he trusted the old Chinese woman. She'd come in on target so far, and there was no reason to believe she would steer them wrong as they approached the stretch.

He didn't want to share the glory with some Johnny-come-lately.

This was his baby and his alone.

Fuck Watley. Fuck Engles. Fuck everyone. When this was over, he would report directly to the Bureau chief. He would be able to write his own ticket.

He sat down on the bed, watched a few moments of a comedy showcase on HBO, then switched to NBC, ABC, CBS, and, finally, an independent station. There was an old movie on. A monster movie.

What did they used to call that in the sixties?

Serendipity.

"Yeah," he said aloud. "Seren-fucking-dipity."

He leaned back on the bed, adjusted the pillow, settled in to watch the movie. He was too charged to sleep.

It was going to be a long night.

But tomorrow was going to be a great day.

Sixty-five

Sue awoke and, for a moment, did not remember where she was. The contours of the room were wrong, the furnishings unfamiliar, and the bed was facing in the wrong direction. Then she saw her grandmother next to her, sitting up, leaning against the backboard of the bed, and the events of the previous evening returned in a rush.

Her grandmother glanced calmly over at her. "I dreamed last night of the black church."

Sue nodded, feeling cold, remembering the dark and frightening images of her own sleep-bound travels. "I did, too."

"It is there that we will find the *cup hu girngsi*. That is where it lives."

The words were spoken with certainty, and Sue sat up, keeping the blanket wrapped around her. She had expected to feel different, to feel . . . something. She had assumed that when the time came, her *Di Lo Ling Gum* would kick in, that she would sense things, know things, but this morning felt the same as every other. Even the intermittent impressions she had received the night before seemed to have deserted her. If she really did have *Di Lo Ling Gum*, what good was it?

Was her grandmother feeling anything?

"So what do we do now?" Sue asked. "Just walk into the church and confront the *cup hu girngsi*?"

"Yes."

Sue blinked, unprepared for that answer. "We don't have to go through some sort of ritual? We don't have to go there at a certain time?"

"No." Her grandmother smiled. "You have seen too many movies."

Sue got out of bed, picked up her robe from where she had placed it on a chair, and put it on. "If it is living in the church," she said, "how come it has not killed the pastor? It does not need him anymore. Why is it keeping him alive?"

"I do not know," her grandmother said, and her voice was troubled. "I do not understand why. That worries me."

Sue sat back down on the bed next to her grandmother. She looked into the old woman's eyes and saw not fear there, not determination, not any of the things she had expected to see. She saw sadness. She saw regret.

"Are we going to die?" she asked.

"I do not know," her grandmother admitted.

This time, Sue knew, she was not lying.

Sixty-six

The town was crawling with reporters, state policemen, and gawkers of all shapes and sizes. The massacre had not gone unnoticed, and the miracle of satellite technology had made sure that the news had been transmitted to everyone in Arizona who could conceivably fuck up today's plans.

The police station was the hub of all this madness, with cameramen lying in wait outside the front door, and a slow but steady trickle of townspeople led in to be interviewed by Steve, Ted, Ben, and Stu.

Robert stood next to the front counter, scanning the room, a major tension headache thumping just below the skin of his right temple. He had been making the rounds of the room, eavesdropping on the interviews, trying to keep track of everything that was going on, but he had given that up and had now decided to let his men perform their jobs without him looking over their shoulders. He had too many other things to think about right now.

He had to think about the *cup hu girngsi.*

He had to find a way for the seven of them to go over to Wheeler's church, armed with spears and a mirror and wearing jade, and kill the vampire in the midst of this media circus.

Jesus, he thought, this was like a damn *Saturday Night Live* sketch. He and Rich had been wrong. They weren't in a horror movie. They were in a comedy. A farce.

He massaged his throbbing head. Rossiter was in his office and had been on the phone for the past half hour, talking to the FBI in Phoenix and Washington, trying to get authorization to shut down the state police investigation. Joe Cash was in the conference room on another phone, talking to his own people, trying to counteract the damage. Rich was leaning against one of the desks talking to Woods, who looked as though he hadn't slept all night. The coroner's face was wan, pale, tired. Rich didn't look much better.

Robert ran a hand through his hair, trying to quell the feelings of doubt that were rising within him. How effective were they going to be if they were all exhausted, exasperated, and not thinking clearly? Right now, he wouldn't trust any of them to go after a high school weenie bopper who'd bought beer with a fake ID, let alone confront a vampire who had just killed upward of thirty people.

Maybe the vampire would be slow and fat and sated after his feast.

Yeah, he thought. Right. And maybe he would just walk in and give himself up, too.

Robert looked over at Sue. She was standing beside her grandmother, who was seated in Stu's chair. Out of everyone in the station, they were the only two who appeared calm and unruffled, and he hoped it was because they had inside information and had concrete assurances the rest of them didn't.

He checked his watch, his headache flaring at the downward movement of his eyes. It was after ten already, nearly ten-thirty. Where was Buford? He'd called the burger stand owner over an hour ago, told him to get his ass over here immediately. Had Buford chickened out?

As if on cue, Buford walked through the door. He did indeed look scared. His face was pale, his clothes disheveled, and he carried a double-barreled shotgun with him into the station. Several people, obviously still shaken by the events of the night before, took a step back at the sight of him, thinking, no doubt, that he was about to open fire, but he strode quickly past them on his way to the front desk.

Robert motioned him over, then gave the high sign to Rich and Woods. The four of them walked through the crowded room to Stu's desk, where Sue and her grandmother waited. He looked at the grandmother, and though he knew she couldn't understand English, he spoke to her. "Okay," he said. "We're all here. Let's go into my office and talk."

"It sounds like there's a whole gang of them," Buford said after he had been briefed on last night's events. "An army."

"That's what some of the survivors are saying."

Sue looked at her grandmother, shook her head. "There is only one."

Steve and Ben were in the room with them, had come in because Robert had asked them to. Maybe only seven of them could go into the church, but he wanted some backup just in case something happened to them.

"I didn't know there really were vampires," Ben said. His voice was shaky. "I thought it was all made up for the movies."

"Now you know," Robert said.

"But why is the vampire afraid of jade?"

"You don't have to know how a television works to turn it on," Sue said. "You don't have to know what a microchip is to use a computer. You don't have to know why the *cup hu girngsi* is afraid of jade. All you need to know is that it is."

"So everything we think we know about vampires is

wrong," Buford said. "They can't be stopped with crosses or holy water or garlic or silver bullets . . ."

"I think some of our legends have a basis in truth," Robert said. "But it's like Sue explained at the meeting, they got distorted over the years." He cleared his throat. "I think it's also a shape-shifter. That's something you all should be aware of. I know we're entering science fiction territory here . . ." He trailed off, grinned. "What the hell am I talking about? We're discussing a damn vampire, and I'm thinking you won't believe that it can change its appearance?" He shook his head. "From what I've heard and been able to gather, the vampire appears as different things to different people. Jesus, obviously. Elvis, according to Emily Frye. La Verona." He paused, looked at Rich. "The Laughing Man. I think maybe it appears to people as their fears. You always hear that in the movies—'It knows what scares you'—but I think it's true here. I think it does know what scares you, and I think it plays on that weakness. We all better be prepared for that."

They were silent.

"I think it can't show up in a mirror," Robert said, "because it *is* a mirror. It's a reflection of our own fears."

"No," Sue said. "It's not. And it can show up in a mirror, in the *baht gwa*. That is why we are bringing the *baht gwa* with us. The *cup hu girngsi* is afraid of its own reflection."

"Maybe it *feeds* off our fears," Buford suggested.

Woods snorted. "Get off this fear kick. You guys've all been watching too many *Twilight Zones*. It's not feeding off our fear. It's not draining our emotions. It doesn't give a damn whether we fear it or hate it or love it. It feeds off our blood and our semen and our urine and our saliva. The fluids of life. Period."

Sue translated, and her grandmother nodded enthusiastically.

"See?" Woods said.

"Then why does it appear as different things to different people?" Robert asked.

"Because," Rich said. It was the first time he'd spoken, and they all turned to look at him. "Because there obviously is a connection between the *cup hu girngsi* and whoever sees it. It does take its form from an image buried in the viewer's mind, but it doesn't appear as a manifestation of a person's fears. It appears as a figure that that person believes can be resurrected." He looked around the room, at each of them. "Think about it. Jesus? Dracula? La Verona? Elvis? I can see people being afraid of Dracula or La Verona. Even Jesus, although that's stretching it. But Elvis? Come on. What I think is happening is that the monster appears not as our fears but as figures who, in our minds, can be resurrected—or cannot be killed. I mean, that's really the only thing these figures have in common: the fact that they have survived death. I think these figures can be from cultural or even personal mythologies, but that's what ties them together. That's what ties together Dracula and the *cup hu girngsi*. I think that's why there's always been such an interest in vampires, why the myths are found in all countries and throughout history. That's what attracts people to them— the idea of everlasting life."

Sue translated. Her grandmother smiled, nodded.

"That's great," Rossiter said. "But I don't give a shit if the vampire represents your repressed homosexual desire for your father or my need to crawl back into my mama's womb. As far as I'm concerned, vampires are creatures that have always been here and always existed. Like sharks. And instead of sitting around chatting about it, we ought to be out there tracking it down and killing it."

"We will," Sue said. "But it's not going outside of the church in the daytime, and we can spend ten minutes talking about it to prepare everyone for what they're going to see, to let everyone know what we're up against.

This isn't a movie. We can't just walk in there, find a coffin, drive a stake through its heart, and live happily ever after. There's more to it than that."

Her grandmother said something in Cantonese. She spoke slowly, and Sue translated slowly, mirroring her grandmother's deliberate speech. "My grandmother says that we don't know the extent of the *cup hu girngsi's* powers. We don't know if it can read minds or control thoughts. But there are a few things we do know: it is afraid of the daylight, it is afraid of jade and willow and mirrors and water. And it can be killed."

"Water?" Robert said.

"The *cup hu girngsi* cannot cross running water," Sue said, but there was no conviction in her voice.

"I hate to burst your grandma's bubble, but Cheri Stevens and Aaron Payne were killed *in* running water. In the river."

"I know. But my grandmother says it cannot cross running water."

A silence settled over them, and it was not a comfortable silence.

"If she's wrong about that . . ." Buford said. He left the thought unfinished.

"Wait a minute," Rich said. "Don't rivers in China flow in a different direction? Don't they flow north instead of south or something?"

Sue's head snapped up. She nodded. "You're right," she said excitedly. "They do. They flow east." She spoke rapidly in Chinese to her grandmother, and the old woman's frown smoothed out, her wrinkled face returning to its normal placidity.

"I dreamed last week of a river of blood that flowed uphill," Sue said.

"We can use this," Buford said thoughtfully. "We can use this information to help us."

"How?" Robert asked. "Drag the vampire to the river?"

"No. We make a fake river. Give ourselves some extra protection."

"Yes," Woods said, catching on. "We dig ditches around the church. We channel water or get some hoses. We make our own fake river and trap the vampire between the streams."

"Exactly."

"That's just dumb," Robert said.

Rich shook his head. "We don't have time to dig ditches."

"We may not have to," Buford said. He looked at Robert. "I have access to hoses, the fire truck. I say we hook those suckers up, point 'em east and let her rip. If worst comes to worst, at least it'll trap him in the church."

"Until the water runs out," Rich said.

"Or until we can think of something else."

Robert nodded slowly. "It just might work. Steve, Ben, you get to work on this."

"Call the water department," Buford said. "Ask for Compton, and tell him to tap off the main valves so we can get some pressure on the hill. The church is on the slope, and pressure's sometimes a problem."

"How long can we keep these streams running?" Robert asked. "How big a reserve do we have to draw from?"

Buford shrugged. "We'll have to ask Compton." He thought for a moment, figuring. "If I remember right, there's a hydrant across the street from the church. But the next closest one's about half a block down, by the old Big A. We're going to need all the hoses we can lay our hands on. I'll call Chief Simmons and get him to open the station. We'll run the water through the truck pump on the far hose, but with the hydrant by the church we'll just have to trust the water pressure."

"Hopefully Compton'll be able to deliver," Robert said.

Buford nodded. "Hopefully." He pushed up the sleeves

on his shirt, looked toward Steve and Ben. "You guys make the calls. I'm going over to the fire station. Tell Simmons to meet me there."

Robert nodded toward Rossiter. "You go with Buford," Robert told the FBI agent.

Rossiter shook his head. "I'm not taking orders from you. I'm in charge of this—"

"No, you're not." Robert faced the agent, and he was steeled with a new resolve. He was terrified, he didn't know if any of them would live through the day, but while they did live, this was his town, and he was calling the shots. He suddenly realized that he had not thought of leaving Rio Verde lately, that he had not mentally planned his escape from town as he had so often in the past. If he made it through this, he decided, he would never again complain about being stuck in this place, in this job. He would thank his lucky stars for his boring, safe, and predictable little life.

There were far worse fates.

Robert motioned toward Sue's grandmother. "She's in charge," he told Rossiter.

"Go with Buford," Sue said. The FBI agent opened his mouth to speak, then shut it again. She knew that he wanted to maintain control. But he was also aware that even if he had an army of FBI agents with him right now, armed to the teeth, it would make no difference. The *cup hu girngsi* could not be fought with conventional weapons, and he knew it.

There was a knock on the office door. Rich, the nearest the door, opened it.

"What is it?" Robert said.

Ted was in the doorway, standing next to a tall, thin, moderately attractive middle-aged woman who was holding a videotape. The woman was nervous and did not look up. Her attention was focused on the tape she was turning over and over in her hands.

"She says she was staying at the Rocking D—" Ted began.

"My husband and I were camping last night, and I saw something flying above the desert." She stopped turning the tape in her hands, held it out. "I thought it was a phoenix. You know, the bird? So I got out my camcorder. It kind of hovered for a while and then flew toward the highway. I got all of it on tape. Our guides never came back, and we were going to go back to our room, but we thought we might get lost and not be able to make it back in the dark, so we decided just to stay there. We found out what happened when we went back to the dude ranch and saw all the police cars . . ." She took a deep breath. "I think you should see the tape."

Robert stood up, walked around his desk, took the videotape from her. "May I keep this and make a copy? I will return it to you."

"Keep it," the woman said. "I never want to see it again."

"Have you looked at it?"

She shivered. "We looked at it."

Robert nodded to Ted. "Take her statement." He turned to the woman. "Thank you again, Ms. . . . ?"

"Singleton. Tracy Singleton."

"Thank you, Ms. Singleton."

Ted escorted the woman down the hall, and Robert turned back toward the others. "We have a VCR in the conference room," he said. "Let's check it out."

"Now we'll get to see him," Woods said. "A camera has no fear, no ideas, no thoughts, no biases. It just records what's there."

"Maybe," Sue said.

They walked down the short paneled hallway to the conference room. Robert switched on the lights, then rolled the TV around to the head of the conference table as the rest of them took their seats. He plugged in the television, and the videotape recorder on the metal shelf beneath it, popping in the tape. He looked around the quiet room. "Ready?"

They all nodded.

"All right."

There was silence in the conference room as the videotape began. Robert found that he was holding his breath, and he forced himself to let out the air and continue breathing. On the screen there was a nighttime view of the desert near the ranch, an off-center composition with too much sand and not enough sky. Then the camera shifted, focused, zoomed, and in the center of the picture, floating in the air, was a tall pale figure that caused goose bumps to ripple over his body, caused his pulse to race with fear.

The cup hu girngsi.

They gasped as they saw it in its true form for the first time. All of them. Even Sue's grandmother drew in her breath sharply. The reality was far worse than Robert had feared. His imaginings had been horrible, but this monstrous figure was beyond anything his mind had been able to conjure. It was neither a dwarf nor a giant but was the size of a tall man. Humanoid, it was extraordinarily thin, almost skeletal, and naked, though it had no genitals. Ribs and bone junctures showed beneath the alabaster skin. It had a baby face—pudgy cheeks, small nose, characterless mouth—but it was an old baby face. There were wrinkles where there should not have been, and the eyes were ancient beyond reason, ancient and corrupt, filled with a sly, knowing evil that belied the innocence of the face's physical characteristics. Although the head was hairless, tufts of unnaturally white and unbelievably long hair grew in unexpected parts of the body, dripping down from the upper forearms, from under the chest, from the knees. The hair blew wildly in the chill desert wind.

The creature smiled. There were no fangs, only an overly large and toothy mouth.

Competing with the images was the soundtrack. Tracy Singleton was narrating, but her voice and observations were entirely superfluous, describing a scene she thought she saw, not the reality actually recorded by the camera. Muffled, far, far in the background, were screams and the sound of shattering glass, the noise of car engines racing and tires peeling out. Overlying this, almost overpowering it, was a liquid whooshing that was somewhere between wind and river, a strange antinoise that made everything seem as if it were happening in a vacuum instead of the real world.

The *cup hu girngsi* stared directly into the camera, an expression of pure malevolent hate on its twisted baby features. Then it sped away, turning from the camera and shrinking to a dot in the distance in less than a second.

The tape ended, the black of night followed by the gray and black dots of videotape static on the screen. The hissing of the speaker, loud and obnoxious though it was, seemed almost soothing after that hellish soundscape.

"So that's what we're up against," Rossiter said. His usual arrogance was gone, replaced by a tone of cowed humility.

Steve crossed himself. "We should get everyone into the churches. The whole town. Hole up there, fight it out. Use 'em like forts."

"Churches won't protect you," Rich said. "The vampire lives in a church."

Robert got up, turned off the VCR, turned off the TV. Sue's grandmother said something in Cantonese.

"Does anyone want to back out?" Sue translated. She looked around the room, at Robert, Rich, Rossiter, Woods, Buford, and the two policemen, her eyes searching each face. "That is what is living inside the church. It's hundreds, maybe thousands of years old. It's killed more people than any of us can imagine. It will not be lying in a coffin. It will not be sleeping. If the church is lighttight, and I think it is, chances are the *cup hu girngsi* will be awake and waiting for us. We may all be killed. If any of you don't want to go through with this, say it now."

No one said a word.

Sue looked at her grandmother.

"Let's do it," Robert said.

Sixty-seven

The wind began as they pulled out of the station parking lot, a cold, gritty gale that carried in tumbleweeds from the surrounding desert and filled the air with blowing sand, effectively cutting visibility to several yards.

Rich stared out the window of Robert's car at the unending cloud of swirling dust. He didn't like this at all. The darkness of night could at least be penetrated by light, but there was no way to nullify the effects of a dust storm.

He wondered if the *cup hu girngsi* had somehow started the freakish wind.

"We'll find them," Robert said gently. "They'll be okay."

"What?"

"Anna and Corrie."

Rich nodded. "Yeah." He gave his brother a reassuring smile. He was fooling himself. He knew that. Despite what Sue's grandmother said, or what Sue *said* her grandmother said, he did not think Corrie and Anna were safe and in hiding. He knew, in his bones, that the *cup hu girngsi* had found them in the church. And the monster did not take prisoners. It killed. Period.

But though he knew this inside, Rich still kept pretending to others he believed his family was safe, half pretending to himself. It was easier this way. He didn't have time to deal with emotions right now. He could not allow himself to experience grief and pain and loss. That would come later. Right now he had a monster to destroy.

He looked out the window, at the vague silhouettes of the few buildings that could be seen through the blowing sand.

The dust storm, he thought, sounded almost like a waterfall.

They were lined up in the street outside the church, waiting. Weapons in hand.

Wheeler's congregation.

Robert rounded the corner and slammed on his brakes, the other patrol car nearly plowing into his rear end.

The street was blocked. Scores of people—maybe a hundred, maybe more—stood in the center of the road. They were visible as little more than an army of shadows behind a curtain of sand, but it was obvious even through the swirling dust that they were clutching shovels and axes and pitchforks—implements that could double as weapons.

The radio crackled, and Rossiter's dry voice came over the tiny speaker. "Welcoming committee."

Several men in the front of the line were cradling rifles or shotguns in their arms, and before Robert even knew what had happened, the front and back windshields of the cruiser exploded in a shatter of sand and safety glass, and a bullet buzzed past his head like a bee.

Immediately, instinctively, he threw the car into reverse and swung back around the corner, nearly colliding with the other patrol car as he swerved out of the line of fire. "Get down!" he ordered. He braked to an abrupt halt just in front of the fire truck. He quickly picked up the mike, pressed down the speak button. "Stay inside," he said. "Don't get out."

He grabbed his rifle from its overhead rack and used the butt to clear out the remaining glass in the windshield.

The wind was dying down slightly, visibility improving, and he could see that the street was clear. The crowd had not followed him around the corner. The people were staying in front of the church. He looked over at Rich, next to him, at Sue and her grandmother, ducking down in the backseat. "Are you all right? Is anyone hurt?"

"We're fine," Sue said.

"Just a little shaken," Rich agreed.

"This is going to be a little tougher than we anticipated," Robert said.

"We have to get into the church," Sue told him. "We have to get in and out of there before dark."

"And we have to set up the hoses," Rich said.

Robert picked up the mike again, spoke into it. "Agent Rossiter? Do you have any idea how we can disperse that crowd?"

Rossiter's voice crackled over the speaker. "You have riot gear, don't you? Gas 'em."

"Shit."

"Would tear gas work?" Rich asked. "It doesn't cause any permanent damage, does it?"

"In this wind? It wouldn't even get half of them. Besides, we only have two canisters, and they're both back at the station."

"Then what are we—"

"Let me handle it." Robert opened the door, held tightly on to his rifle as he stepped out of the patrol car. Behind him, he heard the sound of the fire engine's front door slamming, and out of the corner of his eye he saw Rossiter and Buford step onto the sidewalk, the FBI agent holding a service revolver, Buford clutching his shotgun.

Steve and Ben came out of the other patrol car, guns drawn.

"Hand me that bullhorn," Robert said, and Rich gave it to his brother.

"Testing!" Robert said. His voice was loud enough to

be heard from at least a block away, even with the wind. He looked toward Rossiter, Buford, Steve, and Ben. "Let's go," he said. "But be careful." He looked back toward Rich. "Make sure everyone else stays in the cars. If you hear any shots, get down."

Rich nodded.

The wind had subsided, but sand was still swirling in the air, and Robert wished he had worn sunglasses or goggles. He blinked, trying to protect his eyes against the flying grains that hit his face as he walked forward.

He peeked around the empty office building at the corner.

They were still there, in the middle of the street.

Wheeler was standing in front of them.

He stared through the dust at the preacher, standing with his congregation, and found himself wondering what he would do if Wheeler asked to see a search warrant.

Could this all be a big mistake?

Could May Ling just be a superstitious old woman?

He looked at the huge group of armed people standing in the center of the road in front of the black church. No. There was no mistake. As much as he might like to talk himself out of it, this was real.

He placed the bullhorn to his lips, pressed down on the amplification button. "This is the police!" he said. His voice carried clearly over the dying wind, sounded like the voice of a movie cop, not his own. "Put down your weapons!"

"We don't want you!" someone yelled. "We want the chinks!"

"Put down your weapons!" Robert repeated.

"We'll take you out, too, if we have to!"

The twenty or so men and women standing in a single line in front of the rest of the crowd wore uniforms of underwear, Robert saw, dyed black. He recognized a few of them—Sophocles Johnson holding an ax; Merle Law with what looked like a gas-powered chain saw—but most of the faces were unfamiliar to him.

From behind the people on the street, from the roof of the church, absurdly, came the sounds of hammering, muffled by the wind, as volunteers continued with their construction work, oblivious to the goings-on below.

Robert moved to the center of the intersection. He stood, legs spread, holding the rifle. He'd expected his stance to be at least somewhat threatening, but even the young women in the massive crowd before him did not seem to be cowed.

"Begone!" Wheeler screamed. "Before somebody drops a house on you!"

Robert cleared his throat. He needn't have worried about the preacher asking rational questions about search warrants. He placed the bullhorn to his mouth. "Please disperse!"

"You will never set foot on this sacred land! As Jesus said, 'You are of your father, the devil, and your will is to do your father's desires.' You shall not set foot in the house of the Lord!" Wheeler glared at Robert, then turned, walked back through the crowd toward the church.

"What the fuck was that?" Buford asked.

Robert shrugged. He again cleared his throat, addressed the congregation through the bullhorn. "By the order of the Rio Verde Police Department, you are hereby ordered to disperse! Put down your weapons and move out of the street!"

No one in the crowd moved.

"If you do not vacate the premises, you will be placed under arrest!"

A shot was fired over his head.

"What do we do?" Steve called out nervously.

Buford backed up. "Do we shoot? We can't shoot 'em, can we?"

"Fire on them if they attack," Rossiter said. "Get the ones with the rifles."

Robert turned around, looked back at the cars. Rich, Sue, and Sue's grandmother had gotten out of the patrol car. The grandmother was walking toward the corner. "What are you doing?" he demanded. "Rich, grab her!"

"Leave her alone!" Sue said.

The grandmother reached the corner, walked out from behind the office building into the intersection.

The crowd went crazy. They stormed forward as one, screaming wildly, weapons raised.

"Get ready to fire!" Rossiter said.

And Sue's grandmother started chanting.

He could not hear the words above the noise of the onrushing attackers and his own panicked instructions to his men, but he could see her lips moving, her mouth opening and closing, her almond eyes trained fearlessly on the angry congregation before her. She stood alone, unafraid, a frail, wrinkled old lady who looked like a turtle. He wanted to scream at her, but there was such authority in her stance, such a confident sureness in her gaze, that he allowed himself to hope, to believe, that she knew what she was doing.

She did.

A shot was fired. And another. But that was all. Neither bullet hit its mark, and before he, Rossiter, Buford, Steve, or Ben could fire even a single return shot, it was over. The people in the forefront of the crowd were slowing, stopping. The generic look of single-minded mania that had been imprinted on their faces was leaving, confusion emerging in its stead. Weapons were being lowered. One woman stopped running, stopped walking, sat down on the curb, and began to cry.

"Kill the chinks!" someone in the back of the crowd yelled, but his order went unheeded. More people began to slow, stop, as Sue's grandmother continued chanting.

Sue stepped beside Robert, and he turned to face her. "What's she saying?" he asked.

She shook her head. "I don't know. All I know is that it's something that counteracts the influence of the *cup hu girngsi.*"

"You don't know? What do you mean you don't know?"

"It's not in Cantonese. I can't understand what she's saying."

From the rear of the congregation, a man with a machete strode forward. He was old, sixty or seventy, and looked like a retired bureaucrat or businessman of some sort, but the bland features of his face had been distorted by hate and fury into something else. The old woman's chanting seemed to be having no effect on him. He moved past the first row of now silently milling people, then rushed forward, machete held high. "His will be done!" he shouted.

Rossiter cut him down in midstride. Robert was still deciding whether to hit the man with the butt of his rifle or shoot him in the legs, when the FBI agent's bullet tore through the man's heart. The man fell, dropping the machete. A gushing pool of blood began spreading immediately out from under the body, grains of tan sand blowing onto the top of the sticky red liquid.

"Let's go in," Rossiter said.

The rest of the congregation was in disarray. There were a few others who had not succumbed to the chanting, who were still defiantly holding on to their weapons, but none with the concentrated fury of the fallen man.

"Call an ambulance," Robert ordered Ben. His gaze moved on to Woods, now finally getting out of the other car. "Brad!" he called. "Get over here! We have a man down!"

"He's dead," Rossiter said.

The coroner ran up, knelt next to the body, placed his fingers to the man's wrist and neck, nodded. "He's gone."

"Get the fire truck," Robert said. "I don't know how much time we've got here, how long this is going to last, but we've got to get in there while we can." He turned back toward Ben, who was calling the ambulance from his patrol car. "Bring the weapons!" he yelled. Ben nodded, started the car.

Buford ran back to the fire engine, while the rest of them walked slowly along the sidewalk toward the church. Robert, Rossiter, and Steve kept their guns drawn and ready, but no one made a move toward them, no one even seemed to notice that they were there.

A Jeep pulled behind the fire truck and patrol car as they turned the corner, and Robert saw Chief Simmons and Rand Black inside. The Jeep and truck pulled directly in front of the black church. All three men got out. Buford walked over to his fellow firemen, and they spoke for a moment, then started unrolling hose from the back of the fire engine.

Sue's grandmother had finally stopped chanting, and despite the sounds of crying, the air seemed strangely dead with the cessation of that quiet voice; Robert turned toward Sue. "Can she stop like that? Are they going to revert? Or is that it? Did she cure them?"

Sue translated, listened, translated back. "They will not attack us."

"Steve," Robert ordered, "pick up those weapons. All of them. Lock them in the trunk."

"What should we do with them?" He nodded toward the people milling about. "We can't arrest them all. We don't have enough room in the jail."

"Call Cash. Let the state police handle it. It'll make them feel useful." They reached the steps of the church. He told Rich and Woods, Sue and her grandmother to remain with Ben at the foot of the steps, then walked down the sidewalk to where Buford was screwing the hose onto the side of the fire hydrant. Farther down the block,

Simmons and Rand were hooking another hose up to the hydrant in front of the old Big A building. "How long's it going to take to set these up?" Robert asked.

"Five minutes," Buford said. "If Compton comes through on the water. The chief said he already talked to him. We should be able to swing it."

The ambulance came, sirens blaring, while Buford, Rossiter, Simmons, and Rand were positioning the mouths of the hoses at either side of the church, facing east. Rich stood next to Sue and her grandmother, holding on to the willow spears. Woods made sure that the *baht gwa* leaning against the side of the patrol car did not fall.

Robert authorized removal of the body, helped the ambulance men fill out a preliminary report, and by the time he finally turned back around, the hoses were secured and in place.

"We're ready," Buford said.

Robert nodded. "All right, then. Do it."

Buford got into the truck, started the pump. Simmons and Rand, each manning a hose, opened the nozzles. Twin jets of pressurized water, with enough power for visible back-kicks that nearly knocked the firemen off their feet, exploded forth from the oversize hoses on each side of the church. Sand and dirt were blown instantly out of the ground as the concentrated water carved its own niche in the earth, uprooting weeds and small cacti that were immediately carried away in the newly formed streams.

Robert was impressed. He looked for Sue's grandmother, saw an expression of approval on her lined face, and felt good. He walked over to the fire truck, looked up at Buford. "How long can these be kept up?"

"Don't know," he admitted.

"We'd better get in now, then. We've wasted enough time."

Buford jumped down from the cab, and the two of

them hurried with Rossiter to where the rest of the seven stood waiting. "Ready?" Robert said.

They nodded.

Robert called Steve and Ben over. "You stay out here," he ordered the two policemen. "We're going in. I don't know what's going to happen, but if things get hairy, call for backup. And make sure those state police get their lazy asses over here. We'll do what we have to and be out as soon as we can."

"Be careful," Steve said.

"That's the plan."

Rich passed out flashlights and the spears, and he and Wood carried the *baht gwa* between them across the sidewalk. The seven of them walked through the remnants of Wheeler's army, up the church steps, until they reached the door. Robert had expected the door to be locked, bolted from the inside, maybe with a huge bar of steel like those old cathedrals in the movies. But the black door opened easily when he turned the knob and pushed. The interior of the church was dark and smelled of paint and sawdust . . . and blood.

Sue's grandmother said something.

"Is everyone wearing jade?" Sue asked.

They all nodded.

She and her grandmother pushed past Robert, walked into the church. "Let's find the *cup hu girngsi.*"

What had happened to her *Di Lo Ling Gum?*

Sue walked into the black church, clutching her flashlight and spear. *Di Lo Ling Gum* was supposed to help her, to guide her, but the power lay silent, dormant within her. She received no images or intuitive flashes as she stepped across the church threshold.

She had thought *Di Lo Ling Gum* would be something she could control, something that obeyed her will, but instead it seemed to exist independently of her and to work only when it wanted to.

She found herself wondering what would happen if her grandmother was killed, either by the *cup hu girngsi* or by Pastor Wheeler, who was still around somewhere. She would be expected to take over, lead them, tell them what to do. Yet she had nothing but the vaguest idea of what was supposed to occur.

Why had her grandmother not told her more?

There was a hard knot of fear in the pit of her stomach that made her want to vomit and void her bladder at the same time. She thought she was doing a good job of maintaining a calm outward appearance, but the truth was that she had to convince herself to take each tiny step forward, that she was so terrified she could barely think straight.

She glanced over at her grandmother, who smiled reassuringly at her.

They walked out of the entryway into the chapel.

The fear she'd experienced only seconds before was nothing compared to the powerful new emotion Sue felt now, this gradation of terror that had no name. Every fiber of her being was telling her to get out of here, to turn tail and run, and it took every ounce of courage she had to override that instinct.

The inside of the church looked like a taxidermist's paradise. The walls were festooned with the bodies of bobcats and javelinas, sucked dry and suspended from hooks. Dead hawks hung on wires from the high vaulted ceiling. There was no floor, only hard dirt, and there were three huge openings in the earth, each the size of a small room. Next to each opening were piles of debris.

No, not debris.

Plants and animals.

Sacrifices to the *cup hu girngsi*.

"Jesus," Rich whispered behind her.

She turned her attention toward the front of the

church. At the foot of the altar, a crowd of dead animals was arranged around Jesus' feet. The figure of Jesus itself, impaled on a grossly oversize cross—

She sucked in her breath, took a step forward, shining her flashlight.

Jesus was the dead and mounted body of Jim Hollis.

She stared at the figure. The ranch owner's dried and shriveled form was nailed to the cross with what looked like old railroad spikes, and the spikes had shattered and flattened the withered hands and feet through which they'd been pounded. Hollis's eyes were missing—black holes rimmed with wrinkled skin marking where they had been—and all of the teeth had been knocked out of his mouth.

The martyred figure seemed blasphemous to Sue, and as she turned to look at her companions, she saw the expressions of fear, shock, and revulsion on their faces.

"It is a warning," her grandmother said. "The *cup hu girngsi* is trying to scare us away."

"It's succeeding," Sue said in Cantonese. She translated her grandmother's words into English.

"Where's the vampire?" Rossiter asked, and the sound of his flat, totally unemotional voice made everything seem a little less frightening. It was calming. Sue was suddenly glad the FBI agent was with them.

She translated her grandmother's words as the old woman spoke them: "It is underneath us. The *cup hu girngsi* must spend most of its daylight hours in the earth."

"So we have to go down there?" Robert pointed toward the openings. Sue nodded.

"He can't go over flowing water," Woods said. "Can he go under it?"

Sue had not thought of that. She looked again toward her grandmother, translated the question. Her grandmother frowned, and Sue realized that she had not thought of this possibility either. "We will find out," she said.

Sue repeated the words in English.

The answer did not seem to boost anyone's confidence.

"How do we get down there?" Rich asked.

Robert pointed at two nubs of metal peeking over the rim of the middle hole. "Ladder. If I'm not mistaken, that's where our friend, the illustrious Pastor Wheeler, split to."

"I'll go first," Rossiter volunteered.

Robert nodded. "I'll go last."

It took nearly ten minutes for all of them to climb down. Sue did not like heights, and more than once she thought she would slip, her hands were so sweaty. Finally, she made it safely to the bottom. Her grandmother had a little more difficulty. The old woman's legs were unsteady, her grip weak, and even with Rich climbing directly below her, helping her down, she still needed extra assistance. Woods came after her, periodically reaching down to help hold her hands between one rung and another. When she reached the tunnel floor, she was sweating and out of breath, her overly rapid pulse visible in the throbs of her neck.

Once again, Sue realized how old her grandmother was. And how frail.

What if she had a heart attack before they even found the *cup hu girngsi*? Sue pushed the thought from her mind.

The air down here was dank and fetid. It smelled almost like a sewer or a dump. Almost. But there was another odor here, the stench of death, a dusty, decaying scent that just missed being cloyingly sweet.

Rich climbed halfway back up the ladder, took the *baht gwa* from his brother, handed it down to Woods.

"All here," Robert announced a few moments later as

he hopped off the ladder. He was feigning a confidence he lid not feel, but Sue admired his bravery.

She looked down the length of the tunnel, shining her flashlight. They were all shining their lights, the beams following the eyes and interests of their owners, and it produced a low-level strobe effect that made the high and strangely rounded passage seem that much deeper and darker.

"One of us will die," her grandmother said softly. There was surprise in her voice.

And fear.

She had not expected this.

Sue felt cold. She shone her light on the old woman's face, then quickly moved it away when her grandmother shut her eyes against the beam.

"What did she say?" Robert asked.

"We'd better start walking," Sue said.

She let them think it was a translation.

Rich looked over at Woods, placed his spear in his flashlight hand, and picked up his half of the *baht gwa*. He shone his flashlight into the tunnel ahead. He had expected the other two openings in the floor of the church to empty here as well, but the hole through which they'd come was at the beginning of this passage, which meant that the other openings led to different tunnels altogether. Tunnels heading in other directions.

He hoped they were going the right way.

He didn't want to be caught in this labyrinth when night fell.

"What direction are we heading?" he asked suddenly.

Robert looked at him. "East. Why?"

"The streams."

Robert looked up. "I didn't even think about that." He looked back up through the hole to the church, then glanced down the length of the tunnel, gauging its direction. "Luck of the Irish," he said. "I think we're safe. I think we're between the streams. Assuming that idea works at all."

"If the *cup hu girngsi's* close enough. If the streams don't peter out."

"You know," Buford said, "I bet this empties out by the arroyo."

Robert nodded. "I bet you're right."

They began walking. Multiple flashlight beams scanned the curved sides of the tunnel. Rich looked over at his brother. He could tell from Robert's expression that he felt foolish with the willow spear in his hand, the jade choker around his neck. He would probably have felt more comfortable with his fingers around the butt of a .45, but he obviously knew that his usual modes of thought did not apply down here. In a true show of faith, Robert had even left his rifle outside with Steve. He knew that they were not dealing with a criminal, or even with the type of movie monster that could be taken out by firepower. They were up against something so old and alien that even their knowledge of the supernatural could have no bearing on their actions.

They were entirely in the hands of Sue's grandmother.

Rich, too, would have probably felt more secure if Robert and the FBI agent were packing heat, but he knew that was just conditioning. They were as safe now as they could possibly be under the circumstances.

No matter what happened, he thought, no matter how things turned out, he was proud to be here. Proud to be there with these six people.

Even Rossiter.

They continued walking.

And then he heard it.

The Laughing Man.

His mouth suddenly felt as though it was filled with

cotton, his saliva dried up at the source. The sound was coming from far away, from somewhere deep in the tunnel, but even faint and muffled, he recognized the sound of the Laughing Man. His brain told him that this was merely his own demon projected back at him, that the *cup hu girngsi* looked like that baby-faced monster from the videotape, that no one else probably even heard the sound, but his instinct was stronger than his intellect, and was suddenly deeply and uncontrollably afraid. He knew he could not face the Laughing Man again. He was not brave enough to see it once more.

"Do you hear that?" Sue asked, her voice hushed and fearful. "That laughing?"

Oh, God, Rich thought. She heard it too. He glanced over at Robert. His brother was already looking at him, face pale.

Sue's grandmother said something in Cantonese.

"Noises cannot hurt us," Sue translated. "Ignore them. There will be more."

They shone their lights ahead, toward the source of the sound. The walls of the tunnel before them were no longer smooth, no longer rounded, but looked rough and bulgingly irregular.

Rich was the first to realize why. "Jesus," he breathed.

The tunnel before them was lined with the nude dehydrated bodies of men and women, many more than they would have imagined. As they drew closer, Rich saw that all of them were arranged in grotesque biblical tableaux, cruel, blasphemous parodies of sacred scenes. *Daniel in the lion's den:* Daniel, a castrated child; the lions, dead kittens. *The feeding of the multitudes:* the multitudes, a score of old men, dead rats in their outstretched hands; Jesus, a naked mummified young woman with her breasts removed.

"Holy fuck."

Rich looked up at the sound of his brother's voice.

Robert was a little ways ahead and standing next to Woods, looking at a tableaux on the other side of the passage.

Rich put down his side of the *baht gwa*.

It was Pam Frye, naked and standing between Arn Hewett and another older man. She was made up like a prostitute and obviously supposed to be Mary Magdalene, the rouge and lipstick and overdone eyeshadow appearing frighteningly out of place on the shrunken skeletal child's face. Behind Pam and the others, Mayor Tillis stood as Jesus, holding his hands out in mocking benediction.

Rich swallowed, tasting bile. Rio Verde's dead and missing were here, were all down here, and the extent of the *cup hu girngsi*'s butchery was staggering. The few bodies that had been found in town, the few missing people of whom they were aware, were merely the tip of the iceberg.

The *cup hu girngsi* liked to save its victims.

And play with their bodies.

But why had it left some out where they could be found? Why hadn't it taken Manuel Torres or Terry Clifford down here? Why hadn't it hidden the two teenagers killed in the river?

Because it had wanted them to find the bodies. Because it had been toying with them.

He suddenly realized the enormity of what they were up against.

"How long has it been here?" Robert said softly. "How long has it been in our town?" He pointed toward a shriveled husk of a body lying on the ground at Pam's feet. "That's Lew Rogers. He and his girlfriend skipped town about two years ago. We thought. I figured it was because of all they owed."

On the other side of the passage, Sue gasped, her sharp and sudden intake of breath echoing and unusually loud.

Rich hurried over to where she stood, followed her gaze. It was a nativity scene, only baby Jesus was a tiny, dehydrated, barely formed fetus, connected by a tiny umbilical cord to a mummified Mary whose empty breasts were little more than flattened flaps of dried wrinkled skin.

"That's my friend," Sue whispered. "That's Janine."

Her grandmother spoke in a clear strong voice, and Sue's attention shifted from the manger scene to the old woman.

"What did she say?" Rich asked.

"She says it knows we are coming. It put these here to warn us, to frighten us."

He nodded. "It's trying to scare us away."

Sue shook her head. "No. It wants us to come."

They were all gathered around her now, the other six. They had looked where they'd wanted, had not liked what they'd seen, and had come together around Sue and her grandmother for protection and reassurance. Robert was pensive, Woods and Buford silent and subdued, and even Rossiter's aggressive assurance seemed to have fled. They were a more thoughtful group than they had been up above, more fully aware of what they were facing, but Rich was not sure that was a good thing. They needed some cockiness now, they needed some aggressiveness. They needed the bravery of the foolhardy.

There was none of that now. He felt as though they'd all given up before they'd started, and that frightened him. He thought of Corrie, thought of Anna, tried to tell himself they were up ahead, hostages to the *cup hu girngsi.* He looked at Sue. "Corrie and Anna are not in hiding, are they? They didn't sense danger coming and find some place to hide, did they?"

Sue looked over at her grandmother but did not translate. "I don't think so," she said.

Rich nodded. "I think they're up ahead. I'm going to find them." He held up his spear and flashlight, lifted his half of the *baht gwa.* "Dead or alive, I'm going to find them."

He started forward.

They followed him. As he'd thought, as he'd hoped, his determination seemed to have energized his companions, provided them with renewed purpose, and they strode with him down the center of the earthen tunnel, flashlights trained in unison on the darkness directly before them, no beams sidetracked by the strange staged scenes off to the sides.

The tunnel curved slightly to the left—*underneath the stream?*—and then narrowed. The rounded ceiling grew flatter, rougher.

They stopped walking. Before them was a doorway, a high thin slice in the hardpacked earth that led into even deeper darkness.

And would allow only one of them through at a time.

"I'm going through," Rich announced, putting down the *baht gwa*. His heart was trip-hammering in his chest with attack force, and there was nothing in his life he had ever felt less like doing, but he knew that this was why he was here, this was why he had come. The time for selfishly succumbing to fear had passed.

Robert grabbed his arm, held him back. "You're not going in first. I am."

Rich managed a smile. "You want to hog all the glory for yourself?"

"It's probably a trap. I'm better prepared to deal with something like that than you."

Sue's grandmother slid through the opening.

"Hey!" Robert yelled.

There was no time to argue now. Robert quickly followed the old woman; Rich followed Robert. They walked through, one after the other, in an order that was entirely circumstantial: Sue, Buford, Woods, Rossiter. Buford and the coroner carried the mirror between them as they moved single file through the opening.

The high narrow doorway led into a chamber, a rock room.

The lair of the *cup hu girngsi*.

Rich bumped into his brother and the grandmother as he stepped through. He felt the hard tenseness of his brother's muscles, felt the trembling fear of the old woman as he grabbed her arm to keep her from falling. The undirected beam of his flashlight shone upon the nearest wall, and as he righted himself and stepped out of the way to let Sue through behind him, he saw not dirt, as he would have expected, not rock, but colors, shapes.

Paintings.

His flashlight beam played over the wall, joined by Robert's, then Sue's, then Buford's.

"Mother of shit," Buford breathed.

The walls of the chamber were decorated with an unearthly mural, a pictographic rendering of horrors and atrocities so overwhelmingly evil that he was grateful the flashlights revealed only a small portion of it. He moved closer, tentatively touched the wall. His beam revealed the visages of beings that had either never existed or had lived so long ago that their existence remained unrecorded. There were bodies flayed, souls in torment, every perversity imaginable and many unimaginable depicted in the unholy picture.

He had assumed that the vampire was a creature operating on instinct, not intelligence—a being that existed only to feed. But the mural proved that they were dealing with something much more complex, a creature that was not acting simply on impulses, but a being that was actively and sophisticatedly evil. Whether the mural was a recorded history, depicting scenes that had actually occurred, or whether it was merely an example of artistic expression, it was the product of a profoundly corrupt mind, and Rich grew cold as he tried to imagine the *cup hu girngsi* sitting alone in this underground darkness, painting these painstakingly detailed horrors.

Only his mind did not see that overly tall baby-faced thing from the videotape.

He saw in his mind the Laughing Man.

The idea of the Laughing Man chuckling to himself, alone in the darkness, frightened Rich more than anything else could have.

There was the sound of wind or water, an indeterminate whooshing rush, and all flashlights turned toward the noise. Against the far wall, the beams revealed a throne, an oversize throne made of bones and skulls and animal heads.

Upon the throne sat the Pastor Mr. Wheeler.

Rich looked at the pastor, saw the wildness in his eyes, the bloody Bible on his lap, and for a brief second he thought they'd all been wrong, they'd all been fooled, there was no *cup hu girngsi*, there was only this human fanatic and his cult of human followers who'd been terrorizing the town.

And Corrie and Anna were safe.

Then he heard the laughing, saw the shadow loom next to the throne, felt the temperature drop.

The *cup hu girngsi*.

He backed up, bumped into Sue, and only that contact kept him from running out through that narrow doorway the way he'd come in. He could feel the scream building in his throat. The shadowy figure moved into one of the flashlight beams, and it *was* the Laughing Man. He saw that grinning, characterless face, heard that horrible throaty chuckle.

Then the figure turned toward them, and he saw the faint traces of other faces as well. The structure of the head seemed to shift as the creature moved. Did the monster now have Elvis's lips? Dracula's widow's peak? Oriental eyes? Skin fashioned from sand? Was that Jesus Christ hiding underneath there? He had been right, he realized, but he took no comfort from that fact. The *cup hu girngsi* did indeed draw from mythologies for its appearance, for its form, tapping those deep and primal images that spoke so personally and so eloquently to the holder of the mythology.

"What do we do?" Robert asked Sue.

"Die," the *cup hu girngsi* answered in a whisperlike thunder.

And laughed.

Sue wet her pants.

She did not notice it until she moved closer to her grandmother and felt the warmth spreading outward from her crotch. Under any other circumstances she would have been mortified, would not have been able to think of anything else but the failure of her bladder, but she was so terrified now that the knowledge was simply registered by her brain and then instantly forgotten.

There were other things to think about.

And, under the circumstances, she was not ashamed.

The *cup hu girngsi* looked exactly the same to her as it had on the videotape, and she knew that, unlike the others, her vision was not being filtered through her perceptions. Her grandmother grabbed her hand. She expected some sort of electricity to pass between them, expected to experience a sharing of some kind of power or insight, but there was only the physical contact of that familiar old hand, those bony fingers clutching tightly to her own.

Sue's other hand hurt from clutching the spear.

"What do we do?" she asked her grandmother.

"The *baht gwa.*"

Their whispers were loud in the cavelike chamber, and she wondered if the *cup hu girngsi* understood what they were saying. It had spoken in English. Did it understand

Cantonese? Or did it even need to hear them at all? Could it read their minds?

"The *baht gwa*," Sue repeated. "We need the mirror."

"Right here," Rossiter said. The FBI agent pushed the reflective glass toward her across the hard-packed floor.

The *cup hu girngsi* was gone now. Sue could no longer see it. The tall chamber was nearly smothered in darkness, their own pitiful lights little more than narrow yellow lines in the blackness. It could be anywhere, she knew. It could be way on the other side of the chamber, it could be standing right next to them.

Did there need to be light for it to see itself in the *baht gwa*?

There were so many things she should have asked her grandmother before they started.

She reached for the *baht gwa*, fingers curving over the top of the cold mirror. She pulled it next to her, faced it outward, hid behind it as though it was a shield.

Someone's flashlight was trained on the throne, on Wheeler. The preacher was bending forward, licking the blood off his Bible.

"Is he a *cup hu girngsi*?" Sue asked her grandmother.

"No," the old woman said. "He wants to be, but he is not. He has just been too close. He has been influenced."

Influenced.

"But isn't it trying to turn him into one?"

"The *cup hu girngsi* is vain. It wants people to know of its deeds. That's why it has kept him alive, to spread the word of its actions.

"And that is its downfall." She reached for the mirror and tried to lift it, but the glass was too large and too heavy. Sue saw what she was trying to do, and she lifted one end of the mirror. Rich helped her, and among the three of them, they managed to raise the *baht gwa* to face level.

"Move it slowly," her grandmother said, and Sue translated. She swiveled her body to the left, and Rich did the same, the face of the mirror panning across the darkened room.

There was a flash of light at the far end of the chamber, almost an explosion, and a scream of agony that was loud enough to cause Sue's ears to ring.

"Don't stop!" her grandmother yelled. "You got it! It saw itself!"

"What's happening?" Buford asked. His voice was high, too high, close to panic.

Sue did not answer but kept turning slowly, moving the *baht gwa.*

Another explosion. In the bright light of this one, a brief powder-keg flash against a side wall, she saw swirling red and a naggingly familiar shape, not the *cup hu girngsi* but something else, something she'd seen before and almost recognized.

The creature's voice came out of the shadows. "Dan." It was horrifying but not ugly, a strong, powerful, and undeniably charismatic voice. Sue stared into the darkness. Underneath the fear, underneath the anger and the terror, she felt a weak stirring in her blood, a faint desire to cast off her jade necklace and join Wheeler on the throne of the *cup hu girngsi.* Despite everything, something in the creature's voice spoke to her. She wondered if the others felt it too.

She hoped they didn't.

The creature spoke again in its dulcet tones and strange cadences: "Kill them. Kill the chinks and their fucking friends."

The attraction was gone now, if it had ever been there at all, and only the terror remained. She and Rich continued to turn slowly with the *baht gwa.*

On the throne, Wheeler placed the bloody Bible on the armrest and slid off the raised seat. He looked almost comical as he got off the grotesquely oversize chair, but that impression was as fleeting as it was incorrect. The preacher stood, and there was not merely fanaticism in his face, but a dangerous determination. "Jesus said to kill the fucking chinks. They are evil. They are disciples of the Adversary, and you must smite them in the name of the Lord."

"How come He can't smite us himself?" Robert stepped forward, spear thrust out in front of him, flashlight beam roaming the chamber. He faced Wheeler, shone his light into the preacher's eyes. Wheeler blinked, flinched, drew back. "How come He's so afraid of us? How come He can't touch us himself? Doesn't He like the jade? Huh? Is He afraid of our little sticks? I never heard that Jesus was afraid of jade. I never knew He had a fear of willow branches. I never read that in the Bible."

Wheeler looked from Robert into the darkness to his left. There was confusion on his face, and for a brief moment the mask of fanaticism slipped.

Sue and Rich continued to pan the chamber with the mirror. Stop, she thought. Don't say anything else. Don't ruin it.

"Your followers ran away," Robert continued. "They didn't defend your church at all." He stared at the preacher.

"No!" Wheeler yelled.

"Yes!"

"They must be here for Jesus' rebirth!"

"They decided to skip it."

Someone else's beam, maybe Woods's, maybe Rossiter's, lit upon two dark crumpled forms half hidden behind the irregular bone legs of the throne. Sue knew instinctively what the flashlights had discovered even before her mind recognized the figures.

Corrie.

And Anna.

No, she thought, willing the beams to move on. That's what it wants. That's why it brought them here.

But the lights remained in place, trained on the hunched and blackened forms. Another beam, Buford's, joined the other two. It was obvious now that the figures were dead and nude and female. The woman's face was shoved obscenely into the girl's crotch.

"Your wife. Your daughter." The whisper came from nowhere, came from everywhere. Rich stopped swiveling the mirror.

"No!" Sue said. "Don't listen to it!"

"Pastor Wheeler sucked out their blood and drank it. He fucked them first. He really liked the girl."

Rich screamed. It was supposed to be a word, supposed to be "No," but was far more powerful, a loud primal negation, a full-throated denial that came straight from the depths of his soul. The *baht gwa* slipped from his grasp, and the *cup hu girngsi* loomed out of the blackness, stepping into the flashlight beams as the mirror shattered on the ground. As hard as he could, Rich threw his spear at the monster, but it flew sideways and clattered impotently on the floor.

Wheeler was already upon him. He leaped at Rich's head, and the two of them fell hard on the floor at Sue's feet while Robert, Woods, Rossiter, and Buford rushed forward to help. The two of them rolled in the broken mirror glass. Wheeler was attempting to pull the jade ring from Rich's finger, yanking back the finger itself, breaking it.

One of us will die.

Don't let it be Rich, Sue thought, but she was not sure it was a thought. She was not sure of anything. It was all too confusing, was happening too fast. As if in a drug scene from a sixties movie, everything seemed to be crazily off center, seen through the strobe of the flashlights and the weird angles of the shattered *baht gwa*. She was dimly aware that her grandmother was speaking to her, yelling at her, but amidst the other screaming she could not hear what her grandmother was saying.

The *cup hu girngsi* stood before them, looking just as it had in the videotape, its horridly ancient baby face twisted with hate and a sickening sort of glee. The whiteness of its skin seemed suddenly phosphorescent, lit from the material of its substance and not from the weak beams of the flashlights.

Rich's scream spiraled upward in intensity, shifting from anger to agony, and was cut off suddenly as Sue's flashlight hand was hit with an unexpected wash of liquid warmth. The preacher had bitten into Rich's neck, into the artery, and was vainly trying to drink the spurting blood.

Rossiter and Buford pulled the screaming Wheeler off Rich's spastically convulsing body, and without a word, without a sound, without a second's hesitation, Robert stabbed the preacher through the chest, ramming in his spear as far as it would go, pushing it in farther with the weight of his body as he leaned on it. Wheeler stopped screaming, his eyes bulged, and blood pumped from the skin around the spear and from his still open lips.

This wasn't right. This was not what was supposed to happen.

Sue faced the *cup hu girngsi*, spear thrust outward, dimly aware that her grandmother was doing the same. It was chaos in here, no one knew what they were doing. They were all going to die.

Rossiter was shooting. He had brought a gun, against her grandmother's specific instructions, and he was firing it at the *cup hu girngsi*, the reports echoing painfully in the chamber and blocking out all screams, all other sounds. The first slug ripped a hole through the monster's stomach, and for a brief millisecond there was a glimpse of red, a liquid swirling within the hole, and then the opening was gone, skin covering it up as if it had never existed. The slug immediately after it went through the monster's eye. There was a red hole, and then the eye returned. The other bullets, through the forehead and chest, created equally short-lived wounds that disappeared.

Woods was on one knee, bending over Rich, pressing down on his convulsively jerking body.

Sue pointed her flashlight at the *cup hu girngsi*. Perhaps it had been playing with them. Perhaps, as her grandmother had suggested, it wanted to make its presence known to the world. Perhaps it had merely been bored and wanted a challenge. Whatever the impetus behind its decision to lure them here, it was not playing now. There was demonic purpose in its eyes, determination in its malevolent expression.

And yet—

—it was afraid.

She knew it, knew it instantly, clearly, perfectly. It was not an insight or a revelation, not something that she discovered or that blossomed within her mind, it was simply there, in her brain, as though it was something she had always known.

Di Lo Ling Gum.

She was aware now, also, of the streams on the surface above them. She could feel the power in the twin flows of water even through the layers of dirt and rock above their heads. The streams were weak, beginning to drift at this point, but they were still there and still flowing east.

And they ran in converging paths on either side of the *cup hu girngsi.*

The monster could move neither to the left nor to the right. It could only move toward them or away from them.

It was trapped.

Her grandmother was aware of it, too. Neither of them had spoken, but each was aware of what the other thought and felt, and it was as if they were one mind with two bodies as, willow spears extended, they stepped forward.

Sue sensed that something had been planned, that something big had been about to happen, and that they had stopped it before it started. They had thwarted the *cup hu girngsi,* and it was angry.

But it was even more frightened.

The *cup hu girngsi* hissed. All pretensions of humanity had fled. There was no charismatic dulcet-toned voice, no face or form borrowed from human minds, there was only this spitting, hissing thing, this ancient monster with its hate-twisted baby face and strange skinny body with its long growths of unnatural hair. Inside the terrible mouth, double rows of too many teeth chattered and clicked.

Sue felt pressure in her mind, as though her thoughts were surrounded by a wall, and something huge and powerful was butting against that wall, but it seemed surprisingly easy to keep that pressure at bay. She shoved her spear forward, tried to stab the *cup hu girngsi.*

It backed away, hissed again, a sound like wind, like water.

This close, she could feel the coldness radiating from the monster, waves of increasingly arctic air that felt painful on her skin and made her want to flee, get away.

It was afraid of them.

Her grandmother stepped forward, tried to spear the *cup hu girngsi,* but her weapon swung on a slight arc to the left, and before she had a chance to adjust, to pull back, the creature's long, thin hand swiped toward the old woman's head.

A spear embedded itself in the *cup hu girngsi*'s upper arm, causing it to yank the arm back with a tortured scream.

Another spear flew through the air, hit it in the face.

Rossiter.

Buford.

Sue rushed forward, through the cold, the screaming wind/water sound so loud that it hurt her ears, and with all of her might she shoved her sharpened branch of willow into the monster's stomach.

Blood exploded, flying outward, splashing everything, everyone. The monster's body crumpled, its form instantly losing shape, skin flapping like a deflated balloon as the crimson tide sloshed onto the ground in a truly amazing flood. There were no bones inside the body, no organs, only the blood, an astounding amount of it that continued to flow out of the sinking figure in a seemingly endless stream. It bubbled on the hard floor, boiling, percolating downward through the rock, but on Sue's body it felt cool and flat and dead, and as she glanced quickly around the chamber, she saw that the blood was not hurting or affecting anyone else either.

"He's dead," Woods announced behind her, and for a second she thought he meant the *cup hu girngsi,* but then she realized he was talking about Rich. A twisting hurt ripped through her, and she wished the *cup hu girngsi* was alive so she could kill it again.

Had it ever been alive?

She turned toward her grandmother, threw her arms around the old woman. She felt exhausted all of a sudden, and she needed someone to hold on to. She was dimly aware that the moment's connection the two of them had shared was gone, but she didn't really care. Tears were streaming from her eyes, coursing down her cheeks, but she was not crying. Not yet.

There was movement around her, but she seemed not to know what it was and not to care, the actions of her companions now trivial and irrelevant to her. Her grandmother pulled away from her, touched her cheek, then bent down to pick up her spear.

There was nothing left of the *cup hu girngsi* now but the empty formless hull of its body, and her grandmother began speaking quietly to herself in that unfamiliar dialect as she moved next to it. Pushing up the sleeves of her blouse, the old woman wrapped the leathery skin and its irregular tufts of blood-soaked albino hair around her spear until it resembled a bulging, soggy, rolled-up carpet. She held the wrapped skin in front of her, lifting it as though it weighed nothing, and Sue followed her through the chamber's narrow doorway and down the rounded tunnel the way they'd come.

The others were not following, and Sue did not know what they were doing, but right now that didn't matter.

It was over.

It was done.

She followed her grandmother up the ladder and into the church. The black walls and painted windows seemed glaringly bright after the darkness underground, and the afternoon sunlight streaming through the still-open doors was painful in its intensity.

Unfazed, unhesitating, her grandmother walked through the doorway and, with a grunt and a push, threw the skin and the spear outside, into the sunlight. The skin unfurled a bit and lay on the cement for a moment before it started to hiss and steam. The long tufts of hair blackened, withered; the skin began to bubble. A moment later, there was nothing left but a pool of sticky pinkish liquid on the top of the church steps.

Both she and her grandmother were sweating and soaked with still-wet blood. They looked like monsters themselves, but for the first time in a long while, Sue felt good. It would not last long, she knew. The horrors would catch up with her more quickly than she wanted or probably could handle, but for now she felt fine. She reached out, grabbed her grandmother's frail, wrinkled hand, and the two of them walked outside, into the fresh air, into the desert sunshine.

Sixty-eight

Robert carried his brother's body out of the chamber, out of the tunnel, out of the church. Rich was soaked and sticky with blood, and it was impossible to remove the agonized expression that had cemented itself onto his dying face, but there was no way in hell that he was going to leave his brother alone down here for even one second. He thought of ordering Woods and Rossiter to carry up Connie's and Anna's bodies as well—or what was left of them—but decided that he could not do that. He would come back for them himself.

Both Woods and Buford offered to help him carry Rich, but though the offers were heartfelt, and his brother's body grew heavy almost immediately after picking it up, he had to turn them down. He did need some help on the ladder, and Woods stood below, pushing up, while Robert pulled from above, but once on the surface he again lifted Rich himself and carried him outside, where he finally placed him carefully on the sidewalk.

Rich.

He realized as he looked down at his brother's silently screaming face that he had no family left. Rich had been it. After all the years, after all they'd been through together, after all the times they'd fought, after all the times they'd been there for each other, how could it end like this? Rich's death had not even been heroic. It had been a mistake.

Something he should have been able to prevent.

Schizophrenically, he wanted to call Rich and tell him to grab his camera, get over here, and take some pictures, though he was staring down at Rich's dead body this very moment.

He wanted to cry but knew he could not.

The state police had arrived en masse and had already led away much of Wheeler's congregation. Those who hadn't been arrested yet stood or sat on the ground, staring at nothing, faces blank.

Chief Simmons ran over to meet him, as did Steve, Stu, and Ben. He turned away from them, looking back into the church, not ready to face them yet, not ready to explain what had happened, not ready to make decisions or give orders. There was going to be one major cleanup here. There were a lot of bodies to be brought out from underneath the church. Maybe the state police could call in extra men. Maybe Rossiter could get some FBI agents to help.

The town was still crawling with press and the media, and he knew that there was no way publicity could be voided. What would this news do when it got out, when the whole story was told? What impact would it have? Would it change opinions and perceptions? Would people be looking behind every corner for supernatural beings, jumping at every shadow in fear of vampires? Or would the story of the *cup hu girngsi* be told, ignored, then forgotten? The latter, he suspected. How many tragedies happened each year? Plane crashes, earthquakes, fires? And how many of them did people remember after a day or two? What specifics from past disasters had been retained in the national consciousness?

Very few.

The general public had a short memory.

This, too, would pass. None of *them* would ever forget it, none of the people in Rio Verde, none of the people who had been here today, but to the world at large, this would be just another one of today's sound bites, as ephemeral as yesterday's news.

But this was different, he told himself. This was big. The existence of vampires, of the supernatural, had been proved. Evil had been fought and conquered.

It wasn't different, though. He knew that. Television trivialized, articles distanced. In a week, Rio Verde would be the subject of monologue jokes and tabloid shows.

"Are you okay?" Simmons asked, running up to him.

He nodded, turned toward his men. He didn't have a family anymore, but he still had a town, battered and bruised though it was, and he had never in his life been so glad to see anyone as the men standing before him now. He and the other six—

Rich

—had only been down there for an hour or so, maybe less, but it felt as though they'd been gone forever, and the faces of his officers looked welcome as hell to him right now. "Get—" he started to say, but his voice choked. He looked down at his brother, and in the short space between Rich's Levi's and tennis shoes, he saw that his brother had put on mismatched socks. One brown, one blue.

"Get—" he started to say again.

And he began to cry.

Sixty-nine

In her dream she was suffocating, not able to breathe, though there was nothing obstructing her mouth or nostrils. She was in a green room with green furniture, lying on a green antique fainting couch, and blood covered the floor to the depth of several inches, moving in currents, lapping in waves at the feet of the couch, the tables, the chairs. She was on the couch with Rich, and he was kissing her between the legs, only she kept trying to push him away because she was having her period, and her grandmother was tap dancing in the blood and singing "Singin' in the Rain" in Cantonese.

She awoke feeling tired and sore and emotionally wrung out. Through her window, she could see that the sun had been up for some time, that it was probably close to noon.

Today was Rich's funeral, she realized.

From down the hall, from the living room, she heard her parents arguing, their voices pitched low but still audible. Underneath their voices was the sound of one of her grandmother's Chinese music tapes.

She got out of bed, got dressed.

There were a lot of people at the graveside service, and many of them were people she knew, but Sue stood by herself, preferring to be alone. She looked at the closed casket poised above the open grave and remembered the feel of Rich's hot blood splashing on her hand in the darkness.

She glanced away, looked at the sky.

There were two empty open graves on either side of Rich's, where Corrie and Anna would be buried later this afternoon. She had not known Rich's wife, but she had known his daughter, and she was going to attend the services.

There were going to be a lot of funerals this week.

Including several mass burials.

Were there other *cup hu girngsi* out there? she wondered. Or was that the only one? The FBI agent had claimed—when? Thursday? It seemed like weeks, not days, ago that they had all sat in her living room talking—that he had documented records of thousands of people who'd been killed by a *cup hu girngsi*. Had it been *their* monster? Or were there others, in other states, in other countries?

She didn't want to think about that, could not allow herself to think about that. Not now, not yet, maybe not ever. They had done what they could, and their part was over.

But was it really?

Yes, she told herself.

Her eyes returned to the dark burnished wood of the raised casket. Who would take over the newspaper now? she wondered. Did Robert own it, or were there other relatives to whom it would go? It was a stupid question, but it bothered her. It didn't really matter—she was not going back there, she would not work for the newspaper again—but, still, it nagged at her.

What was she going to do? She wasn't needed at the restaurant. Not really. Her parents could survive without her. She had some money saved up. Maybe she could get a job in Phoenix or Mesa or Scottsdale or Tempe, work during the day, go to a community college at night. Her family could come and visit her on their days off. It was only a couple of hours' drive.

She wanted to get away from Rio Verde.

She needed to get away from Rio Verde.

The casket was lowered into the grave, the sound of the machinery creaky in the afternoon silence, and she found herself thinking of those negatives and proofsheets of Corrie that were still hanging in the newspaper office.

More than anything else, more than the faces of the mourners around her, more than the words of the pastor, it was the thought of those photos that brought home to her the sense of loss. A man. A woman. Passion. Love. A child. All gone. Tears welled in her eyes as she thought of the first night she had met Rich, in the empty classroom at the high school. She realized that she could not remember the editor's voice. She would know it if she heard it, but she could not call it to mind.

The casket was lowered, dirt was thrown, words were said, people started to leave, many of them crying. Sue looked up, saw Robert on the other side of the grave. Through her tears, she smiled at him, he smiled at her, but neither of them made the effort to speak. She knew how he felt, she could feel his pain almost as clearly as her own, but she had nothing to say to him.

Could they have done something sooner? It seemed so obvious to her now: the killings had begun at the same time that Wheeler had started adding on to his church. Was there some way they could have discovered this earlier, before everything had gone so far? Couldn't common sense have told them what was happening? Had they really had to wait for her grandmother's *Di Lo Ling Gum* to kick in?

Maybe, maybe not. She didn't know, and she would never know. But she did know one thing: *laht sic* was not set in stone. She did not have to wait passively to see what fate had in store for her. She could act instead of react, make her own decisions, steer her own course, live her own life.

But maybe that, too, was *lait sic*.

Maybe.

She turned away from the gravesite. The day was cool and clear, the sky a deep-sea blue, the kind of day Rich would have loved. In the distance, she heard the sound of hammers and buzzsaws—the black church being dismantled.

Her grandmother had wanted to come to the funeral, had asked to come, but Sue had asked her not to. She did not know why, but she had not wanted her family to be here with her. Her grandmother, somehow, had understood.

She walked across the newly installed squares of grass, and saw Carole as she headed back to the car. The secretary turned in her direction, attempted a wave, but Sue hurriedly moved away.

As she walked, as her feet carried her over the recently restored ground, something shifted inside of her, something changed. The sadness and despair that had begun to take root within her disappeared, and she felt inappropriately light-headed, almost giddy. She knew, suddenly, with certainty, that everything was going to be all right, that she would be okay, that she and her family would live long and happy lives.

It was a strange, childishly simple thing to think, but it was what she wanted to hear, what she needed to hear, and it affected her in a way that nothing else could have.

Di Lo Ling Gum?

Perhaps it was. Or perhaps it was simply a voice within herself. Perhaps it was merely what she wanted to believe.

She didn't care. All she knew was that she suddenly wanted to go home, to see her parents, to see John and her grandmother, to be with them.

She looked back at Robert, now standing alone with the pastor at the edge of the grave, and thought that maybe later, maybe tomorrow, she would call him, talk to him.

No matter what happened from here on in, no matter what life threw at her, everything was going to turn out all right, everything was going to be okay.

She got in the station wagon, turned on the radio, and headed for home.

About the Author

BENTLEY LITTLE was born in Arizona—a month after his mother attended the world premiere of *Psycho*. He now lives in California. He has worked as a newspaper reporter/photographer, video arcade attendant, window washer, rodeo gatekeeper, telephone book deliveryman, library aide, typesetter, furniture mover, salesclerk, and technical writer. He is the author of THE MAILMAN, DEATH INSTINCT and the Bram Stoker Award-winning THE REVELATION.

His girlfriend, Wai Sau, is Chinese.